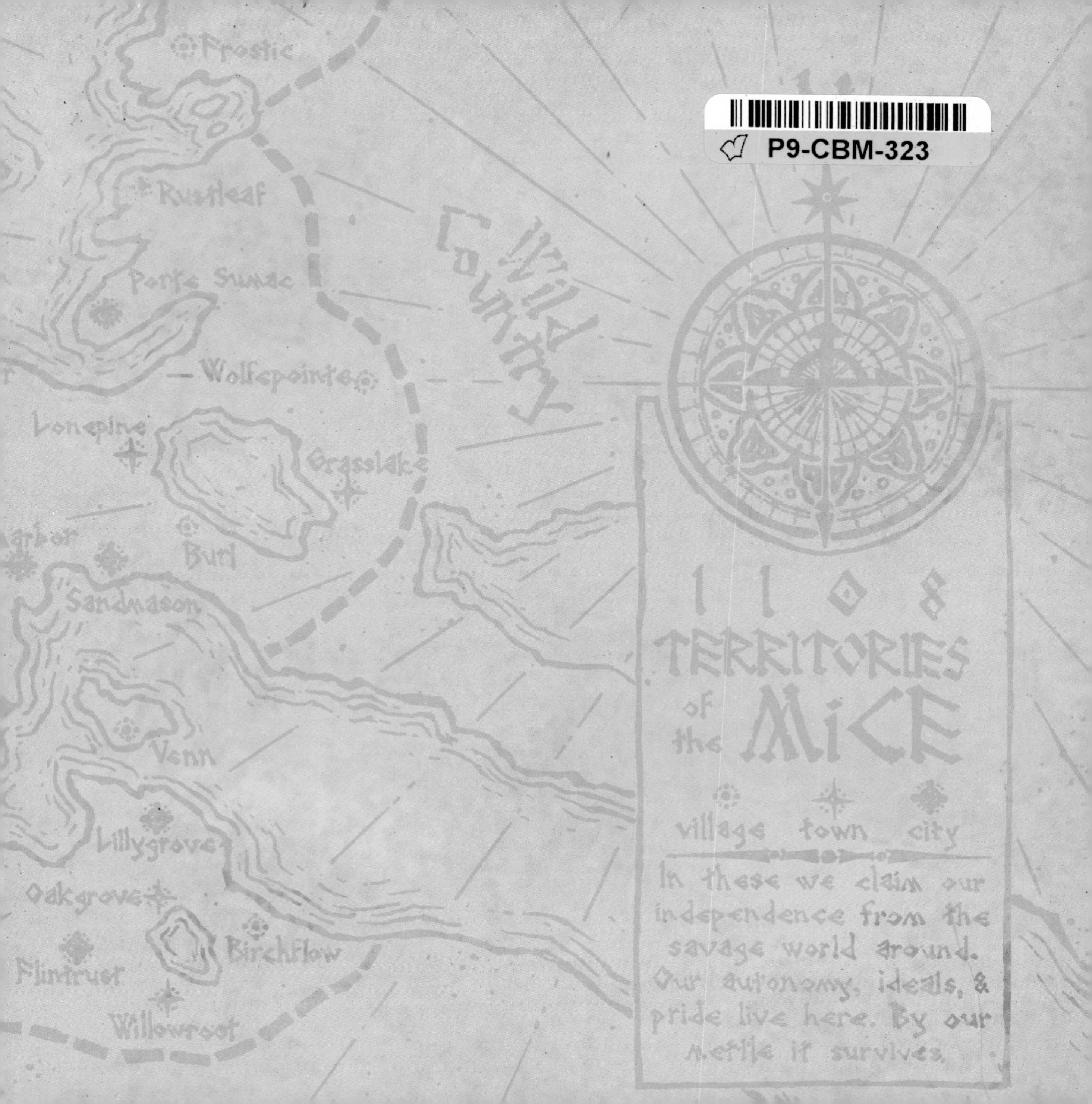
Frostic
Rustleaf
Wild Country
Ponte Sumac
Wolfepointe
Lonepine
Grasslake
Arbor
Burl
Sandmason
Venn
Lillygrove
Oakgrove
Birchflow
Flintrust
Willowroot
1108
TERRITORIES of the MICE
village town city
In these we claim our independence from the savage world around. Our autonomy, ideals, & pride live here. By our mettle it survives.

MOUSE GUARD™
THE BLACK AXE

ARCHAIA ENTERTAINMENT LLC
WWW.**ARCHAIA**.COM

FOR MY WIFE JULIA

SPECIAL THANKS TO:

MY PARENTS, JESSE GLENN, MIKE DAVIS, EMERSON JONES,
SEYTH MIERSMA, JEREMY BASTIAN, NATE PRIDE, KATIE COOK,
ALEX SHEIKMAN, SEAN RUBIN, DUNCAN FEGREDO,
C.P. WILSON III, SHANE-MICHAEL VIDAURRI, MIKE MIGNOLA,
MARK SMYLIE, ERIC LYNCH,
AND TERRY JONES

MOUSE GUARD™
THE BLACK AXE

STORY & ART BY
DAVID PETERSEN

Rebecca Taylor, *Editor*

Archaia Entertainment LLC

Jack Cummins, *President & COO*   Stephen Christy, *Editor-in-Chief*
Mark Smylie, *Chief Creative Officer*   Mel Caylo, *Marketing Manager*
Mike Kennedy, *Publisher*   Scott Newman, *Production Manager*

Published by **Archaia**

Archaia Entertainment LLC
1680 Vine Street, Suite 1010
Los Angeles, California, 90028
www.archaia.com

ARCHAIA™
NEW STORIES. NEW WORLDS.

MOUSE GUARD Volume Three: THE BLACK AXE Collected Edition Hardcover. June 2013. FIRST PRINTING.

10 9 8 7 6 5 4 3 2 1

ISBN: 1-936393-06-9
ISBN 13: 978-1-936393-06-0

Printed in **China**.

PREFACE

WELCOME TO THE WORLD OF CELANAWE.

MOUSE GUARD: THE BLACK AXE LURES US INTO BELIEVING MICE FLY BIRDS, BUILD SHIPS, AND KILL FOXES. THAT FERRETS LIVE IN GREAT HALLS, THAT WEASELS WEAR SKULLS, AND THAT MICE CAROUSE WITH THE BEST OF THEM.

THE DETAIL OF THE MEDIEVAL PERIOD IS AUTHENTIC AND FEELS JUST AS IT SHOULD. THE COSTUMES, THE BOOKS, THE INNS, THE HOUSES, THE LIBRARIES, ALL LOOK AS IF THEY WERE MADE IN THE MIDDLE AGES.

I CANNOT PRAISE DAVID PETERSEN TOO HIGHLY FOR HIS STORYTELLING. HE KNOWS EXACTLY WHEN TO SAY WHAT IS HAPPENING IN THE TEXT AND DIALOGUE, AND EXACTLY WHEN TO LEAVE IT TO THE PICTURES TO TELL THE STORY.

MOREOVER, YOU ACTUALLY CARE FOR THE CREATURES IN THE TALE. FOR EXAMPLE, THE FERRETS WHEN YOU FIRST SEE THEM ARE COARSE AND DANGEROUS, BUT YOU DISCOVER THEY HAVE A CODE OF HONOR THAT ELEVATES THEM, AND WHEN THE KING'S SON IS BROUGHT IN DEAD, YOU FEEL FOR THE KING'S GRIEF. THE IMAGES OF THE FERRETS AT EM'S FUNERAL ARE SIMPLY STUNNING.

CELANAWE HIMSELF IS A GREAT HERO – QUIET BUT RESOURCEFUL AND DETERMINED – WHILE STILL BEING A MOUSE.

THE TALE OF *THE BLACK AXE* IS TRUE TO THE SPIRIT OF THE MEDIEVAL PERIOD AND A WONDERFUL READ. I HOPE YOU ENJOY IT AS MUCH AS I DID.

TERRY JONES
LONDON MARCH 2013

CONTENTS

PROLOGUE

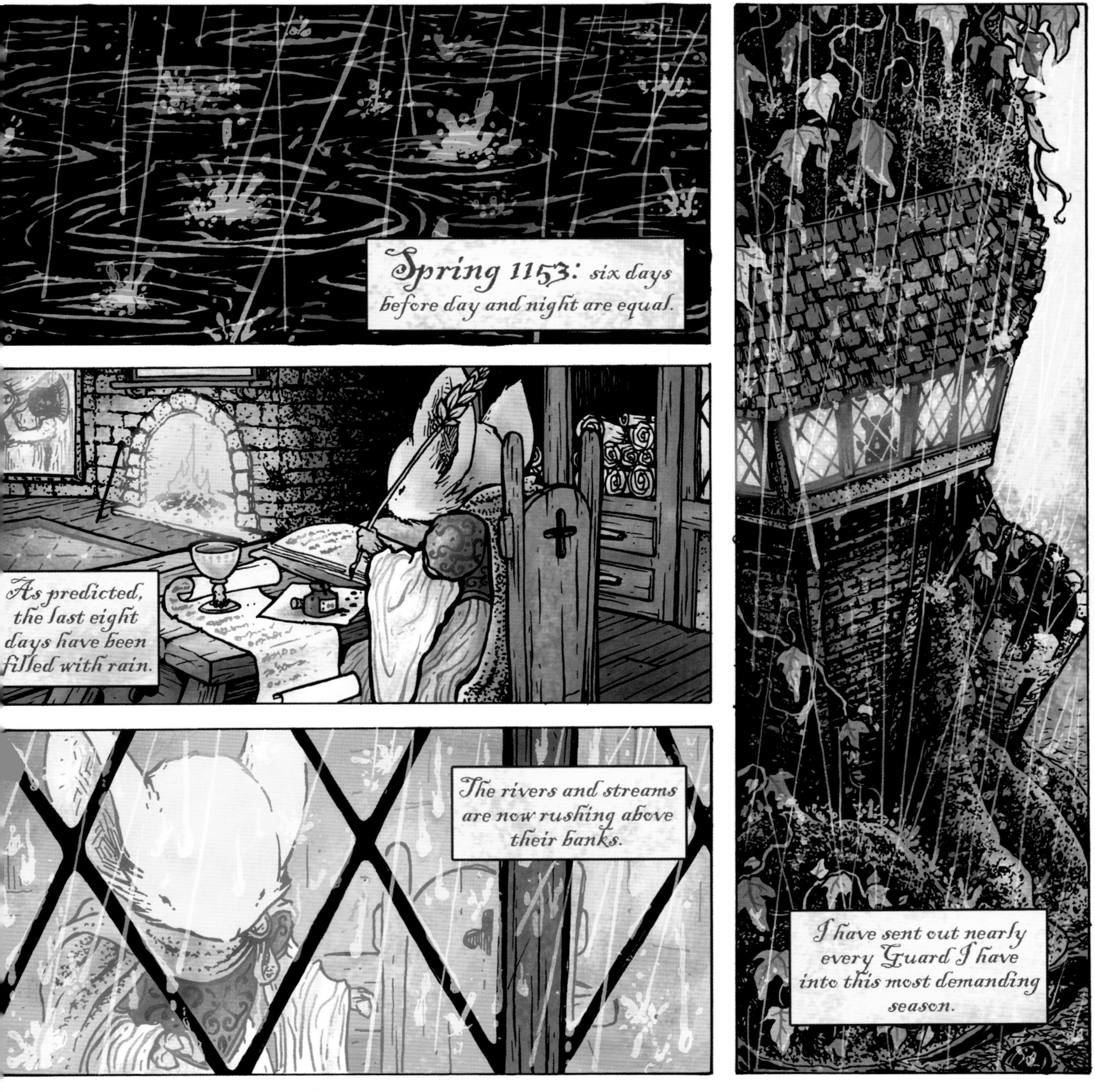
Spring 1153: six days before day and night are equal.
As predicted, the last eight days have been filled with rain.
The rivers and streams are now rushing above their banks.
I have sent out nearly every Guard I have into this most demanding season.

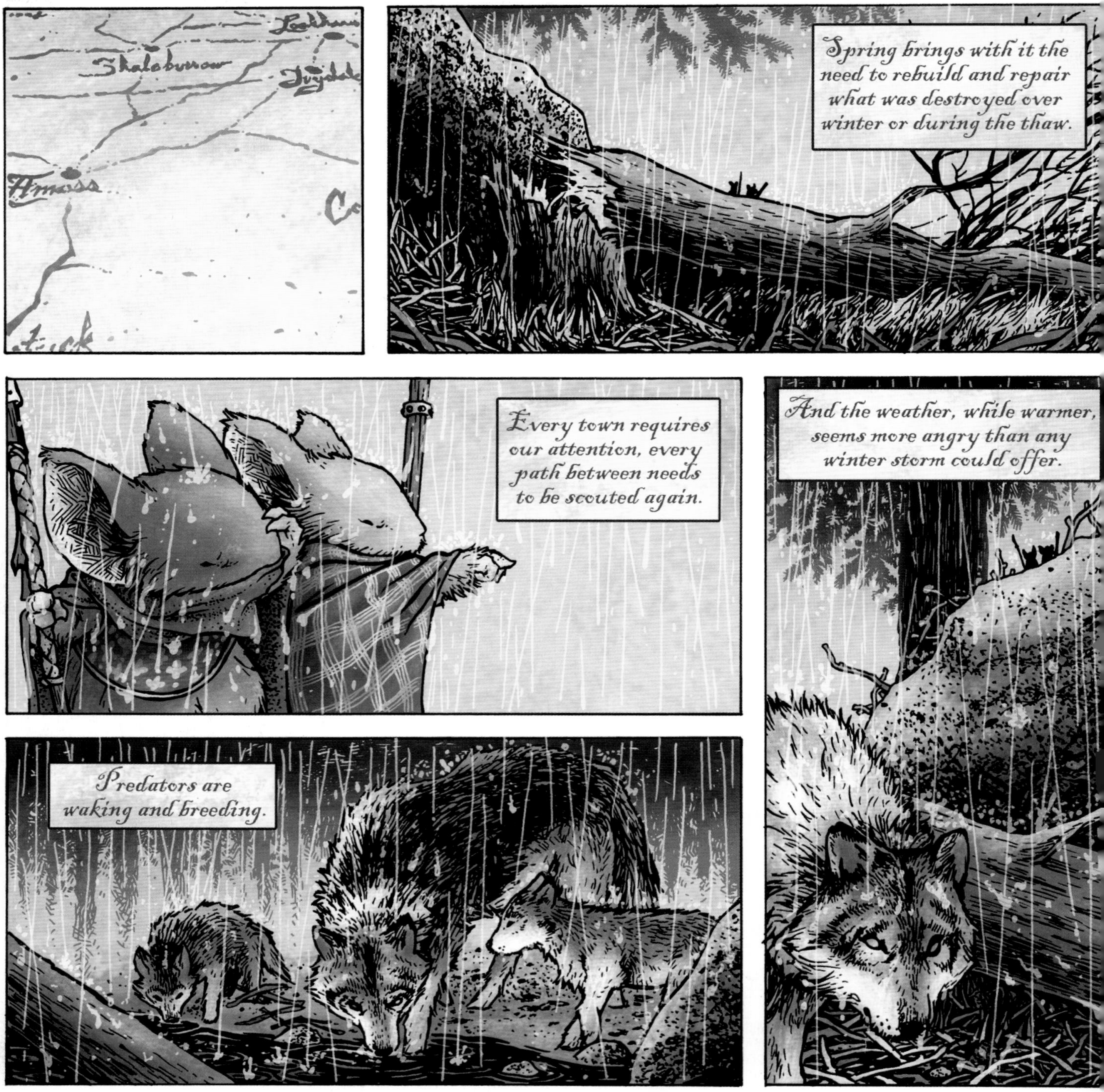
Shaleburrow
Amassa
Spring brings with it the need to rebuild and repair what was destroyed over winter or during the thaw.
Every town requires our attention, every path between needs to be scouted again.
Predators are waking and breeding.
And the weather, while warmer, seems more angry than any winter storm could offer.

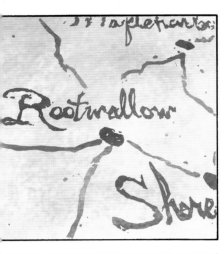

Rootwallow Shore

My mice are working mainly in pairs to cover all the ground our work takes us through.

Three full moon cycles have come and gone since our youngest Guard, Lieam, vanished.

I can spare none to search for him though.

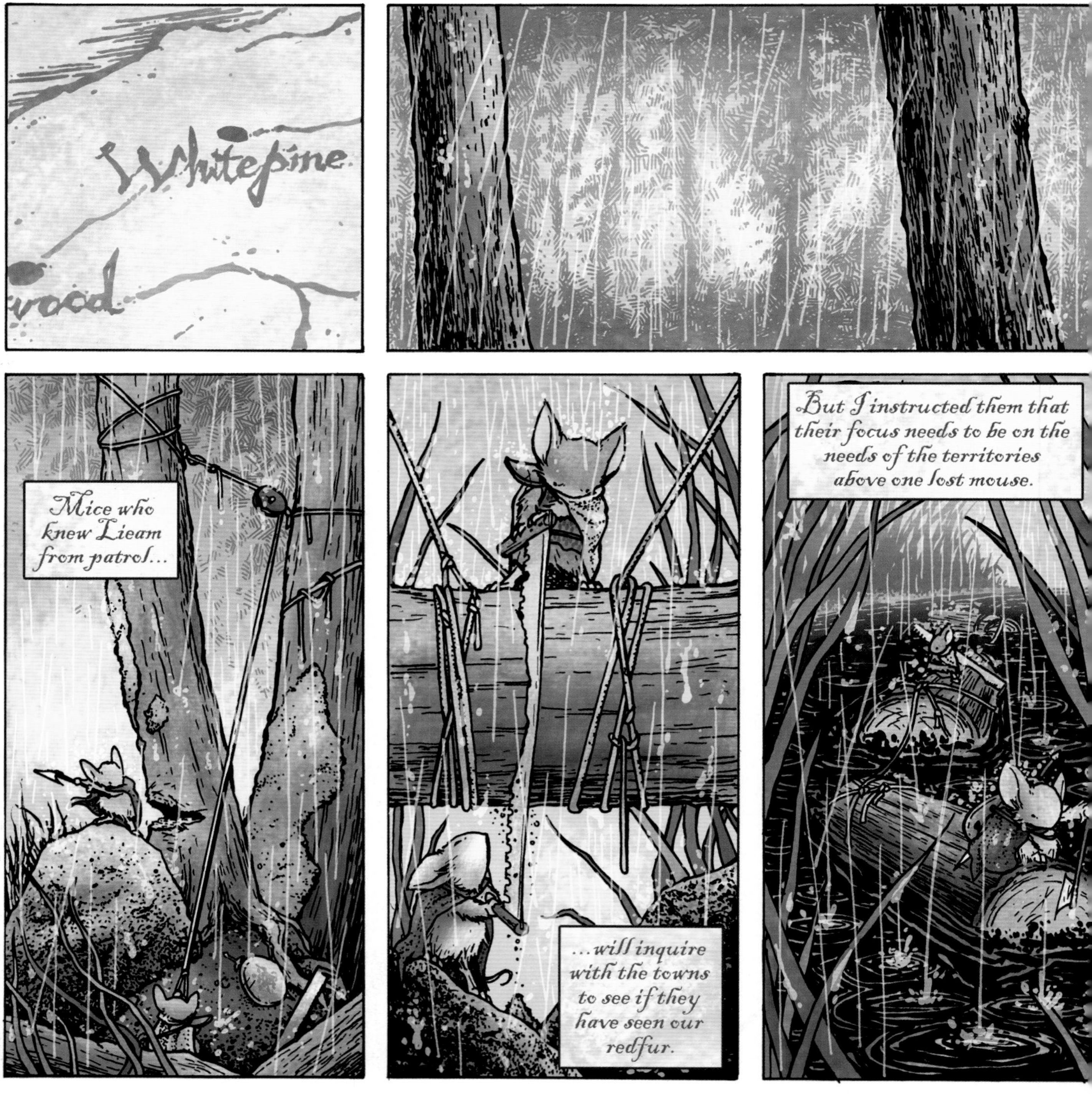
Whitepine
wood
Mice who knew Lieam from patrol...
...will inquire with the towns to see if they have seen our redfur.
But I instructed them that their focus needs to be on the needs of the territories above one lost mouse.

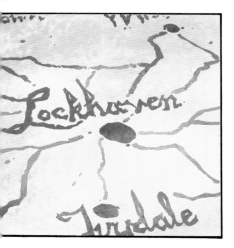

Lockhaven

Tirdale

Later matriarchs might think me cold-hearted for not spending more resources on a Guard whose acts have made such notable entries in this journal for the last thirteen seasons.

I am inclined to believe Saxon knows more than he is letting on about Lieam, but I see the worry in his and Kenzie's faces as well.

I assure any who read this that I wish for nothing but the safe return of that mouse.

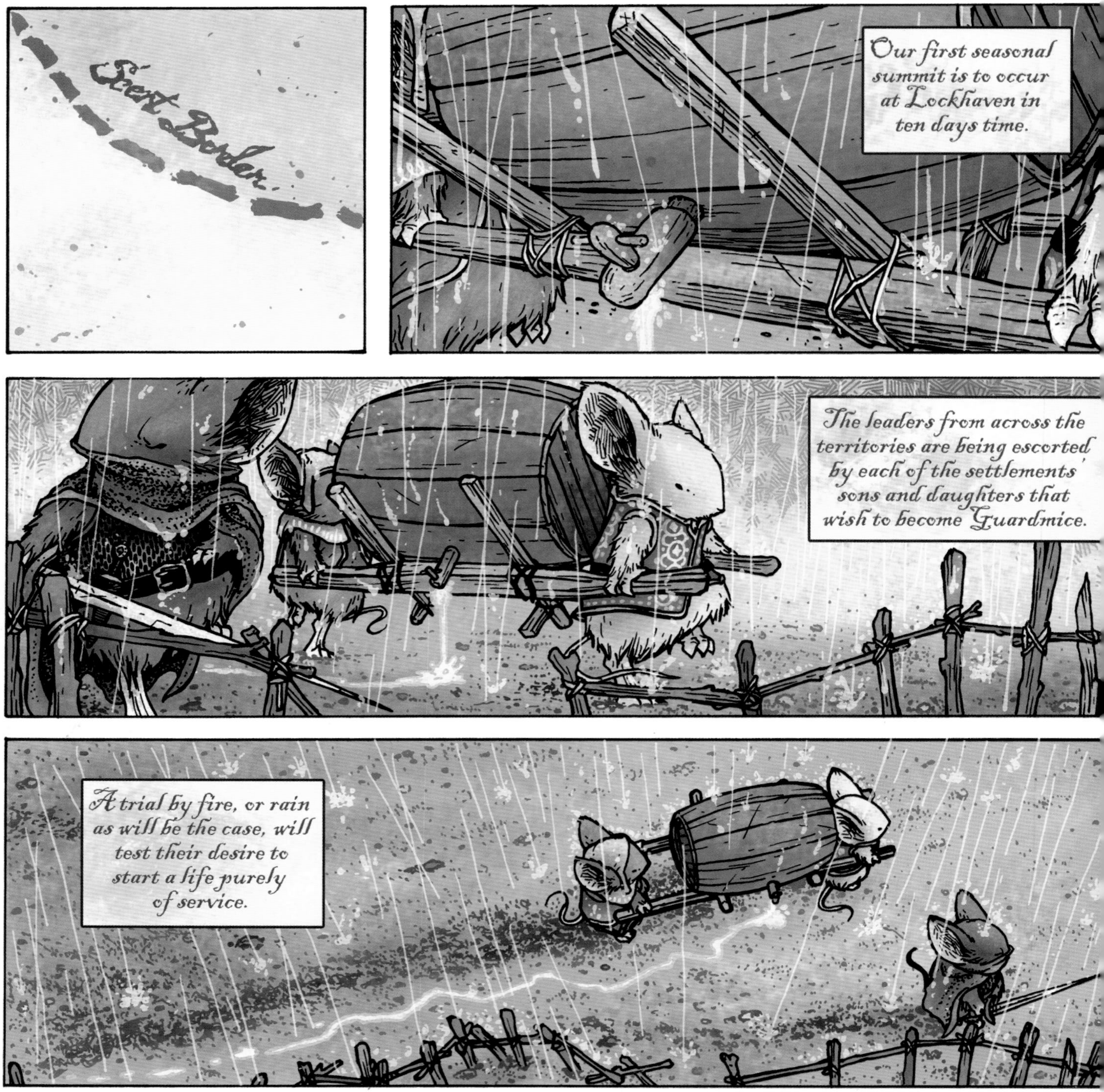
Scent Border
Our first seasonal summit is to occur at Lockhaven in ten days time.
The leaders from across the territories are being escorted by each of the settlements' sons and daughters that wish to become Guardmice.
A trial by fire, or rain as will be the case, will test their desire to start a life purely of service.

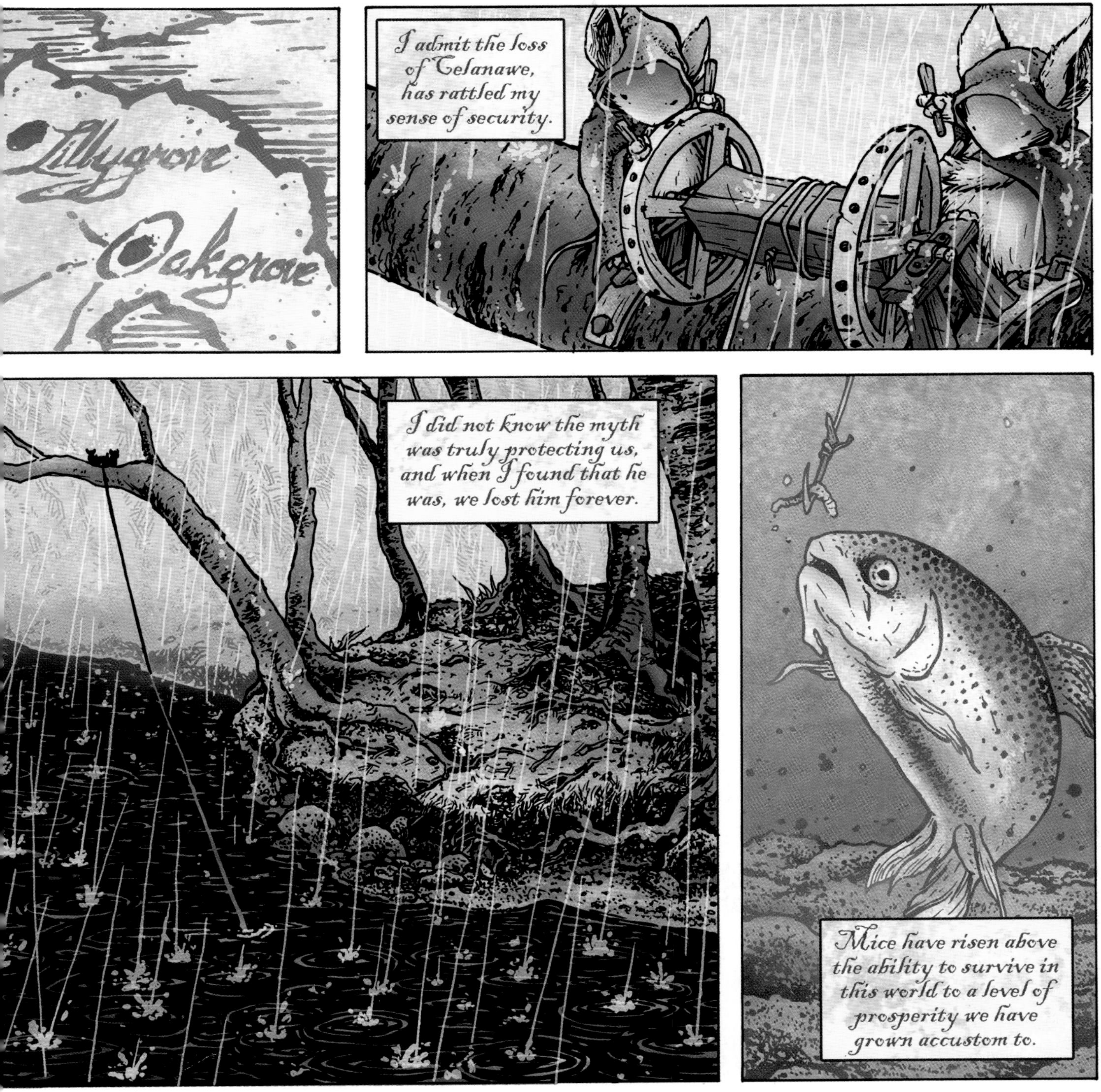
Lillygrove
Oakgrove
I admit the loss of Celanawe, has rattled my sense of security.
I did not know the myth was truly protecting us, and when I found that he was, we lost him forever.
Mice have risen above the ability to survive in this world to a level of prosperity we have grown accustom to.

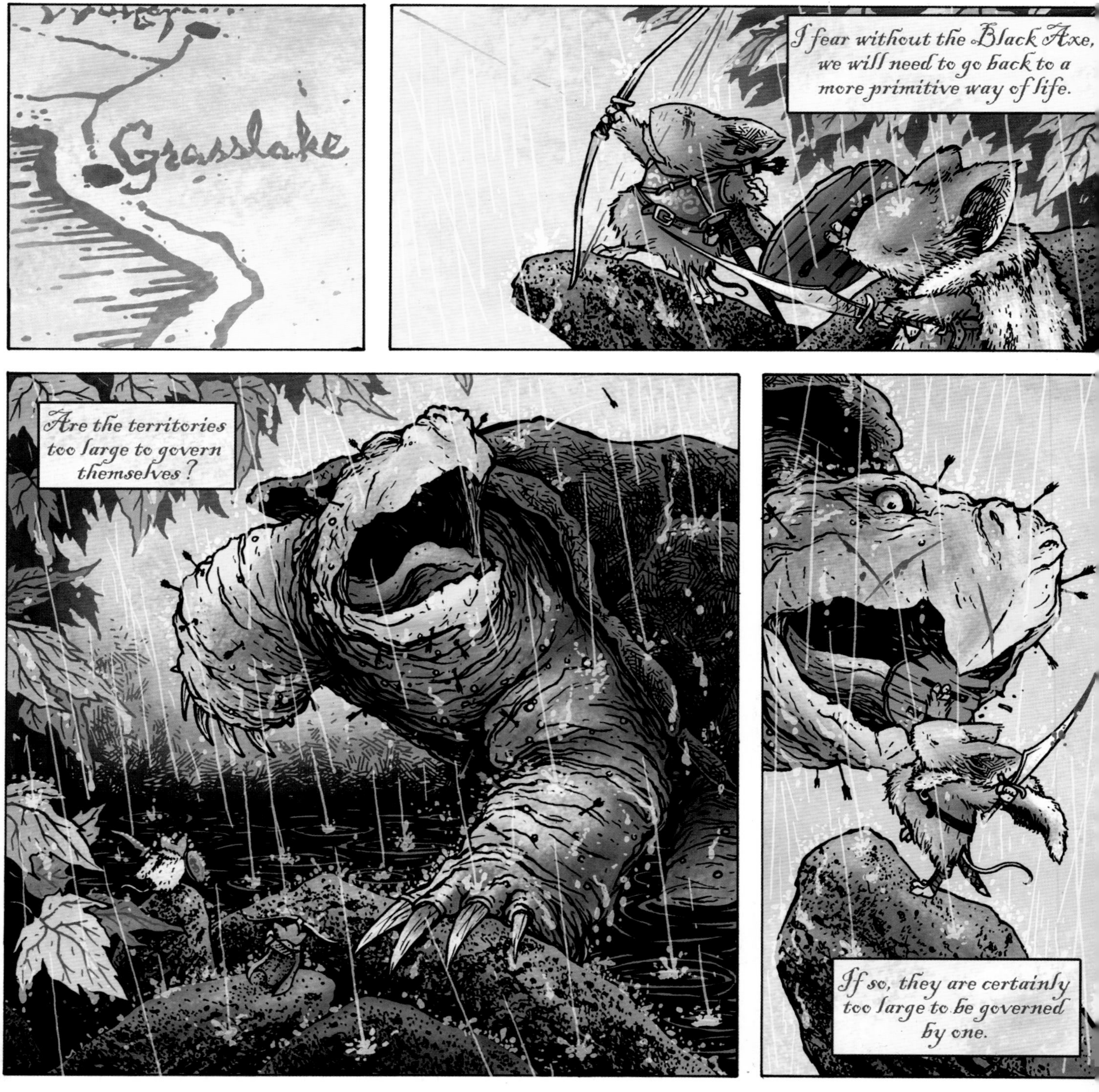
Grasslake
I fear without the Black Axe, we will need to go back to a more primitive way of life.
Are the territories too large to govern themselves?
If so, they are certainly too large to be governed by one.

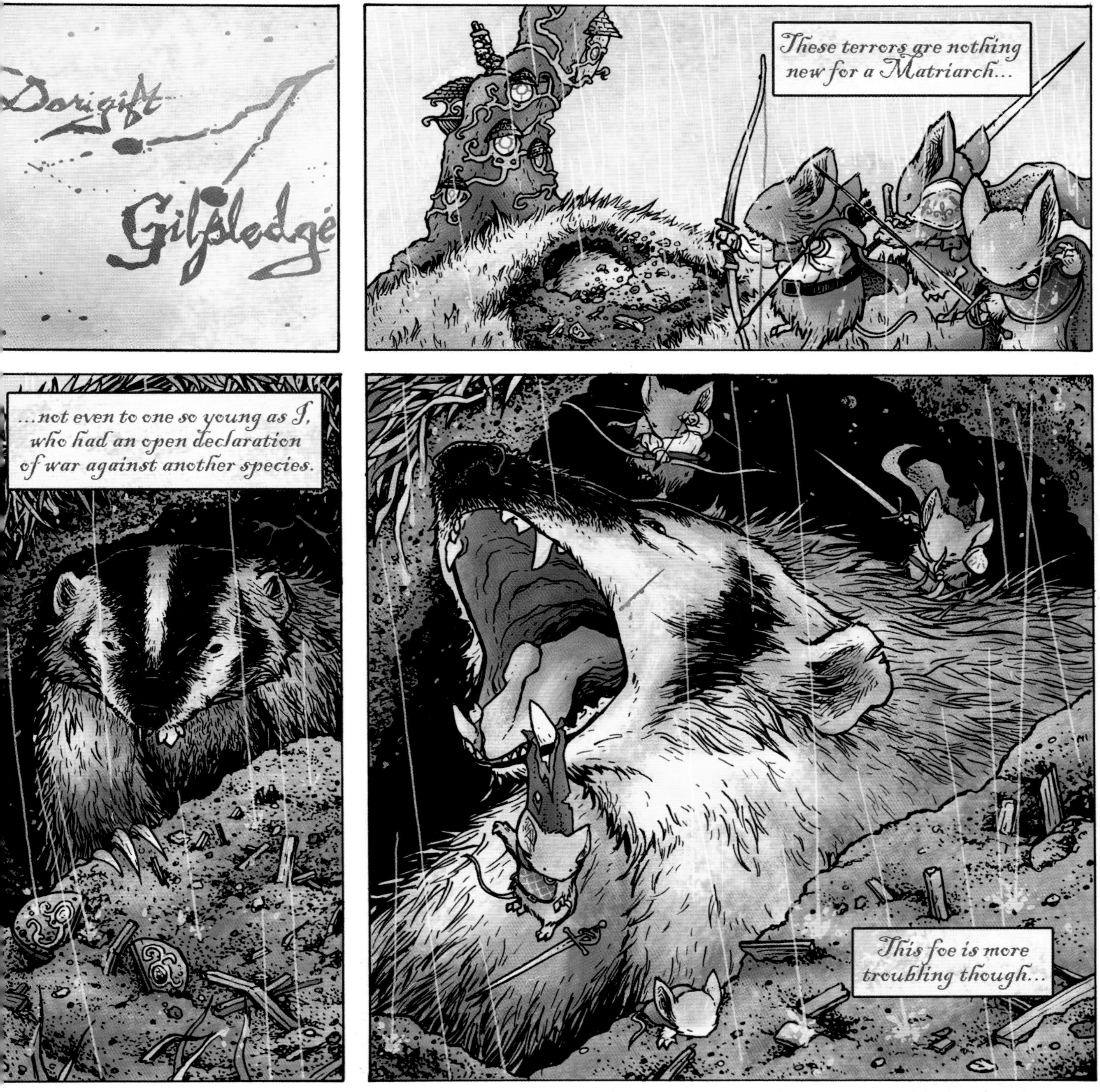
Darigift
Gilpledge
These terrors are nothing new for a Matriarch...
...not even to one so young as I, who had an open declaration of war against another species.
This foe is more troubling though...

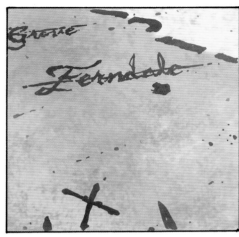

...It has no one name, no face, no home.

It looms like a dark giant...

half asleep...

half awake.

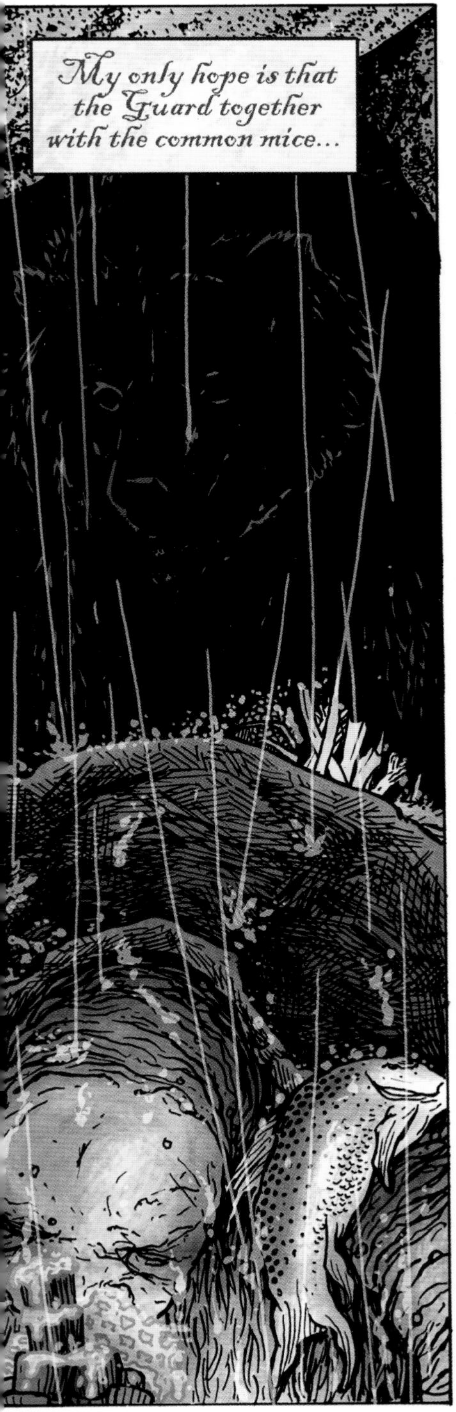
My only hope is that the Guard together with the common mice...

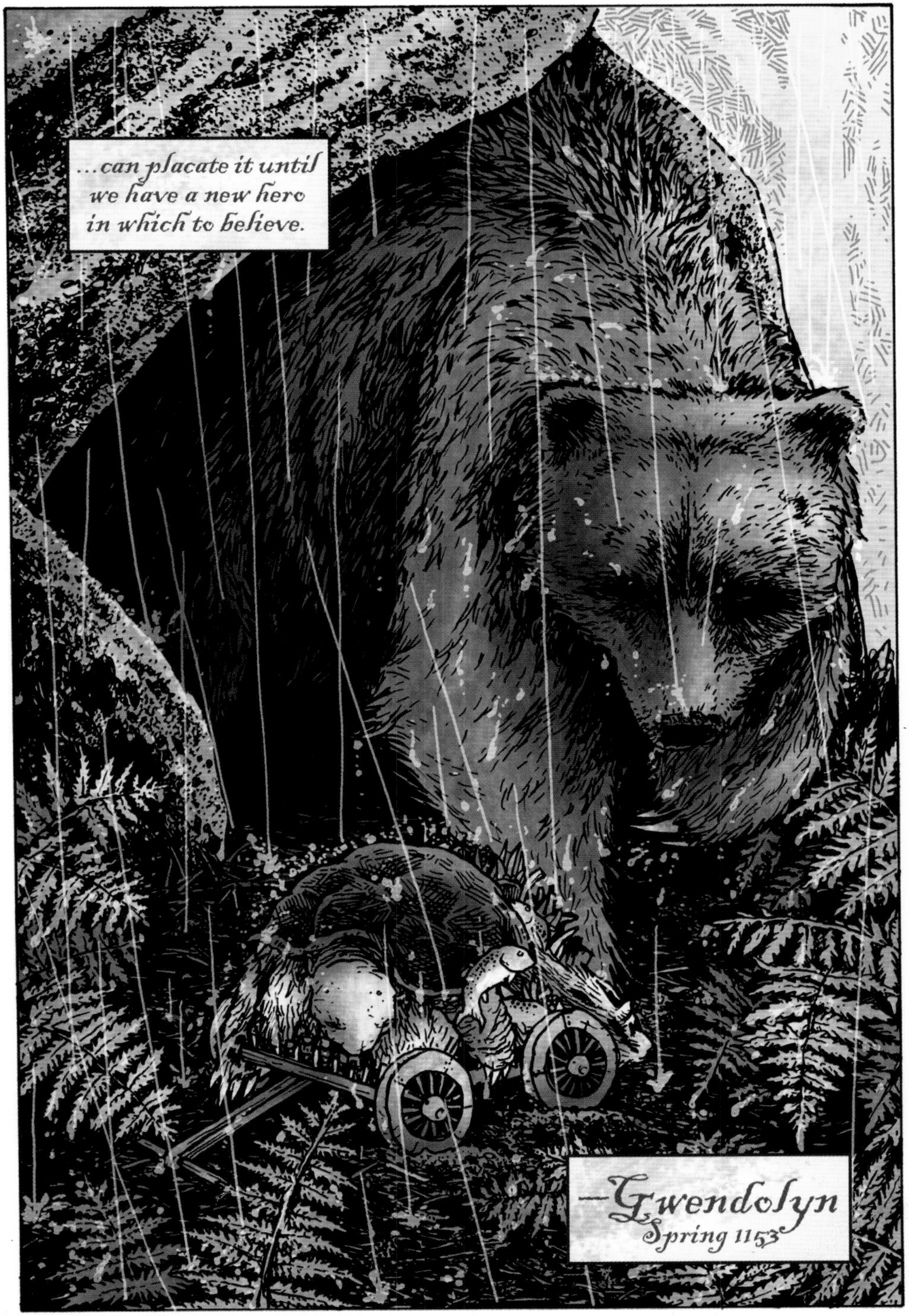
...can placate it until we have a new hero in which to believe.
—Gwendolyn
Spring 1153

THE BLACK AXE

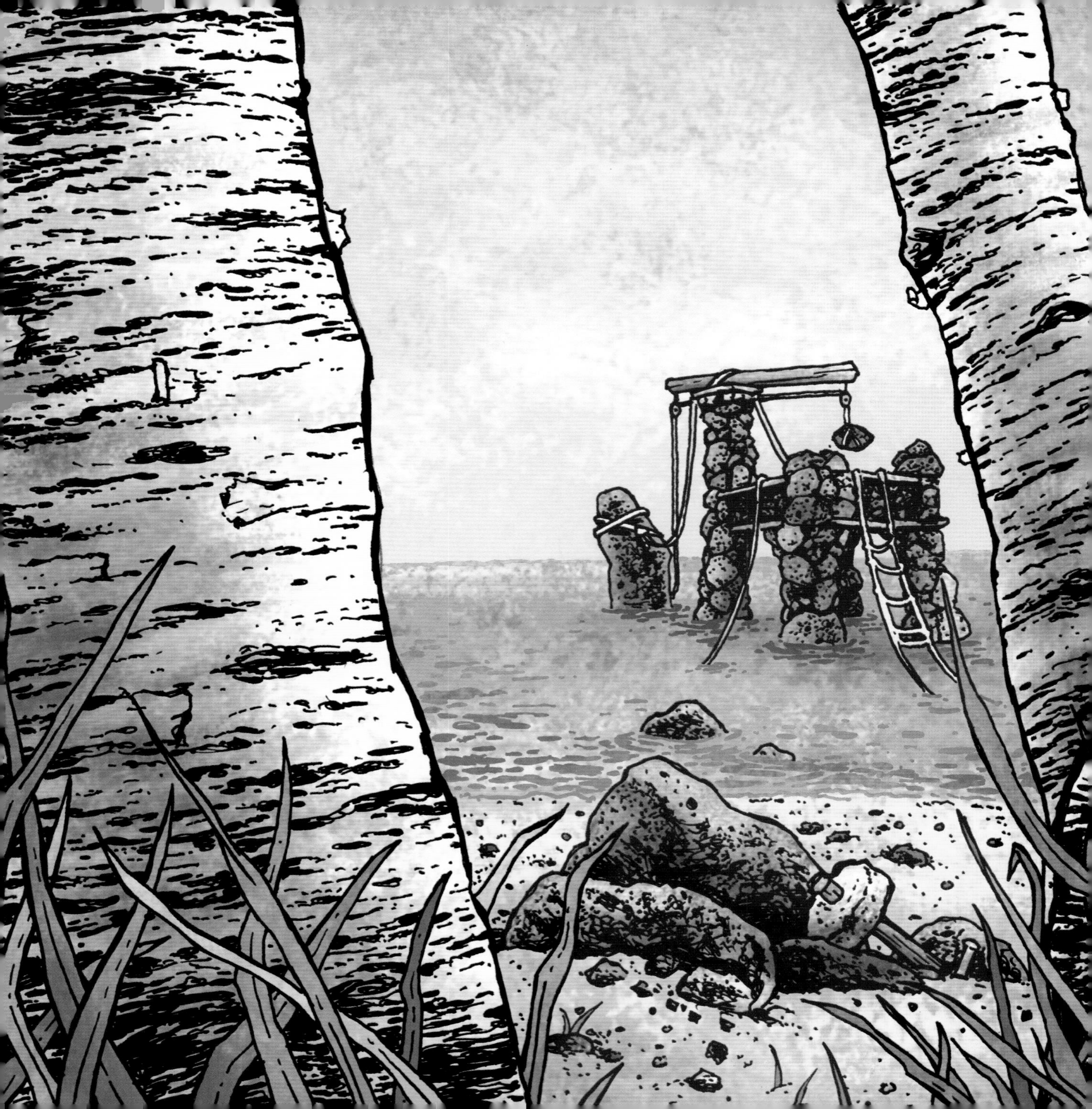

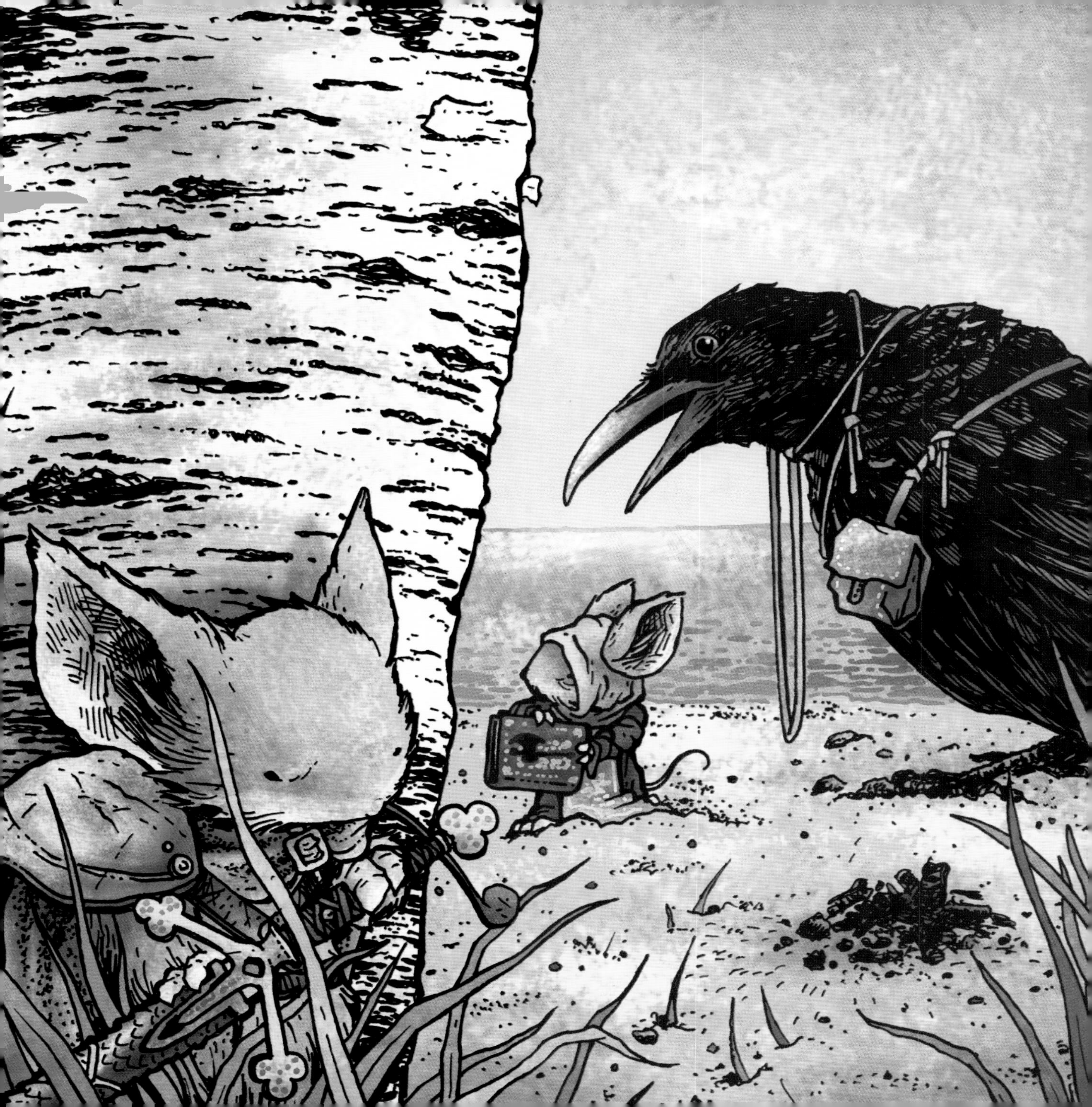

IN SECRET, THE **BLACK AXE** WORKED HIS WILL TOWARD THE LAND. AND LO, THE BEASTS OF FUR WHO STAND ON FOUR AND GROWL WITH GREAT RUMBLING THROATS, LIVED IN FEAR. THE FEATHERED AND THE SCALED TOO SHIVERED AT THE UNKNOWN MOUSE WITH HIS BEAKED BLADE. HIS WEAPON WAS MIGHTY AND HIS DUTY WAS JUST.

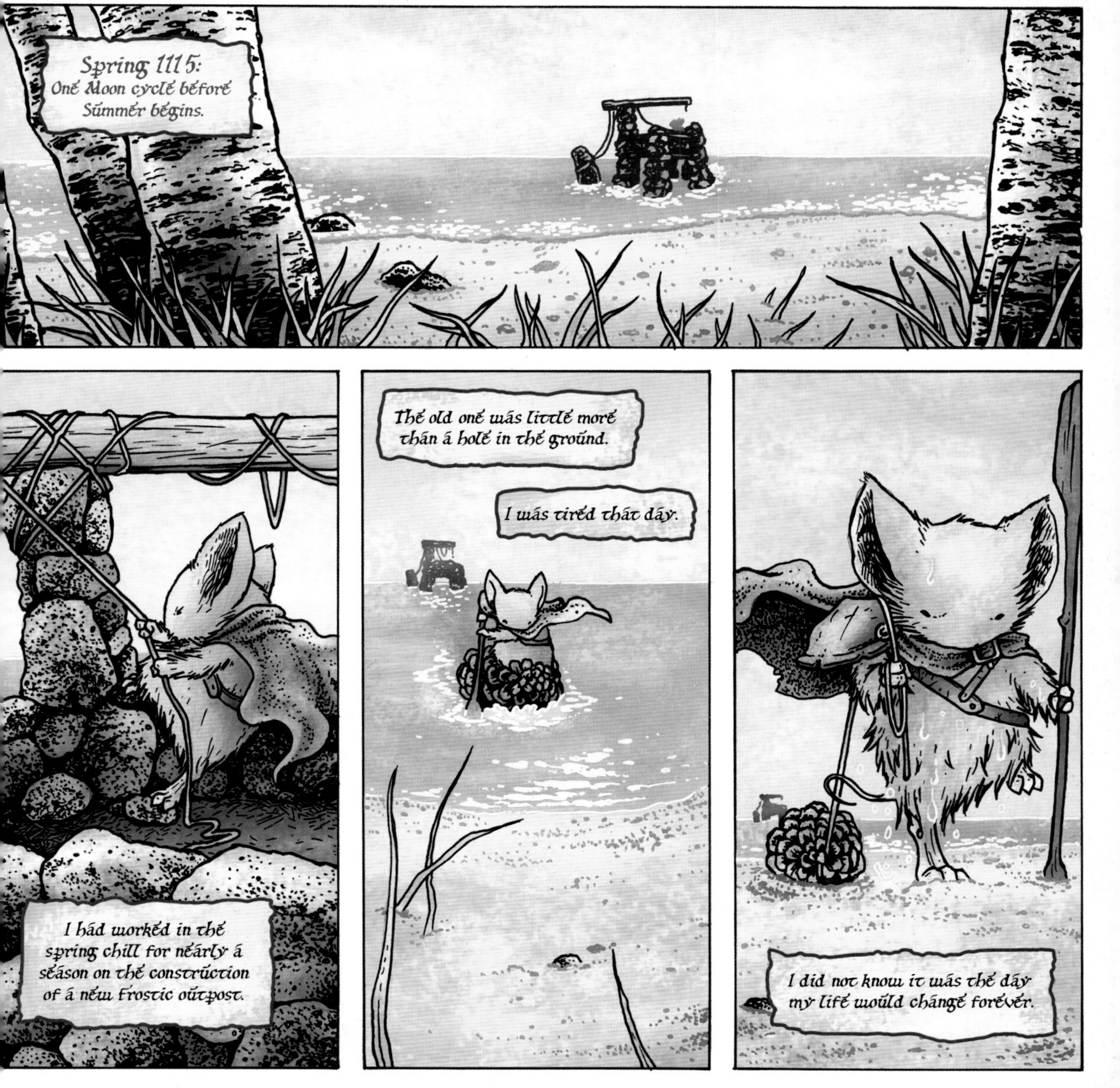
Spring 1115:
One Moon cycle before Summer begins.
I had worked in the spring chill for nearly a season on the construction of a new Frostic outpost.
The old one was little more than a hole in the ground.
I was tired that day.
I did not know it was the day my life would change forever.

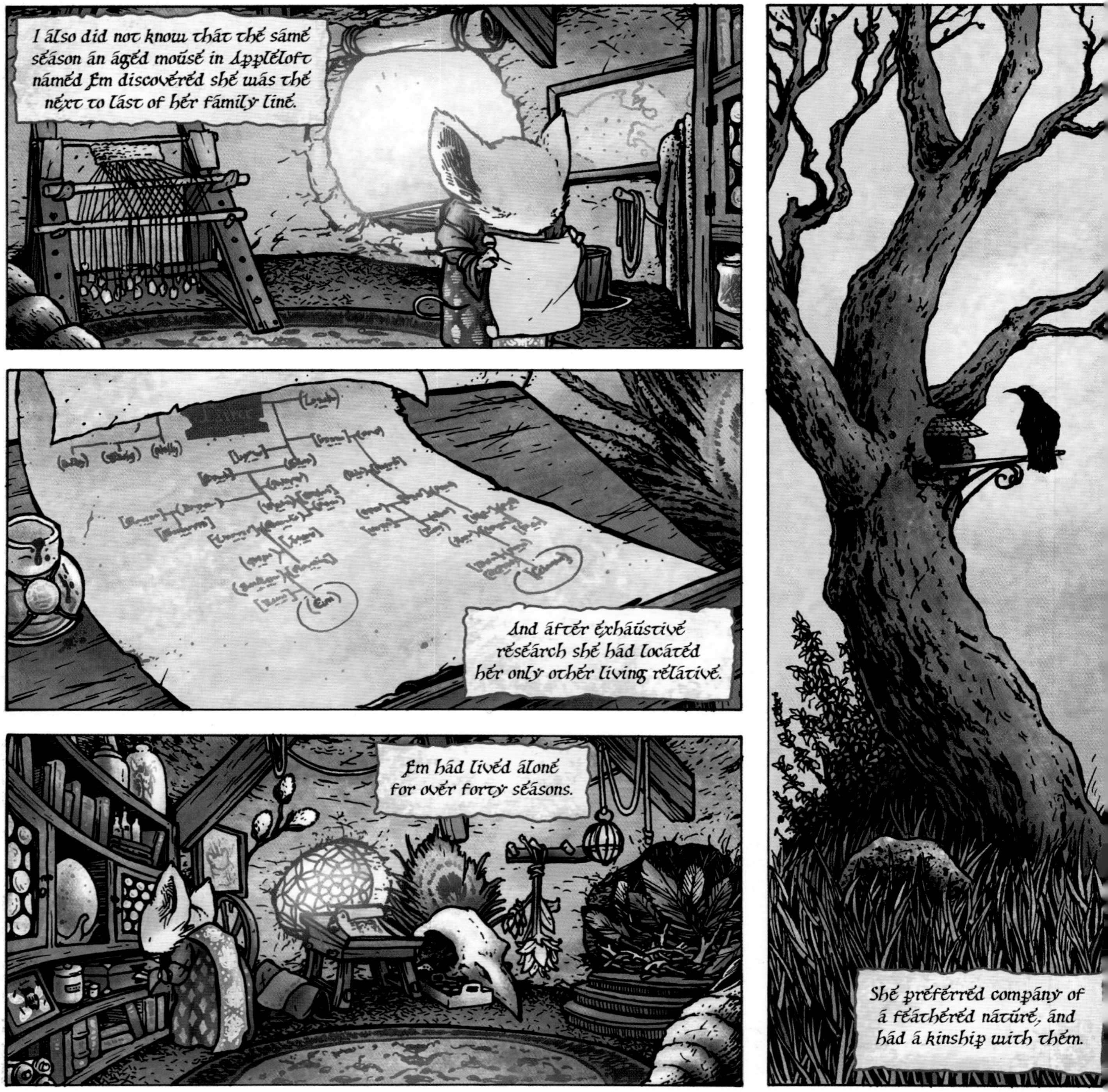
I also did not know that the same season an aged mouse in Appleloft named Em discovered she was the next to last of her family line.
And after exhaustive research she had located her only other living relative.
Em had lived alone for over forty seasons.
She preferred company of a feathered nature, and had a kinship with them.

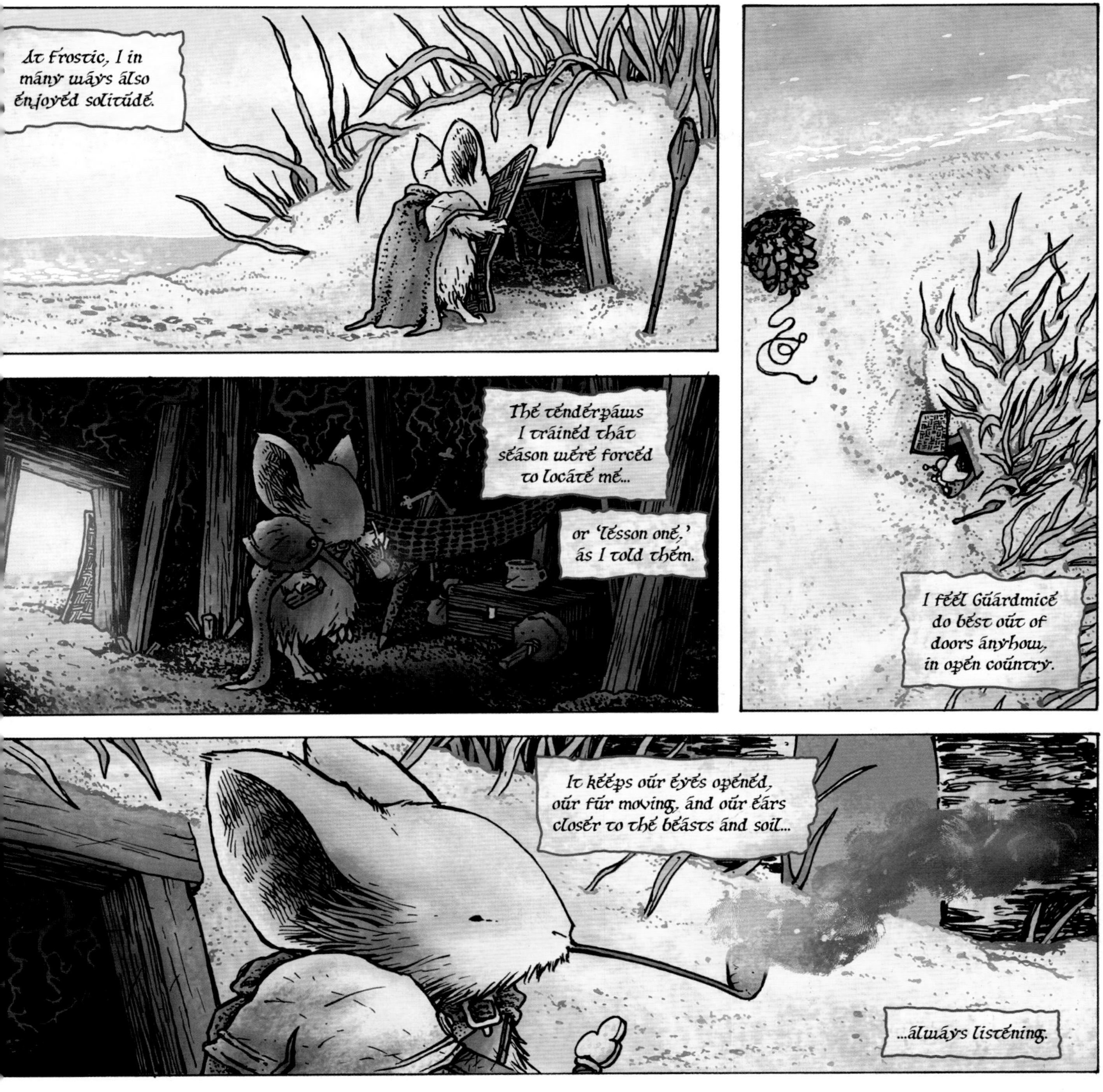
At Frostic, I in many ways also enjoyed solitude.
The tenderpaws I trained that season were forced to locate me...
or 'lesson one,' as I told them.
I feel Guardmice do best out of doors anyhow, in open country.
It keeps our eyes opened, our fur moving, and our ears closer to the beasts and soil...
...always listening.

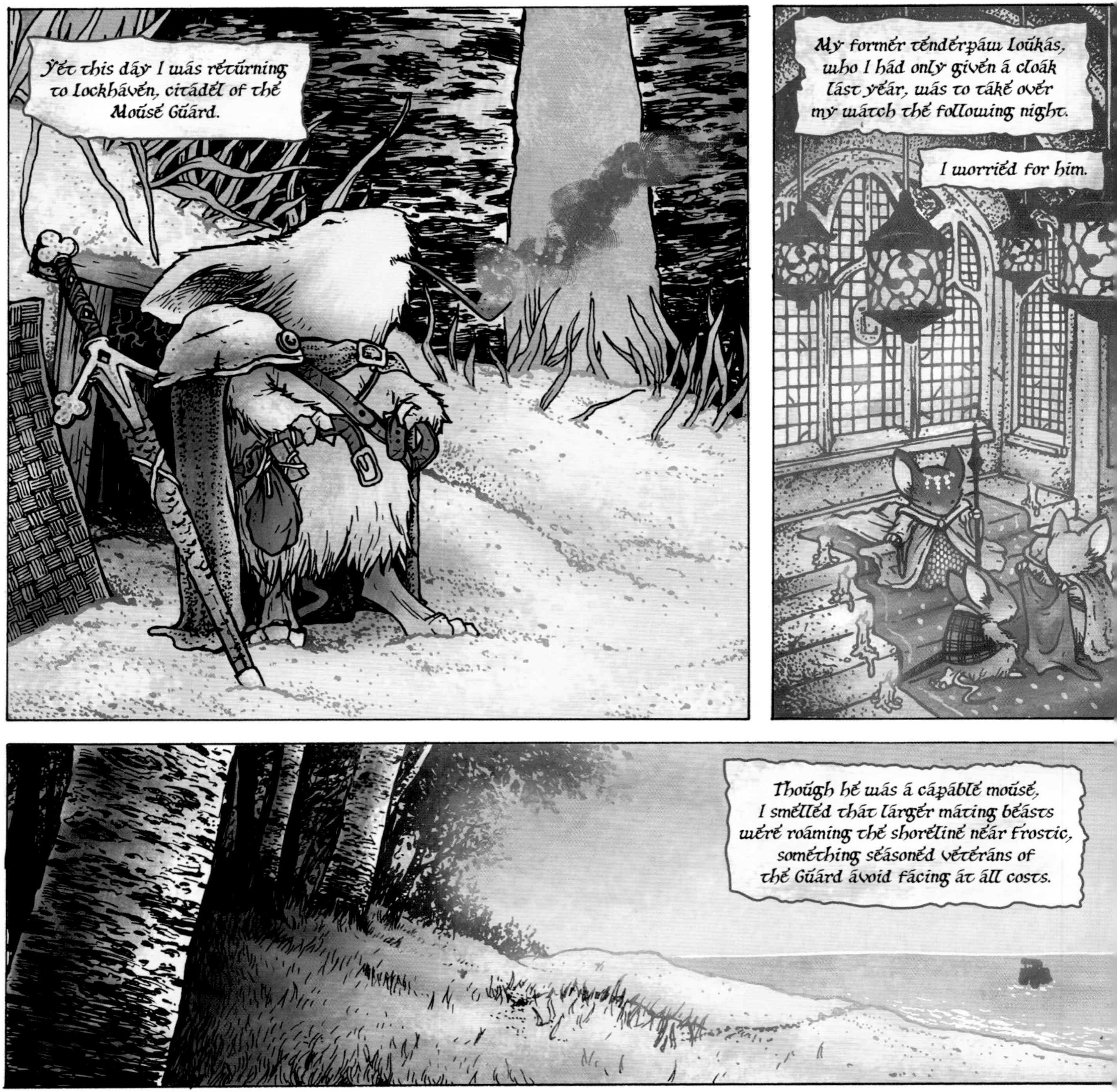
Yet this day I was returning to Lockhaven, citadel of the Mouse Guard.
My former tenderpaw Loukas, who I had only given a cloak last year, was to take over my watch the following night.
I worried for him.
Though he was a capable mouse, I smelled that larger mating beasts were roaming the shoreline near Frostic, something seasoned veterans of the Guard avoid facing at all costs.

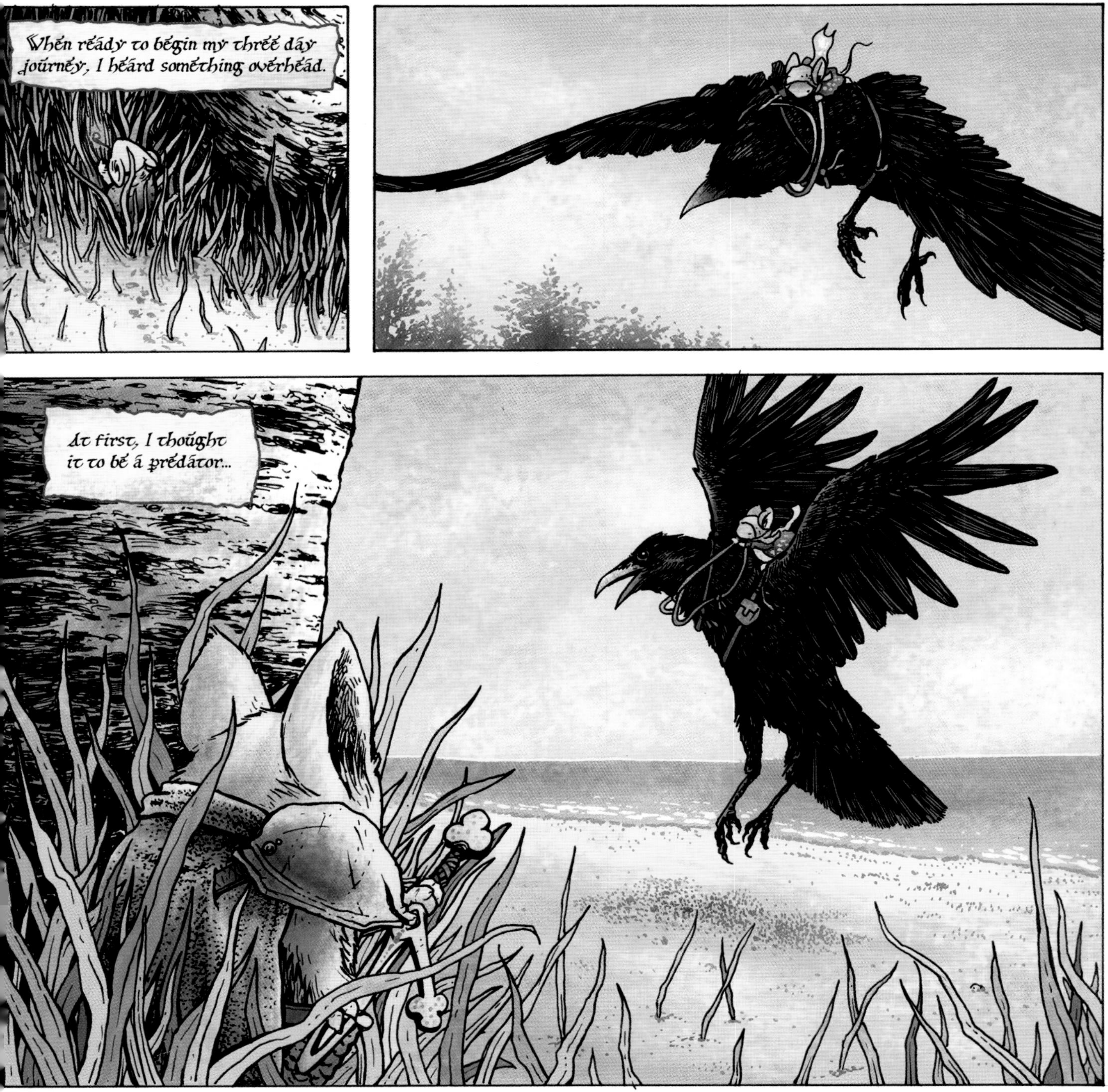
When ready to begin my three day journey, I heard something overhead.
At first, I thought it to be a predator...

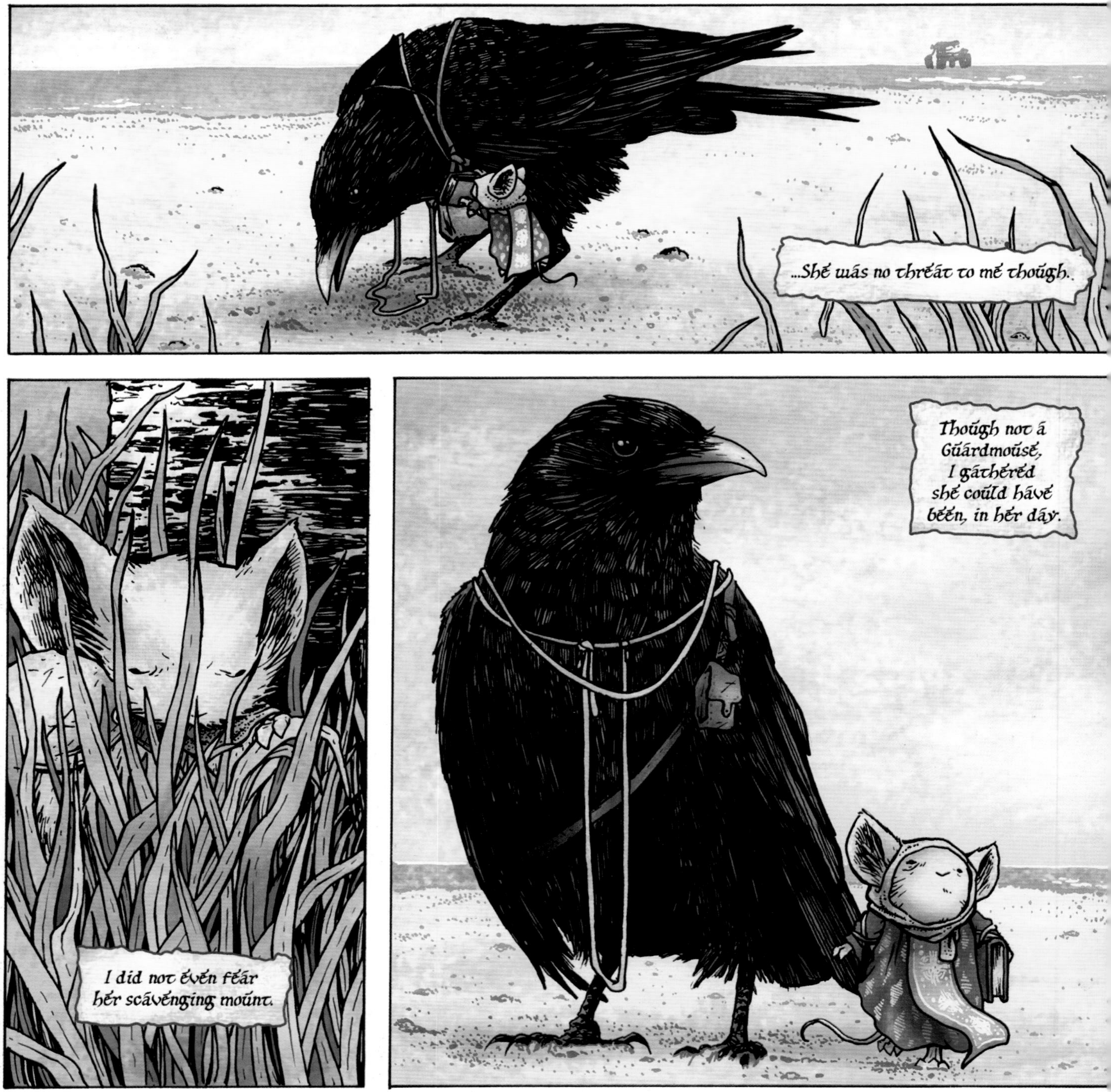
...She was no threat to me though.
I did not even fear her scavenging mount.
Though not a Guardmouse, I gathered she could have been, in her day.

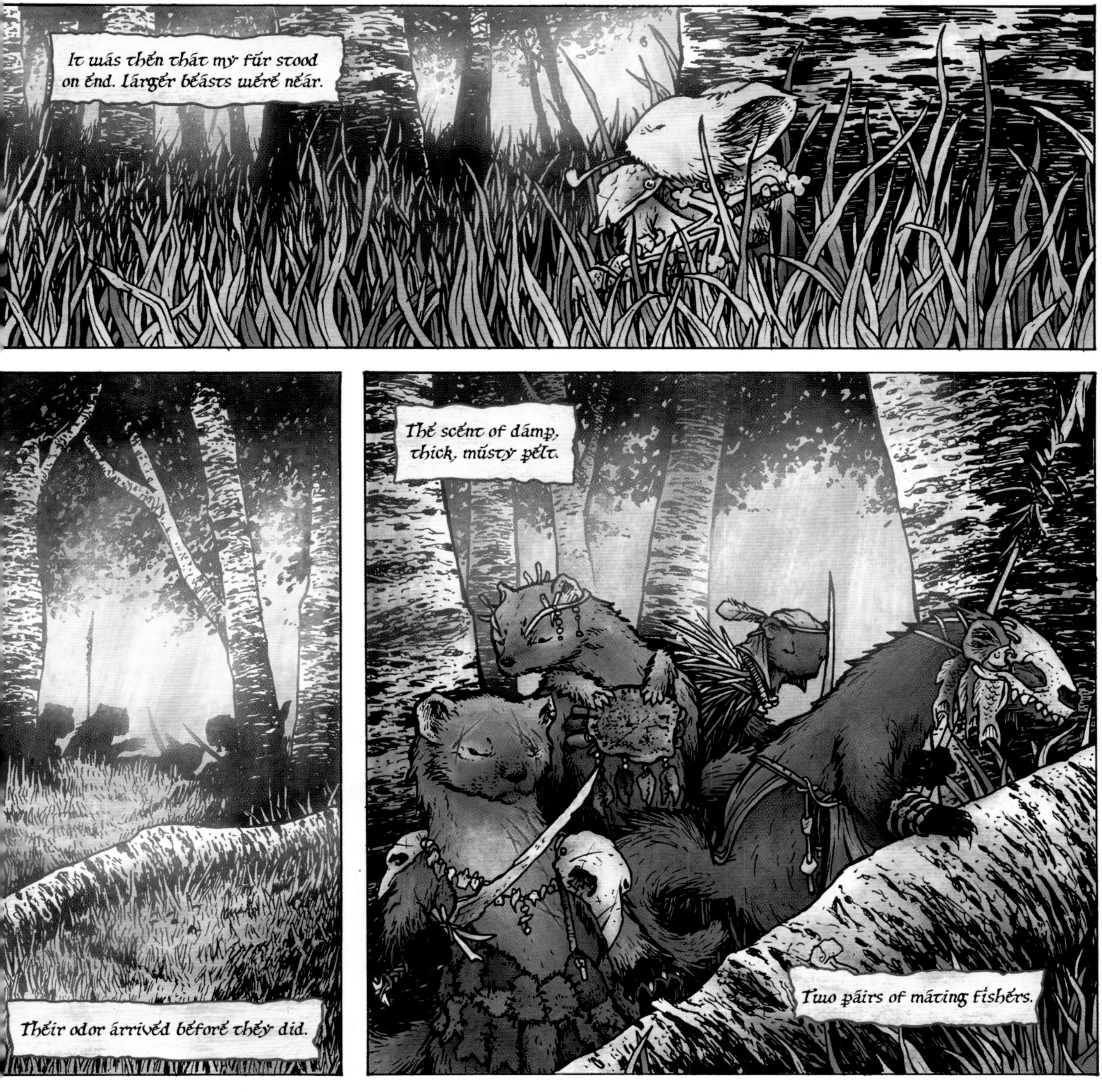
It was then that my fur stood on end. Larger beasts were near.
Their odor arrived before they did.
The scent of damp, thick, musty pelt.
Two pairs of mating fishers.

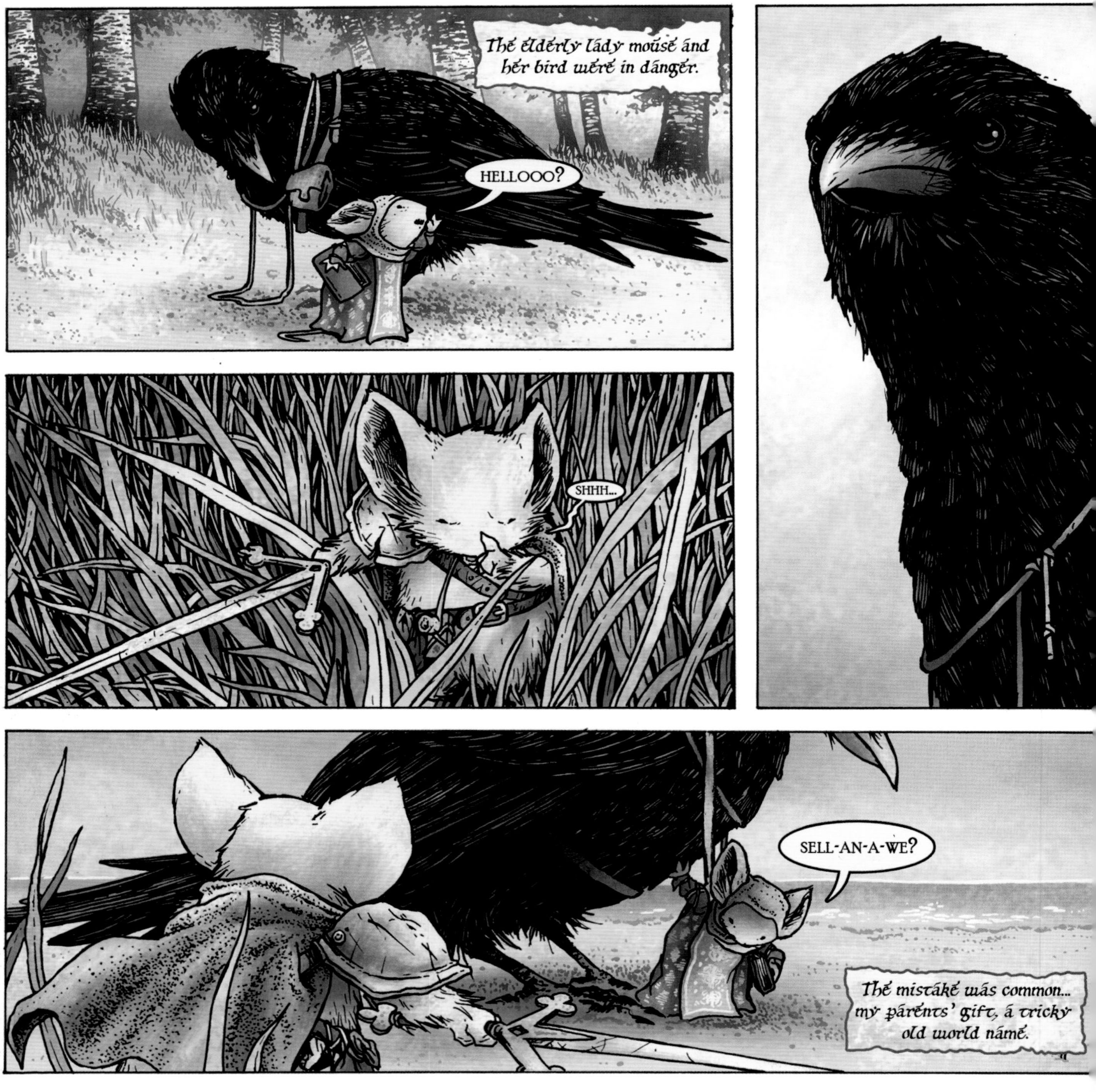
The elderly lady mouse and her bird were in danger.
HELLOOO?
SHHH...
SELL-AN-A-WE?
The mistake was common... my parents' gift, a tricky old world name.

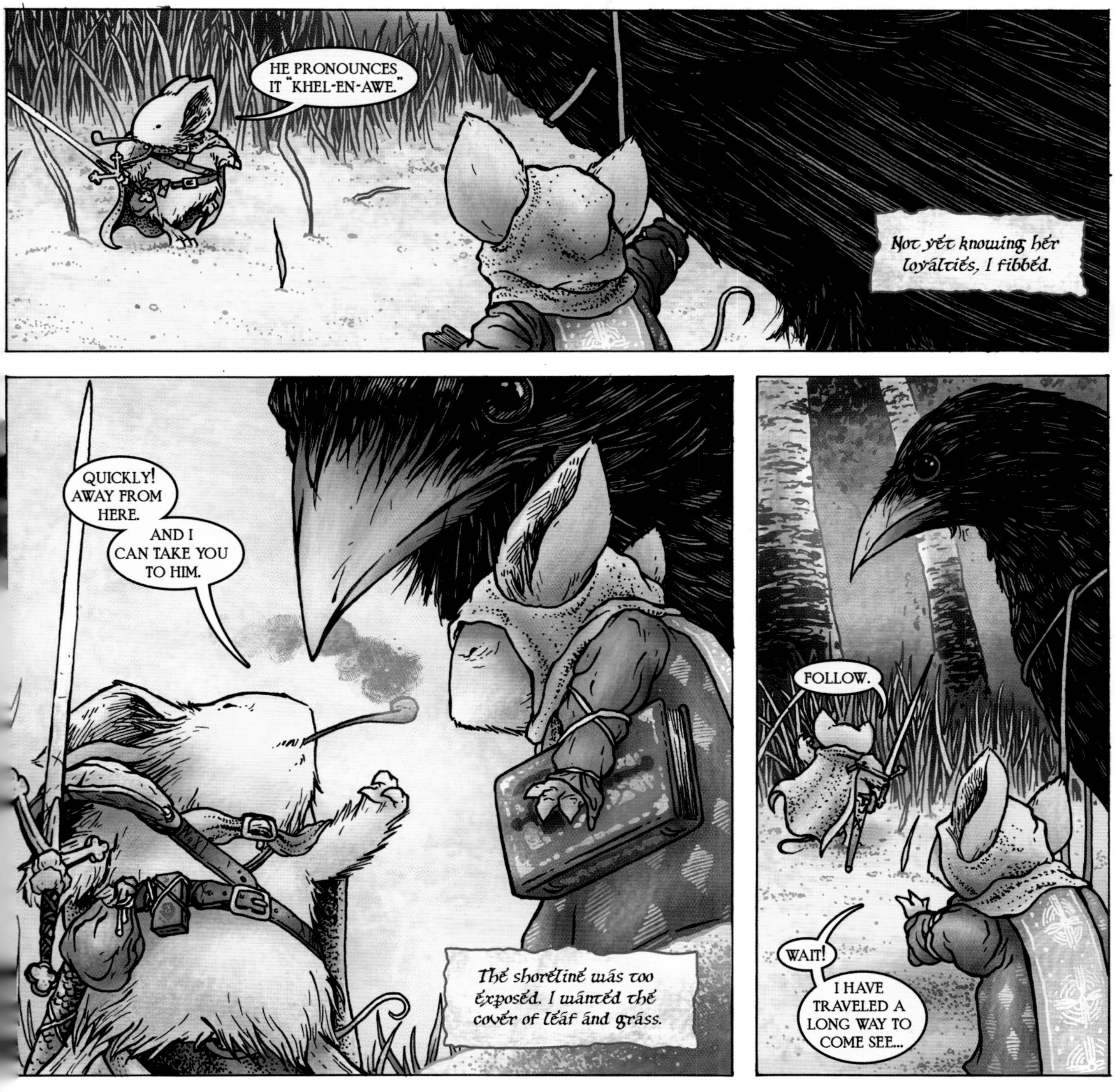

HE PRONOUNCES IT "KHEL-EN-AWE."
Not yet knowing her loyalties, I fibbed.
QUICKLY! AWAY FROM HERE.
AND I CAN TAKE YOU TO HIM.
The shoreline was too exposed. I wanted the cover of leaf and grass.
FOLLOW.
WAIT!
I HAVE TRAVELED A LONG WAY TO COME SEE...

"...YOU."

Something I learned training tenderpaws: lead and they will follow.

"TAKE ME NO FURTHER...

...FOR **YOU** ARE CELANAWE,

SON OF MAREIN, DAUGHTER OF BLACKBUR, SON OF HOLTON, SON OF DALTON."

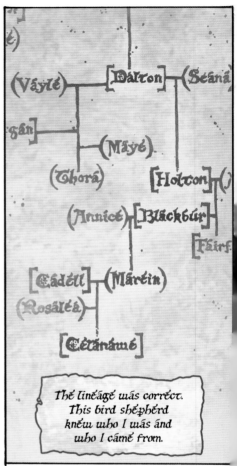

(Vayle) — [Dalton] — (Seana

gan — (Maye)

(Thora) — [Holton] — (

(Annice) — [Blackbur]

[Fairf

[Cadell] — (Marein)

(Rosalea)

[Celanawe]

The lineage was correct. This bird shepherd knew who I was and who I came from.

"WE ARE KIN YOU AND I

FROM LOCK-HAVEN I HAVE FLOWN...

...AND FROM APPLELOFT BEFORE THAT.

I HAVE THE AUTHORITY OF—

WE MUST LEAVE THIS PLACE MAKING NO SOUND.

FOR WE ARE HUNTED..."

CAW CAW

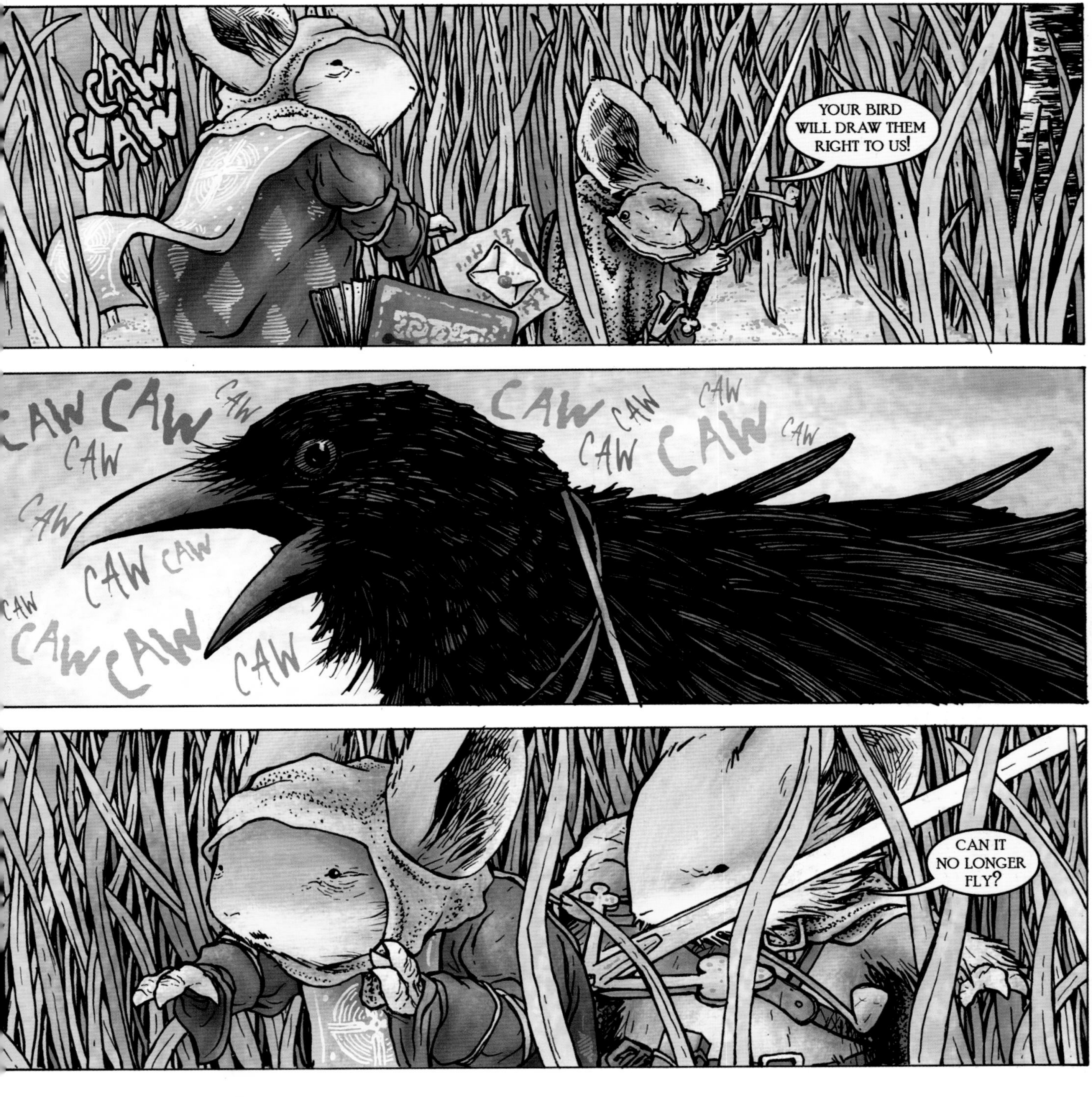

CAW CAW
YOUR BIRD WILL DRAW THEM RIGHT TO US!
CAW CAW CAW CAW CAW CAW CAW CAW CAW CAW CAW CAW CAW CAW CAW CAW CAW
CAN IT NO LONGER FLY?

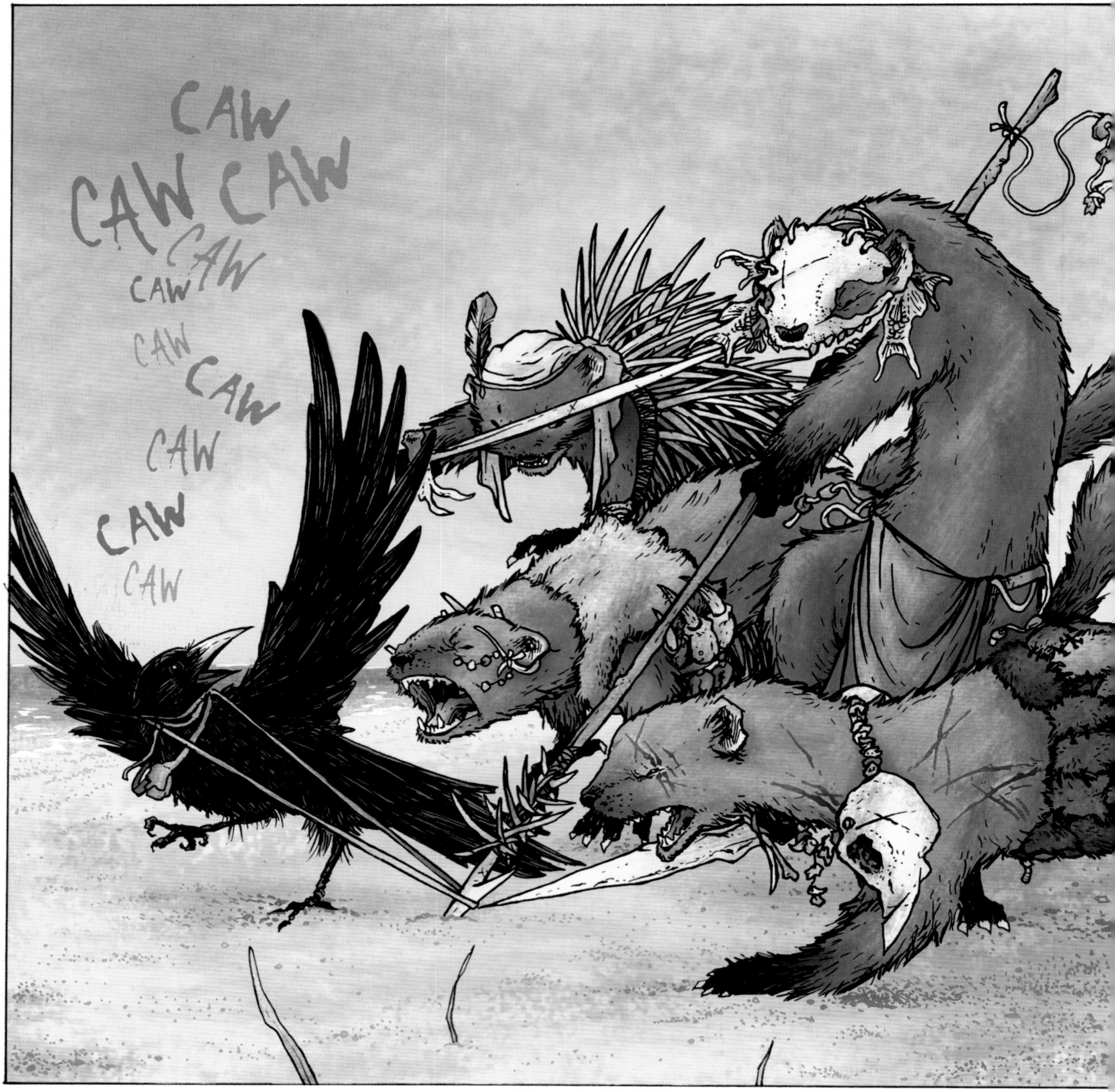
CAW
CAW CAW CAW
CAW
CAW
CAW
CAW
CAW
CAW
CAW

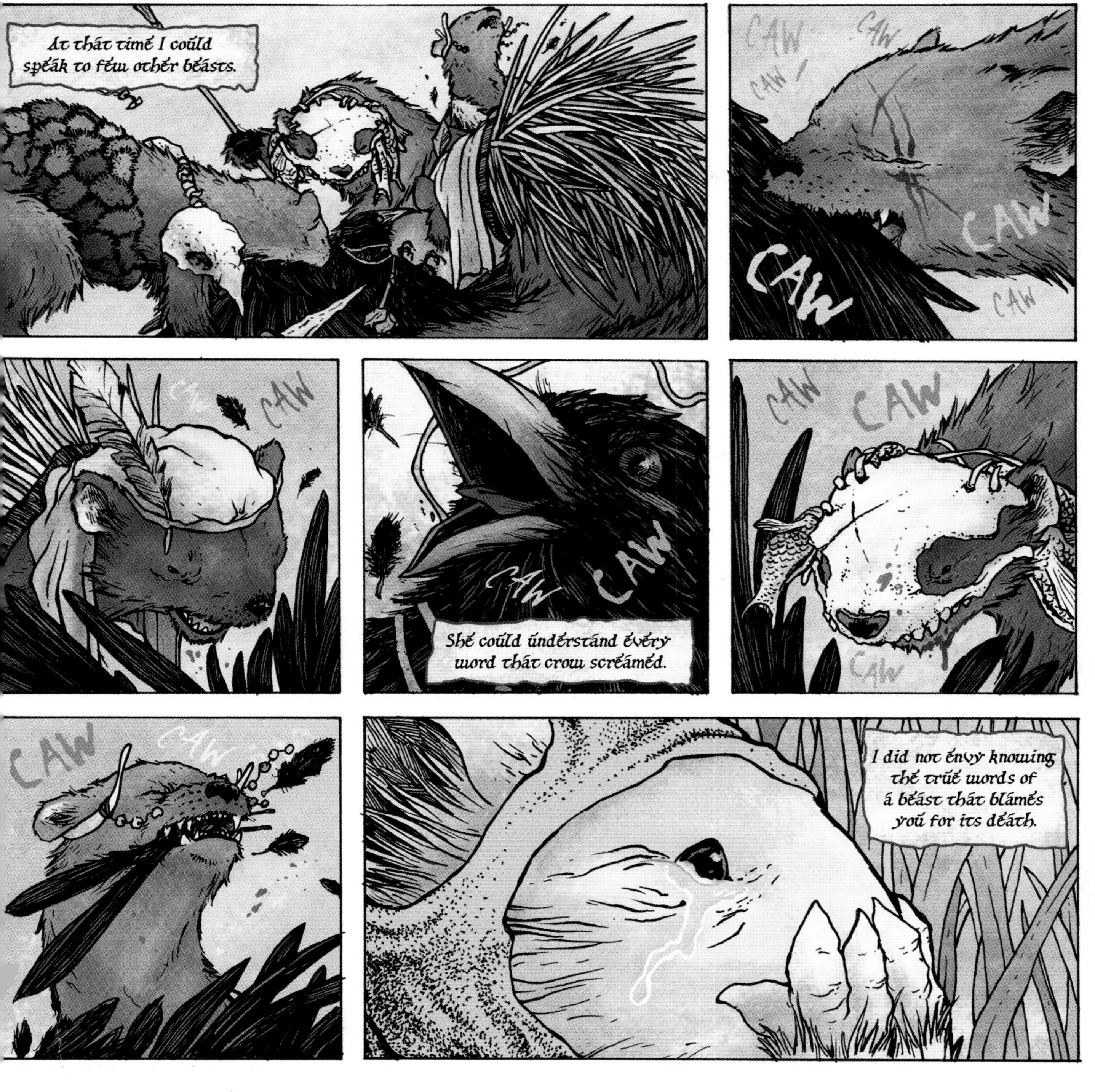

At that time I could speak to few other beasts.
CAW
CAW
CAW
CAW
CAW
CAW
CAW
CAW
CAW
CAW
She could understand every word that crow screamed.
CAW
CAW
CAW
CAW
CAW
I did not envy knowing the true words of a beast that blames you for its death.

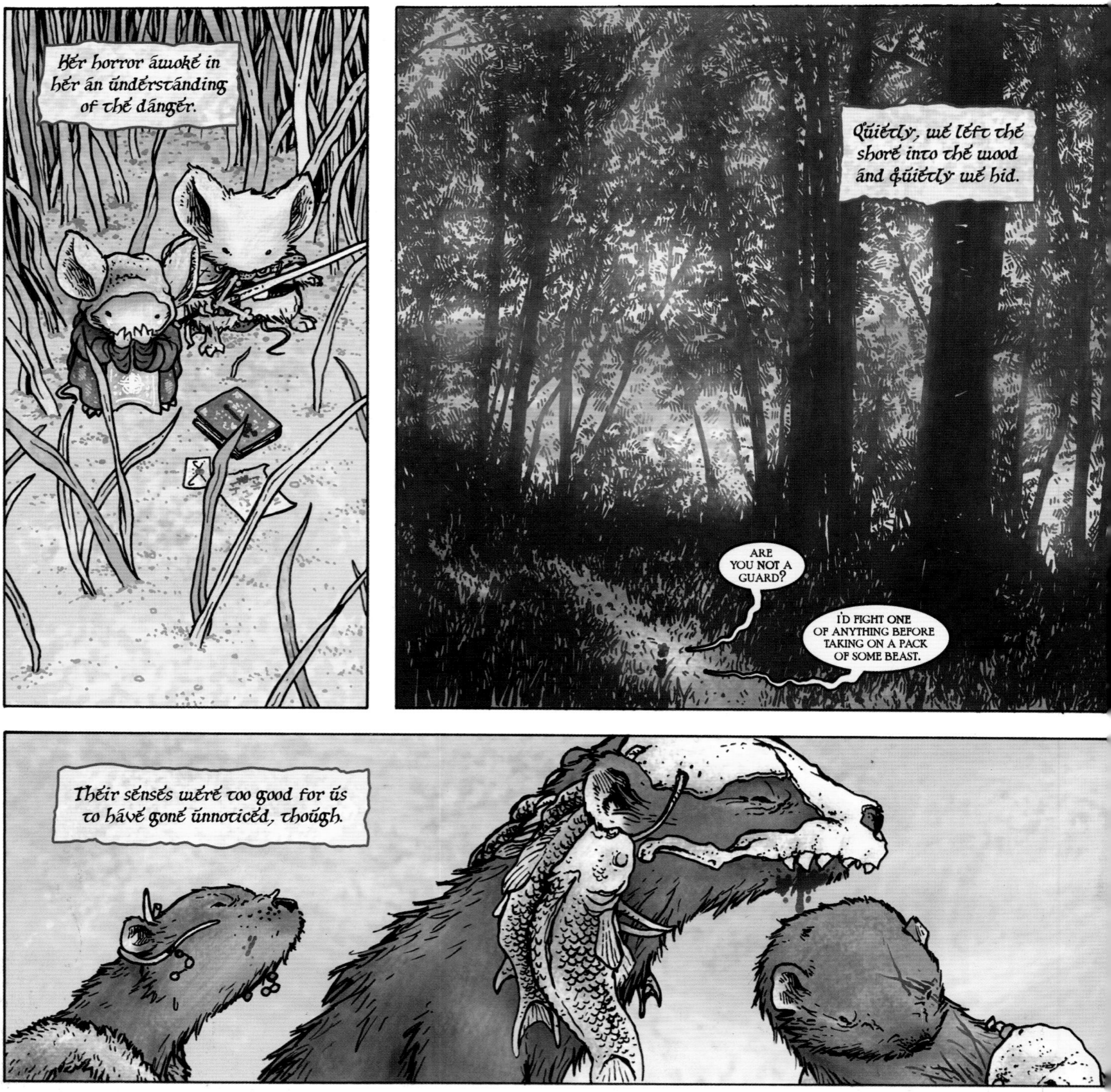
Her horror awoke in her an understanding of the danger.
Quietly, we left the shore into the wood and quietly we hid.
ARE YOU NOT A GUARD?
I'D FIGHT ONE OF ANYTHING BEFORE TAKING ON A PACK OF SOME BEAST.
Their senses were too good for us to have gone unnoticed, though.

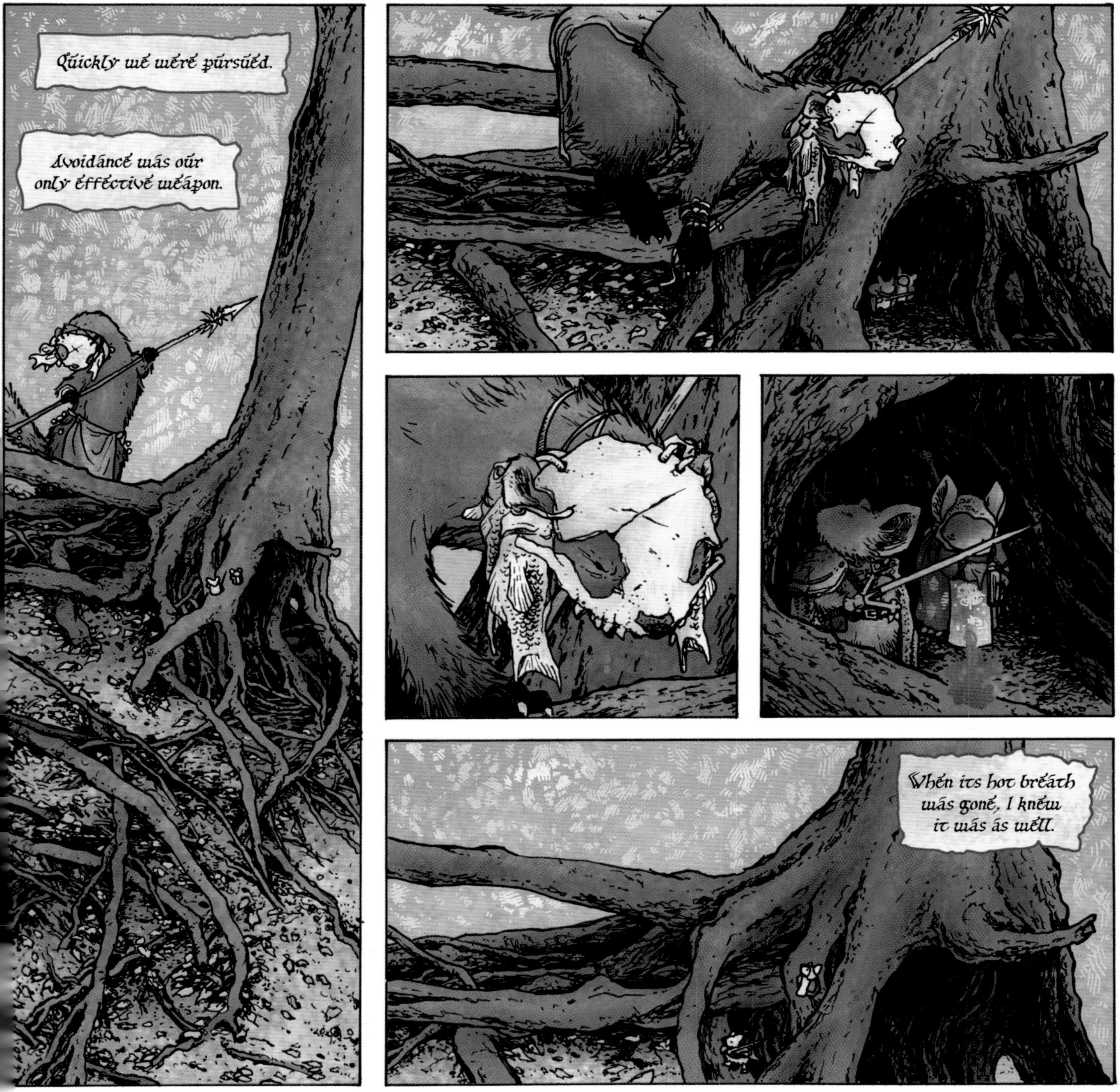
Quickly we were pursued.
Avoidance was our only effective weapon.
When its hot breath was gone, I knew it was as well.

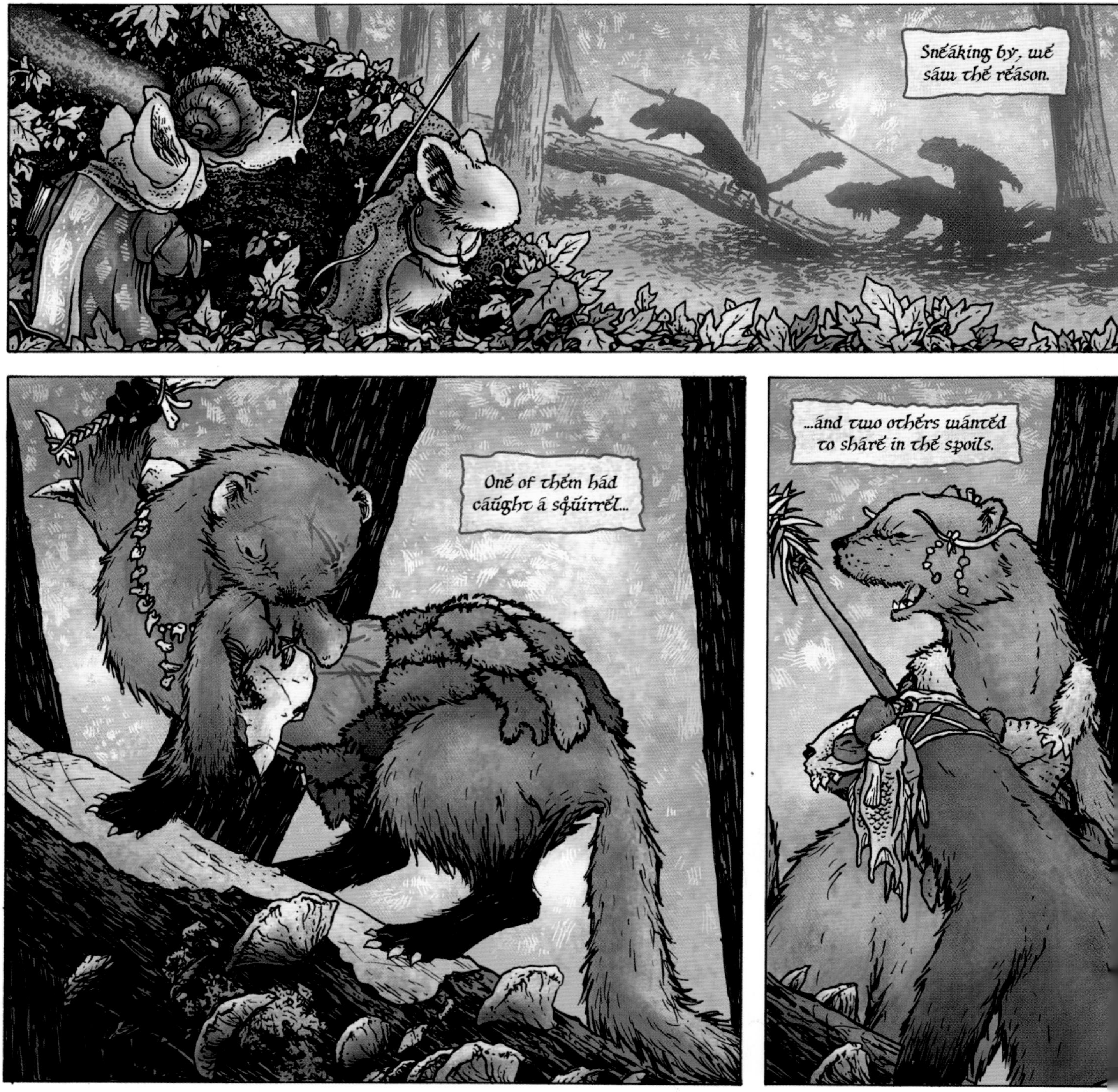
Sneaking by, we saw the reason.
One of them had caught a squirrel...
...and two others wanted to share in the spoils.

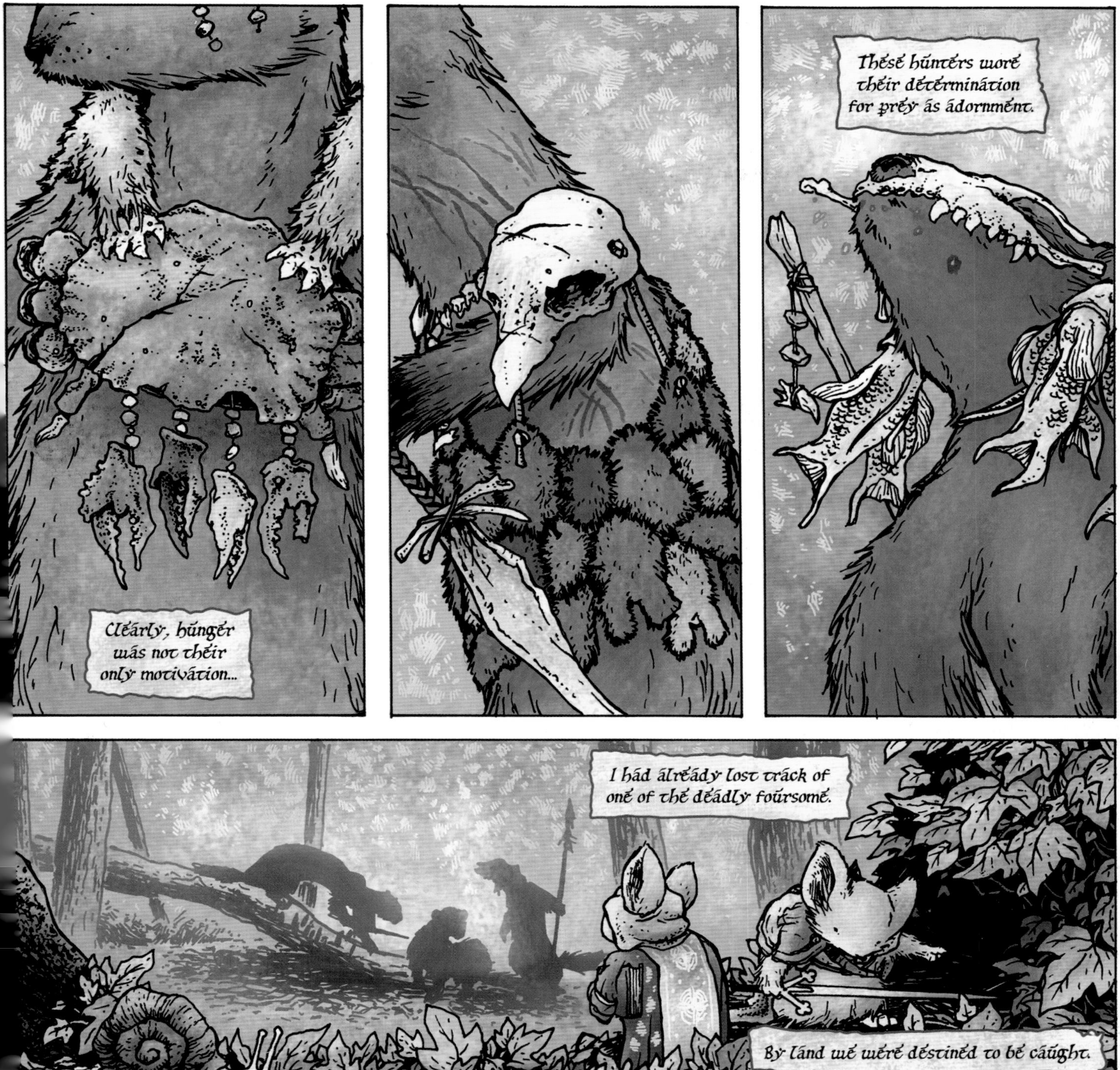
Clearly, hunger was not their only motivation...
These hunters wore their determination for prey as adornment.
I had already lost track of one of the deadly foursome.
By land we were destined to be caught.

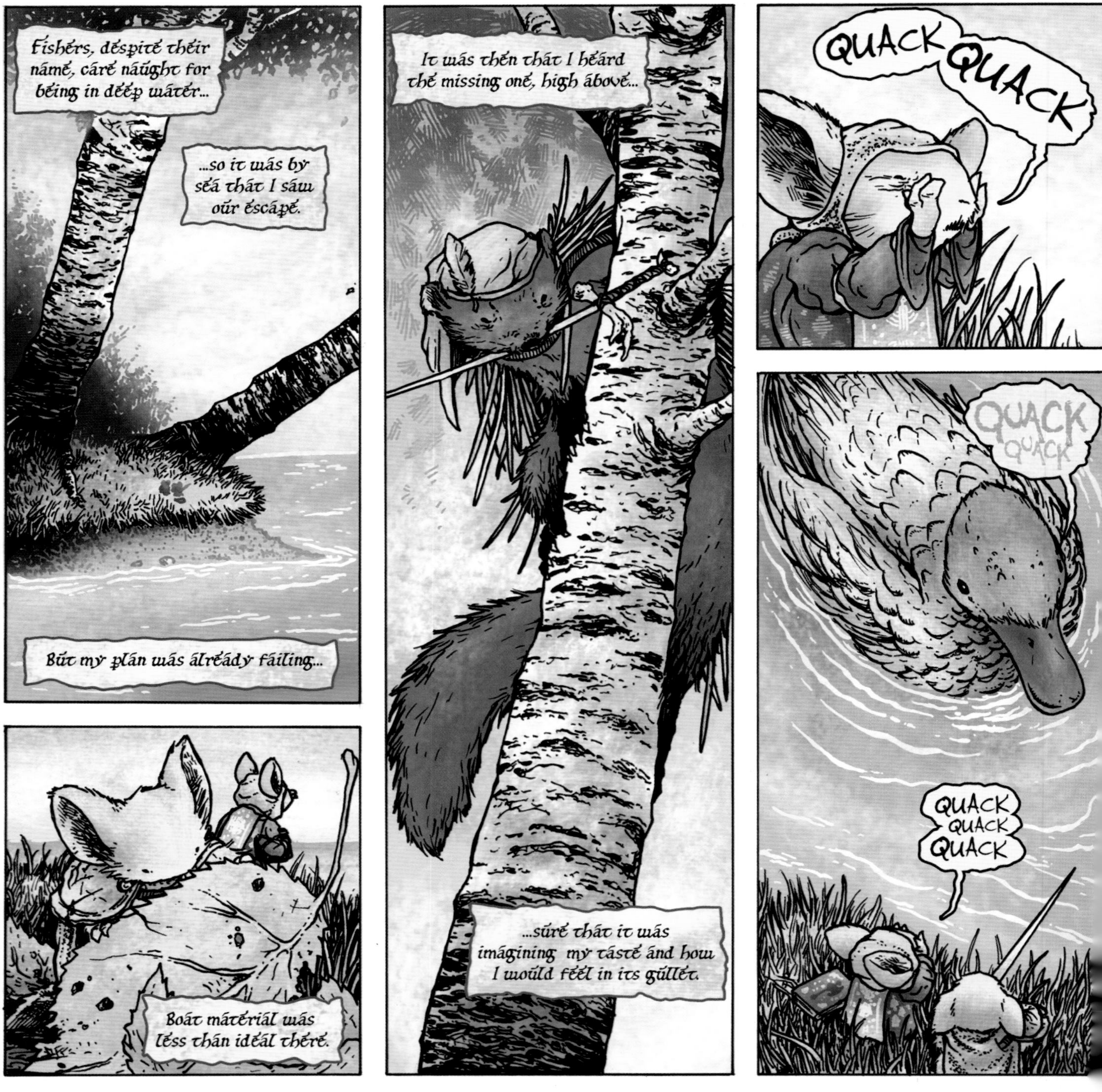
Fishers, despite their name, care naught for being in deep water...
...so it was by sea that I saw our escape.
But my plan was already failing...
Boat material was less than ideal there.
It was then that I heard the missing one, high above...
...sure that it was imagining my taste and how I would feel in its gullet.
QUACK QUACK QUACK
QUACK QUACK
QUACK QUACK QUACK

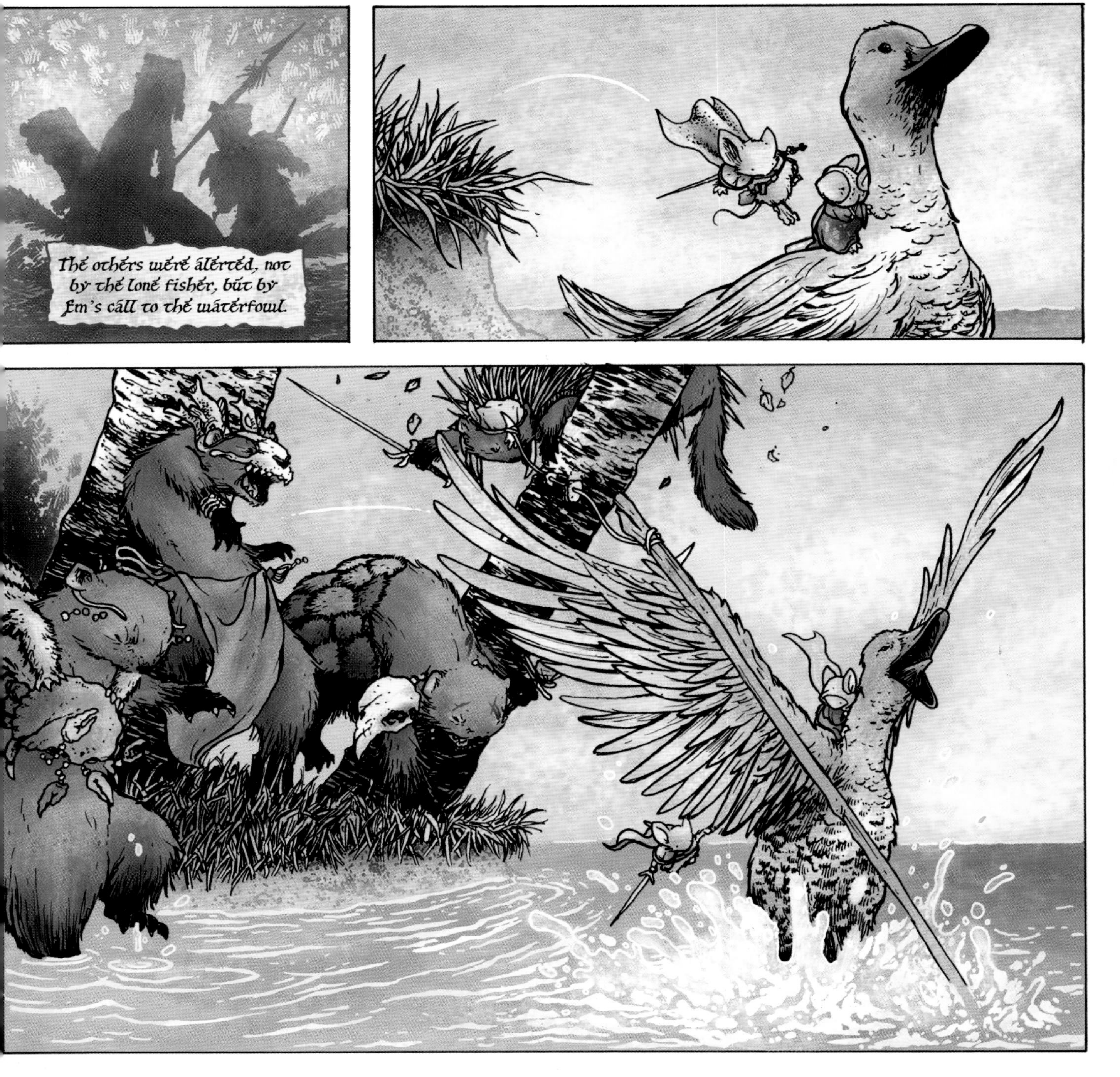
The others were alerted, not by the lone fisher, but by Em's call to the waterfowl.

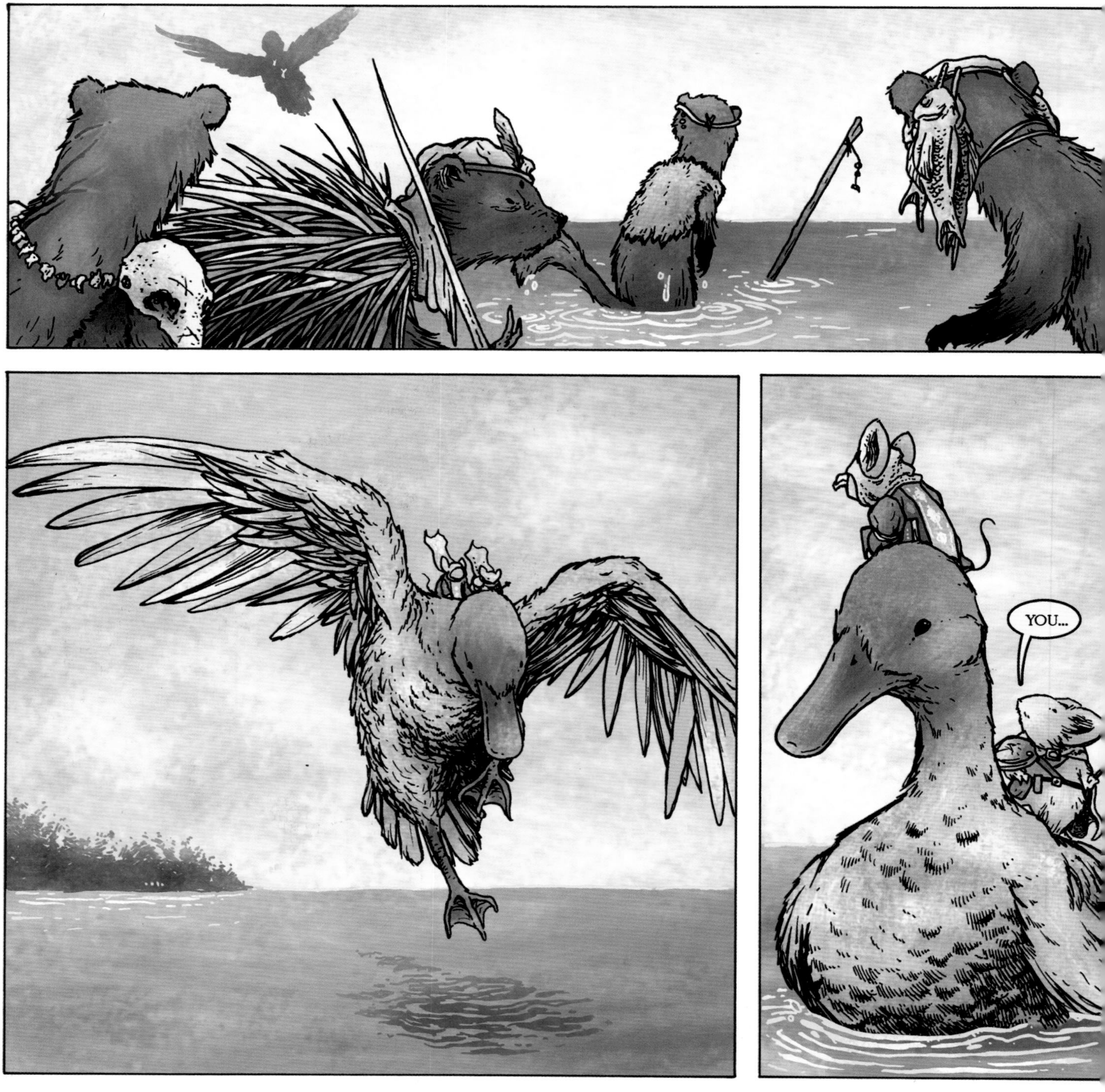
YOU...

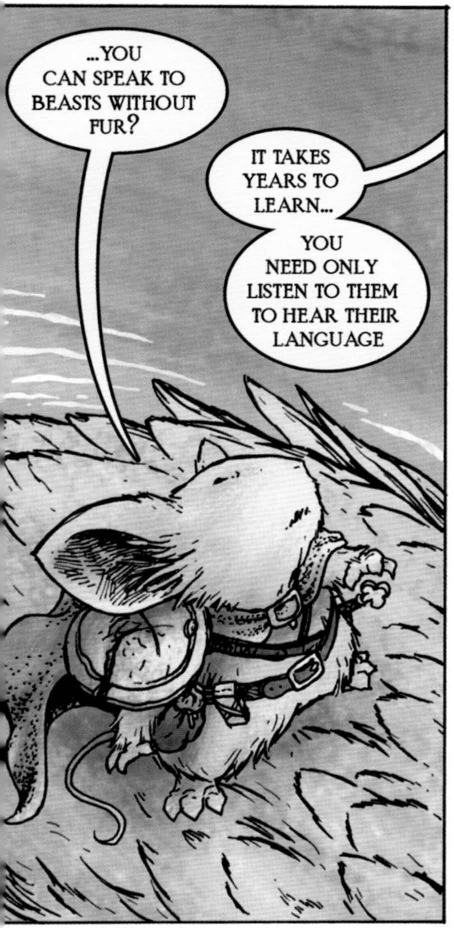
...YOU CAN SPEAK TO BEASTS WITHOUT FUR?
IT TAKES YEARS TO LEARN...
YOU NEED ONLY LISTEN TO THEM TO HEAR THEIR LANGUAGE

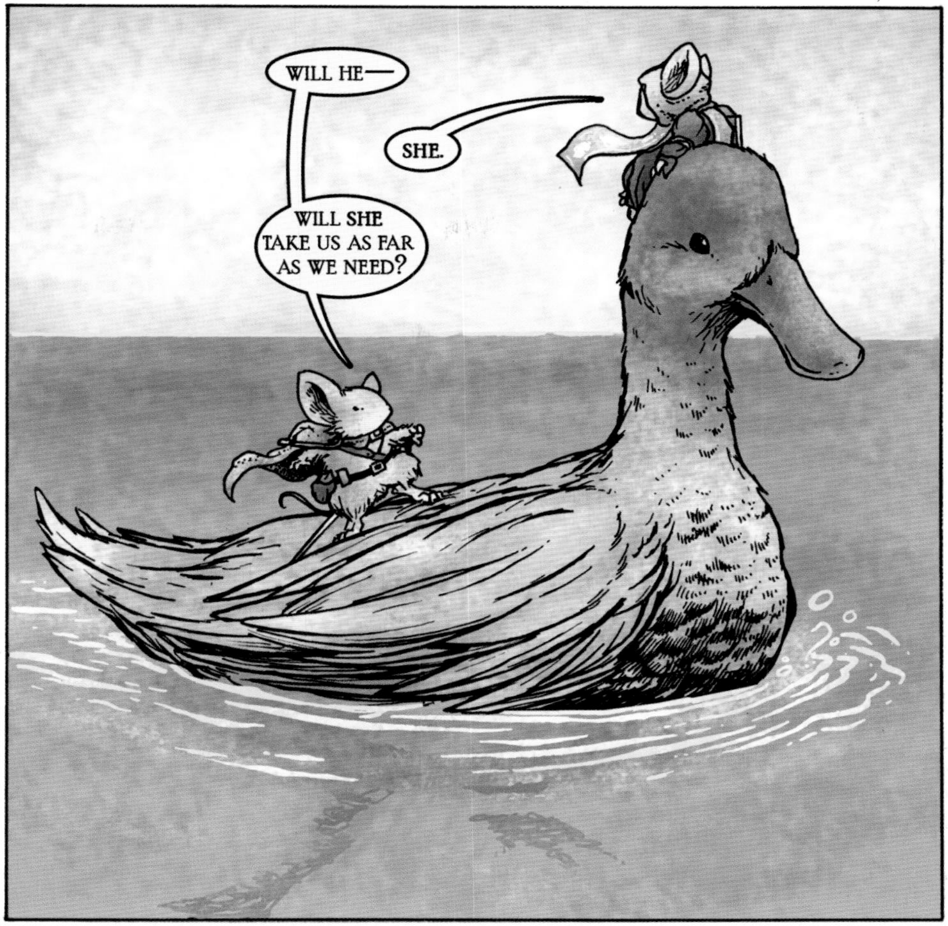
WILL HE—
SHE.
WILL SHE TAKE US AS FAR AS WE NEED?

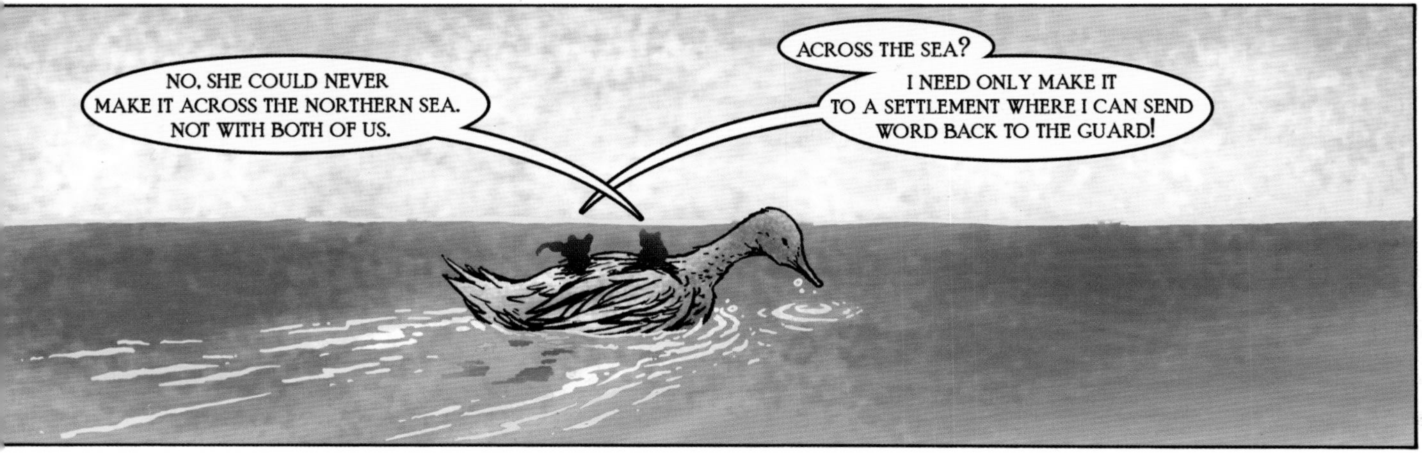
NO. SHE COULD NEVER MAKE IT ACROSS THE NORTHERN SEA. NOT WITH BOTH OF US.
ACROSS THE SEA?
I NEED ONLY MAKE IT TO A SETTLEMENT WHERE I CAN SEND WORD BACK TO THE GUARD!

I HAVE AUTHORIZATION FROM YOUR MATRIARCH.

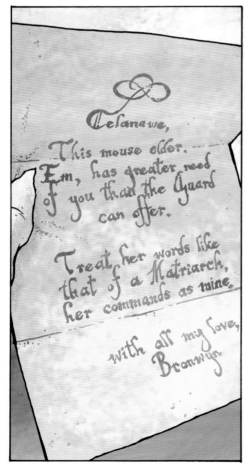

Celanawe,

This mouse elder, Em, has greater need of you than the Guard can offer.

Treat her words like that of a Matriarch, her commands as mine.

With all my love,
Bronwyn

AS YOU WISH, M'LADY.

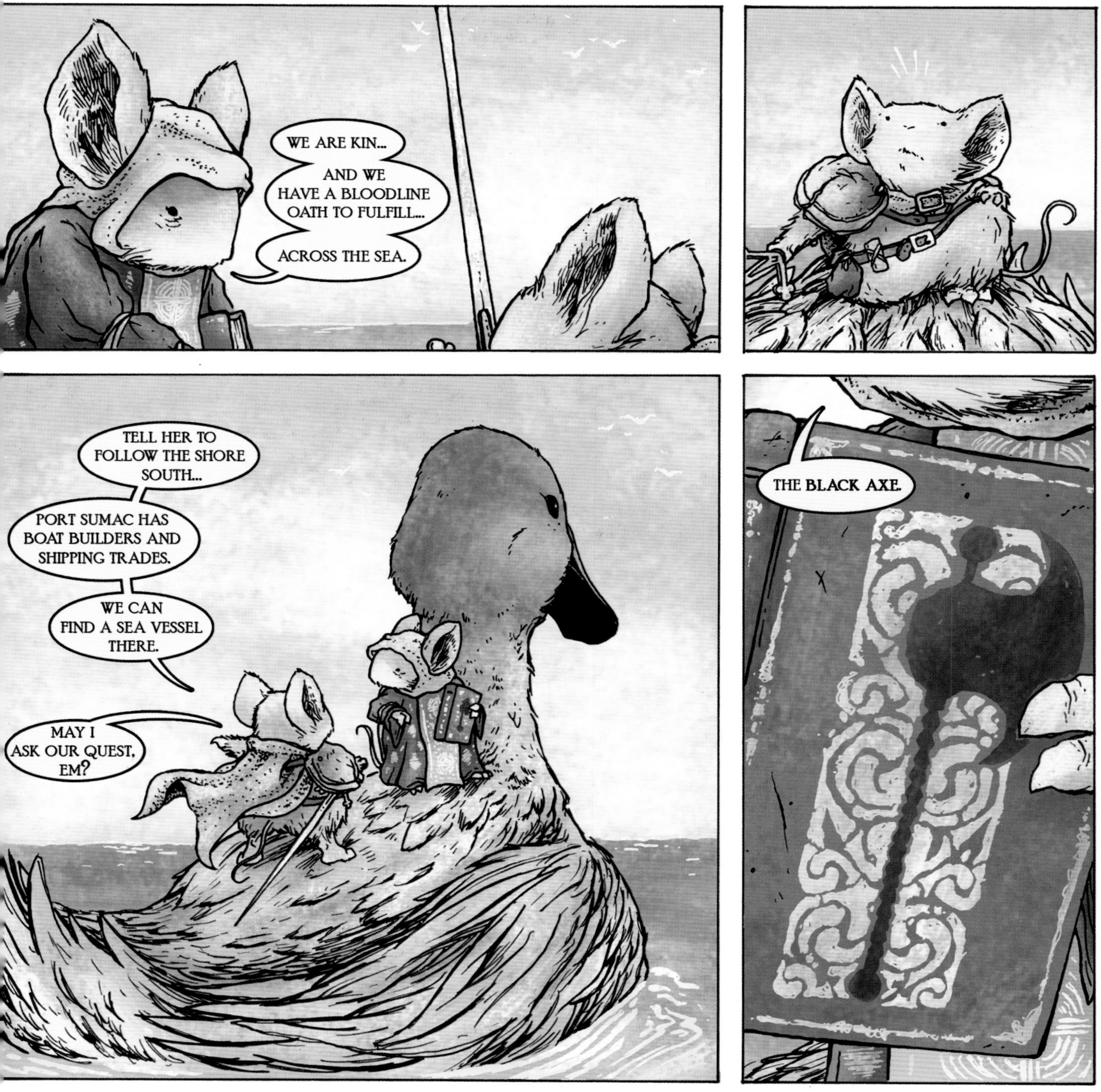
WE ARE KIN...
AND WE HAVE A BLOODLINE OATH TO FULFILL...
ACROSS THE SEA.
TELL HER TO FOLLOW THE SHORE SOUTH...
PORT SUMAC HAS BOAT BUILDERS AND SHIPPING TRADES.
WE CAN FIND A SEA VESSEL THERE.
MAY I ASK OUR QUEST, EM?
THE BLACK AXE.

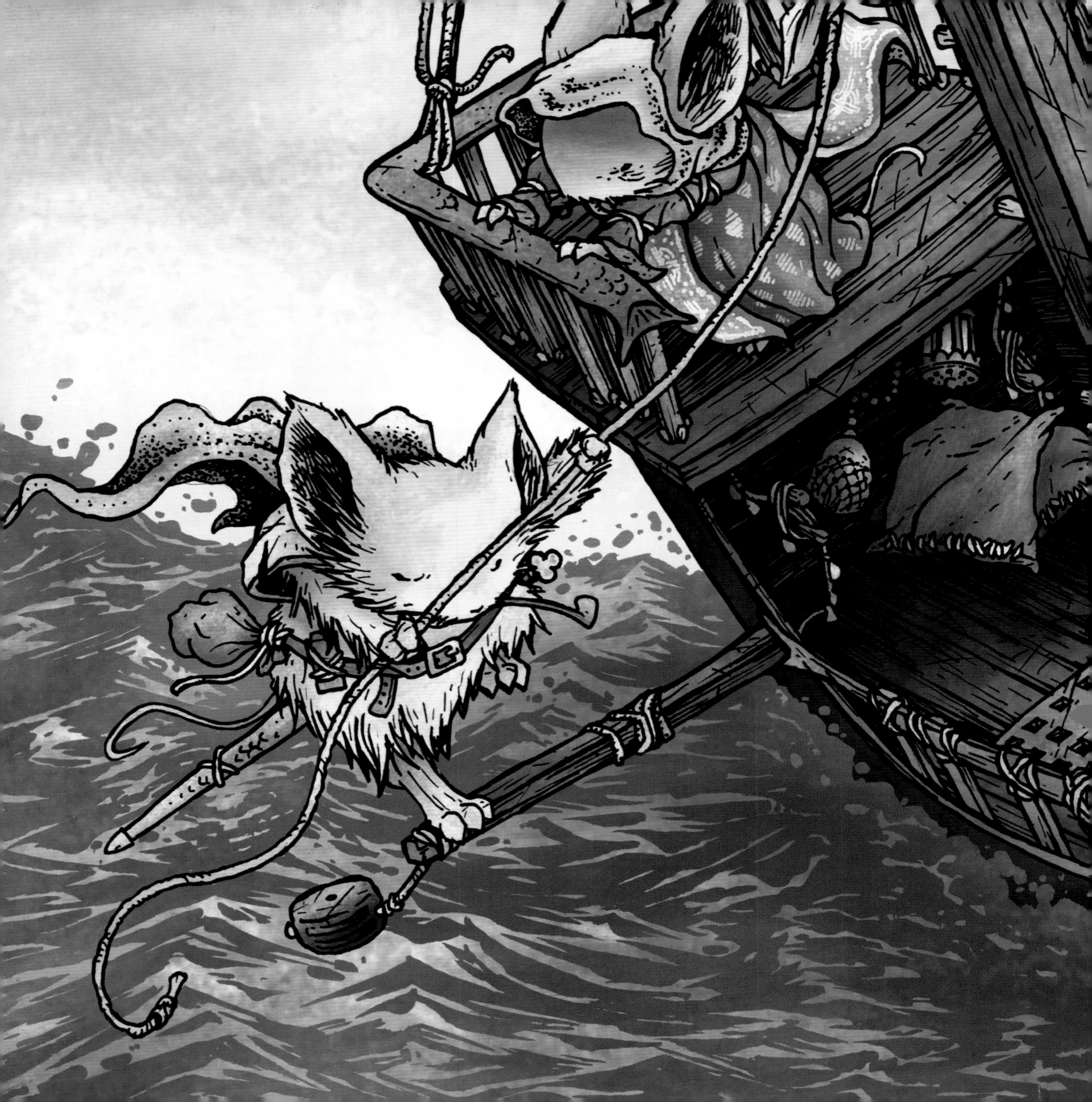

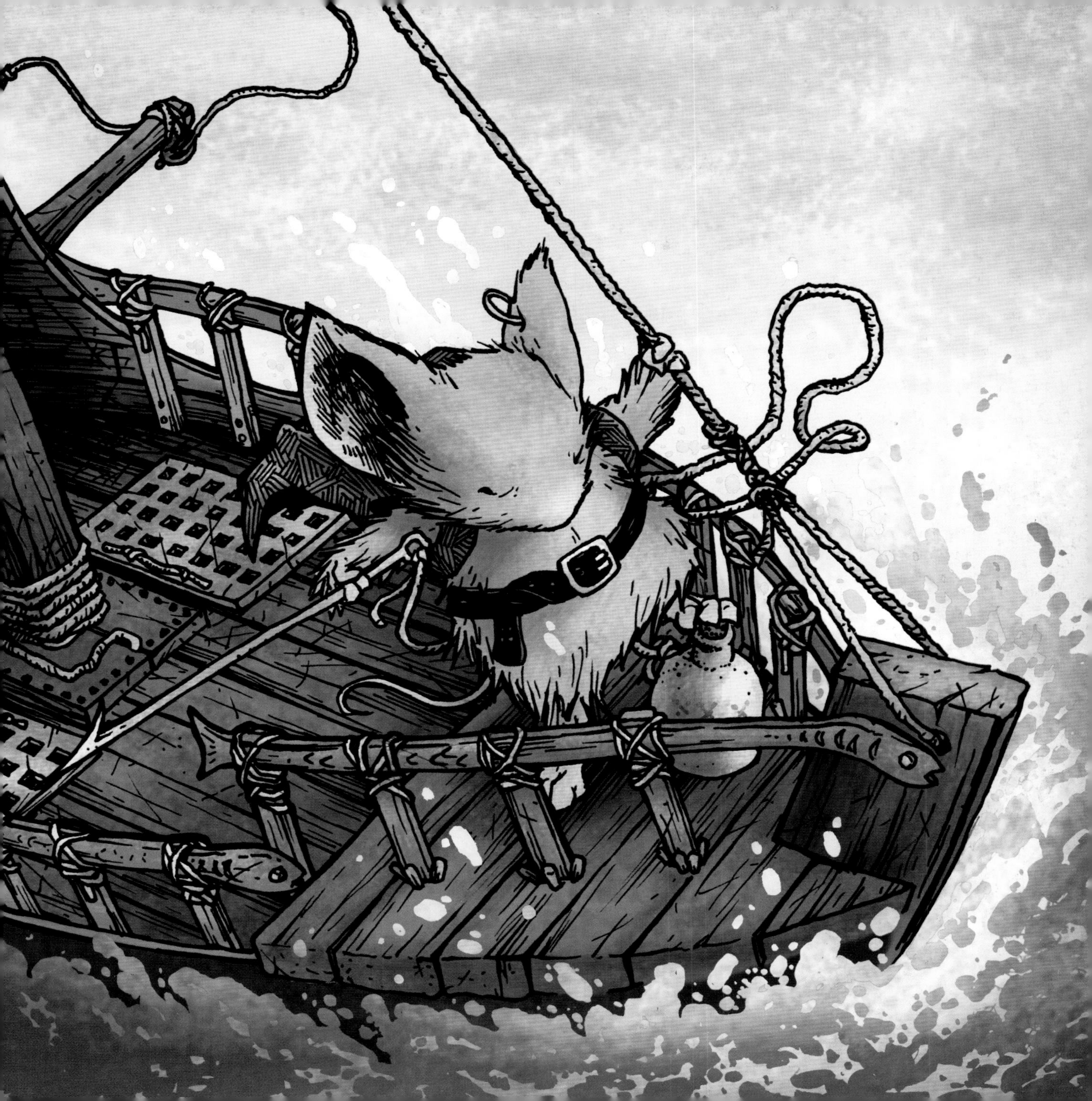

CHAPTER TWO

On the backs of winged beasts and furred giants, strode the Black Axe

They took no notice of him, for his movements were quiet and his soul calm.

The land was wide and vast and he could round all that was from rising till setting of the moon.

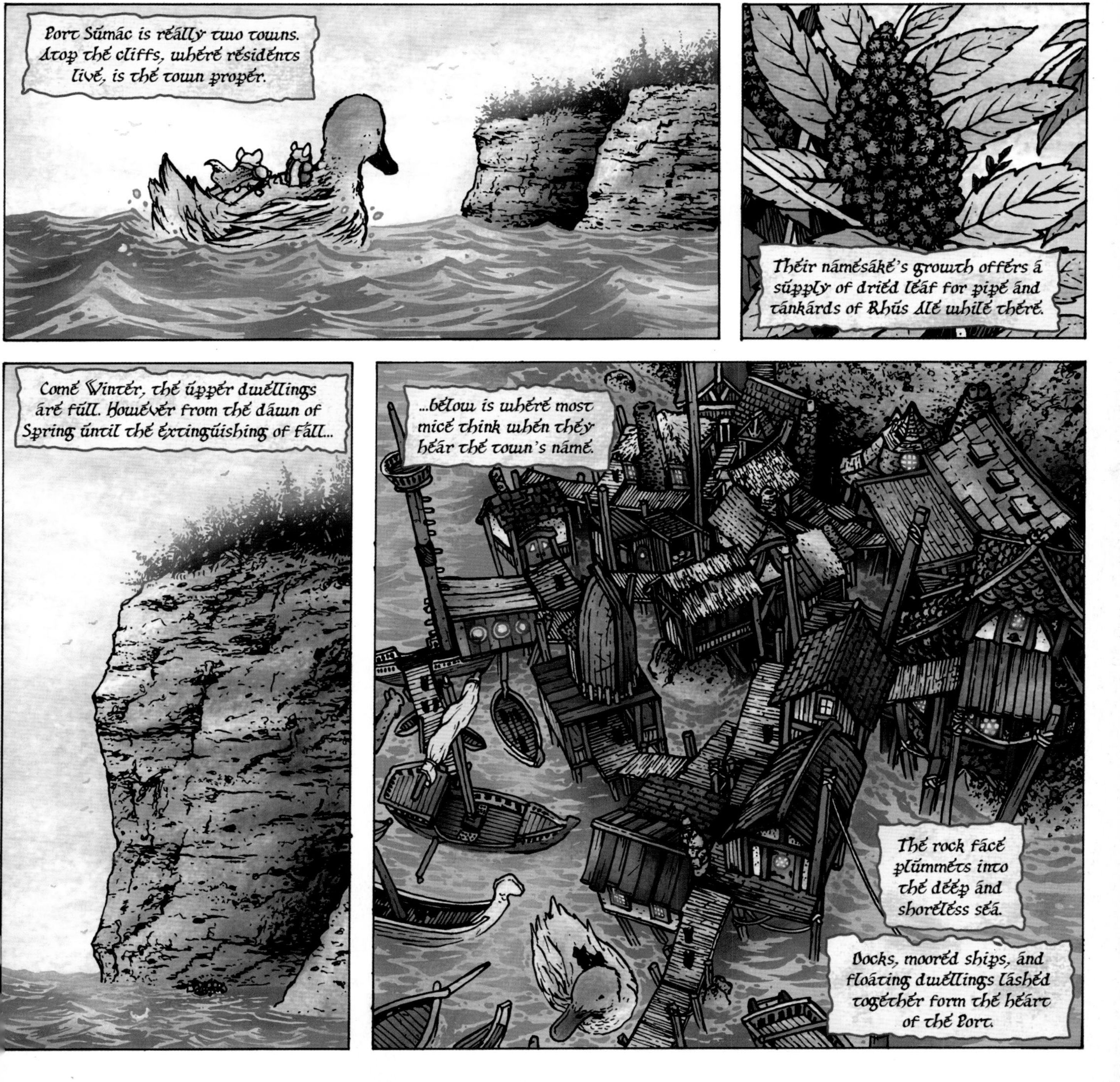
Port Sumac is really two towns. Atop the cliffs, where residents live, is the town proper.
Their namesake's growth offers a supply of dried leaf for pipe and tankards of Rhus Ale while there.
Come Winter, the upper dwellings are full. However from the dawn of Spring until the extinguishing of fall...
...below is where most mice think when they hear the town's name.
The rock face plummets into the deep and shoreless sea.
Docks, moored ships, and floating dwellings lashed together form the heart of the Port.

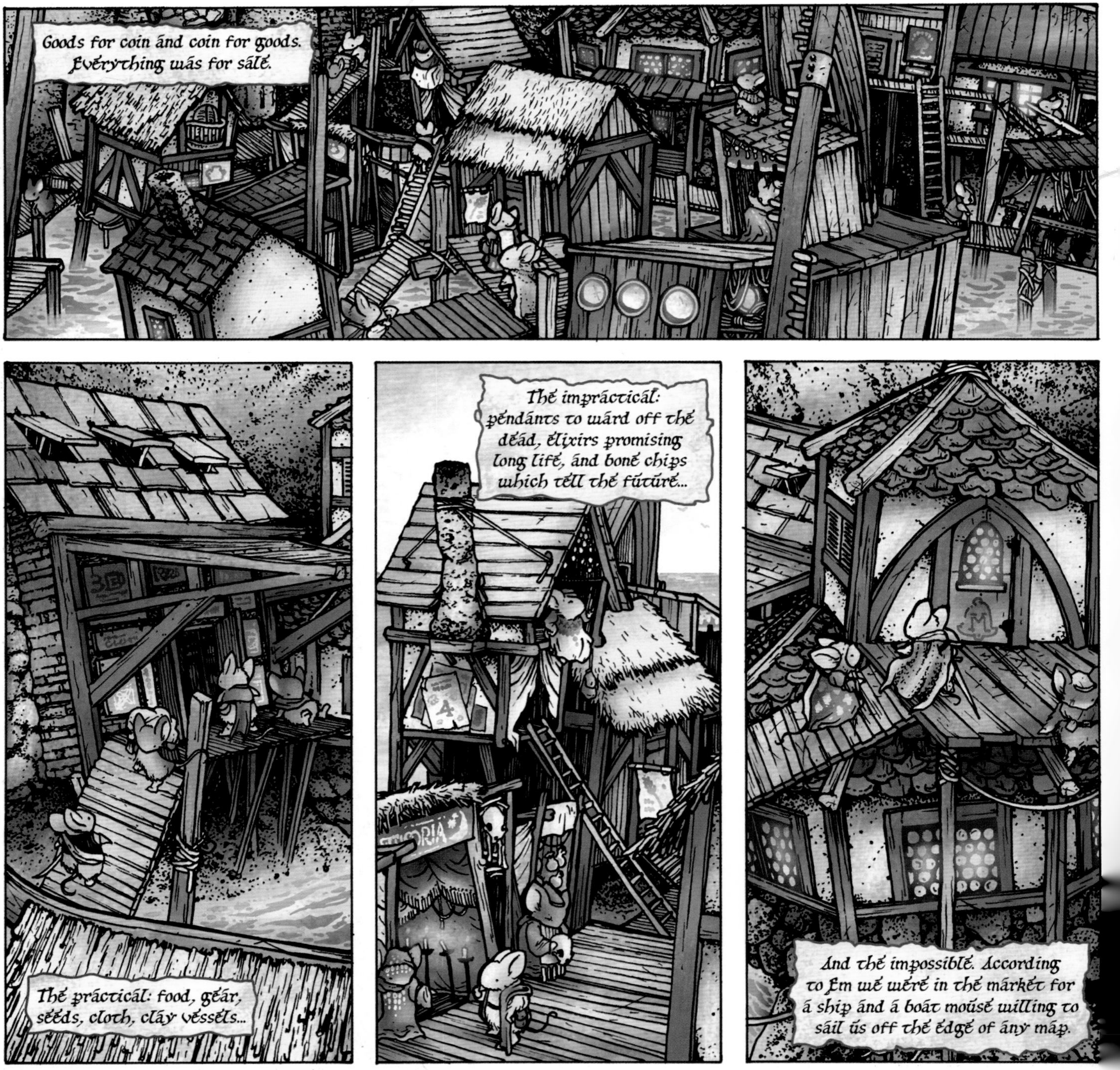

Goods for coin and coin for goods. Everything was for sale.
The practical: food, gear, seeds, cloth, clay vessels...
The impractical: pendants to ward off the dead, elixirs promising long life, and bone chips which tell the future...
And the impossible. According to Em we were in the market for a ship and a boat mouse willing to sail us off the edge of any map.

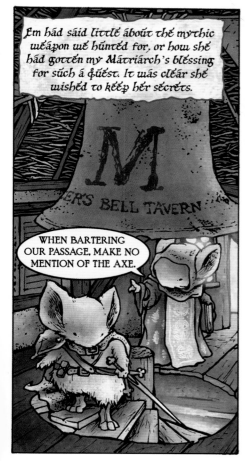

Em had said little about the mythic weapon we hunted for, or how she had gotten my Matriarch's blessing for such a quest. It was clear she wished to keep her secrets.

WHEN BARTERING OUR PASSAGE, MAKE NO MENTION OF THE AXE.

HOW DO YOU EXPECT ME TO DO THAT?

A CLEVER GUARD YOU ARE, I AM SURE YOU WILL MANAGE...

UNLESS YOU NEED AN AGED LADY MOUSE TO DEAL WITH THESE SCOUNDRELS.

The Mariner's Bell catered to the filthiest, crookedest, and greediest mice in the territories. Everything had a price: ruling power, murder, even mice themselves.

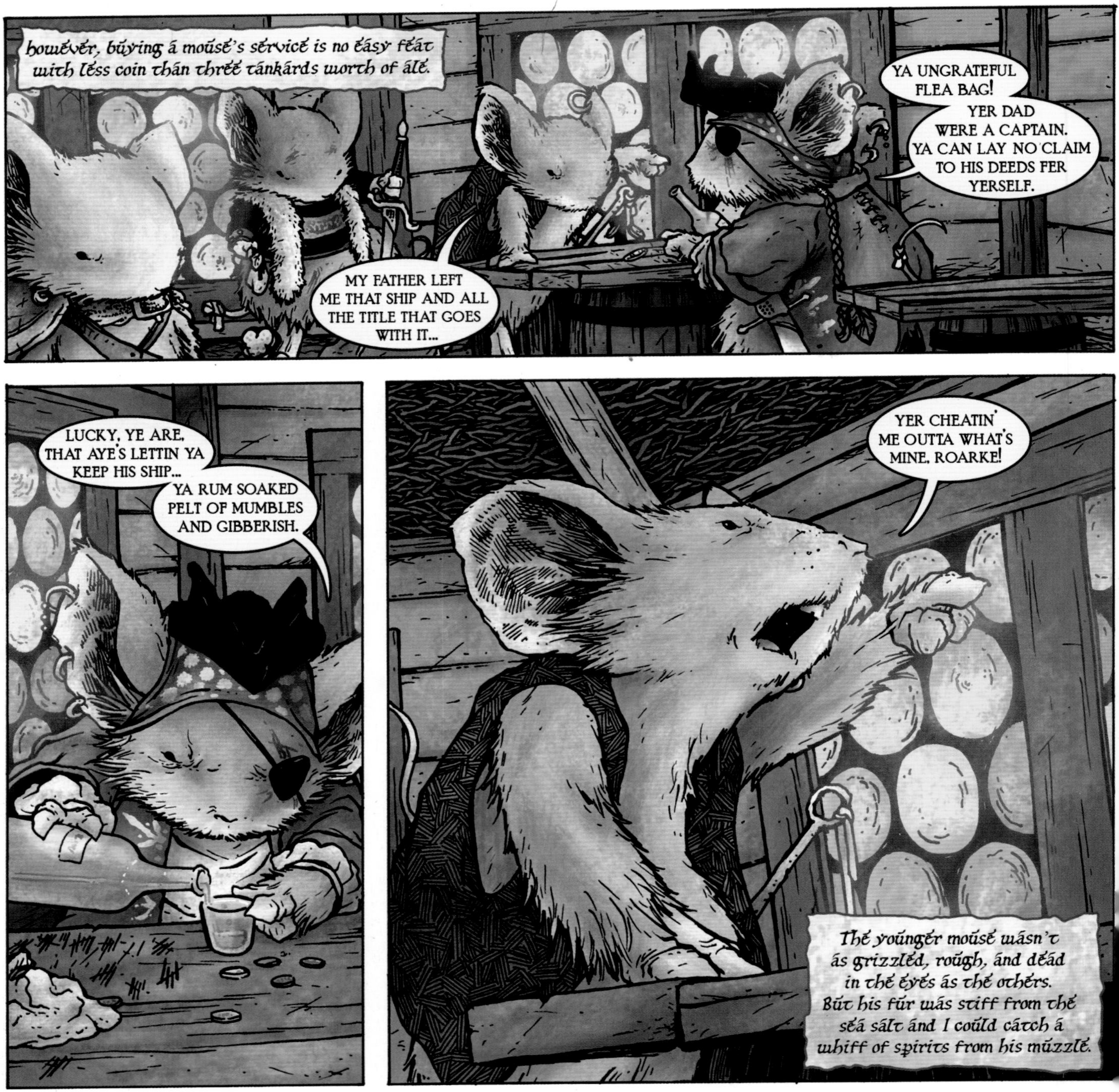
however, buying a mouse's service is no easy feat with less coin than three tankards worth of ale.
YA UNGRATEFUL FLEA BAG!
YER DAD WERE A CAPTAIN. YA CAN LAY NO CLAIM TO HIS DEEDS FER YERSELF.
MY FATHER LEFT ME THAT SHIP AND ALL THE TITLE THAT GOES WITH IT...
LUCKY, YE ARE, THAT AYE'S LETTIN YA KEEP HIS SHIP...
YA RUM SOAKED PELT OF MUMBLES AND GIBBERISH.
YER CHEATIN' ME OUTTA WHAT'S MINE, ROARKE!
The younger mouse wasn't as grizzled, rough, and dead in the eyes as the others. But his fur was stiff from the sea salt and I could catch a whiff of spirits from his muzzle.

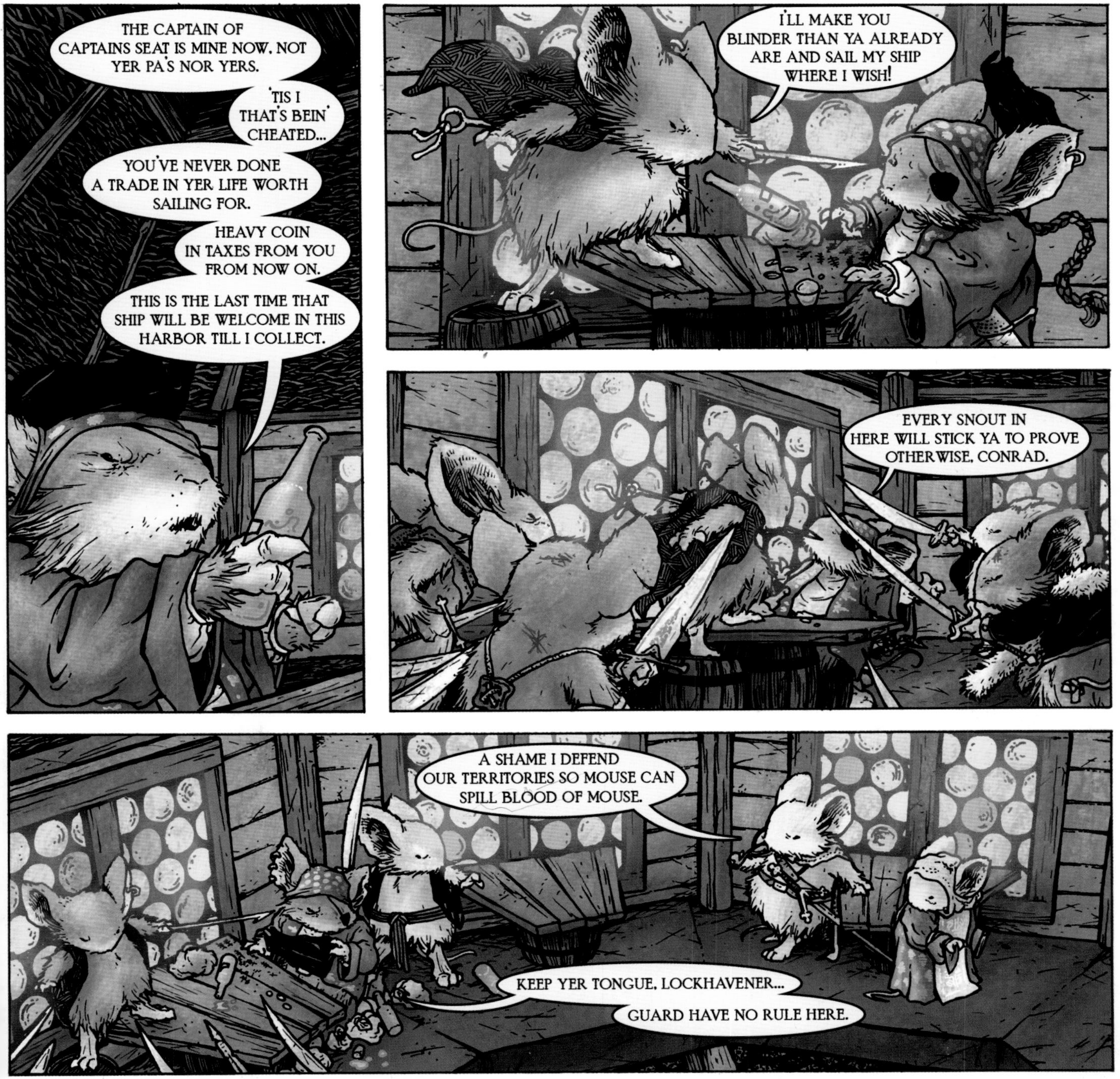

THE CAPTAIN OF CAPTAINS SEAT IS MINE NOW, NOT YER PA'S NOR YERS.
'TIS I THAT'S BEIN' CHEATED...
YOU'VE NEVER DONE A TRADE IN YER LIFE WORTH SAILING FOR.
HEAVY COIN IN TAXES FROM YOU FROM NOW ON.
THIS IS THE LAST TIME THAT SHIP WILL BE WELCOME IN THIS HARBOR TILL I COLLECT.
I'LL MAKE YOU BLINDER THAN YA ALREADY ARE AND SAIL MY SHIP WHERE I WISH!
EVERY SNOUT IN HERE WILL STICK YA TO PROVE OTHERWISE, CONRAD.
A SHAME I DEFEND OUR TERRITORIES SO MOUSE CAN SPILL BLOOD OF MOUSE.
KEEP YER TONGUE, LOCKHAVENER...
GUARD HAVE NO RULE HERE.

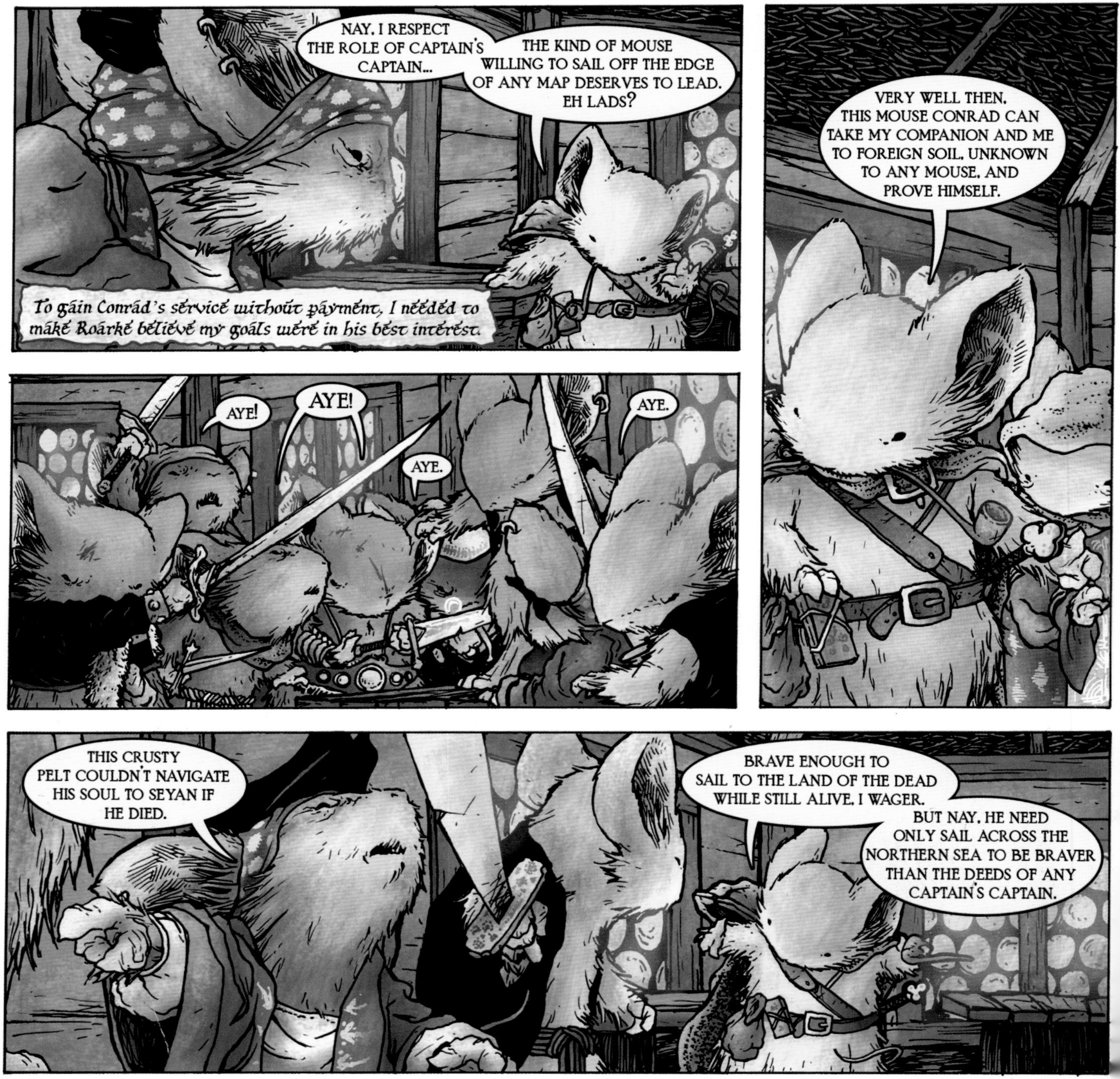
NAY, I RESPECT THE ROLE OF CAPTAIN'S CAPTAIN...
THE KIND OF MOUSE WILLING TO SAIL OFF THE EDGE OF ANY MAP DESERVES TO LEAD. EH LADS?
To gain Conrad's service without payment, I needed to make Roarke believe my goals were in his best interest.
VERY WELL THEN. THIS MOUSE CONRAD CAN TAKE MY COMPANION AND ME TO FOREIGN SOIL, UNKNOWN TO ANY MOUSE, AND PROVE HIMSELF.
AYE!
AYE!
AYE.
AYE.
THIS CRUSTY PELT COULDN'T NAVIGATE HIS SOUL TO SEYAN IF HE DIED.
BRAVE ENOUGH TO SAIL TO THE LAND OF THE DEAD WHILE STILL ALIVE, I WAGER.
BUT NAY, HE NEED ONLY SAIL ACROSS THE NORTHERN SEA TO BE BRAVER THAN THE DEEDS OF ANY CAPTAIN'S CAPTAIN.

HAR! IF HE GOES FURTHER THAN THE HORIZON AND RETURNS WITH THINGS MY EYE HAS NEVER SEEN, HE WON'T JUST BE ON THE COUNCIL OF CAPTAINS, I'LL MAKE HIM CAPTAIN OF IT!

A BLOOD AGREEMENT THEN?

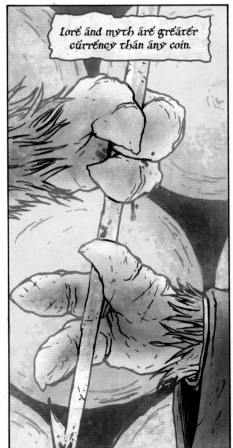

Lore and myth are greater currency than any coin.

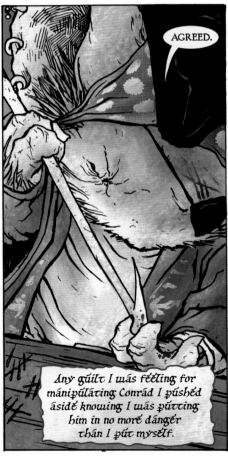

AGREED.

Any guilt I was feeling for manipulating Conrad I pushed aside knowing I was putting him in no more danger than I put myself.

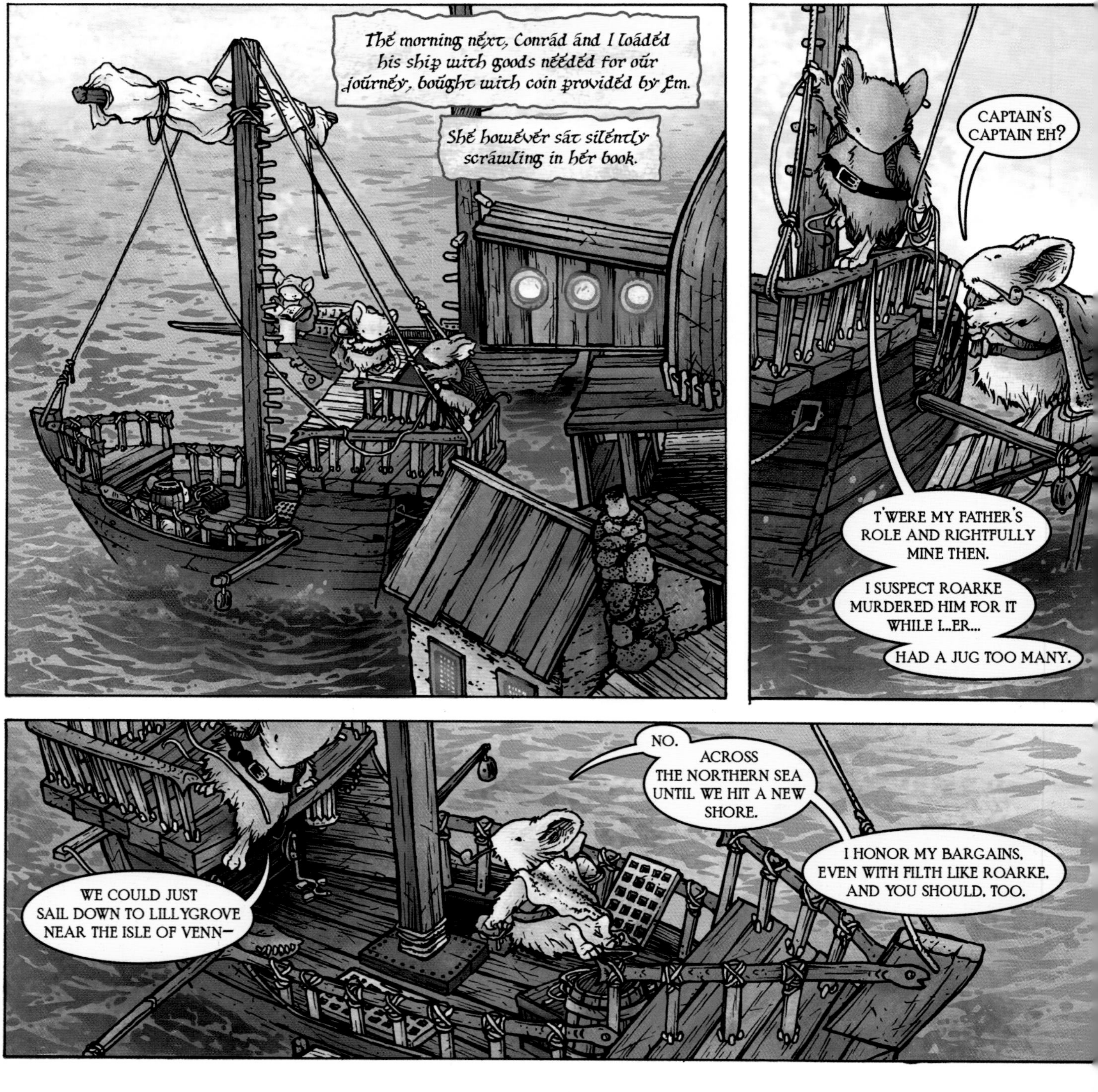
The morning next, Conrad and I loaded his ship with goods needed for our journey, bought with coin provided by Em.
She however sat silently scrawling in her book.
CAPTAIN'S CAPTAIN EH?
T'WERE MY FATHER'S ROLE AND RIGHTFULLY MINE THEN.
I SUSPECT ROARKE MURDERED HIM FOR IT WHILE I...ER...
HAD A JUG TOO MANY.
WE COULD JUST SAIL DOWN TO LILLYGROVE NEAR THE ISLE OF VENN—
NO.
ACROSS THE NORTHERN SEA UNTIL WE HIT A NEW SHORE.
I HONOR MY BARGAINS, EVEN WITH FILTH LIKE ROARKE, AND YOU SHOULD, TOO.

I questioned my own judgement that day. I was blindly following Em off the edge of the world for a mythological axe that no mouse had seen in twenty seasons.

Was I no better than Conrad? Manipulated into this quest?

Only because I knew my matriarch Bronwyn's writing, her script, her seal, would I honor Em's request.

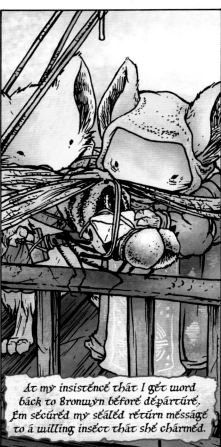

At my insistence that I get word back to Bronwyn before departure, Em secured my sealed return message to a willing insect that she charmed.

She assured me it understood when she told it "Lockhaven."

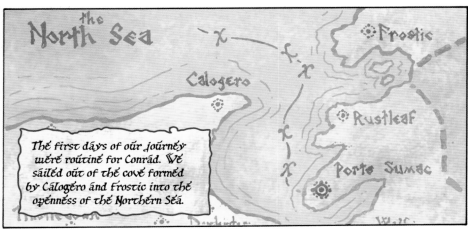

The North Sea

Frostic

Calogero

Rustleaf

Porte Sumac

The first days of our journey were routine for Conrad. We sailed out of the cove formed by Calogero and Frostic into the openness of the Northern Sea.

Early on, I tried to plot our course by map. Once we lost sight of land, this became impossible.

Conrad said he had little use for maps anyhow.

Em, however, would make note of stars once they appeared, finding constellations to guide us.

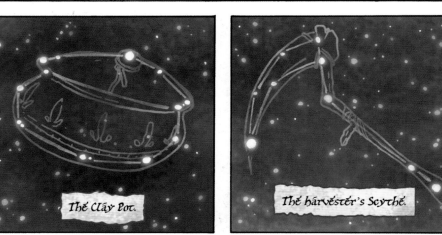

The Clay Pot.

The harvester's Scythe.

The Heron.

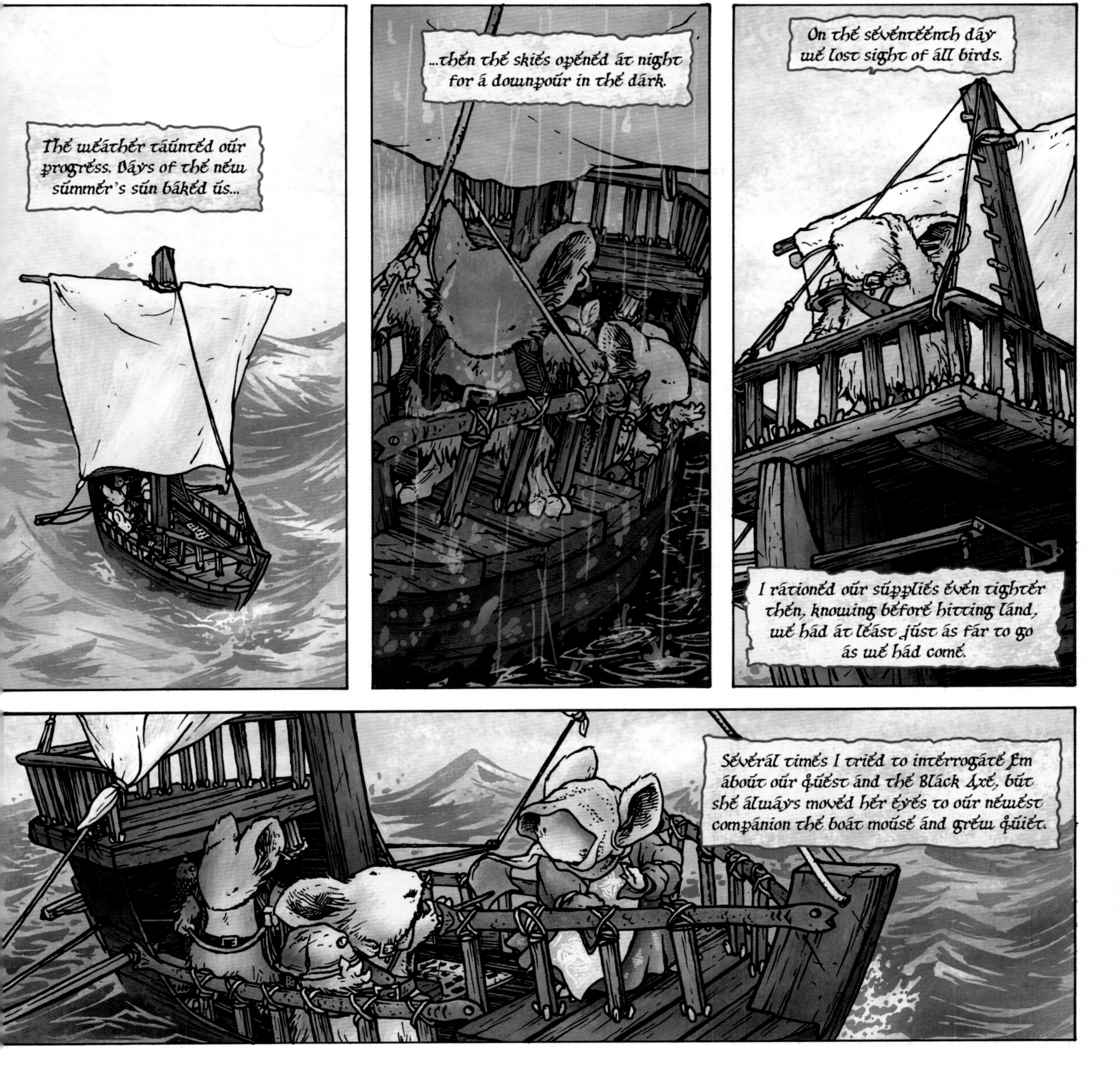
The weather taunted our progress. Days of the new summer's sun baked us...
...then the skies opened at night for a downpour in the dark.
On the seventeenth day we lost sight of all birds.
I rationed our supplies even tighter then, knowing before hitting land, we had at least just as far to go as we had come.
Several times I tried to interrogate Em about our quest and the Black Axe, but she always moved her eyes to our newest companion the boat mouse and grew quiet.

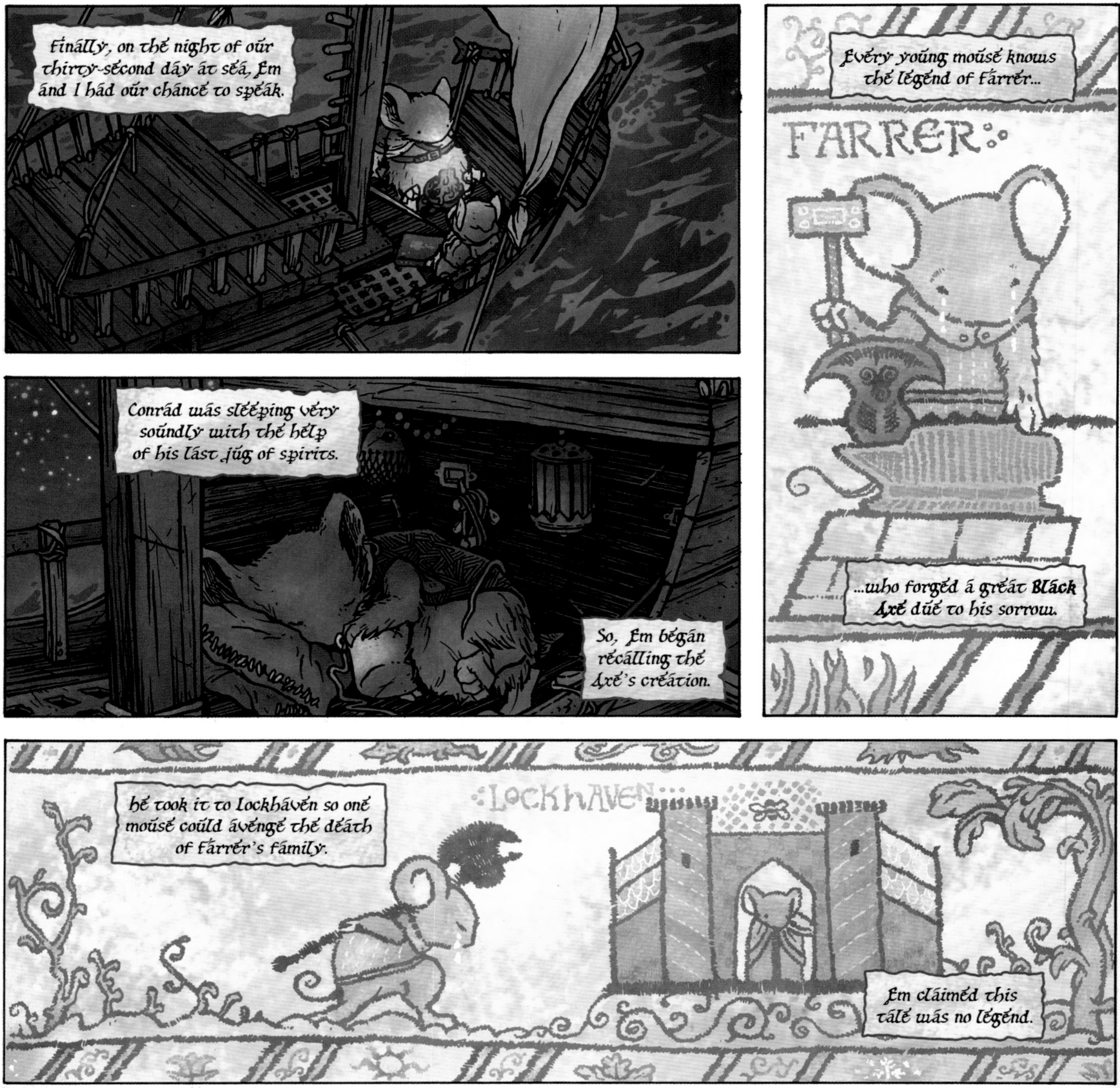
Finally, on the night of our thirty-second day at sea, Em and I had our chance to speak.
Every young mouse knows the legend of Farrer...
FARRER
Conrad was sleeping very soundly with the help of his last jug of spirits.
So, Em began recalling the Axe's creation.
...who forged a great Black Axe due to his sorrow.
He took it to Lockhaven so one mouse could avenge the death of Farrer's family.
LOCKHAVEN
Em claimed this tale was no legend.

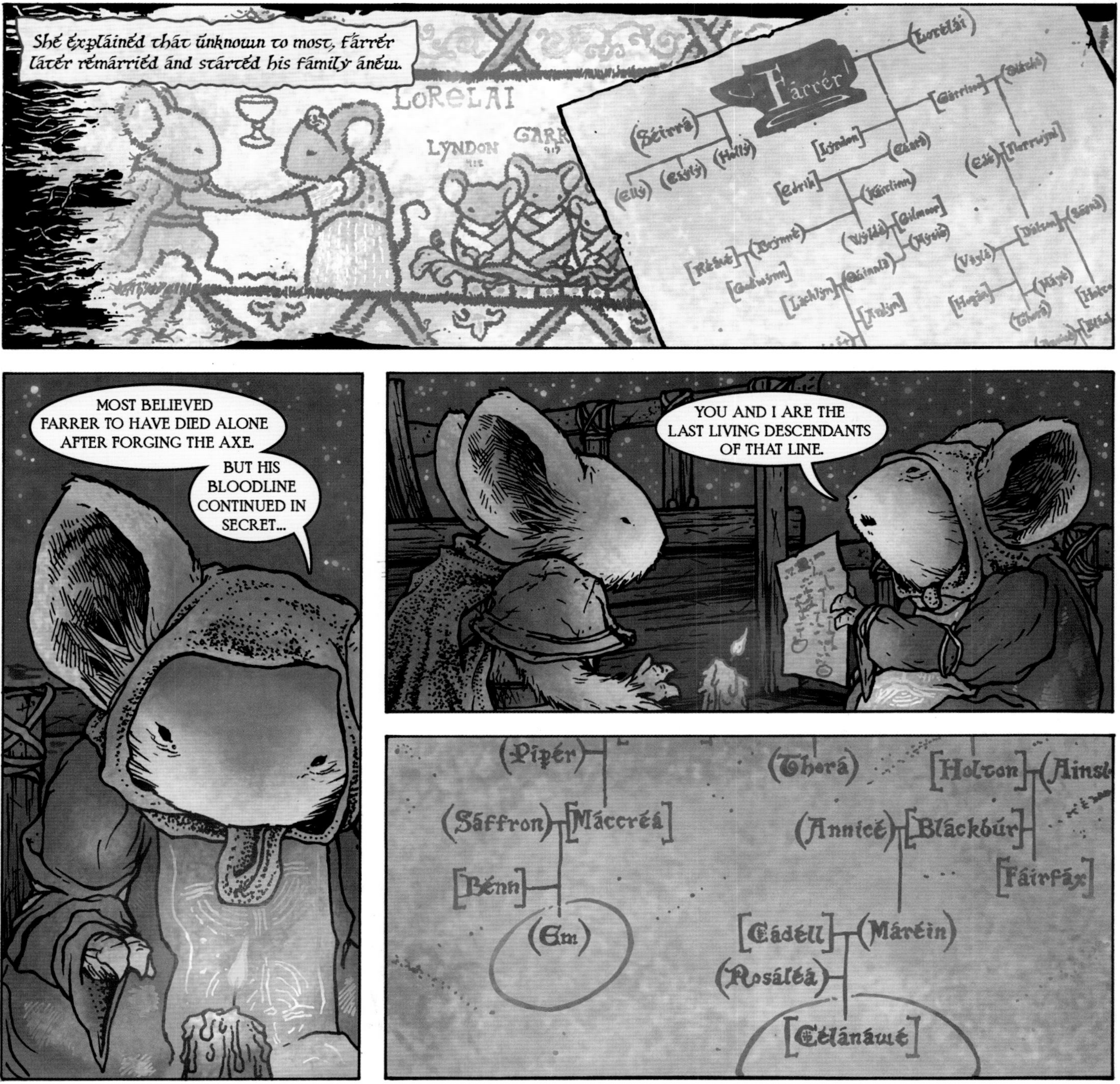
She explained that unknown to most, Farrer later remarried and started his family anew.
LORELAI
LYNDON
GARR
Farrer
Lorelai
MOST BELIEVED FARRER TO HAVE DIED ALONE AFTER FORGING THE AXE.
BUT HIS BLOODLINE CONTINUED IN SECRET...
YOU AND I ARE THE LAST LIVING DESCENDANTS OF THAT LINE.
(Piper)
(Thera)
[Holton]
(Saffron)
[Maccrea]
(Annice)
[Blackbur]
[Fairfax]
[Benn]
(Em)
[Cadell]
(Martin)
(Rosalea)
[Celanawe]

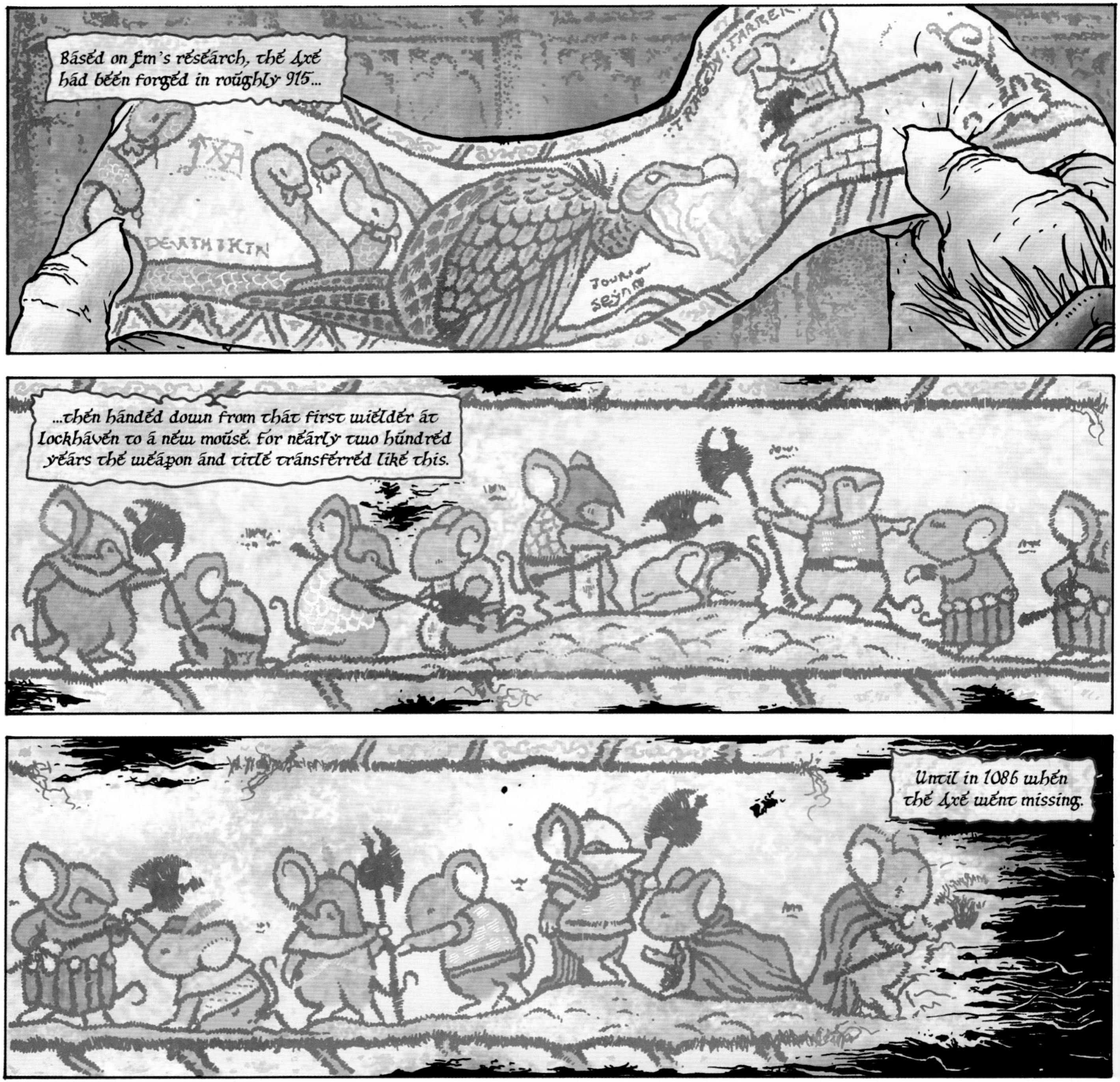
Based on Em's research, the Axe had been forged in roughly 915...
...then handed down from that first wielder at Lockhaven to a new mouse. For nearly two hundred years the weapon and title transferred like this.
Until in 1086 when the Axe went missing.

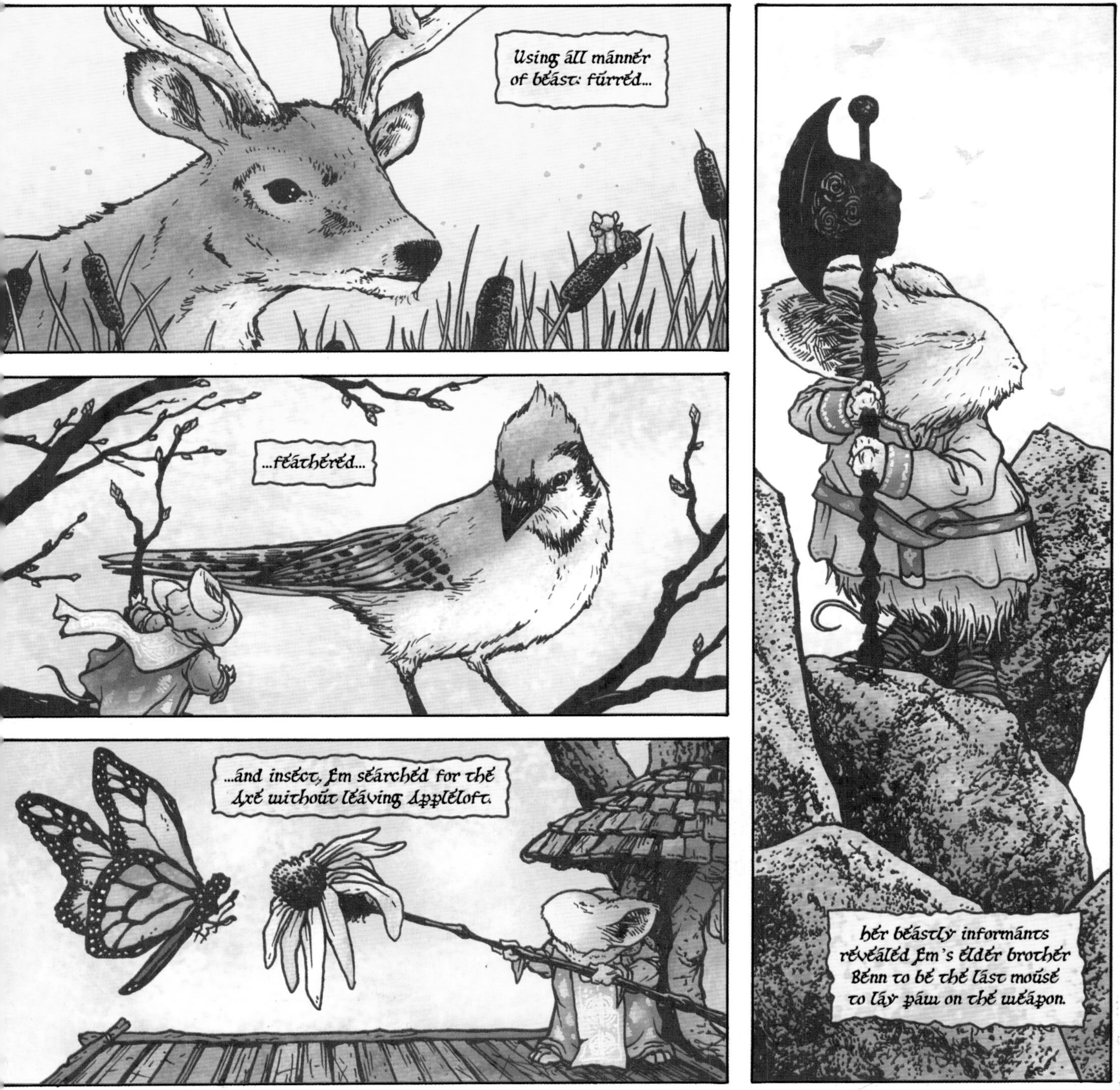
Using all manner of beast: furred...
...feathered...
...and insect, Em searched for the Axe without leaving Appleloft.
Her beastly informants revealed Em's elder brother Benn to be the last mouse to lay paw on the weapon.

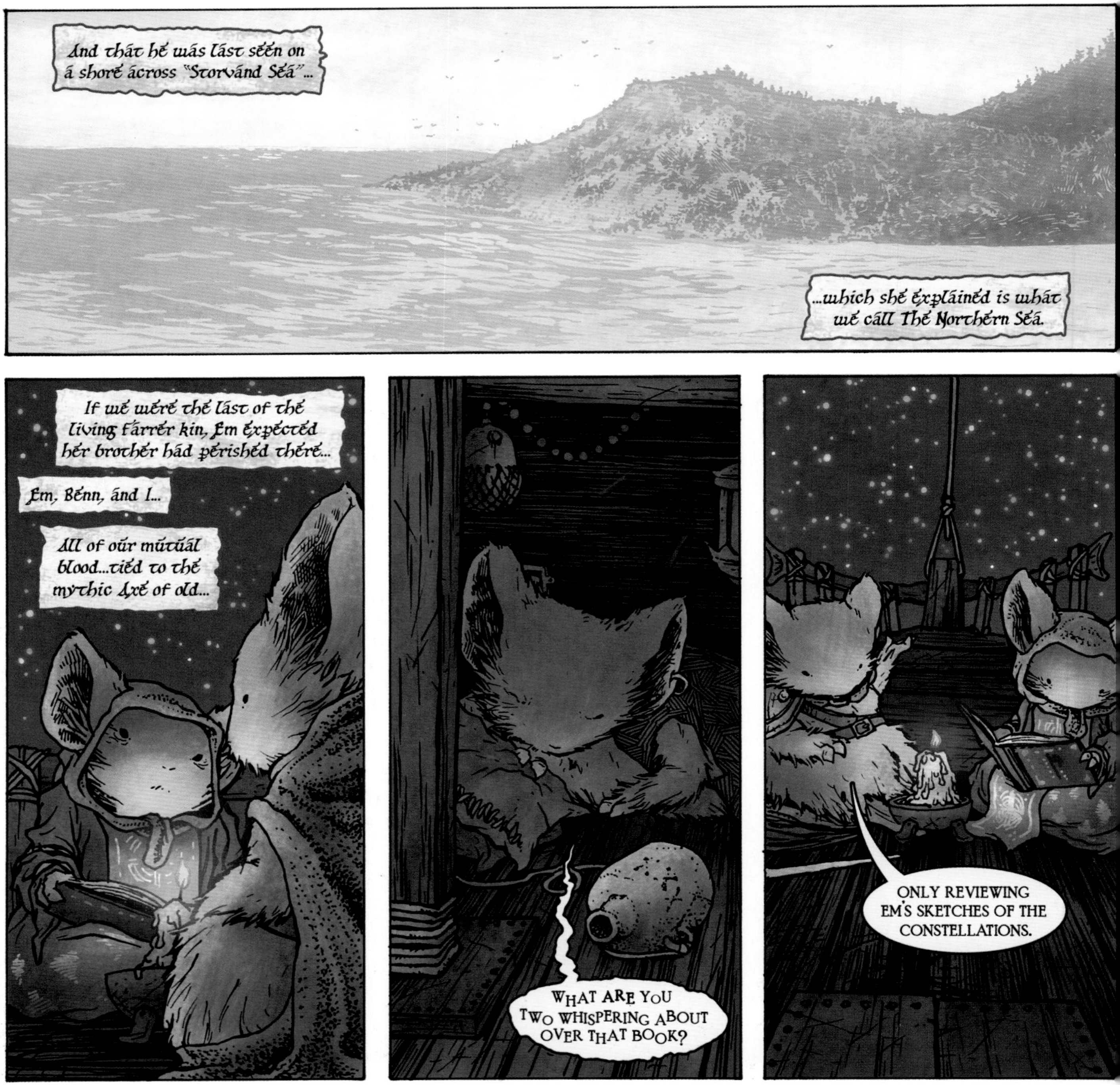
And that he was last seen on a shore across "Storvand Sea"...
...which she explained is what we call The Northern Sea.
If we were the last of the living Farrer kin, Em expected her brother had perished there...
Em, Benn, and I...
All of our mutual blood...tied to the mythic Axe of old...
WHAT ARE YOU TWO WHISPERING ABOUT OVER THAT BOOK?
ONLY REVIEWING EM'S SKETCHES OF THE CONSTELLATIONS.

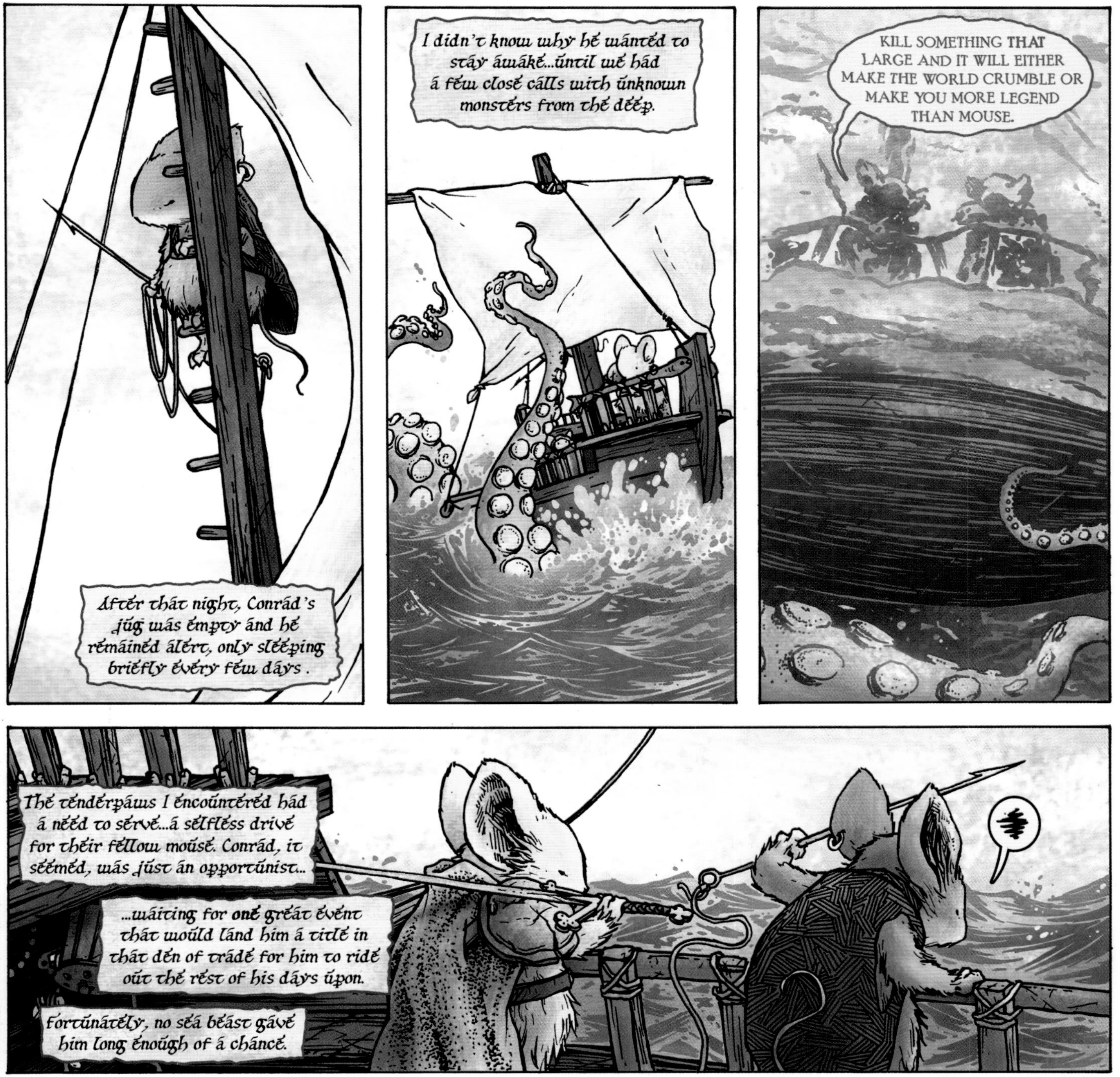
After that night, Conrad's jug was empty and he remained alert, only sleeping briefly every few days.
I didn't know why he wanted to stay awake...until we had a few close calls with unknown monsters from the deep.
KILL SOMETHING THAT LARGE AND IT WILL EITHER MAKE THE WORLD CRUMBLE OR MAKE YOU MORE LEGEND THAN MOUSE.
The tenderpaws I encountered had a need to serve...a selfless drive for their fellow mouse. Conrad, it seemed, was just an opportunist...
...waiting for one great event that would land him a title in that den of trade for him to ride out the rest of his days upon.
Fortunately, no sea beast gave him long enough of a chance.

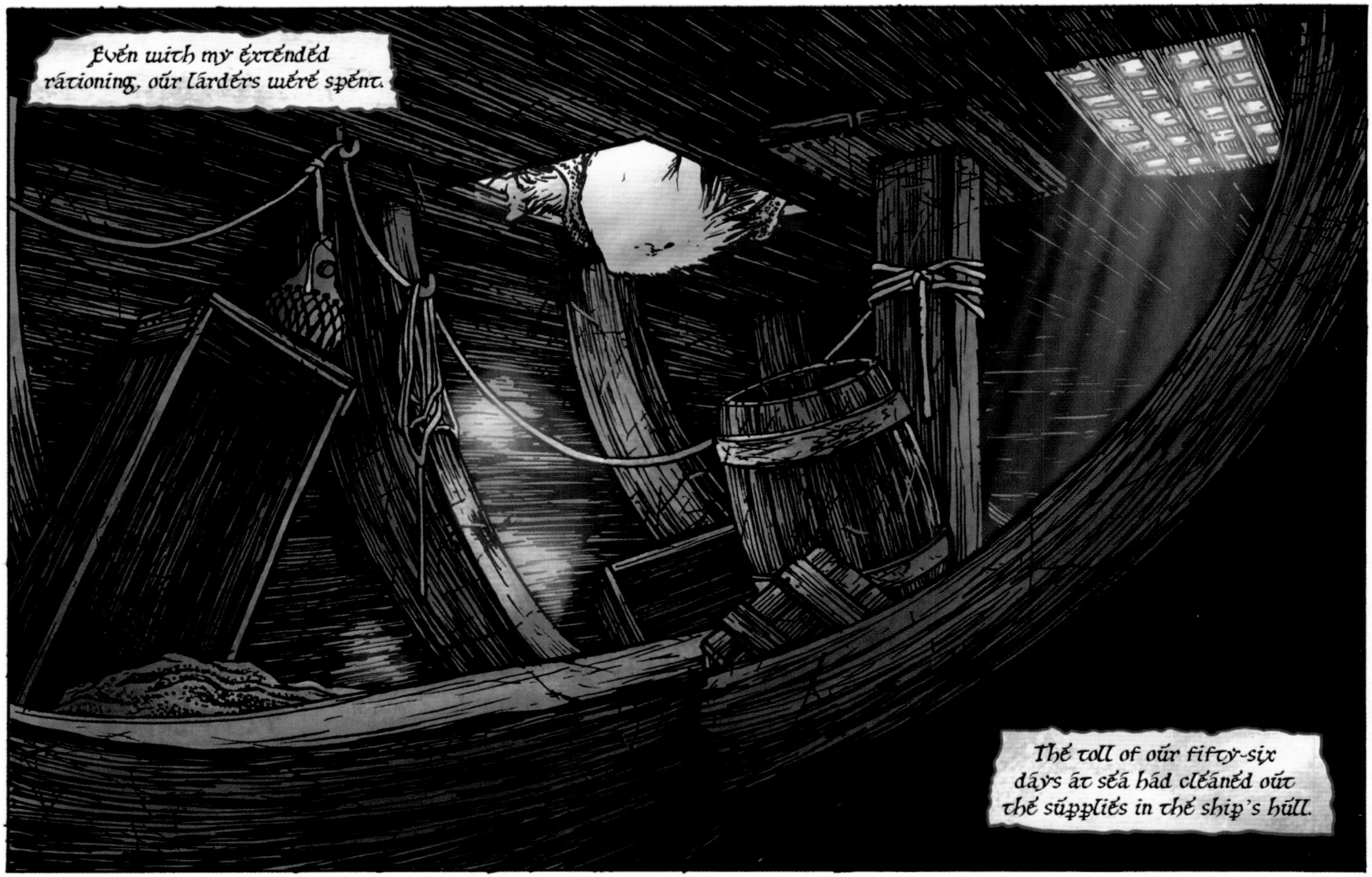
Even with my extended rationing, our larders were spent.
The toll of our fifty-six days at sea had cleaned out the supplies in the ship's hull.

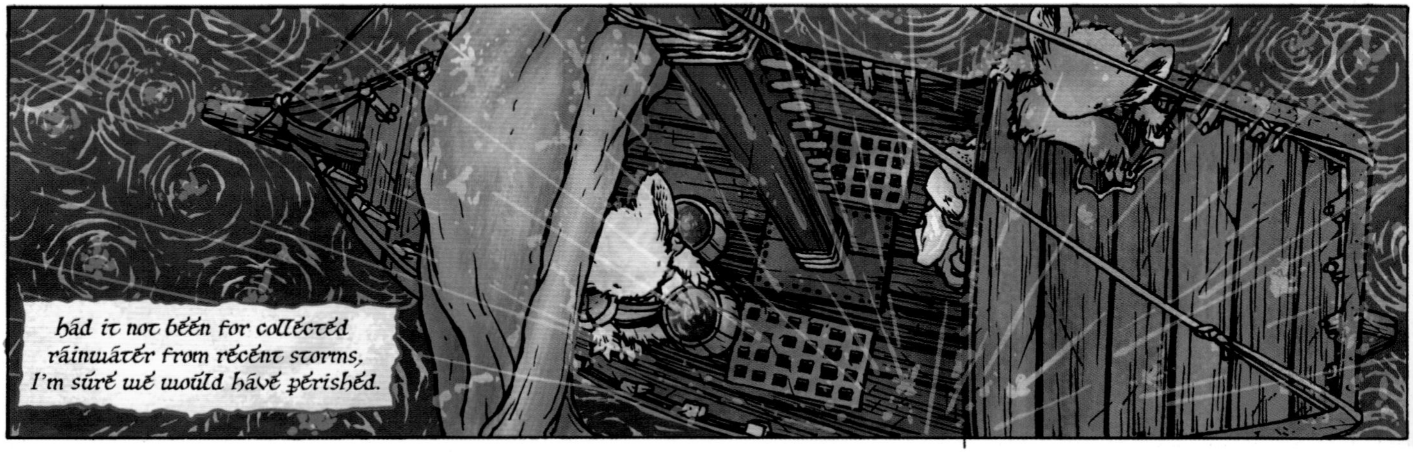
had it not been for collected rainwater from recent storms, I'm sure we would have perished.

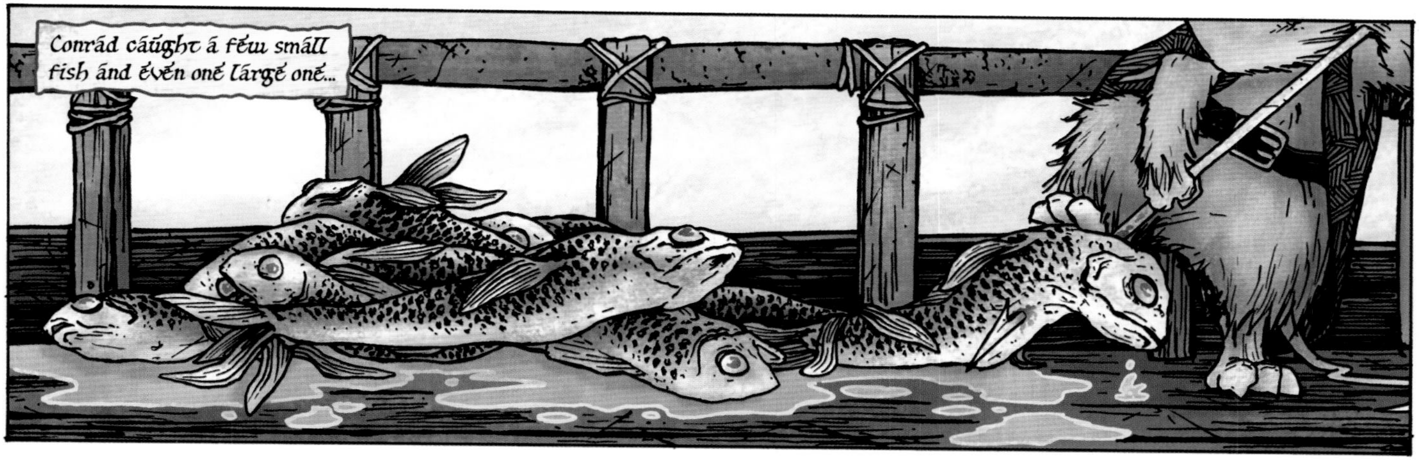
Conrad caught a few small fish and even one large one...

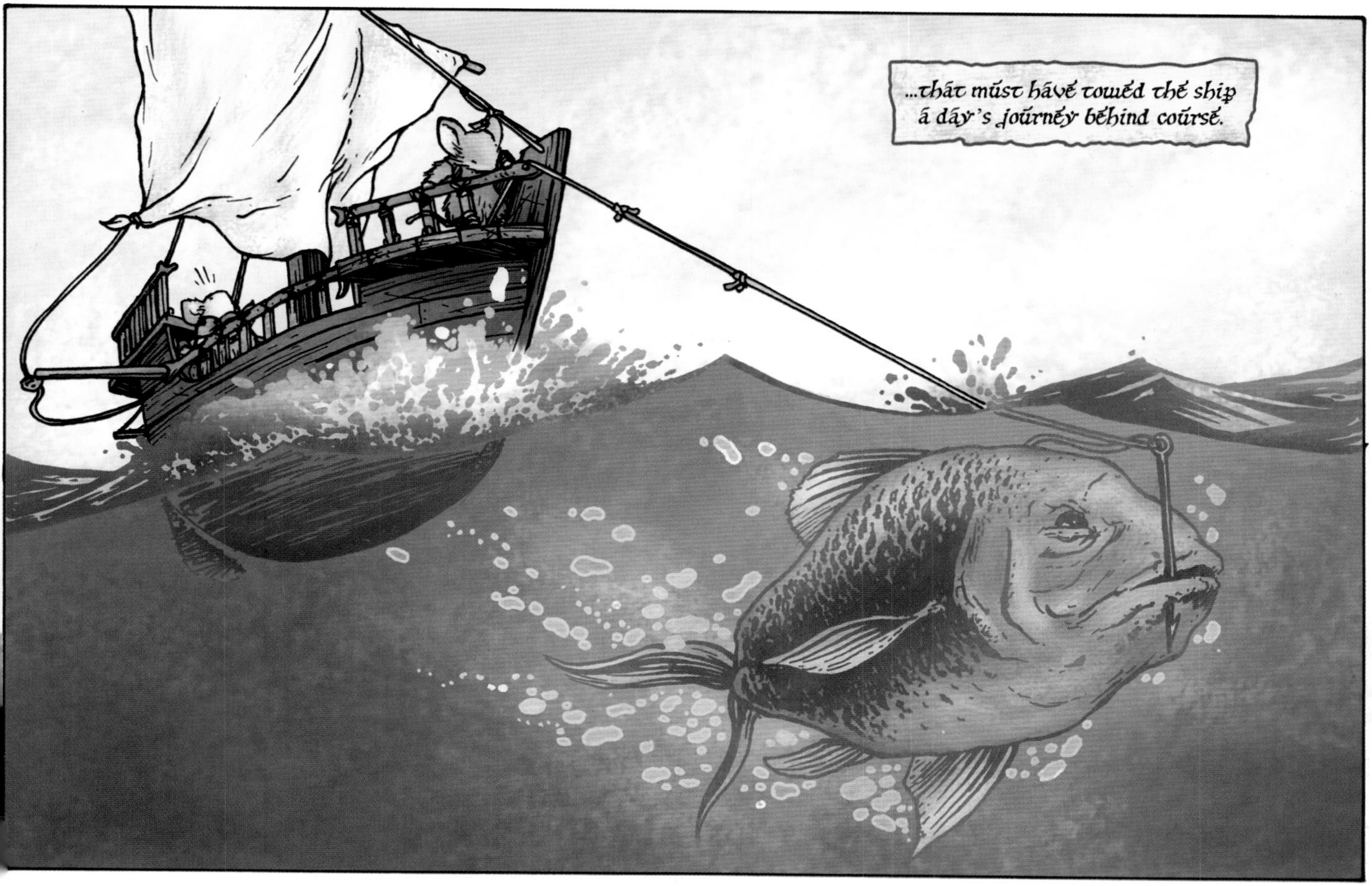
...that must have towed the ship a day's journey behind course.

Conrád convincéd Ém ánd mé to pártáké in thé spoils.

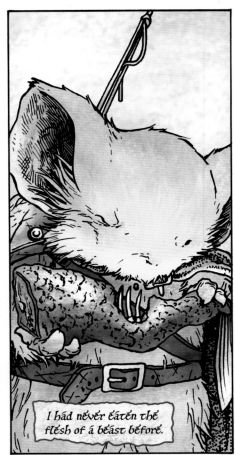

I hád névér éátén thé flésh of á béást beforé.

BLEARRH

It would táké néár stárvátion beforé I would do it ágáin.

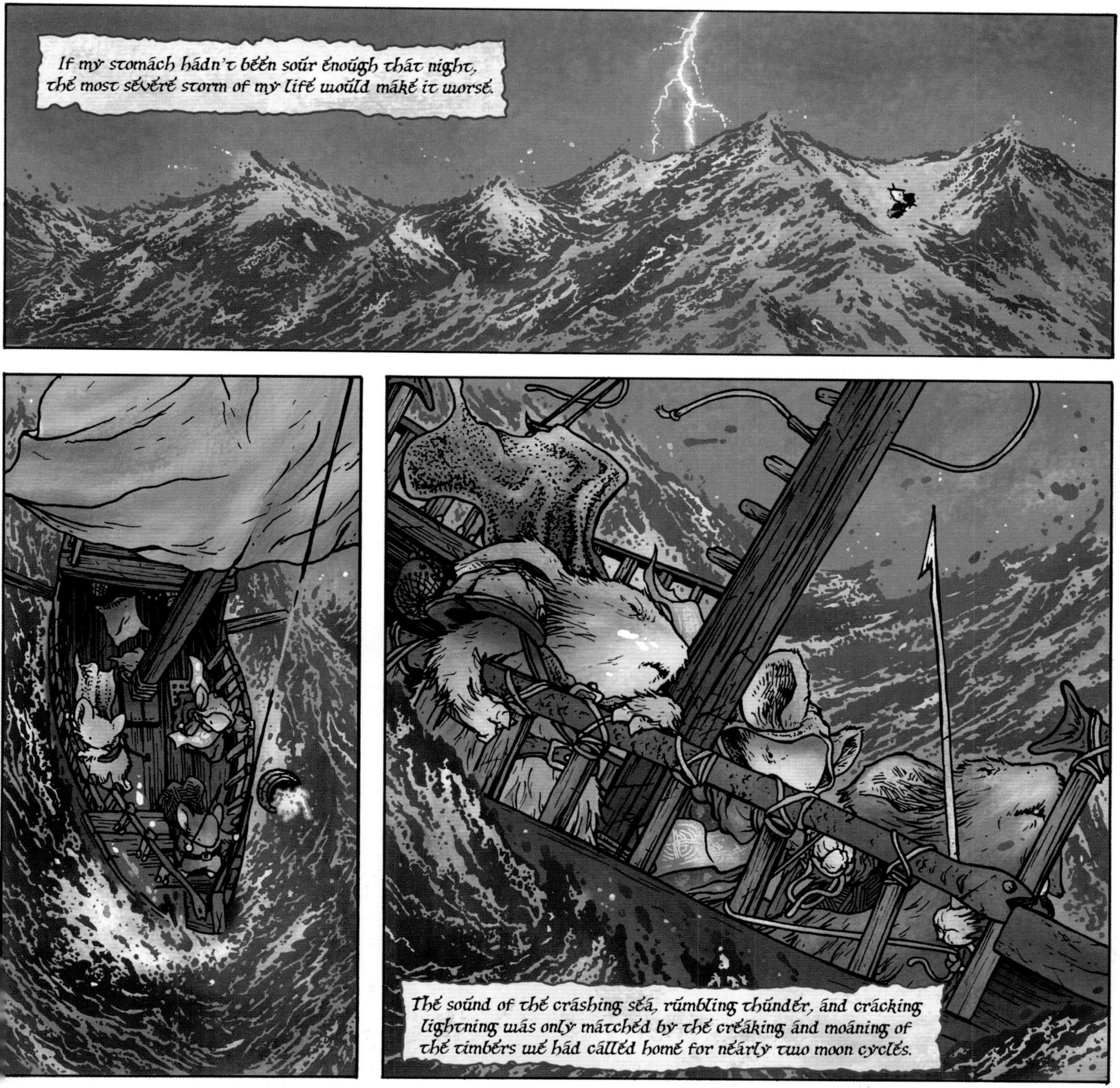
If my stomach hadn't been sour enough that night, the most severe storm of my life would make it worse.
The sound of the crashing sea, rumbling thunder, and cracking lightning was only matched by the creaking and moaning of the timbers we had called home for nearly two moon cycles.

Seeing the impending swell, we lashed any loose item of value to ourselves.

When it crashed onto us, the ship was torn asunder and swallowed by the inky wetness.

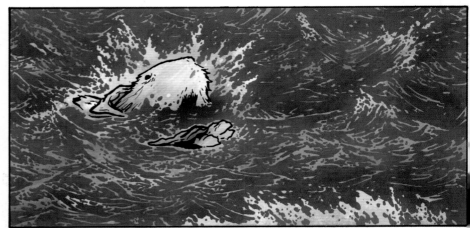

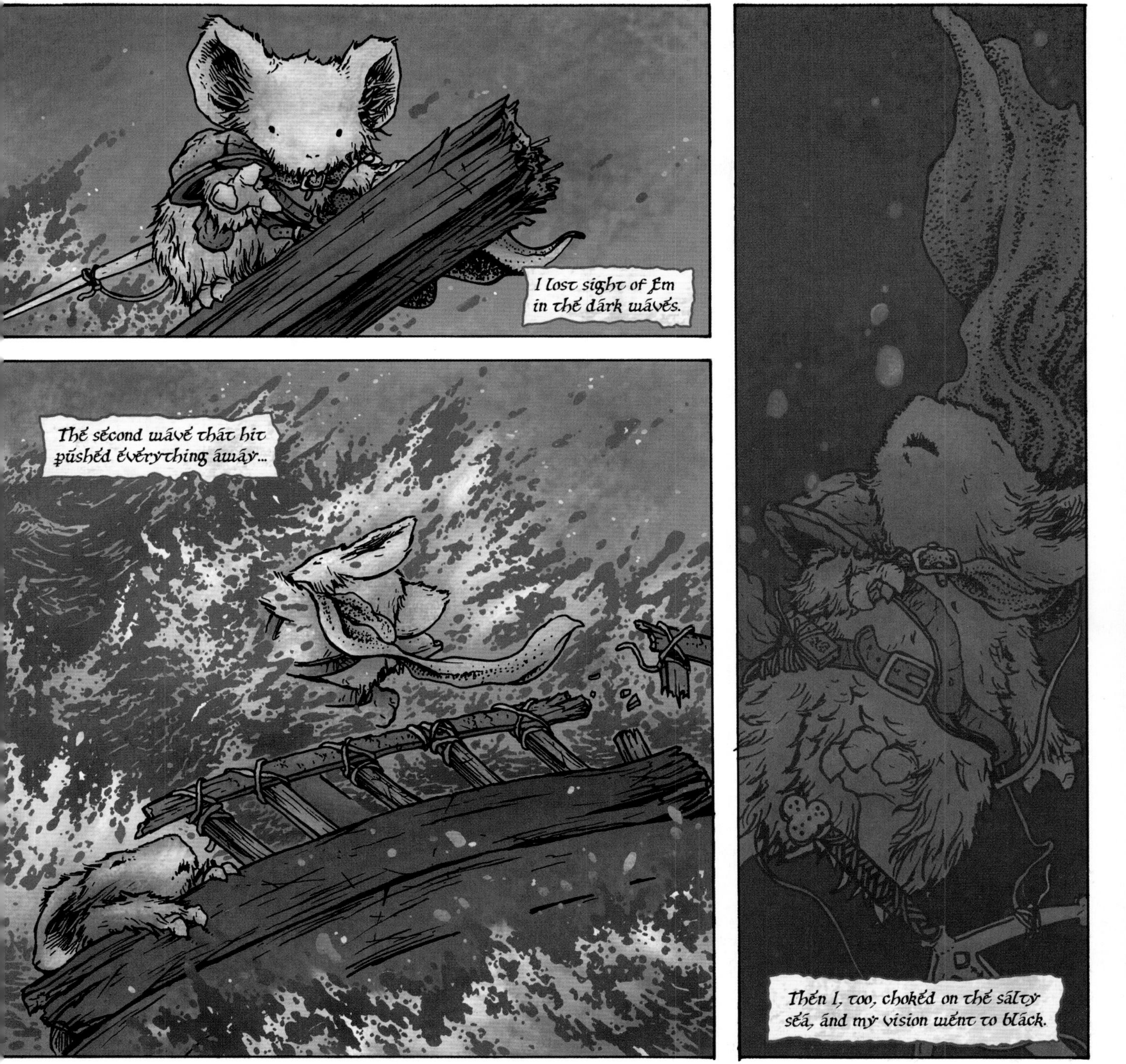
I lost sight of Em in the dark waves.
The second wave that hit pushed everything away...
Then I, too, choked on the salty sea, and my vision went to black.

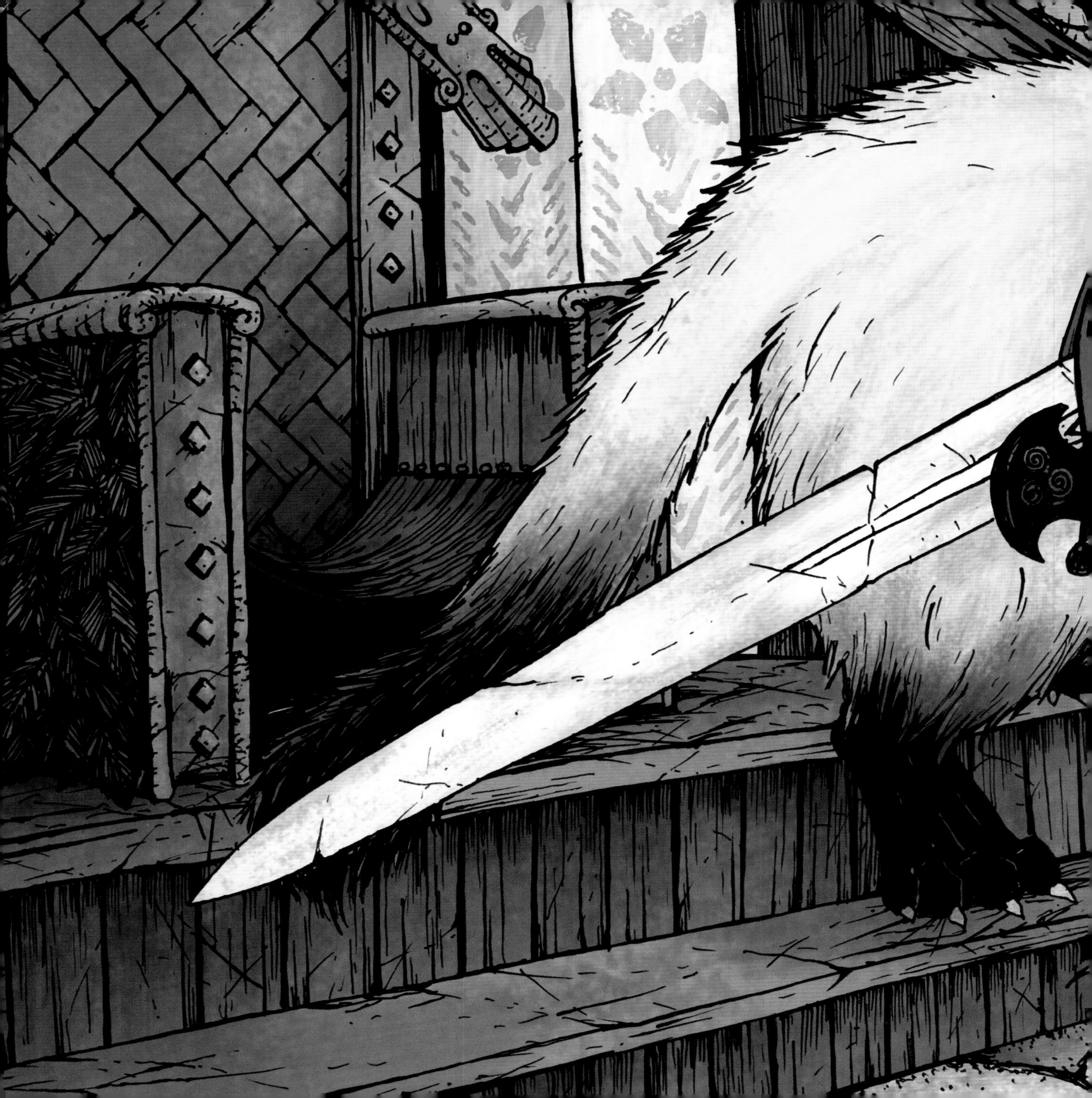

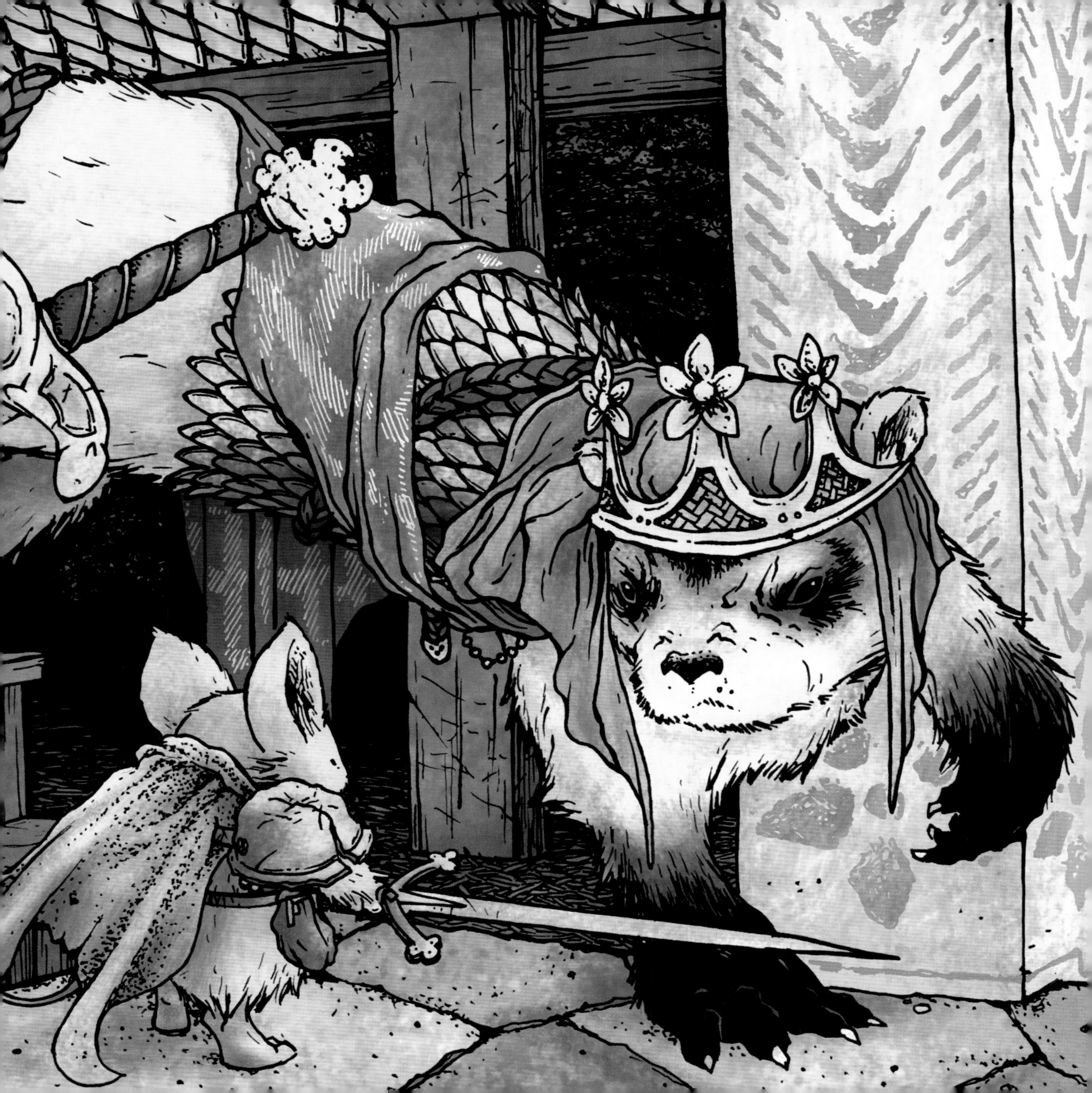

CHAPTER THREE

The blade of the axe was honed, but not
as sharp as the tongue and mind of
its wielder. For he had the
cunning of Reinhard,
first of the
Vulpes

Rare was
the time when
blood did not need
to be spilled for prosperity
to spread for mice, but when it did
not it was due to the Black Axe's words
entering like a poison into the veins of his prey

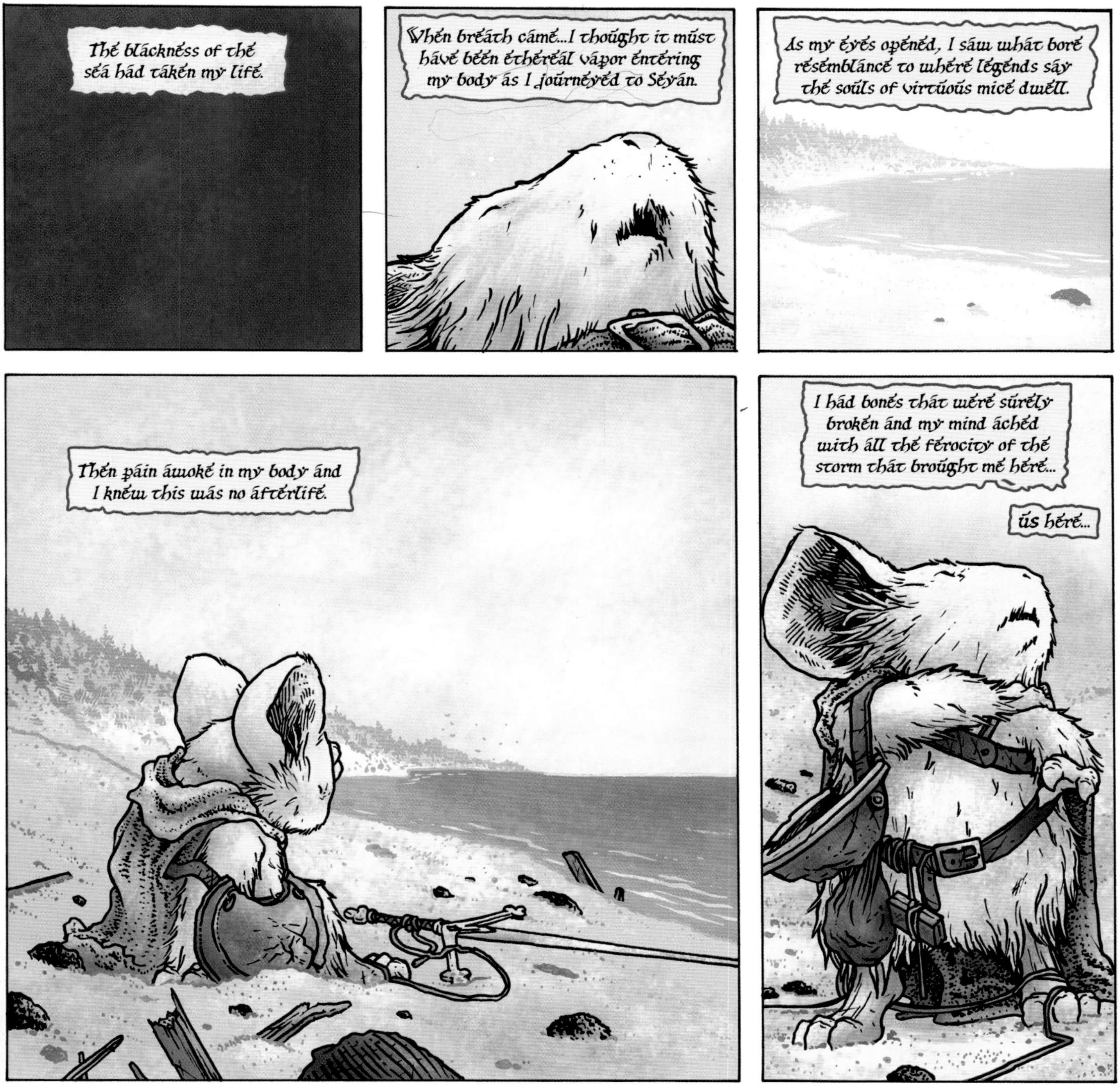
The blackness of the sea had taken my life.
When breath came...I thought it must have been ethereal vapor entering my body as I journeyed to Seyan.
As my eyes opened, I saw what bore resemblance to where legends say the souls of virtuous mice dwell.
Then pain awoke in my body and I knew this was no afterlife.
I had bones that were surely broken and my mind ached with all the ferocity of the storm that brought me here...
us here...

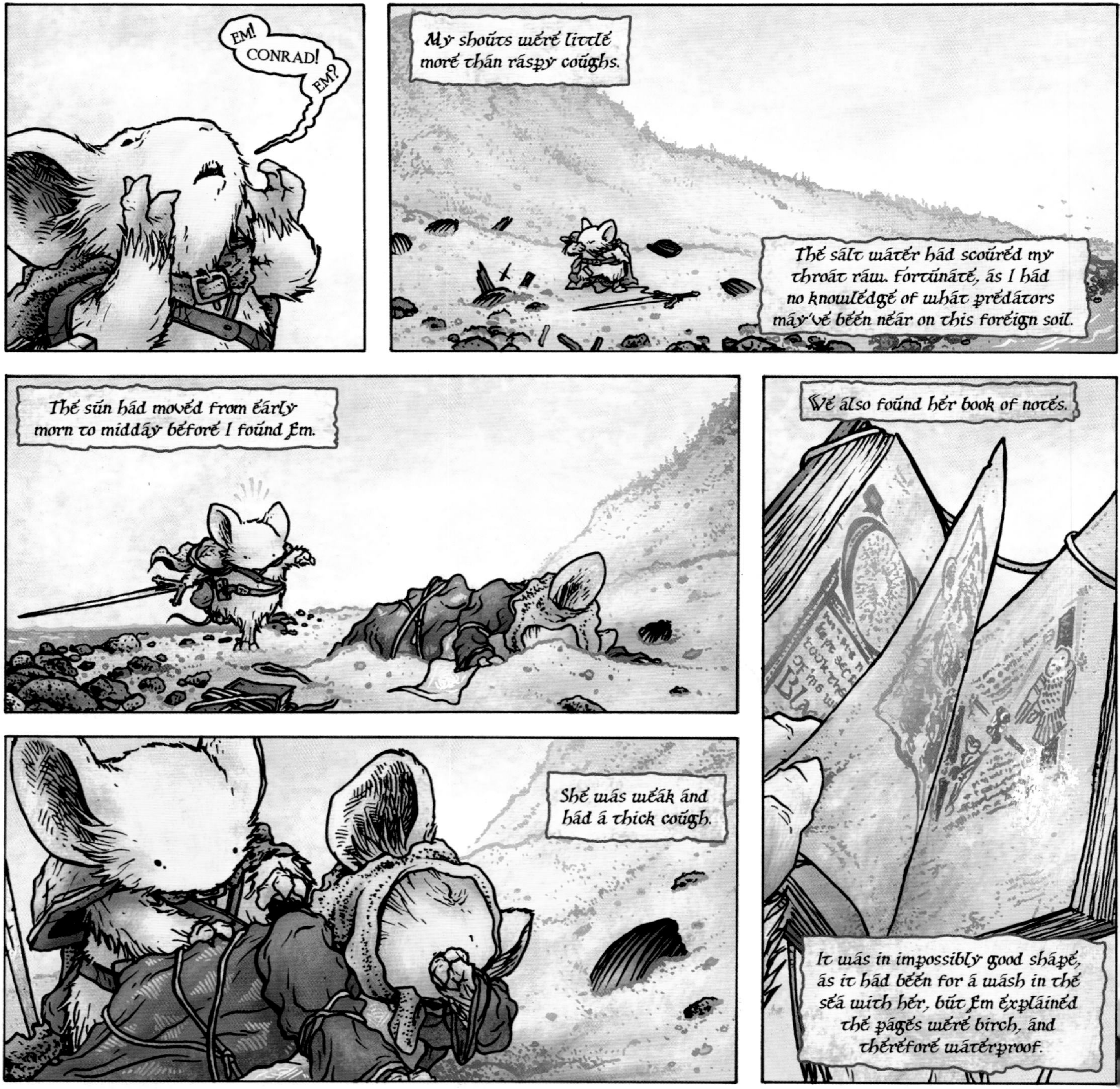
EM!
CONRAD!
EM?
My shouts were little more than raspy coughs.
The salt water had scoured my throat raw. Fortunate, as I had no knowledge of what predators may've been near on this foreign soil.
The sun had moved from early morn to midday before I found Em.
She was weak and had a thick cough.
We also found her book of notes.
It was in impossibly good shape, as it had been for a wash in the sea with her, but Em explained the pages were birch, and therefore waterproof.

In neither direction along the shore did we find Conrad. I silently mourned him as we searched.

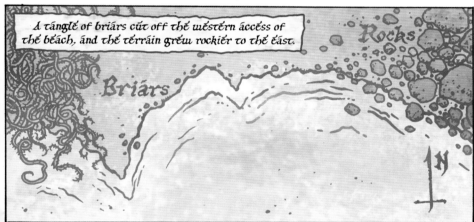

A tangle of briars cut off the western access of the beach, and the terrain grew rockier to the east.

Briars

Rocks

Was this even the land we had set out for?

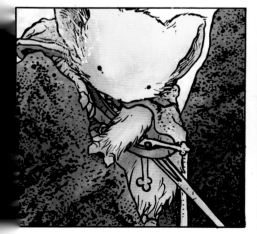

The skeleton and clothes of one of our own, tucked in the stones, told us it was.

BENN!

HOW CAN YOU BE CERTAIN?

THE...THE TUNIC CAME FROM MY LOOM. I WOVE IT AS A GIFT TO MY BROTHER...

Crows arrived and bore witness to her grief.

CAW CAW CAW

CAW CAW caw CAW CAW CAW caw CAW CAW caw CAW caw CAW CAW caw CAW caw CAW

The flock claimed to fm that twenty seasons ago this mouse came to these shores with an axe, and the one who slew him marched to the "hall in the hill."

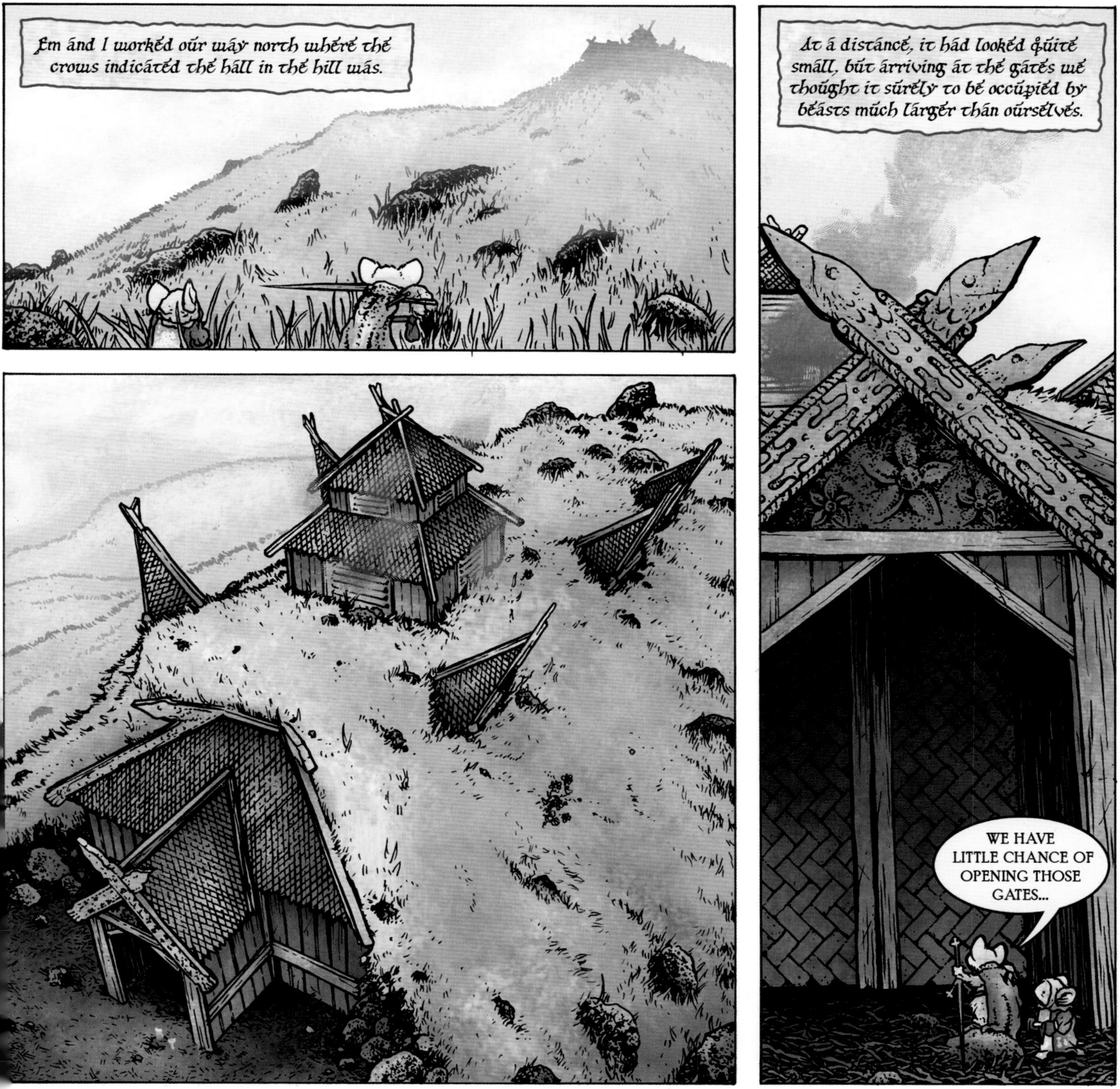
Em and I worked our way north where the crows indicated the hall in the hill was.
At a distance, it had looked quite small, but arriving at the gates we thought it surely to be occupied by beasts much larger than ourselves.
WE HAVE LITTLE CHANCE OF OPENING THOSE GATES...

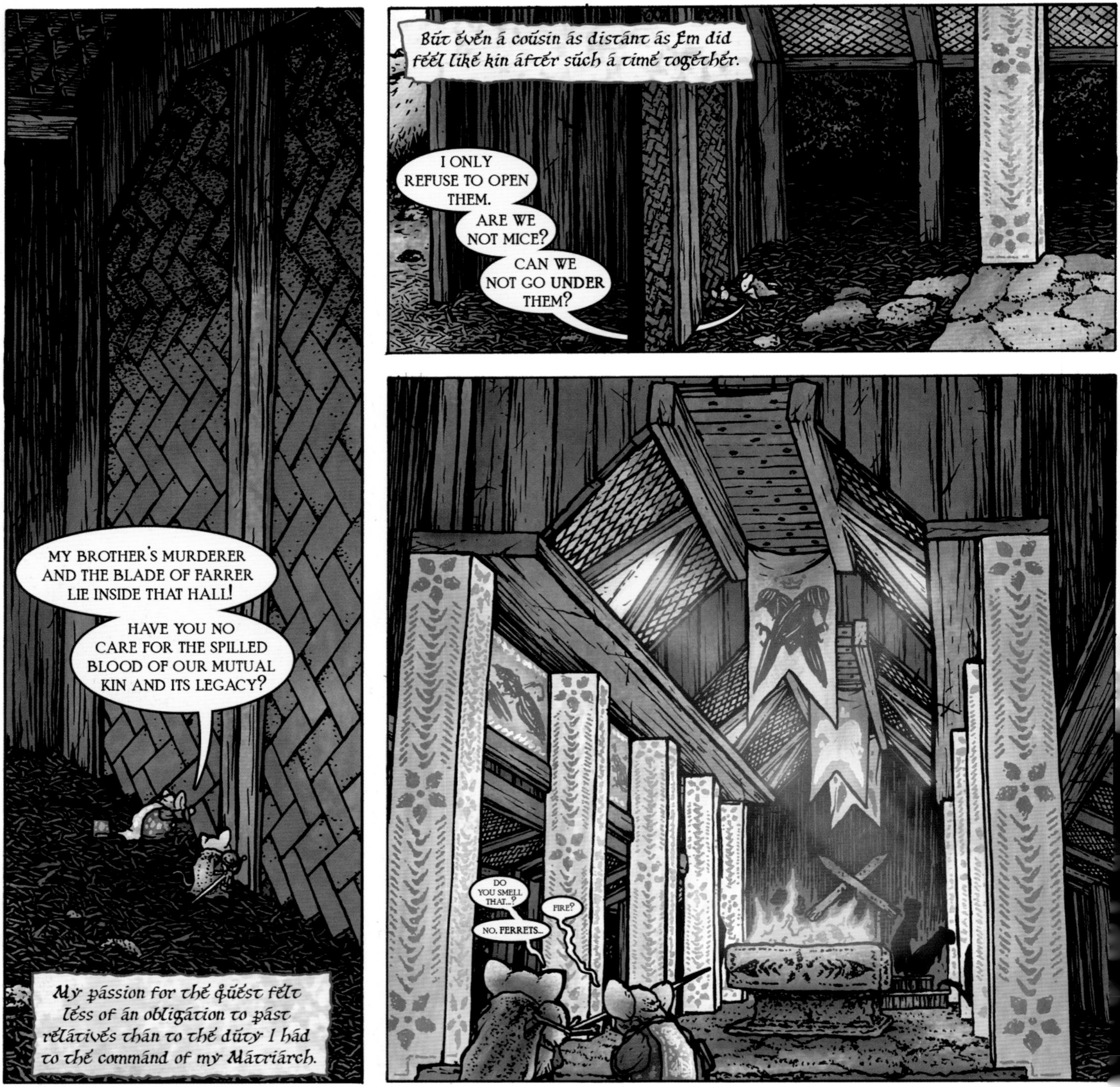
MY BROTHER'S MURDERER AND THE BLADE OF FARRER LIE INSIDE THAT HALL!
HAVE YOU NO CARE FOR THE SPILLED BLOOD OF OUR MUTUAL KIN AND ITS LEGACY?
My passion for the quest felt less of an obligation to past relatives than to the duty I had to the command of my Matriarch.
But even a cousin as distant as Em did feel like kin after such a time together.
I ONLY REFUSE TO OPEN THEM.
ARE WE NOT MICE?
CAN WE NOT GO UNDER THEM?
DO YOU SMELL THAT...?
FIRE?
NO. FERRETS...

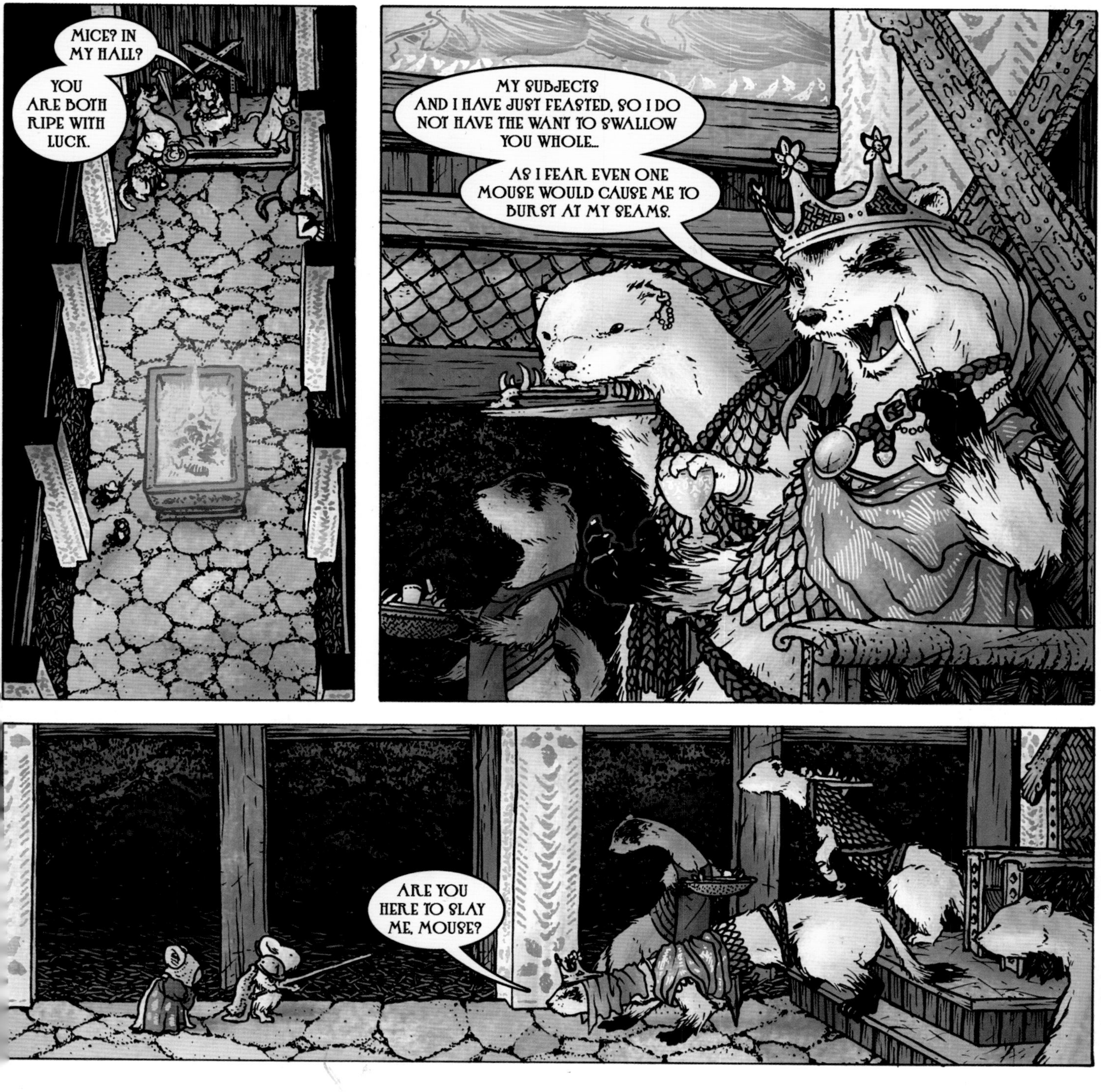
MICE? IN MY HALL?
YOU ARE BOTH RIPE WITH LUCK.
MY SUBJECTS AND I HAVE JUST FEASTED, SO I DO NOT HAVE THE WANT TO SWALLOW YOU WHOLE...
AS I FEAR EVEN ONE MOUSE WOULD CAUSE ME TO BURST AT MY SEAMS.
ARE YOU HERE TO SLAY ME, MOUSE?

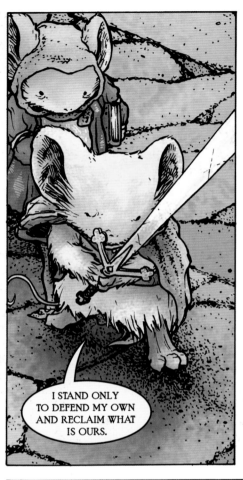

I STAND ONLY TO DEFEND MY OWN AND RECLAIM WHAT IS OURS.

YOURS? THERE ARE NO LONGER MICE ON THIS LAND, OR IS THAT WHAT YOU HAVE COME TO RECLAIM?

THE TWO OF YOU ARE TO REPOPULATE MY ISLAND OF ILDUR?

SHE LOOKS A BIT OLD TO BEAR YOUR FRUIT, SWORDMOUSE.

WATCH YOUR TONGUE, SHE IS MY KIN AND ELDER.

THE ONLY REASON I SEE FOR THERE BEING NAUGHT BUT THE BONES OF MICE HERE IS A FAT FERRET OF A KING.

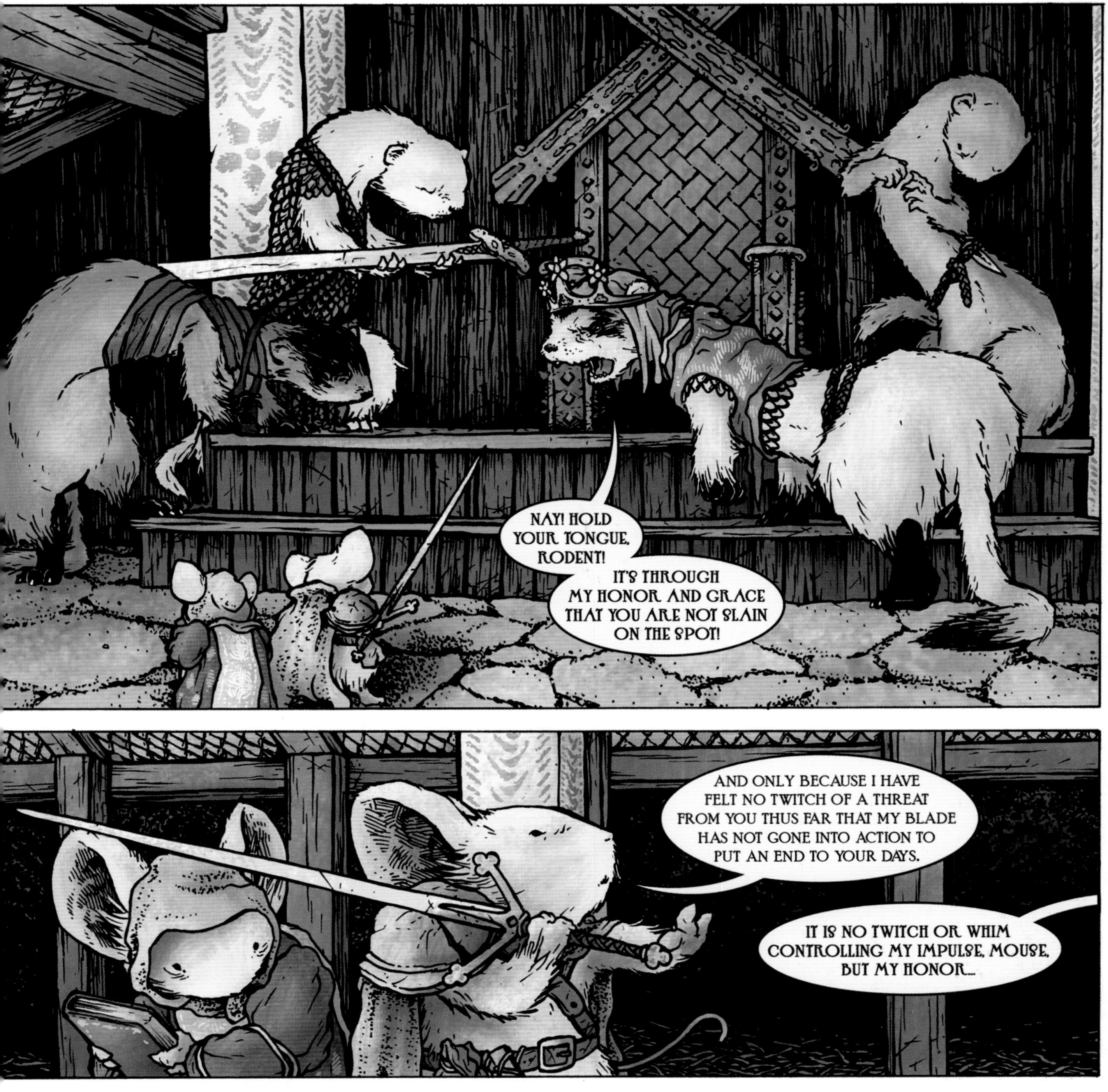
NAY! HOLD YOUR TONGUE, RODENT!
IT'S THROUGH MY HONOR AND GRACE THAT YOU ARE NOT SLAIN ON THE SPOT!
AND ONLY BECAUSE I HAVE FELT NO TWITCH OF A THREAT FROM YOU THUS FAR THAT MY BLADE HAS NOT GONE INTO ACTION TO PUT AN END TO YOUR DAYS.
IT IS NO TWITCH OR WHIM CONTROLLING MY IMPULSE, MOUSE, BUT MY HONOR...

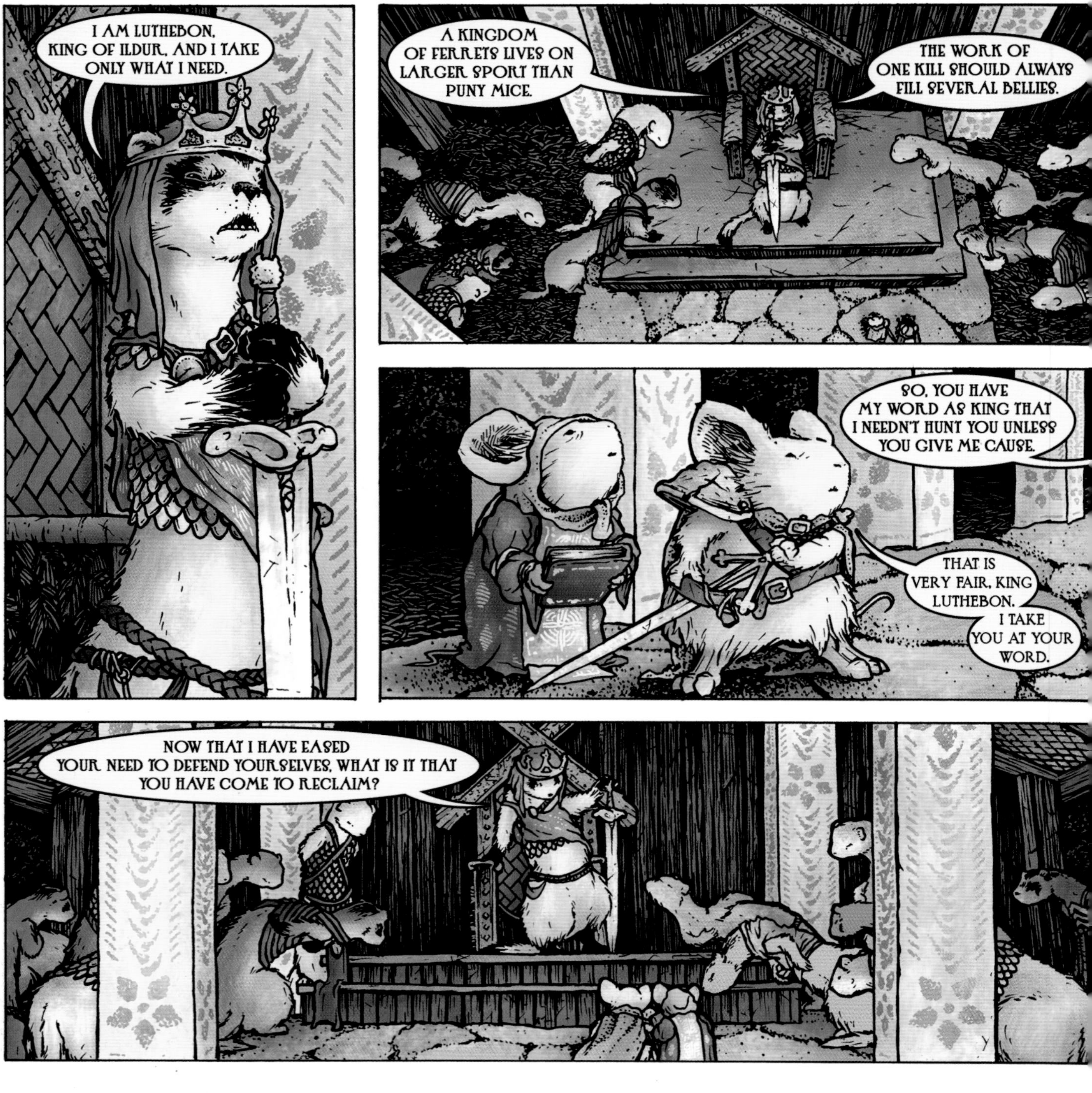
I AM LUTHEBON, KING OF ILDUR, AND I TAKE ONLY WHAT I NEED.
A KINGDOM OF FERRETS LIVES ON LARGER SPORT THAN PUNY MICE.
THE WORK OF ONE KILL SHOULD ALWAYS FILL SEVERAL BELLIES.
SO, YOU HAVE MY WORD AS KING THAT I NEEDN'T HUNT YOU UNLESS YOU GIVE ME CAUSE.
THAT IS VERY FAIR, KING LUTHEBON.
I TAKE YOU AT YOUR WORD.
NOW THAT I HAVE EASED YOUR NEED TO DEFEND YOURSELVES, WHAT IS IT THAT YOU HAVE COME TO RECLAIM?

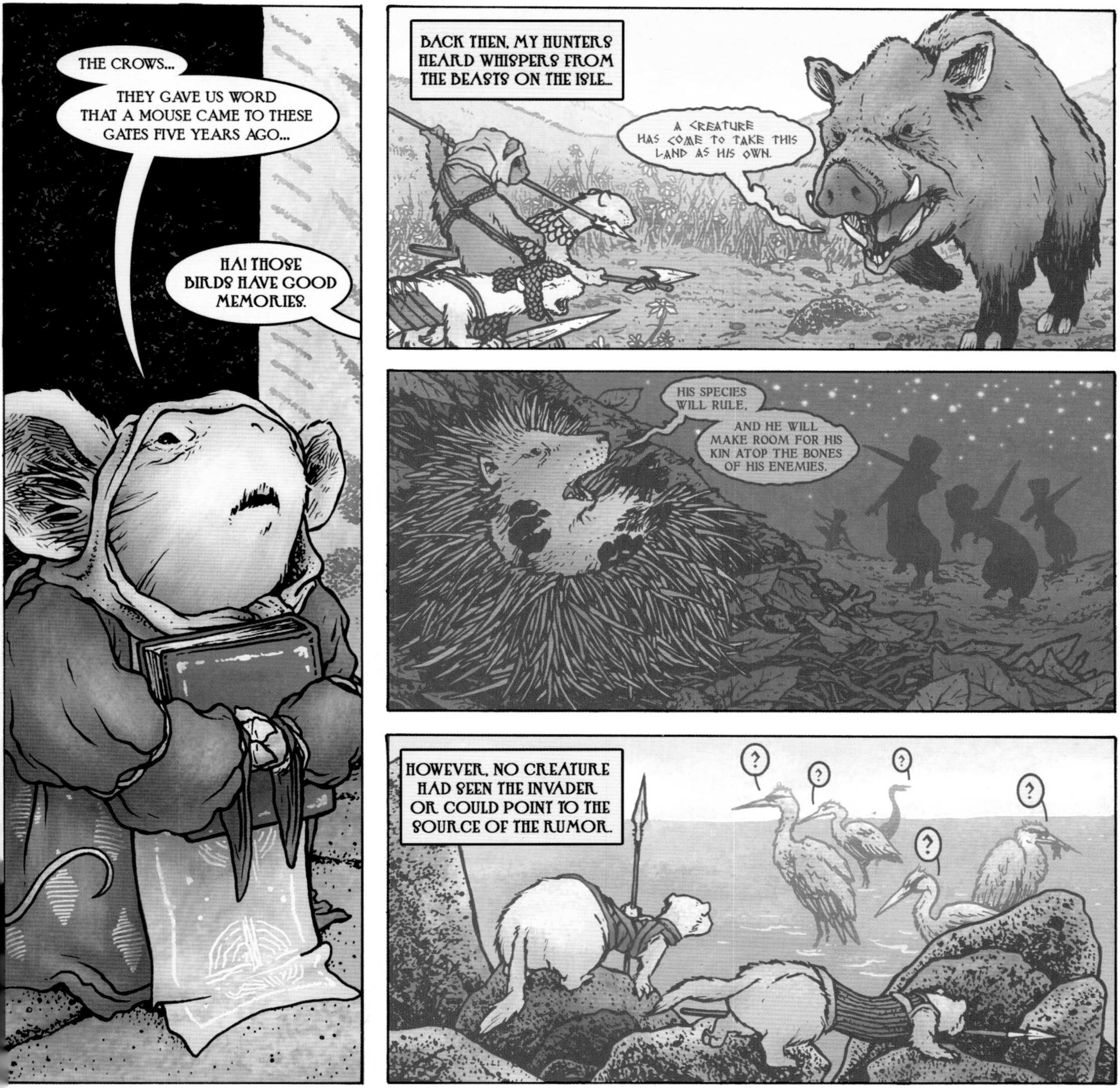
THE CROWS...
THEY GAVE US WORD THAT A MOUSE CAME TO THESE GATES FIVE YEARS AGO...
HA! THOSE BIRDS HAVE GOOD MEMORIES.
BACK THEN, MY HUNTERS HEARD WHISPERS FROM THE BEASTS ON THE ISLE...
A CREATURE HAS COME TO TAKE THIS LAND AS HIS OWN.
HIS SPECIES WILL RULE,
AND HE WILL MAKE ROOM FOR HIS KIN ATOP THE BONES OF HIS ENEMIES.
HOWEVER, NO CREATURE HAD SEEN THE INVADER OR COULD POINT TO THE SOURCE OF THE RUMOR.
?
?
?
?
?

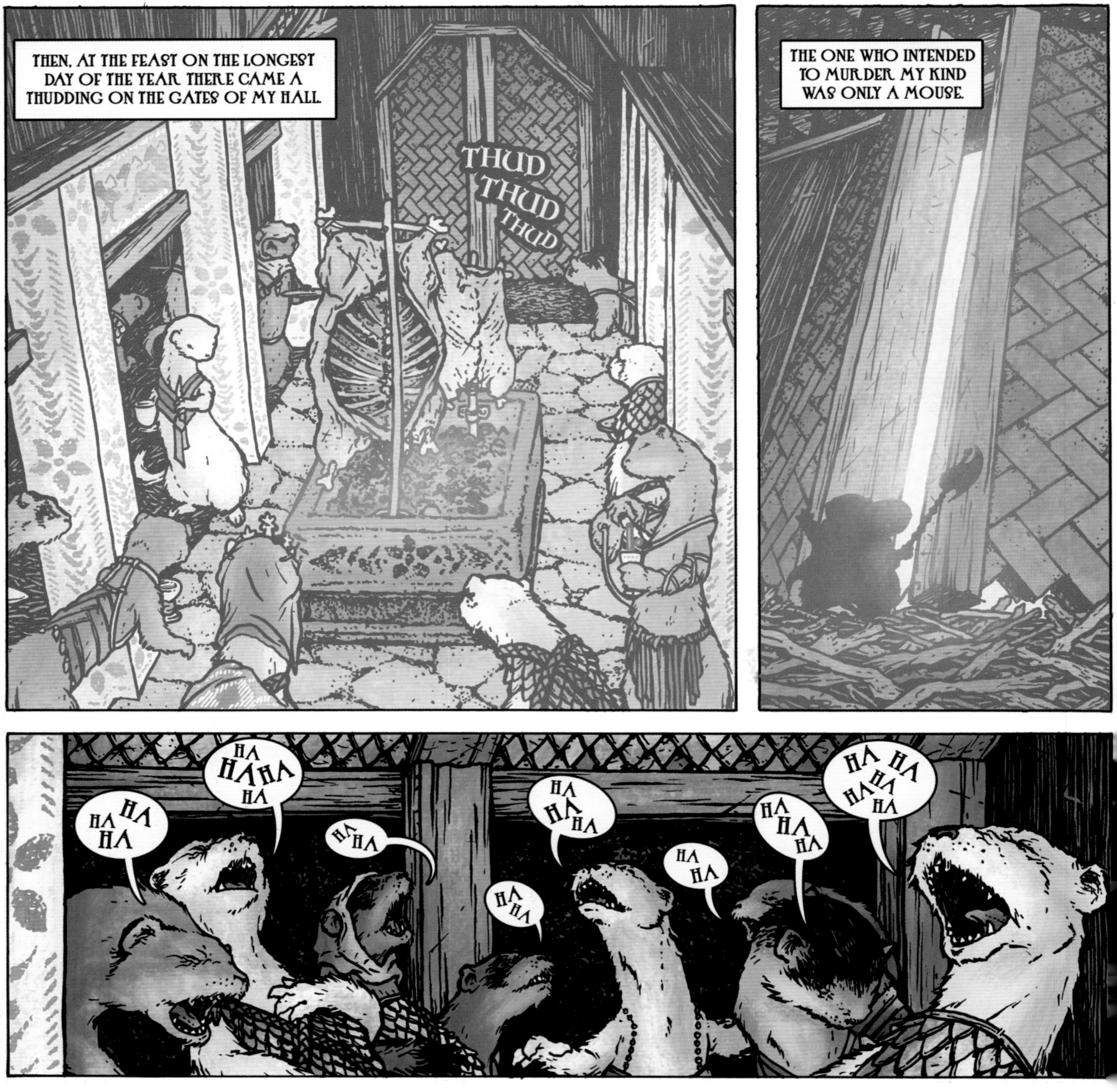
THEN, AT THE FEAST ON THE LONGEST DAY OF THE YEAR THERE CAME A THUDDING ON THE GATES OF MY HALL.
THUD THUD THUD
THE ONE WHO INTENDED TO MURDER MY KIND WAS ONLY A MOUSE.
HA HA HA
HA HA HA HA
HA HA
HA HA
HA HA HA HA
HA HA
HA HA HA HA
HA HA HA HA HA HA

MY SUBJECTS LAUGH BECAUSE WITH EASE I CLEAVED THE UPSTART IN TWO AND SWALLOWED BOTH PARTS WHOLE...

CLOTHES, BONES, AND ALL.

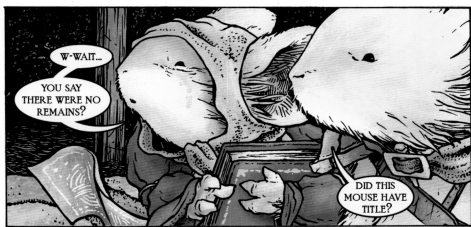

W-WAIT...

YOU SAY THERE WERE NO REMAINS?

DID THIS MOUSE HAVE TITLE?

"MEREK." AND THIS IS THE WEAPON HE RAISED AGAINST ME.

Our quest.

Proof the tale of Farrer was more than a story scribbled on paper, knit in cloth, and whispered into our ears.

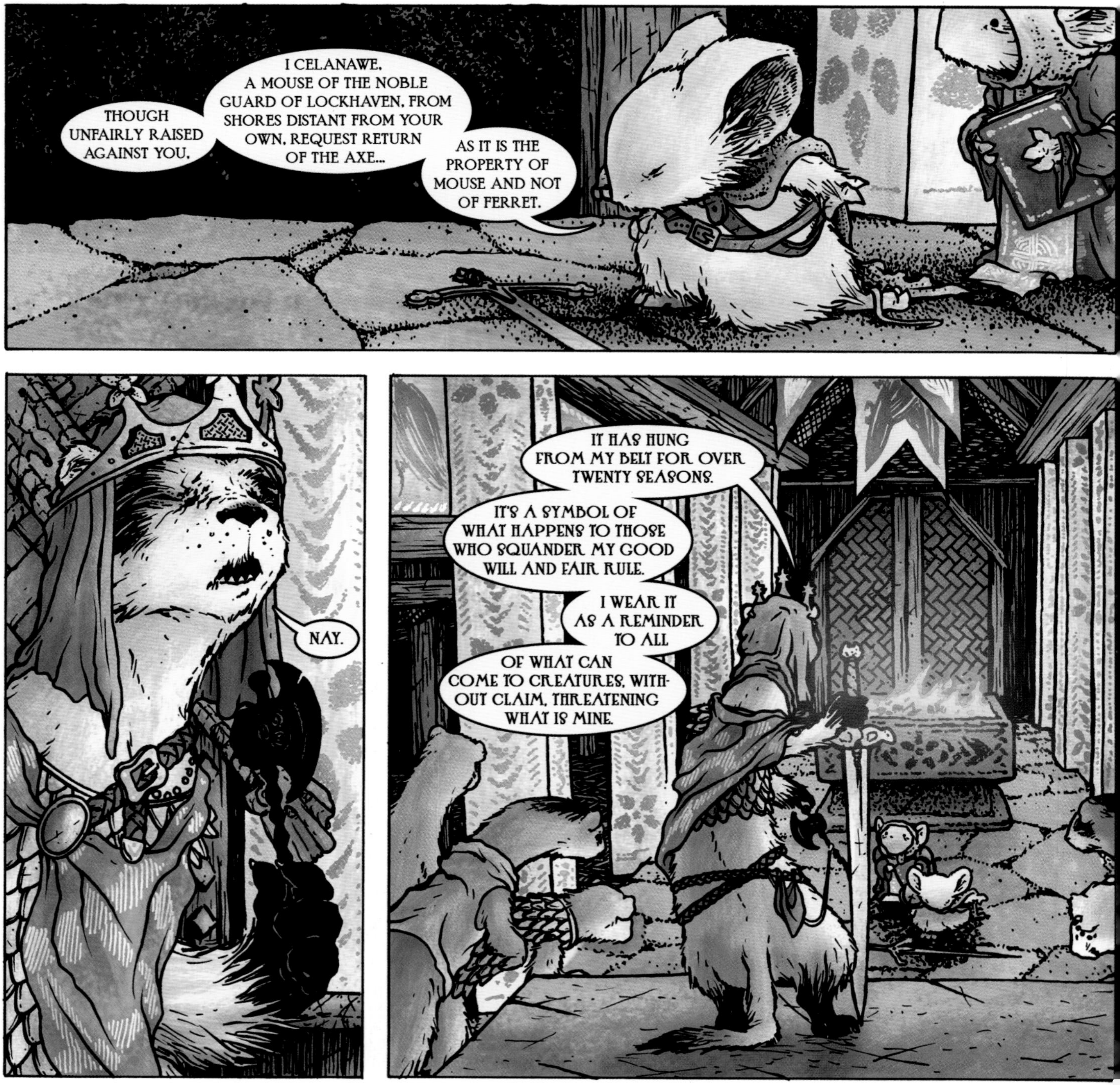
THOUGH UNFAIRLY RAISED AGAINST YOU,
I CELANAWE, A MOUSE OF THE NOBLE GUARD OF LOCKHAVEN, FROM SHORES DISTANT FROM YOUR OWN, REQUEST RETURN OF THE AXE...
AS IT IS THE PROPERTY OF MOUSE AND NOT OF FERRET.
NAY.
IT HAS HUNG FROM MY BELT FOR OVER TWENTY SEASONS.
IT'S A SYMBOL OF WHAT HAPPENS TO THOSE WHO SQUANDER MY GOOD WILL AND FAIR RULE.
I WEAR IT AS A REMINDER TO ALL
OF WHAT CAN COME TO CREATURES, WITH-OUT CLAIM, THREATENING WHAT IS MINE.

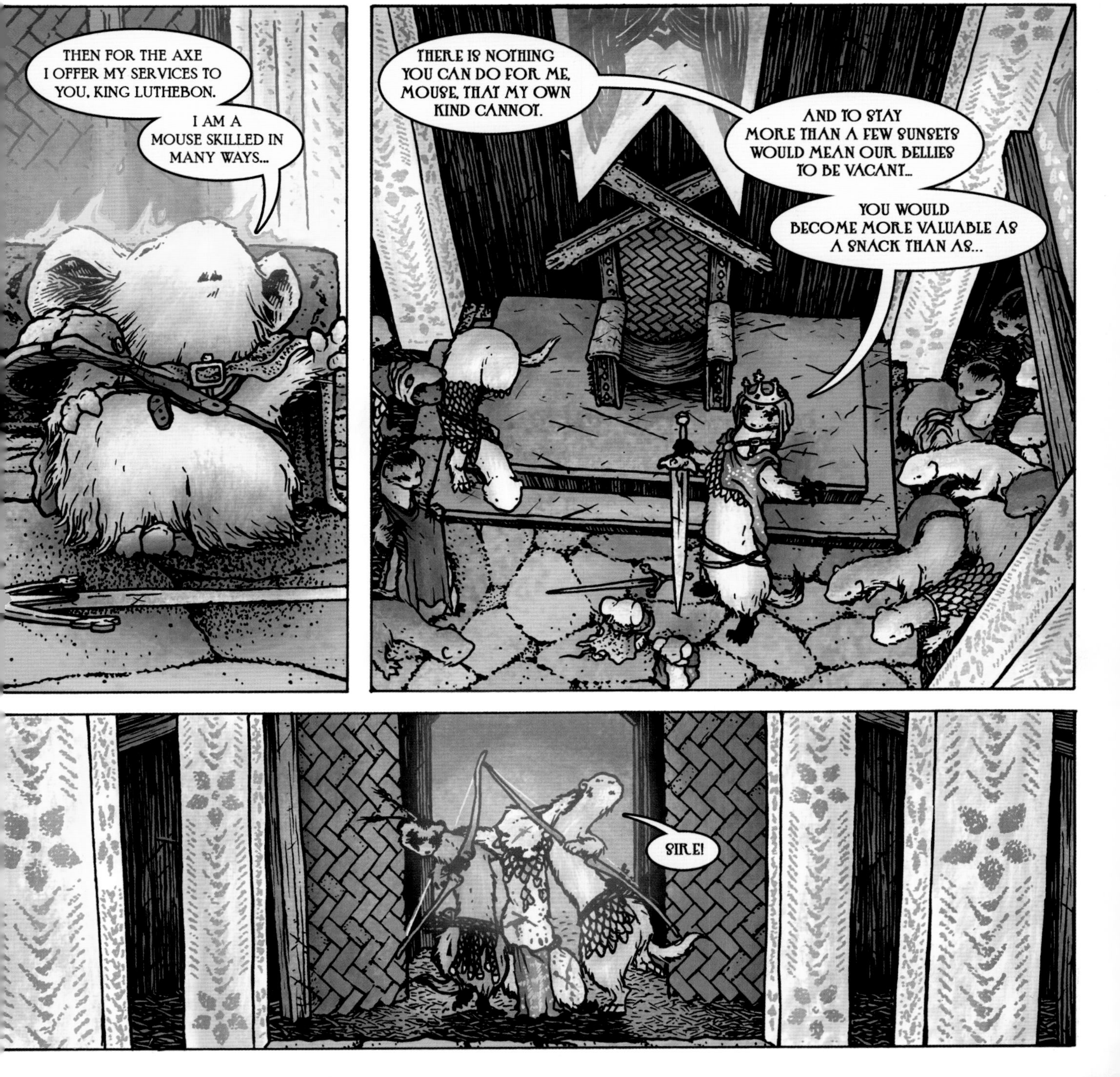
THEN FOR THE AXE I OFFER MY SERVICES TO YOU, KING LUTHEBON.
I AM A MOUSE SKILLED IN MANY WAYS...
THERE IS NOTHING YOU CAN DO FOR ME, MOUSE, THAT MY OWN KIND CANNOT.
AND TO STAY MORE THAN A FEW SUNSETS WOULD MEAN OUR BELLIES TO BE VACANT...
YOU WOULD BECOME MORE VALUABLE AS A SNACK THAN AS...
SIRE!

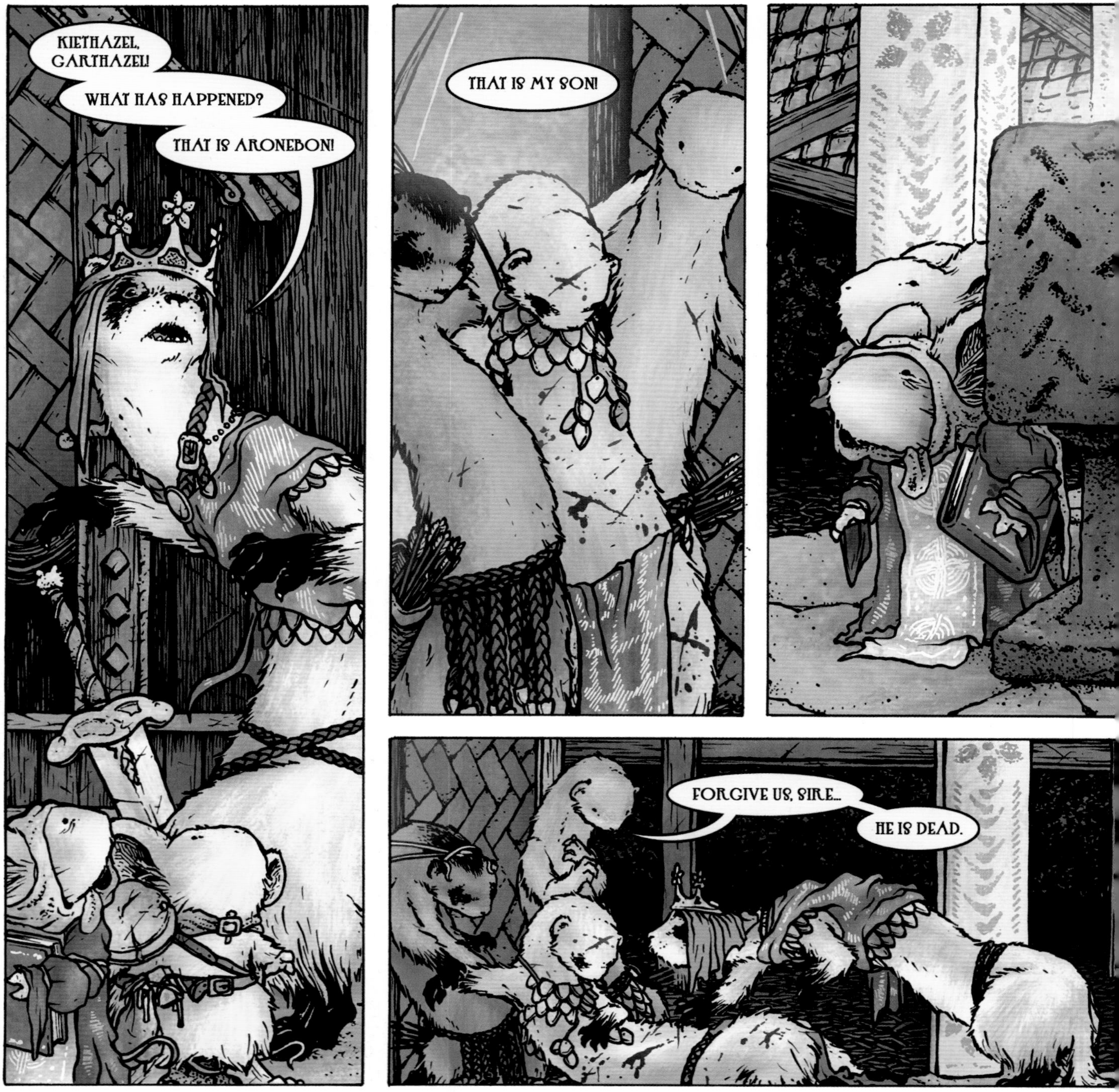
KIETHAZEL, GARTHAZEL!
WHAT HAS HAPPENED?
THAT IS ARONEBON!
THAT IS MY SON!
FORGIVE US, SIRE...
HE IS DEAD.

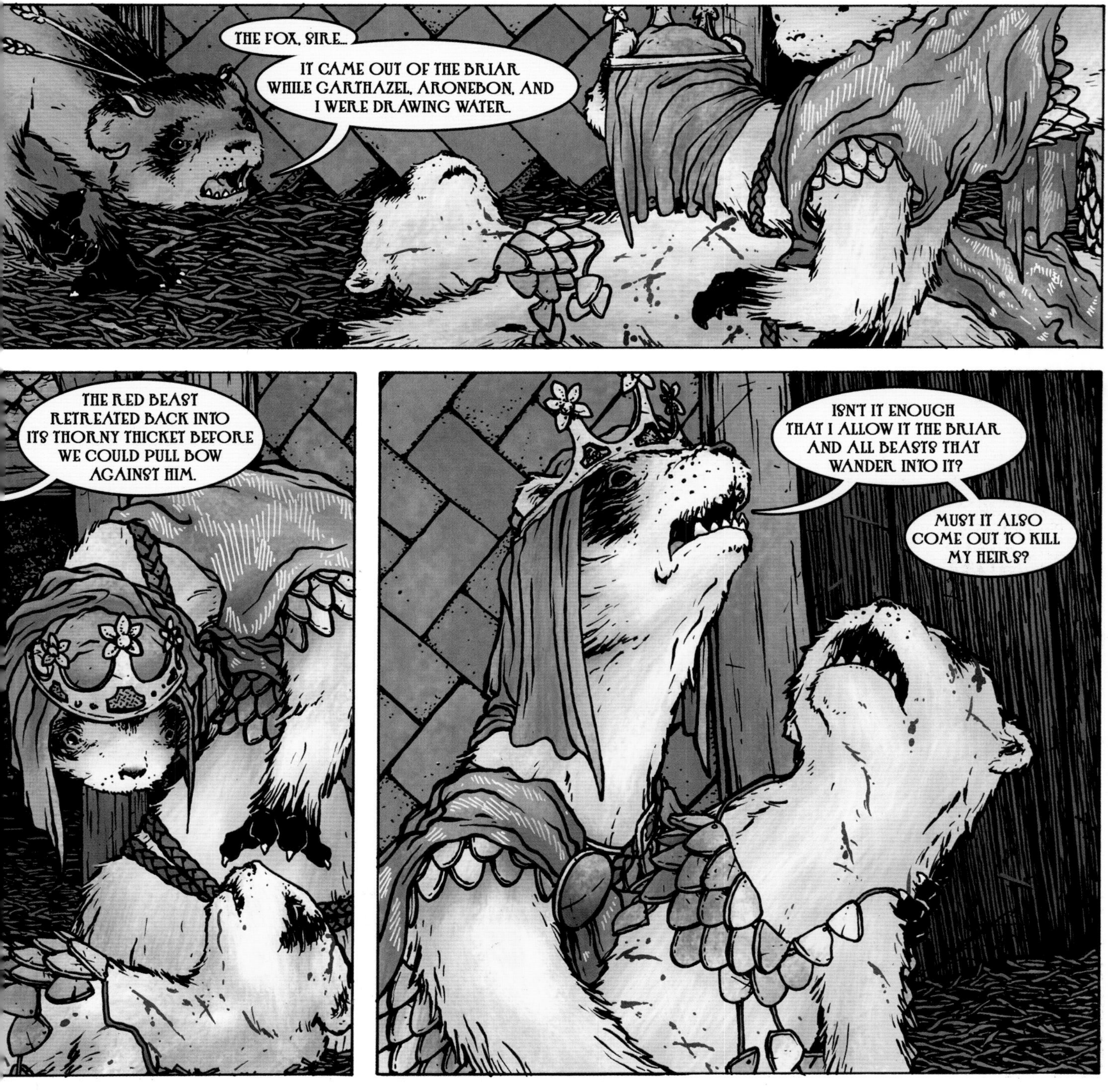
THE FOX, SIRE...
IT CAME OUT OF THE BRIAR WHILE GARTHAZEL, ARONEBON, AND I WERE DRAWING WATER.
THE RED BEAST RETREATED BACK INTO ITS THORNY THICKET BEFORE WE COULD PULL BOW AGAINST HIM.
ISN'T IT ENOUGH THAT I ALLOW IT THE BRIAR AND ALL BEASTS THAT WANDER INTO IT?
MUST IT ALSO COME OUT TO KILL MY HEIRS?

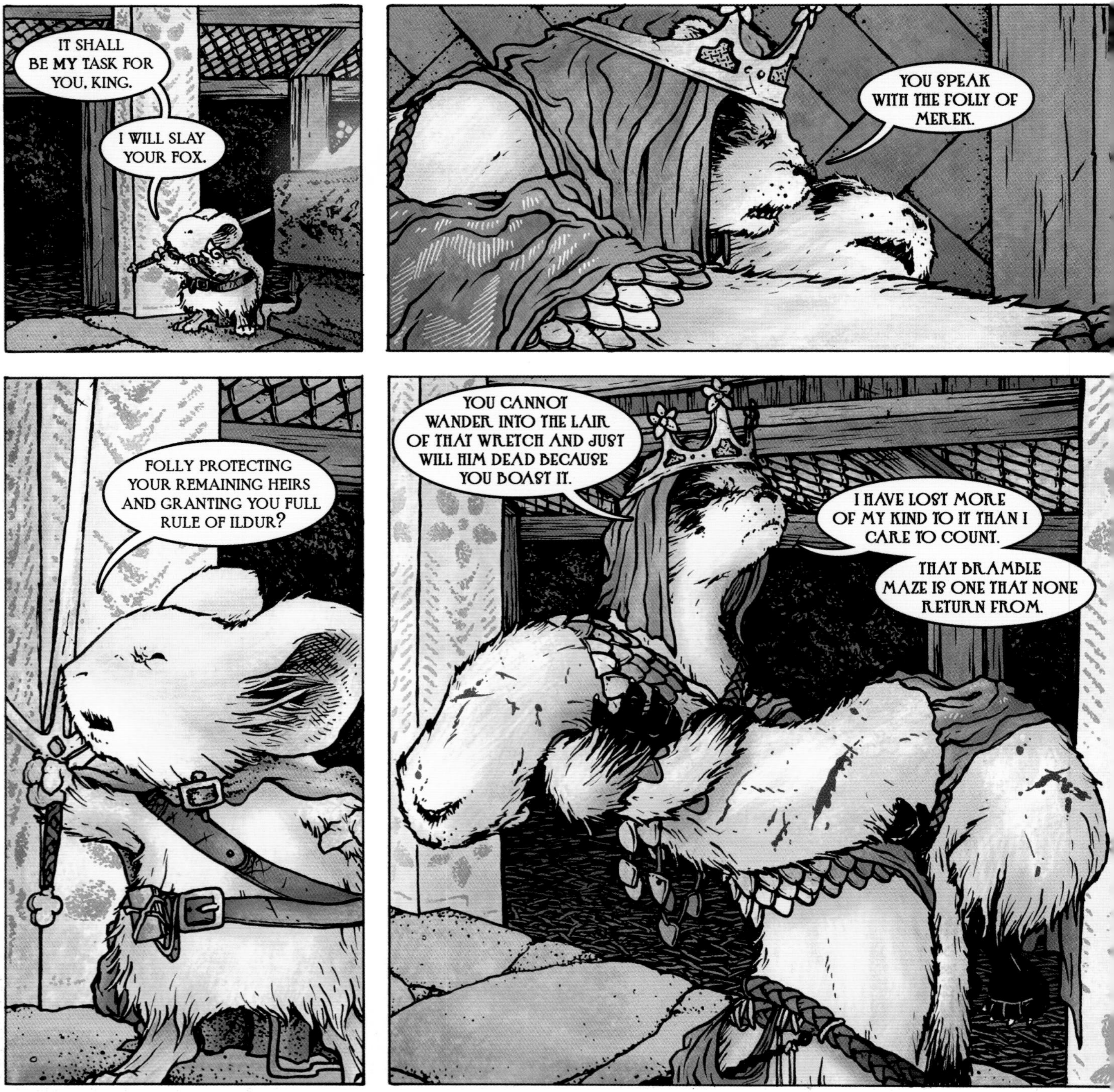
IT SHALL BE MY TASK FOR YOU, KING.
I WILL SLAY YOUR FOX.
YOU SPEAK WITH THE FOLLY OF MEREK.
FOLLY PROTECTING YOUR REMAINING HEIRS AND GRANTING YOU FULL RULE OF ILDUR?
YOU CANNOT WANDER INTO THE LAIR OF THAT WRETCH AND JUST WILL HIM DEAD BECAUSE YOU BOAST IT.
I HAVE LOST MORE OF MY KIND TO IT THAN I CARE TO COUNT.
THAT BRAMBLE MAZE IS ONE THAT NONE RETURN FROM.

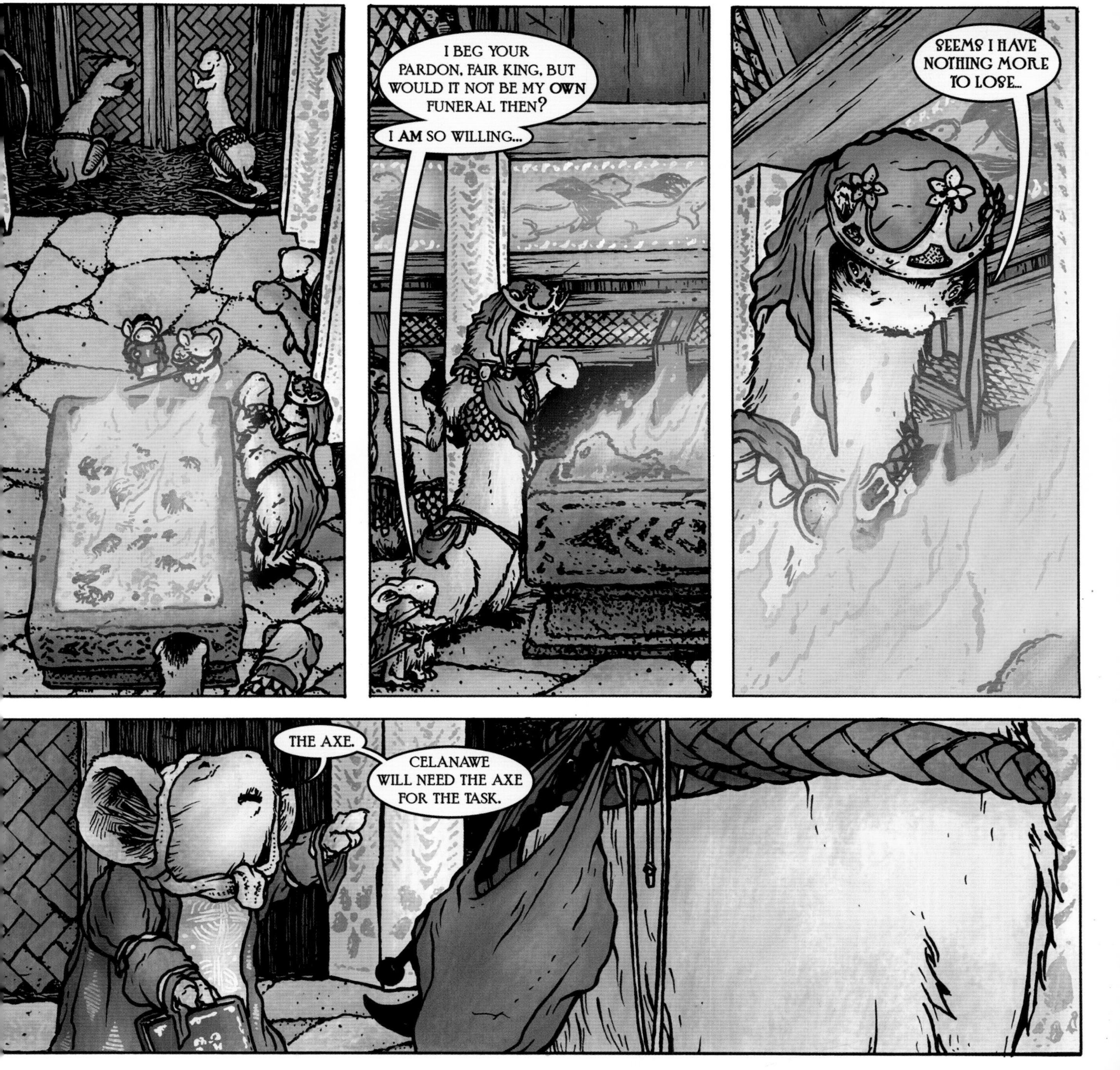
I BEG YOUR PARDON, FAIR KING, BUT WOULD IT NOT BE MY OWN FUNERAL THEN?
I AM SO WILLING...
SEEMS I HAVE NOTHING MORE TO LOSE...
THE AXE.
CELANAWE WILL NEED THE AXE FOR THE TASK.

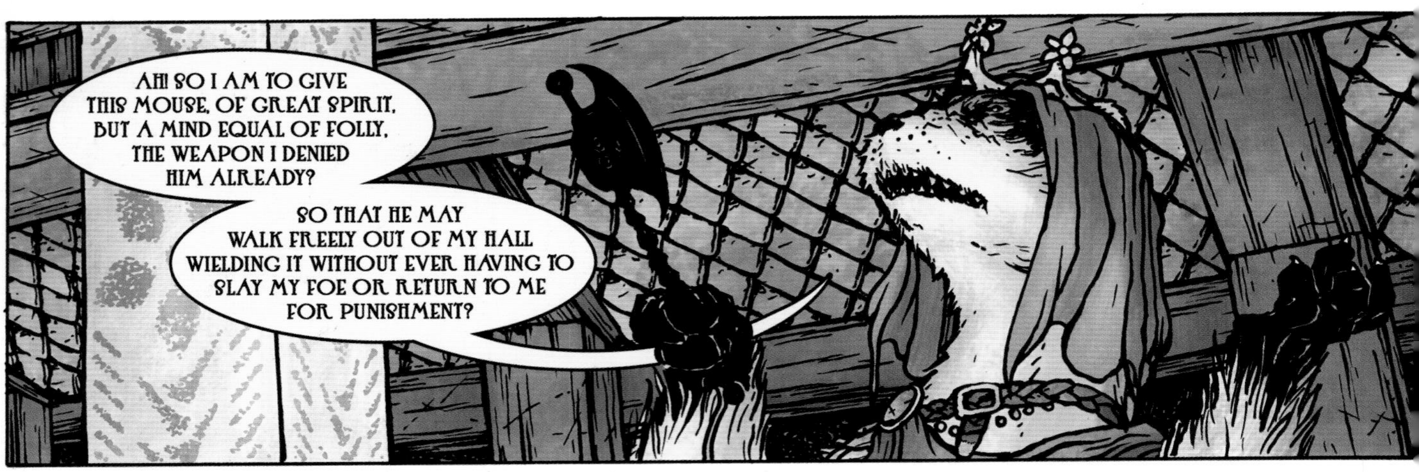
AH! SO I AM TO GIVE THIS MOUSE, OF GREAT SPIRIT, BUT A MIND EQUAL OF FOLLY, THE WEAPON I DENIED HIM ALREADY?
SO THAT HE MAY WALK FREELY OUT OF MY HALL WIELDING IT WITHOUT EVER HAVING TO SLAY MY FOE OR RETURN TO ME FOR PUNISHMENT?

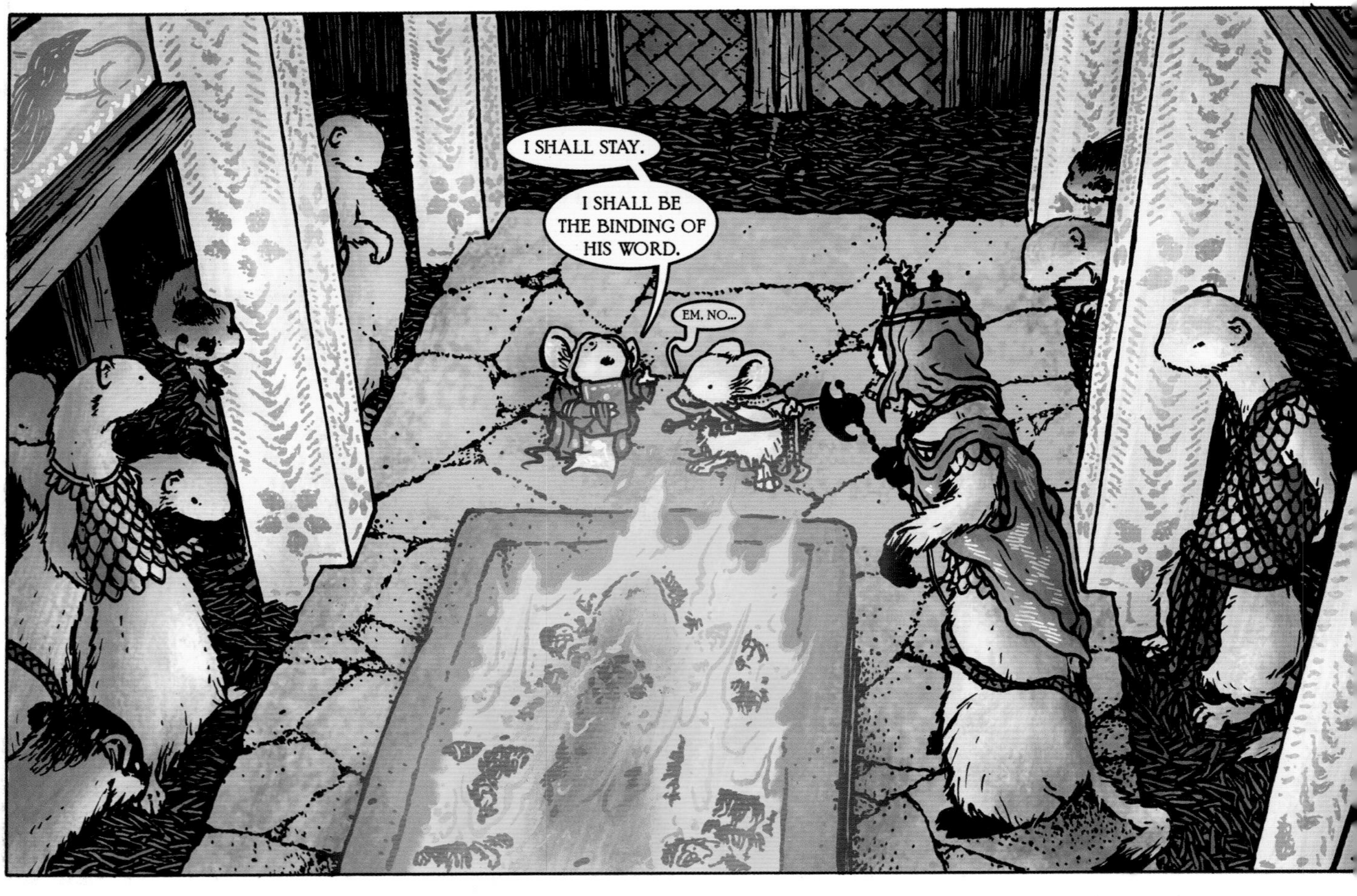
I SHALL STAY.
I SHALL BE THE BINDING OF HIS WORD.
EM, NO...

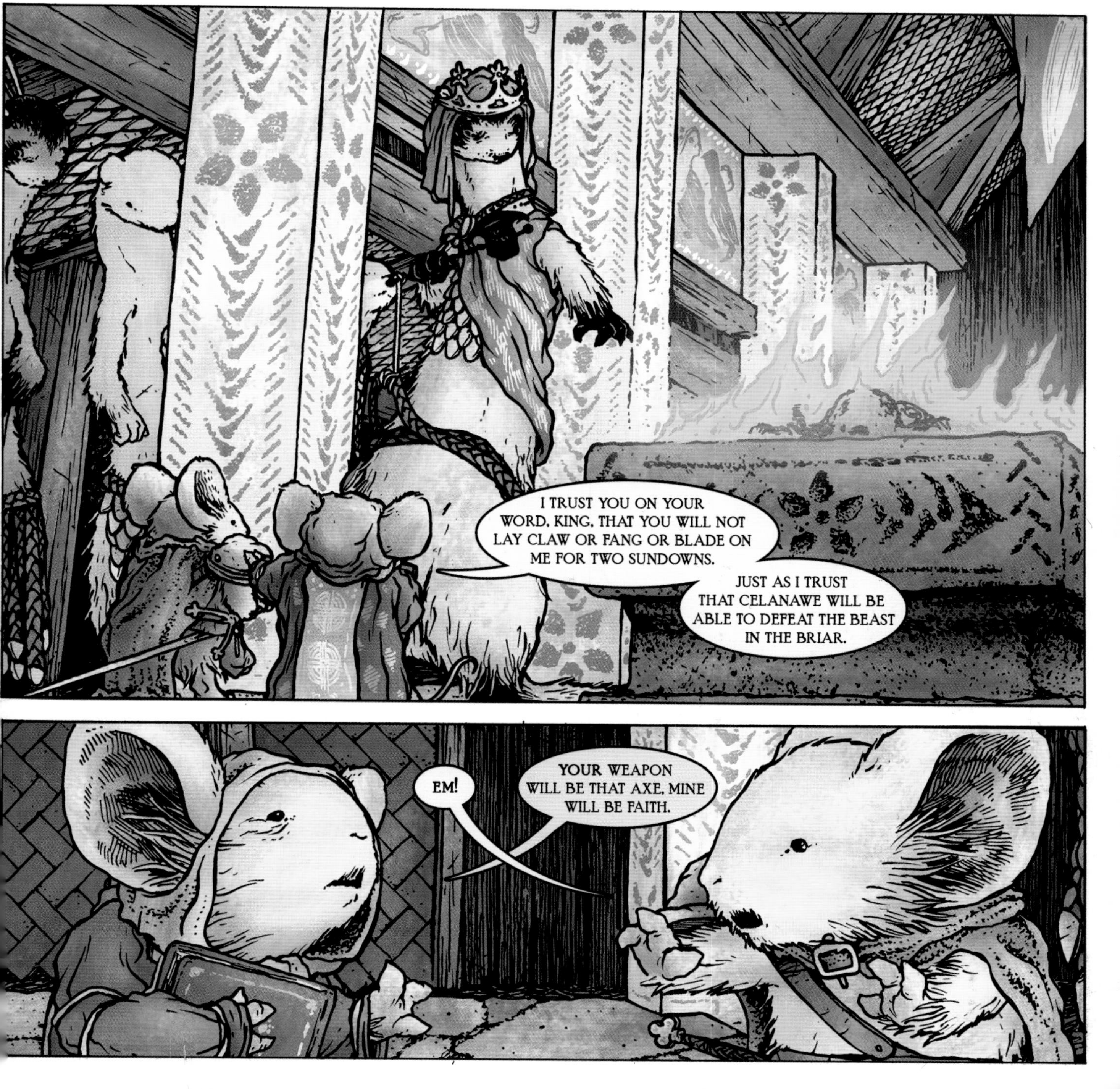
I TRUST YOU ON YOUR WORD, KING, THAT YOU WILL NOT LAY CLAW OR FANG OR BLADE ON ME FOR TWO SUNDOWNS.
JUST AS I TRUST THAT CELANAWE WILL BE ABLE TO DEFEAT THE BEAST IN THE BRIAR.
EM!
YOUR WEAPON WILL BE THAT AXE, MINE WILL BE FAITH.

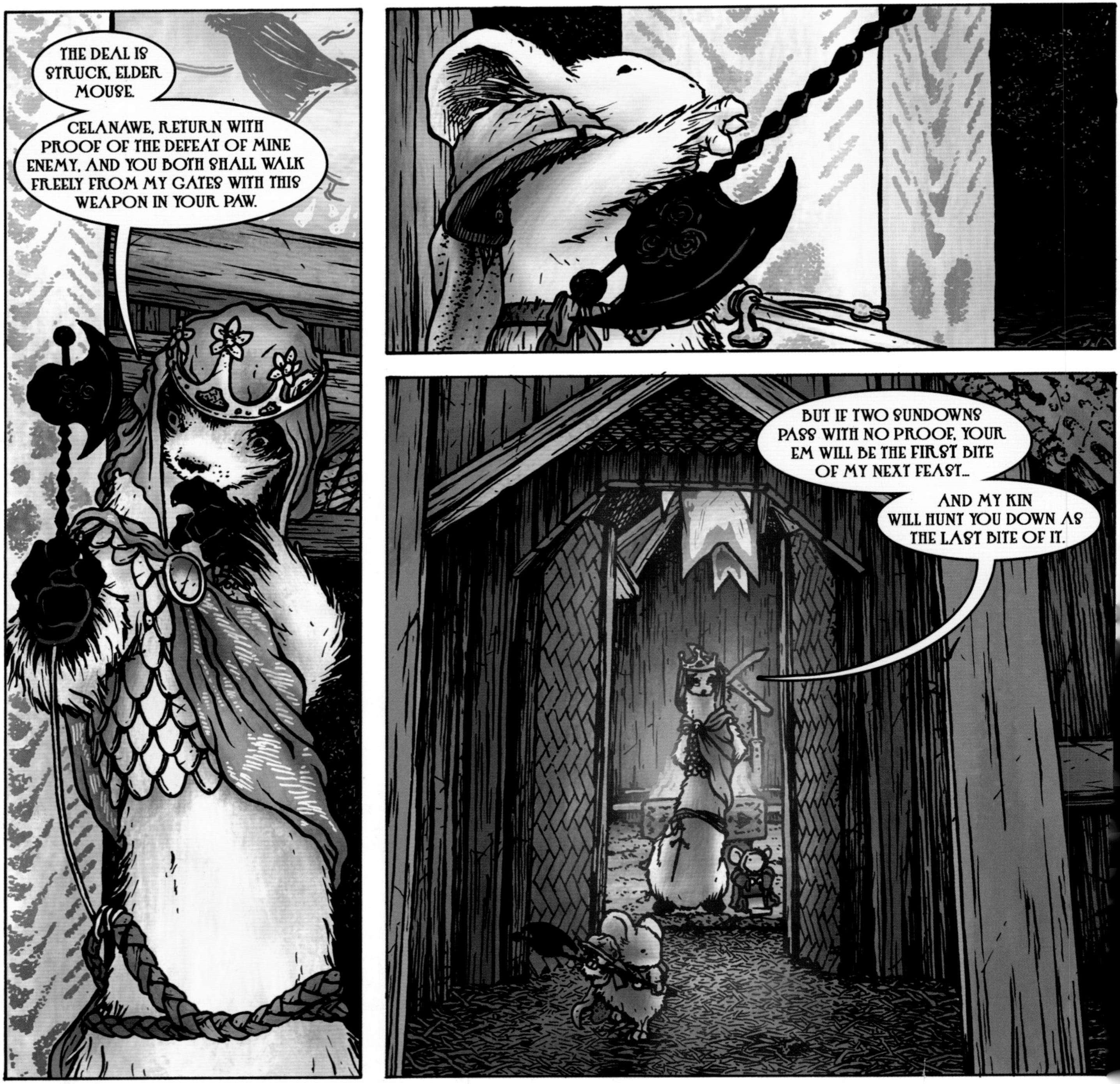
THE DEAL IS STRUCK, ELDER MOUSE.
CELANAWE, RETURN WITH PROOF OF THE DEFEAT OF MINE ENEMY, AND YOU BOTH SHALL WALK FREELY FROM MY GATES WITH THIS WEAPON IN YOUR PAW.
BUT IF TWO SUNDOWNS PASS WITH NO PROOF, YOUR EM WILL BE THE FIRST BITE OF MY NEXT FEAST...
AND MY KIN WILL HUNT YOU DOWN AS THE LAST BITE OF IT.

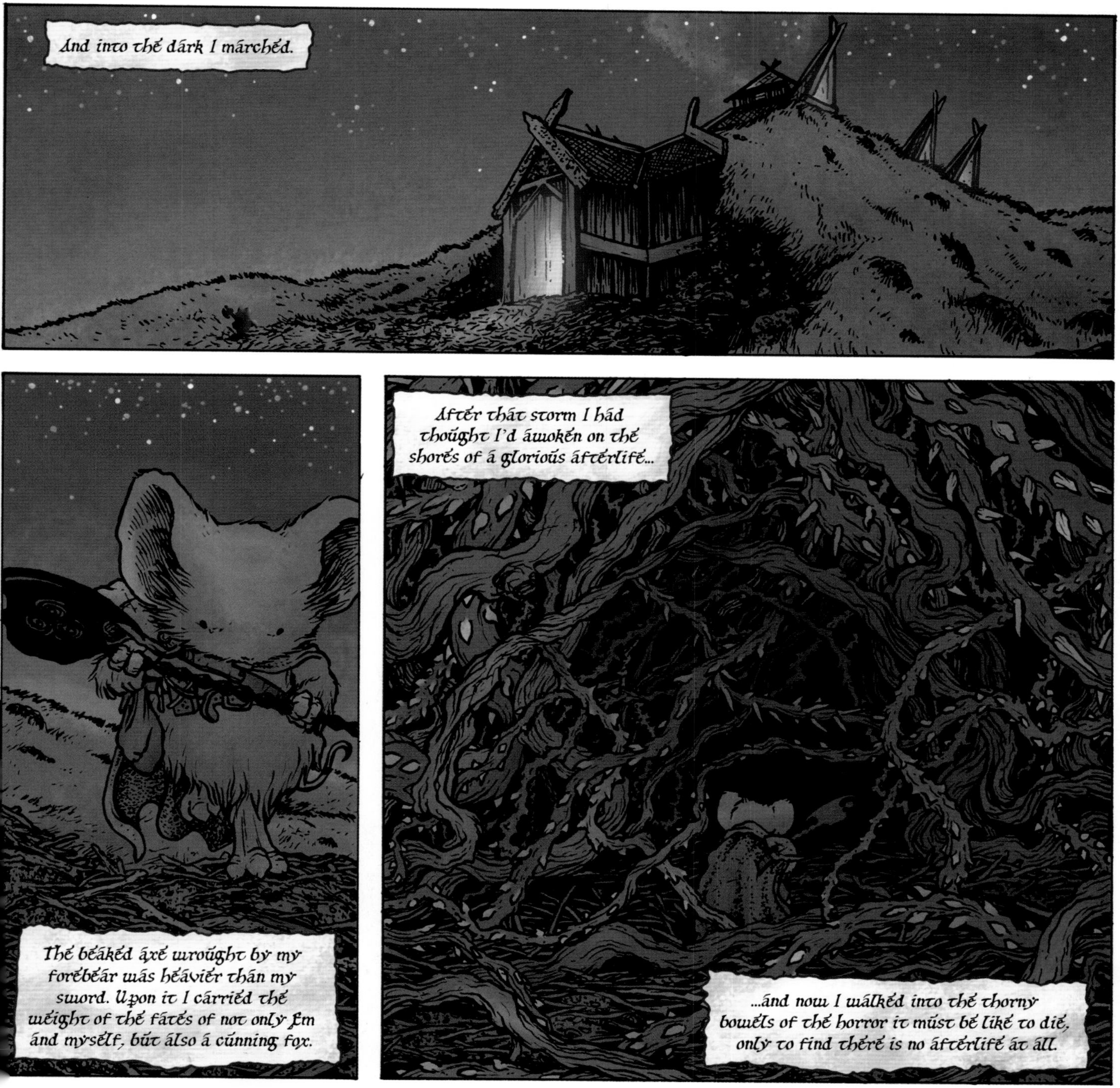
And into the dark I marched.
After that storm I had thought I'd awoken on the shores of a glorious afterlife...
The beaked axe wrought by my forebear was heavier than my sword. Upon it I carried the weight of the fates of not only Em and myself, but also a cunning fox.
...and now I walked into the thorny bowels of the horror it must be like to die, only to find there is no afterlife at all.

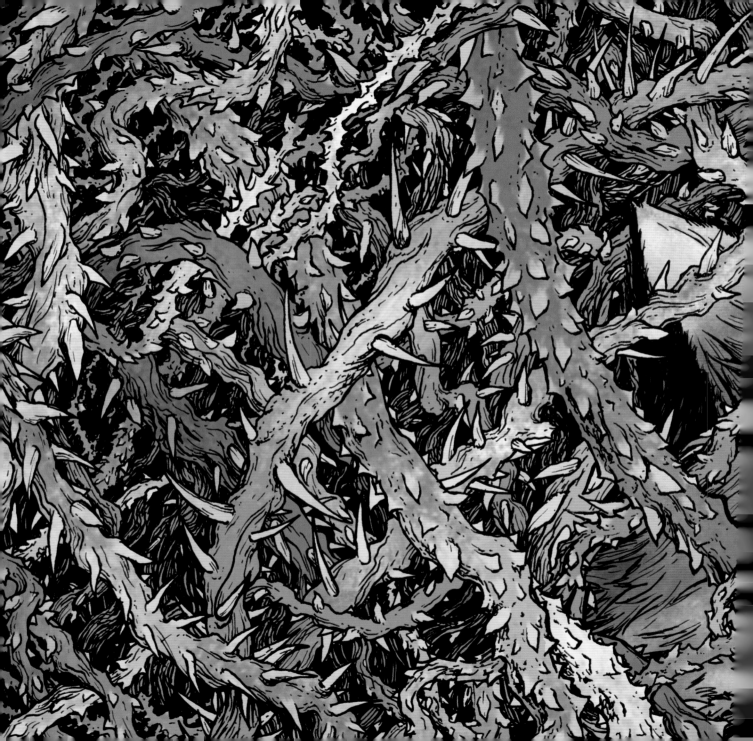

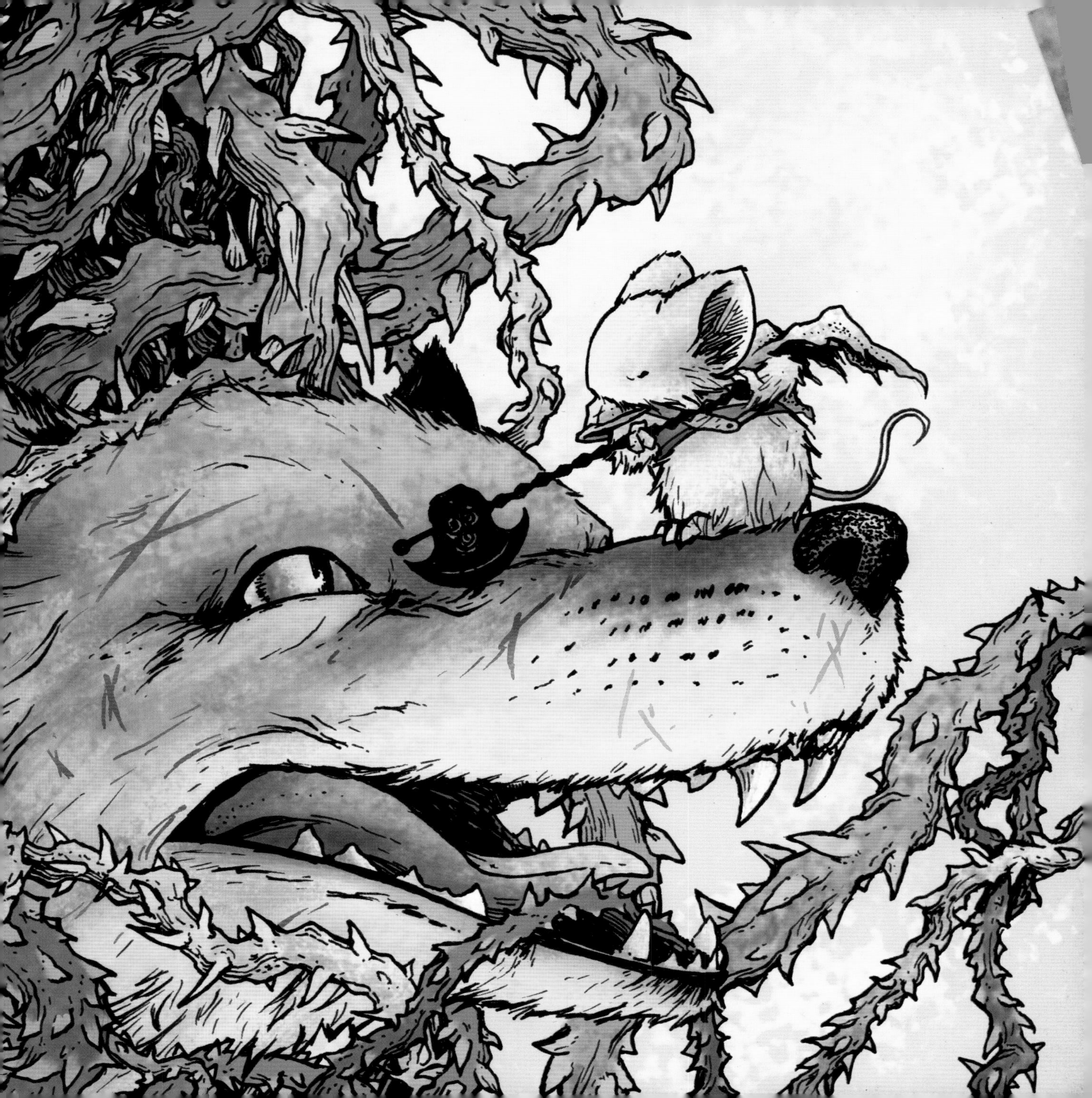

CHAPTER FOUR

At the shore of the great large lake, the battle-for-all began ⚜

Lupis showed snarled tooth and wicked claw.

Buteo soared above with eyes that could see all.

Vulpes sculled about with tactics above all others.

Serpentes rode low with venom for a blade.

The Black Axe took seven suns worth of time on each of them and their kin that followed them to battle and when the moon had showed every phase the great lake shone scarlet with the life ❈ of the Black Axe's victims. ❈

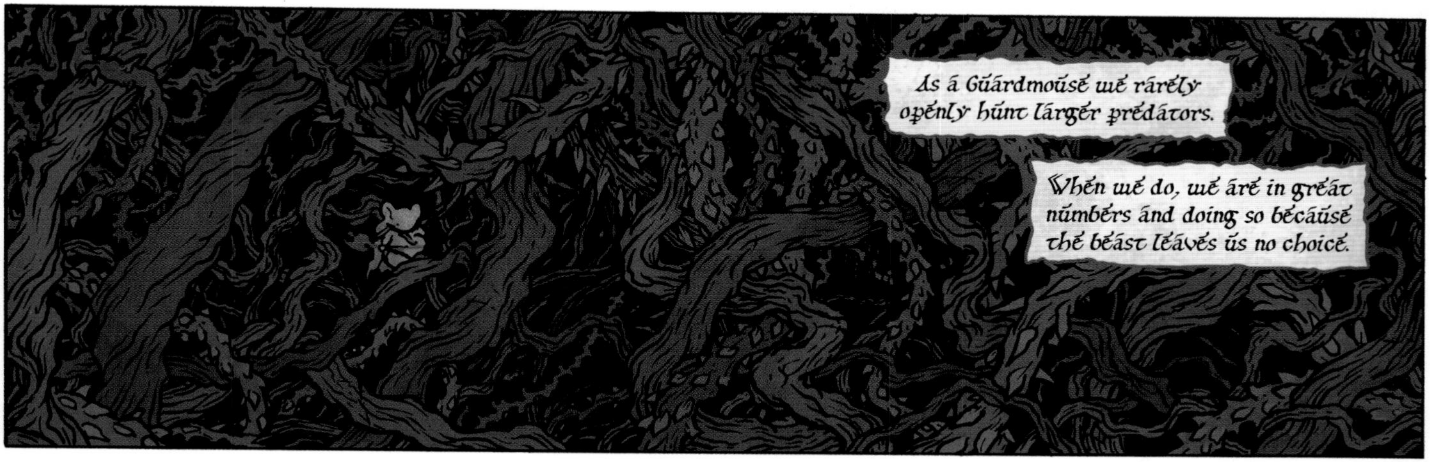
As a Guardmouse we rarely openly hunt larger predators.
When we do, we are in great numbers and doing so because the beast leaves us no choice.

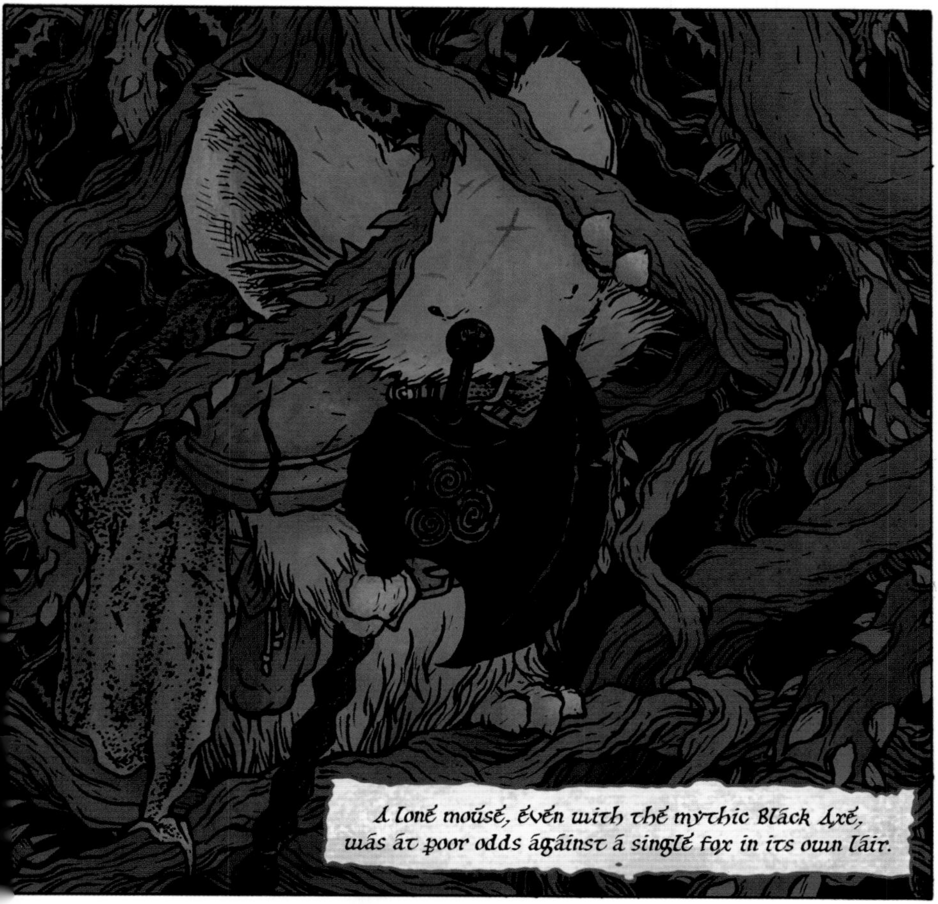
A lone mouse, even with the mythic Black Axe, was at poor odds against a single fox in its own lair.

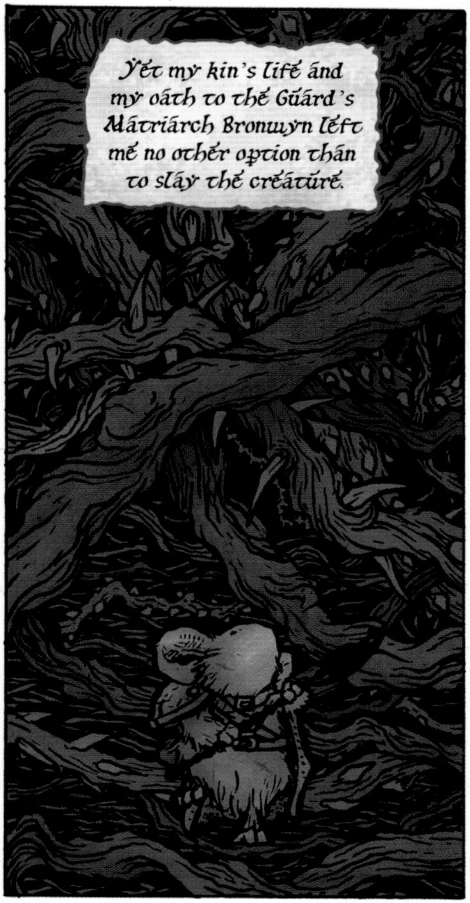
Yet my kin's life and my oath to the Guard's Matriarch Bronwyn left me no other option than to slay the creature.

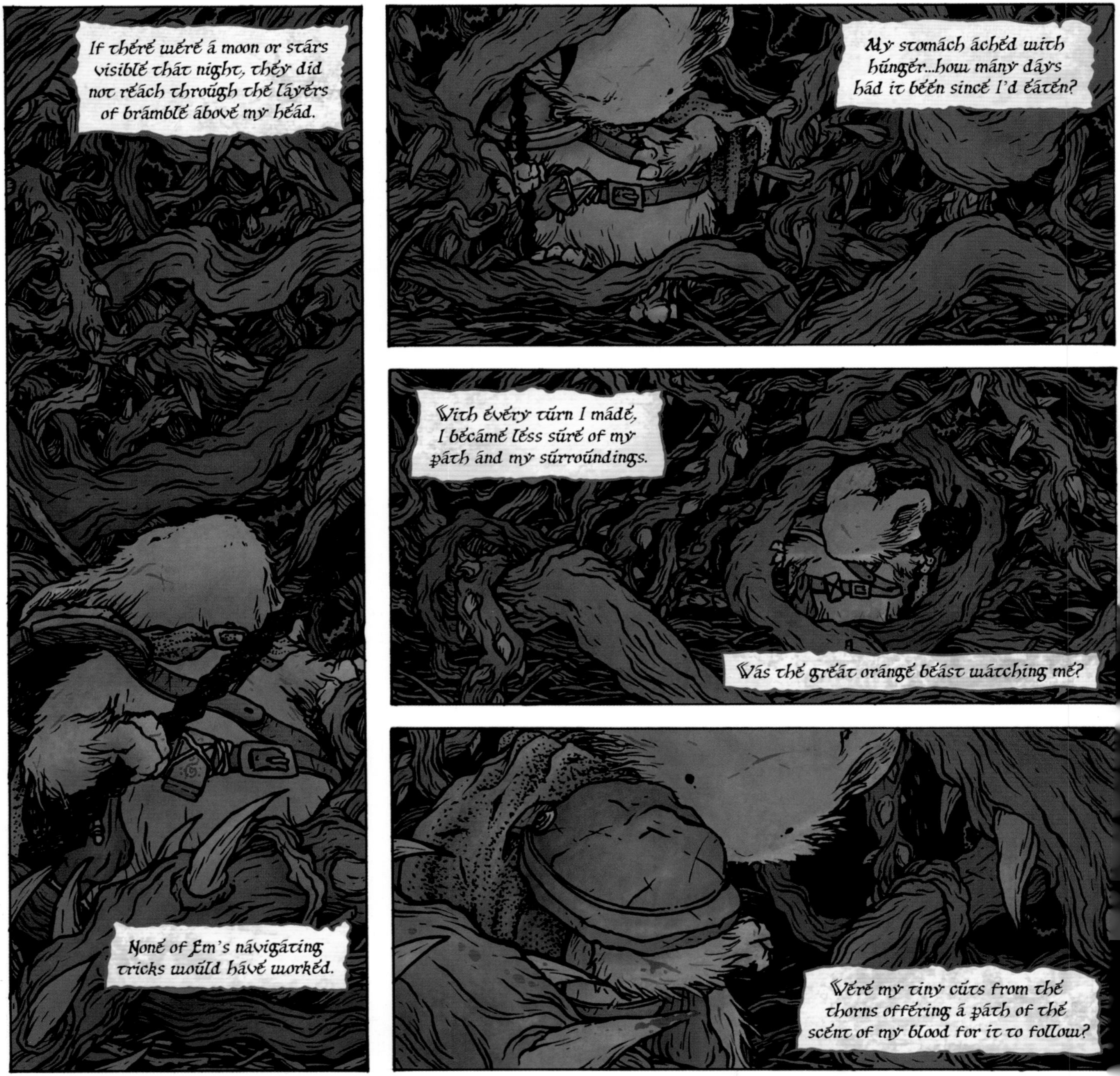
If there were a moon or stars visible that night, they did not reach through the layers of bramble above my head.
None of Em's navigating tricks would have worked.
My stomach ached with hunger...how many days had it been since I'd eaten?
With every turn I made, I became less sure of my path and my surroundings.
Was the great orange beast watching me?
Were my tiny cuts from the thorns offering a path of the scent of my blood for it to follow?

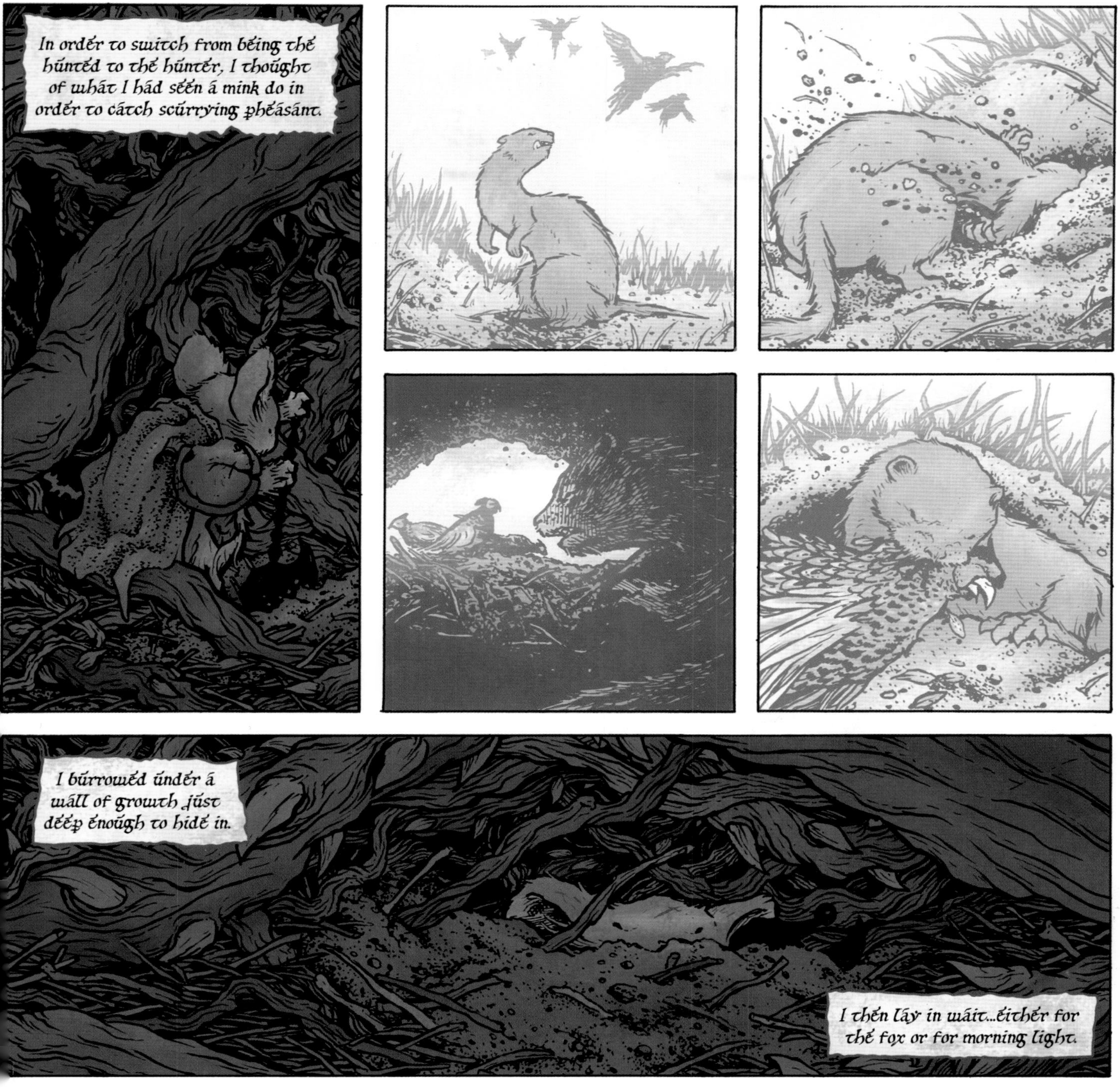
In order to switch from being the hunted to the hunter, I thought of what I had seen a mink do in order to catch scurrying pheasant.
I burrowed under a wall of growth just deep enough to hide in.
I then lay in wait...either for the fox or for morning light.

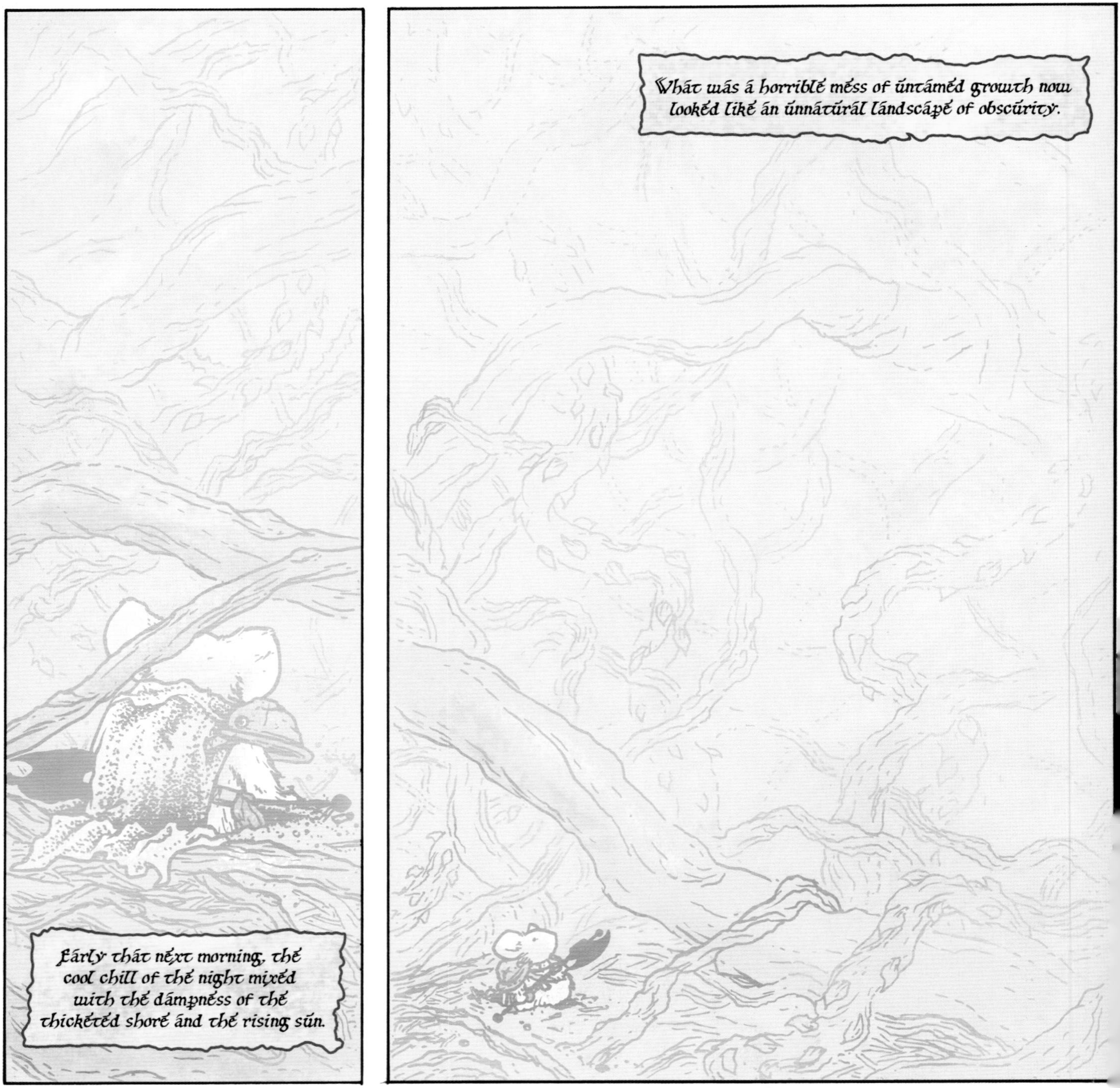
Early that next morning, the cool chill of the night mixed with the dampness of the thicketed shore and the rising sun.
What was a horrible mess of untamed growth now looked like an unnatural landscape of obscurity.

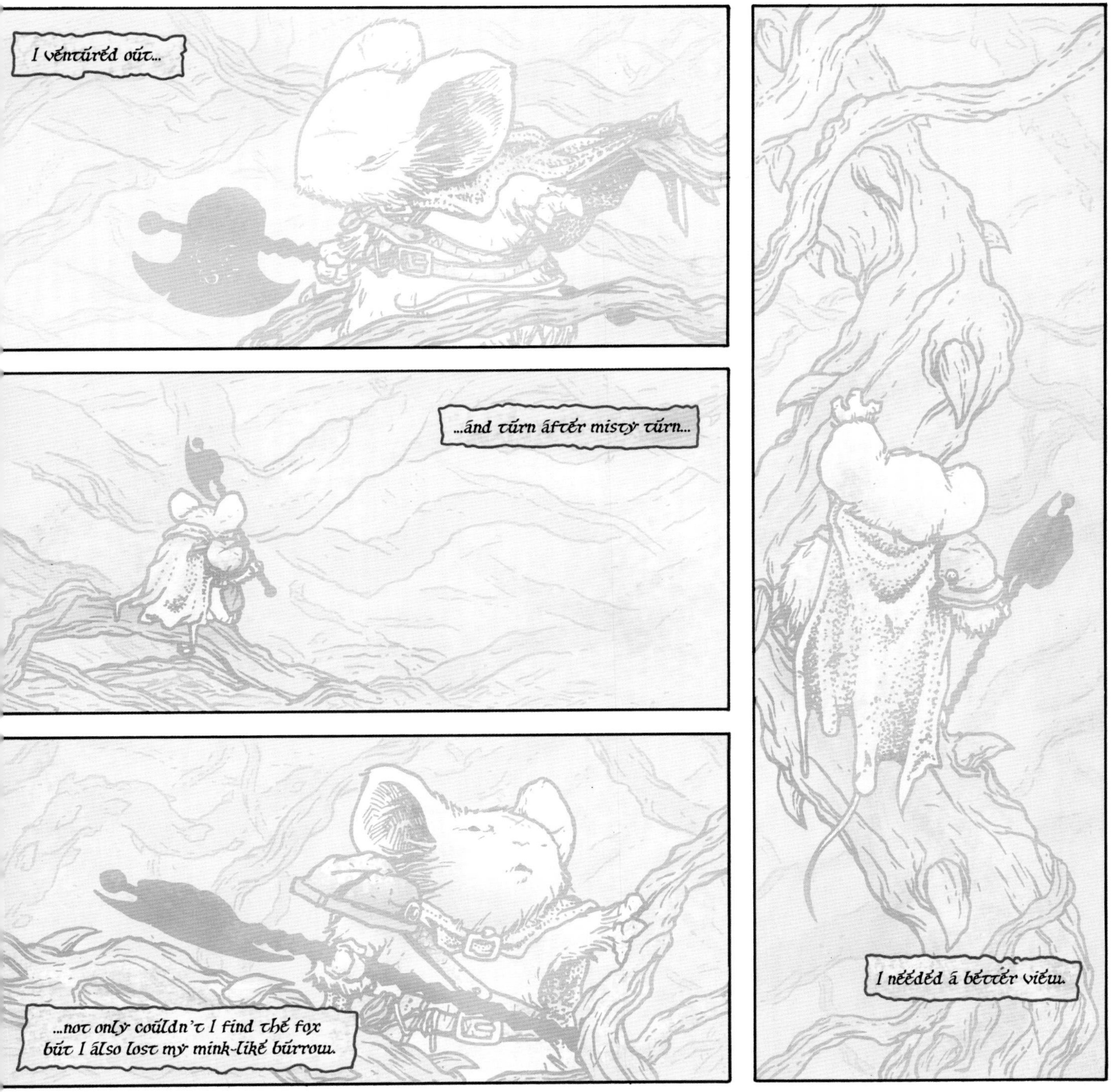
I ventured out...
...and turn after misty turn...
...not only couldn't I find the fox but I also lost my mink-like burrow.
I needed a better view.

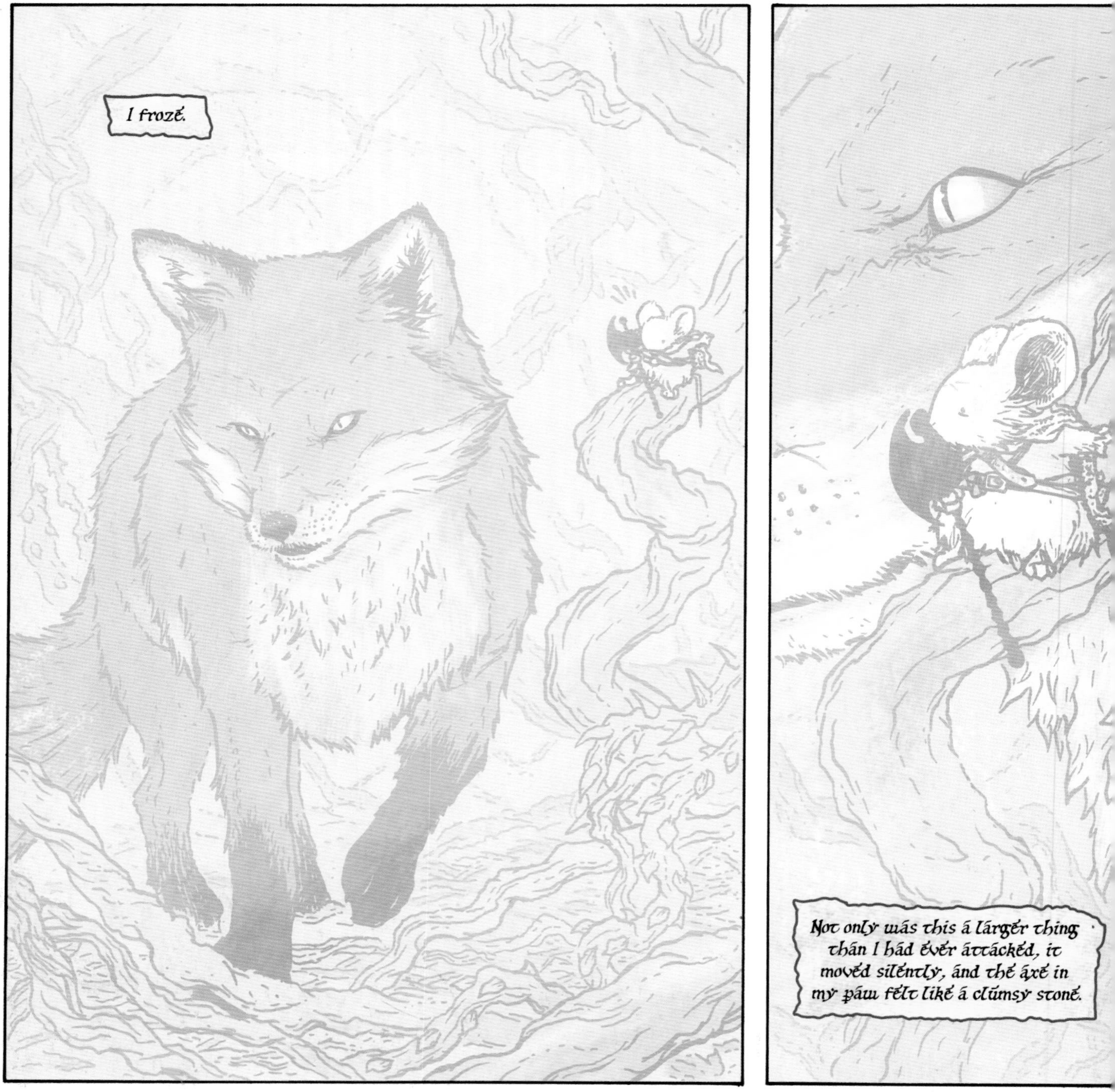
I froze.
Not only was this a larger thing than I had ever attacked, it moved silently, and the axe in my paw felt like a clumsy stone.

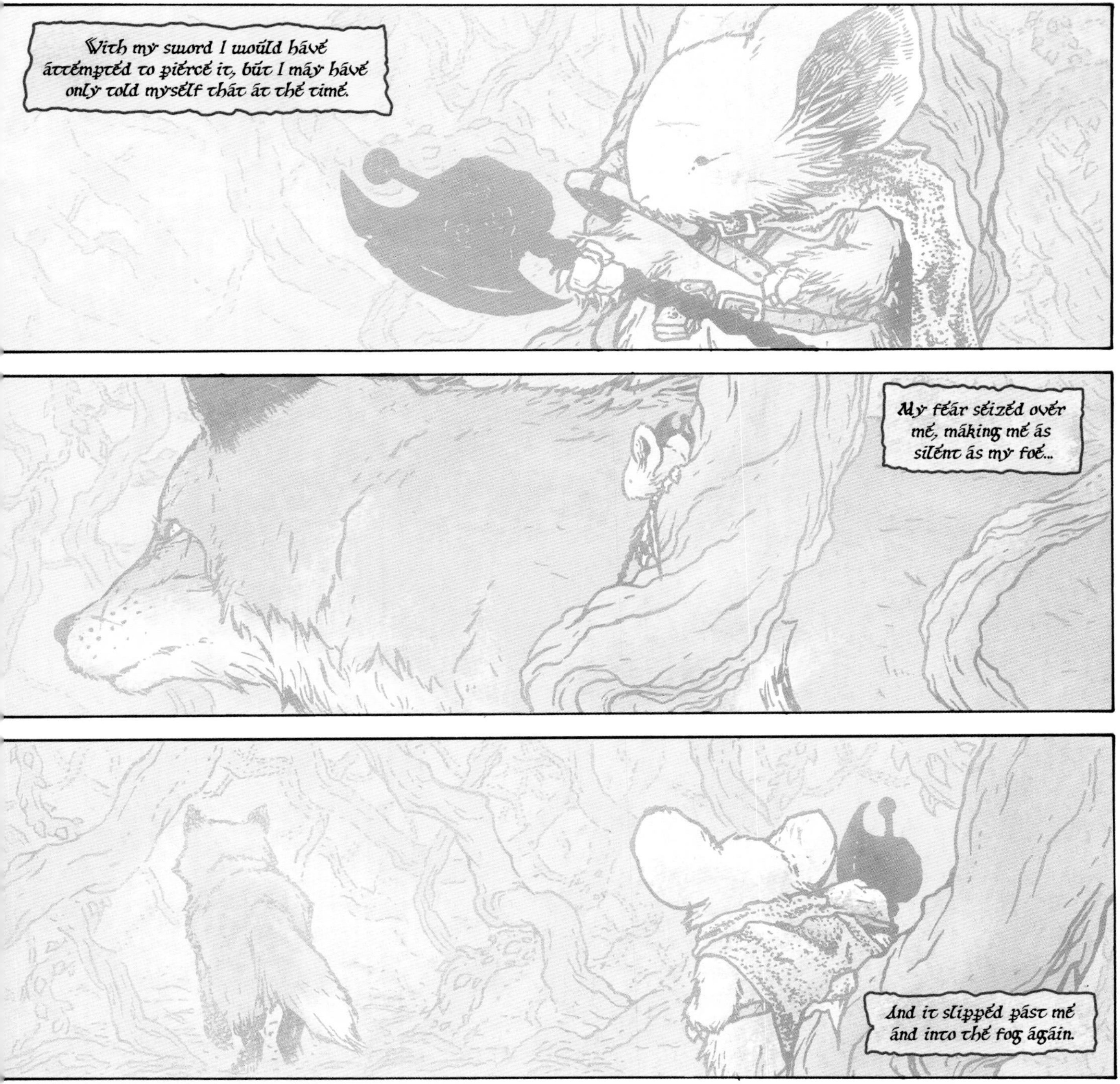
With my sword I would have attempted to pierce it, but I may have only told myself that at the time.
My fear seized over me, making me as silent as my foe...
And it slipped past me and into the fog again.

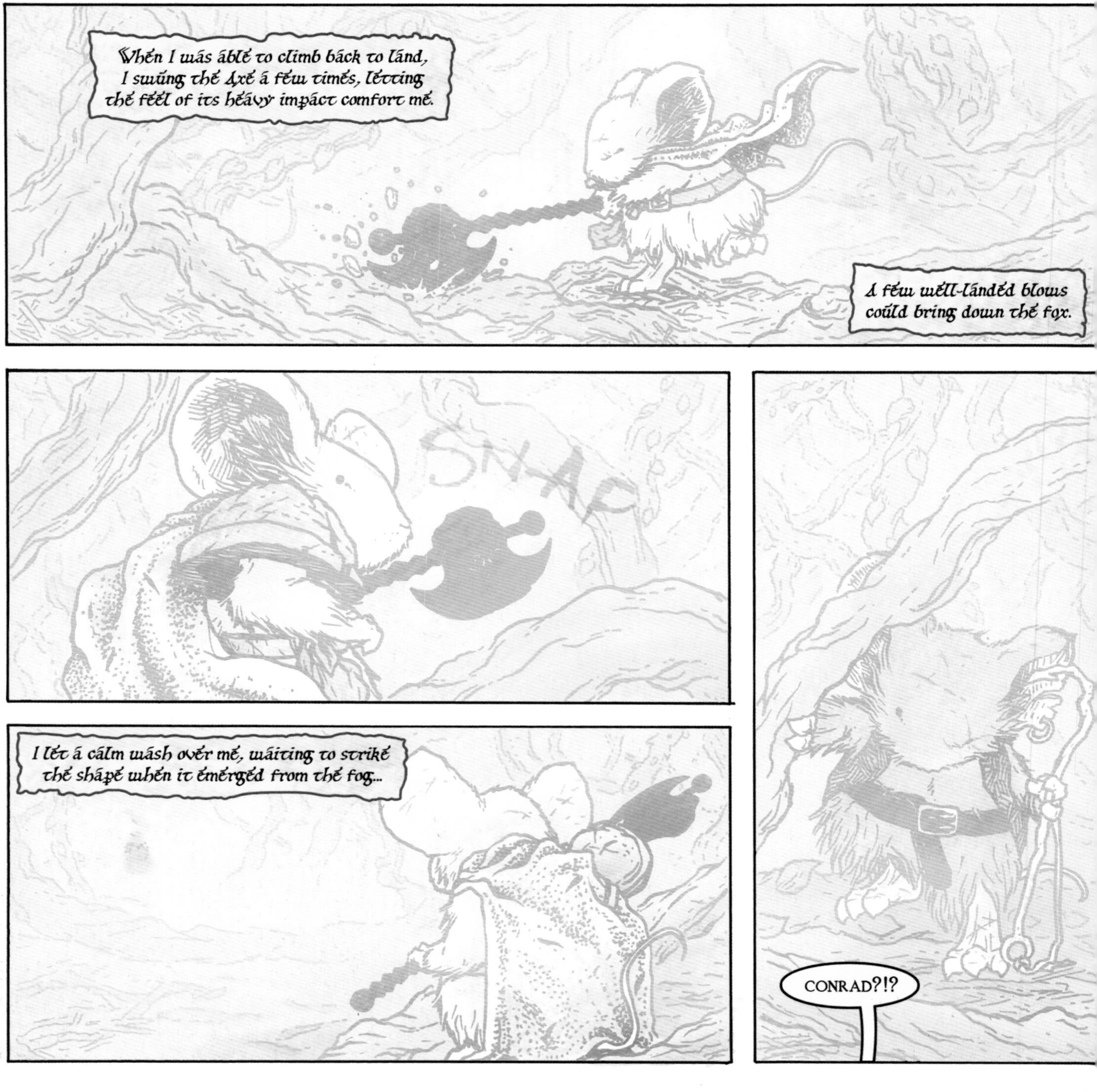
When I was able to climb back to land, I swung the Axe a few times, letting the feel of its heavy impact comfort me.
A few well-landed blows could bring down the fox.
SNAP
I let a calm wash over me, waiting to strike the shape when it emerged from the fog...
CONRAD?!?

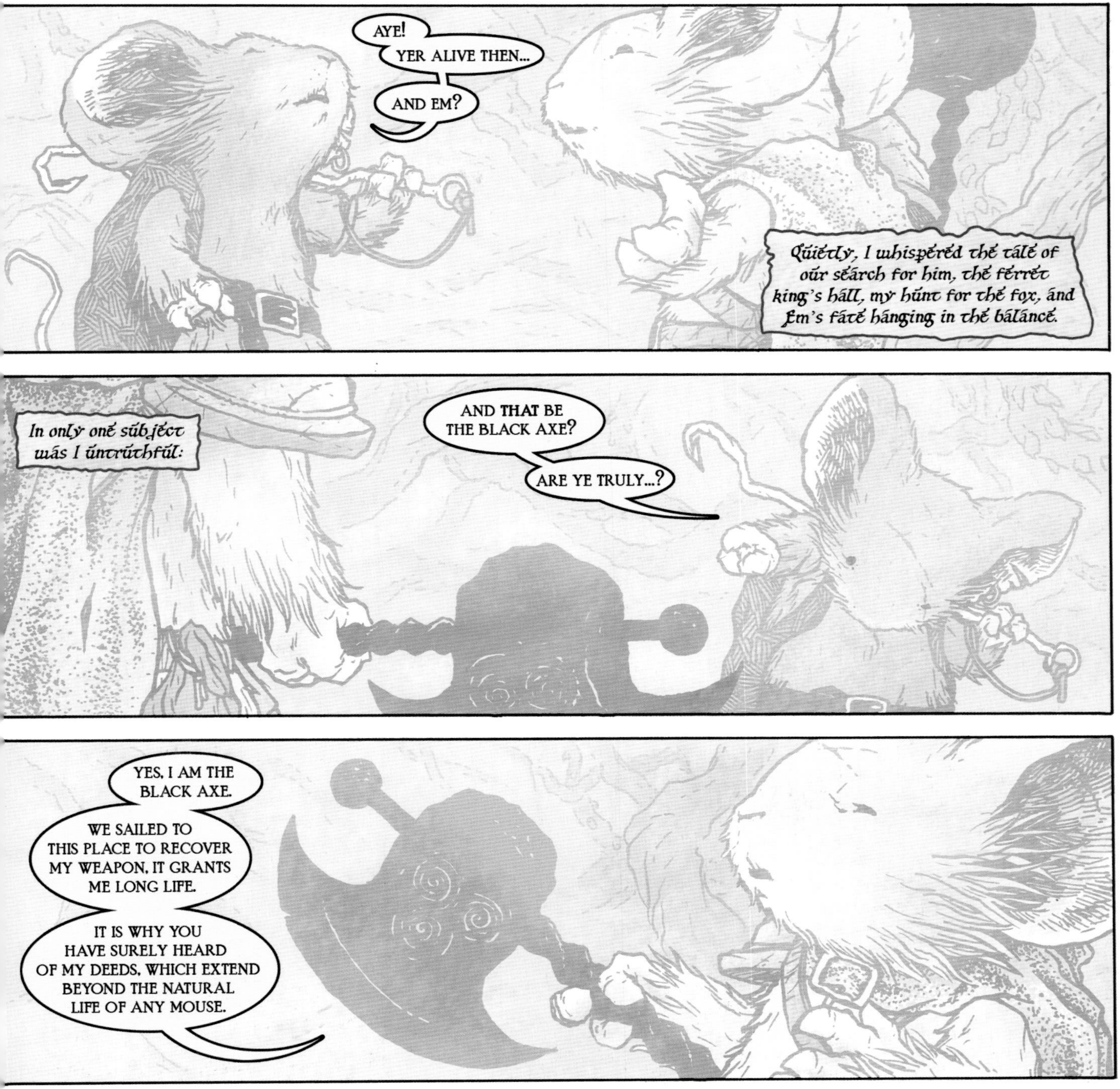
AYE!
YER ALIVE THEN...
AND EM?
Quietly, I whispered the tale of our search for him, the ferret king's hall, my hunt for the fox, and Em's fate hanging in the balance.
In only one subject was I untruthful:
AND THAT BE THE BLACK AXE?
ARE YE TRULY...?
YES, I AM THE BLACK AXE.
WE SAILED TO THIS PLACE TO RECOVER MY WEAPON, IT GRANTS ME LONG LIFE.
IT IS WHY YOU HAVE SURELY HEARD OF MY DEEDS, WHICH EXTEND BEYOND THE NATURAL LIFE OF ANY MOUSE.

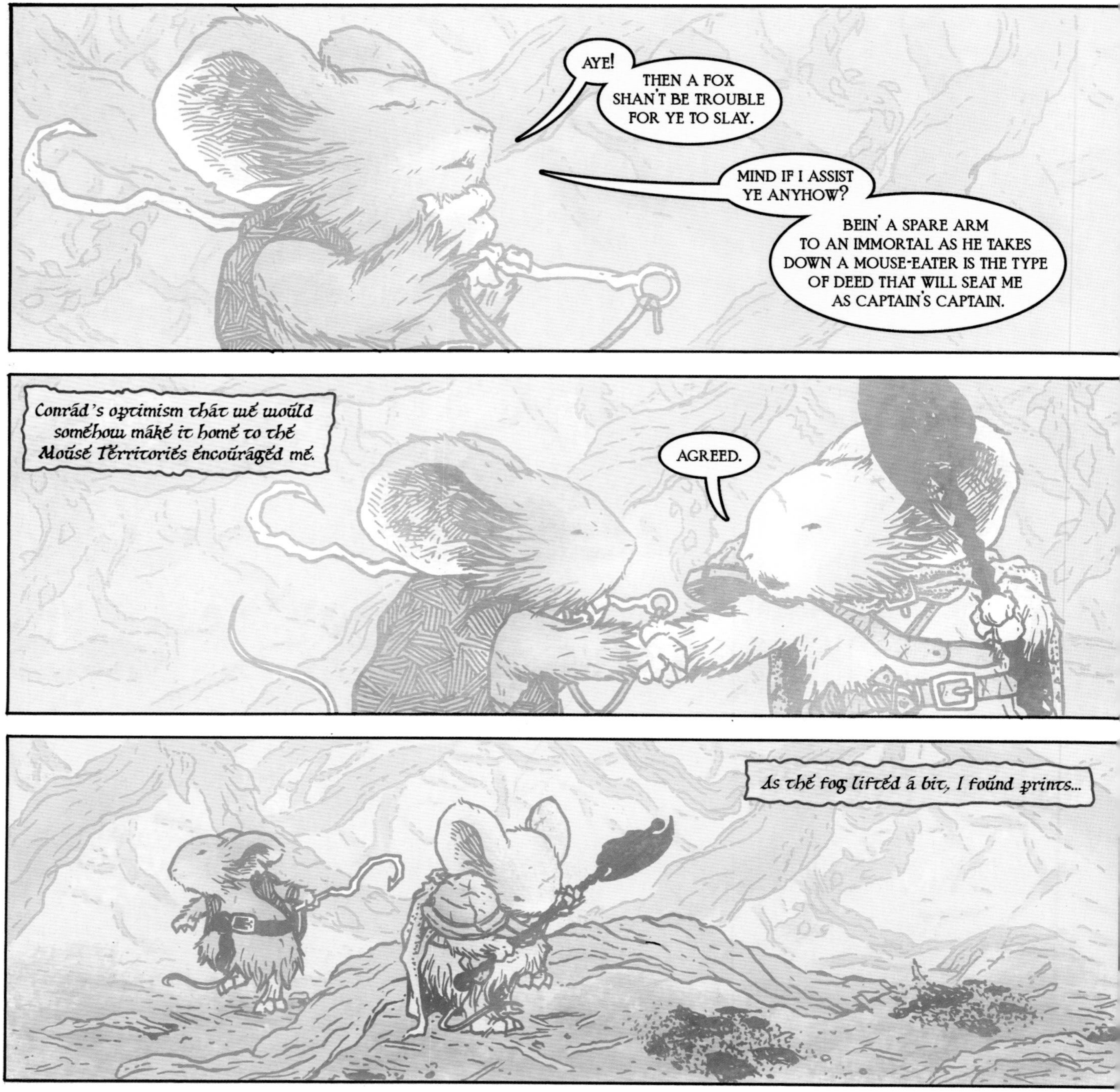
AYE!
THEN A FOX SHAN'T BE TROUBLE FOR YE TO SLAY.
MIND IF I ASSIST YE ANYHOW?
BEIN' A SPARE ARM TO AN IMMORTAL AS HE TAKES DOWN A MOUSE-EATER IS THE TYPE OF DEED THAT WILL SEAT ME AS CAPTAIN'S CAPTAIN.
Conrad's optimism that we would somehow make it home to the Mouse Territories encouraged me.
AGREED.
As the fog lifted a bit, I found prints...

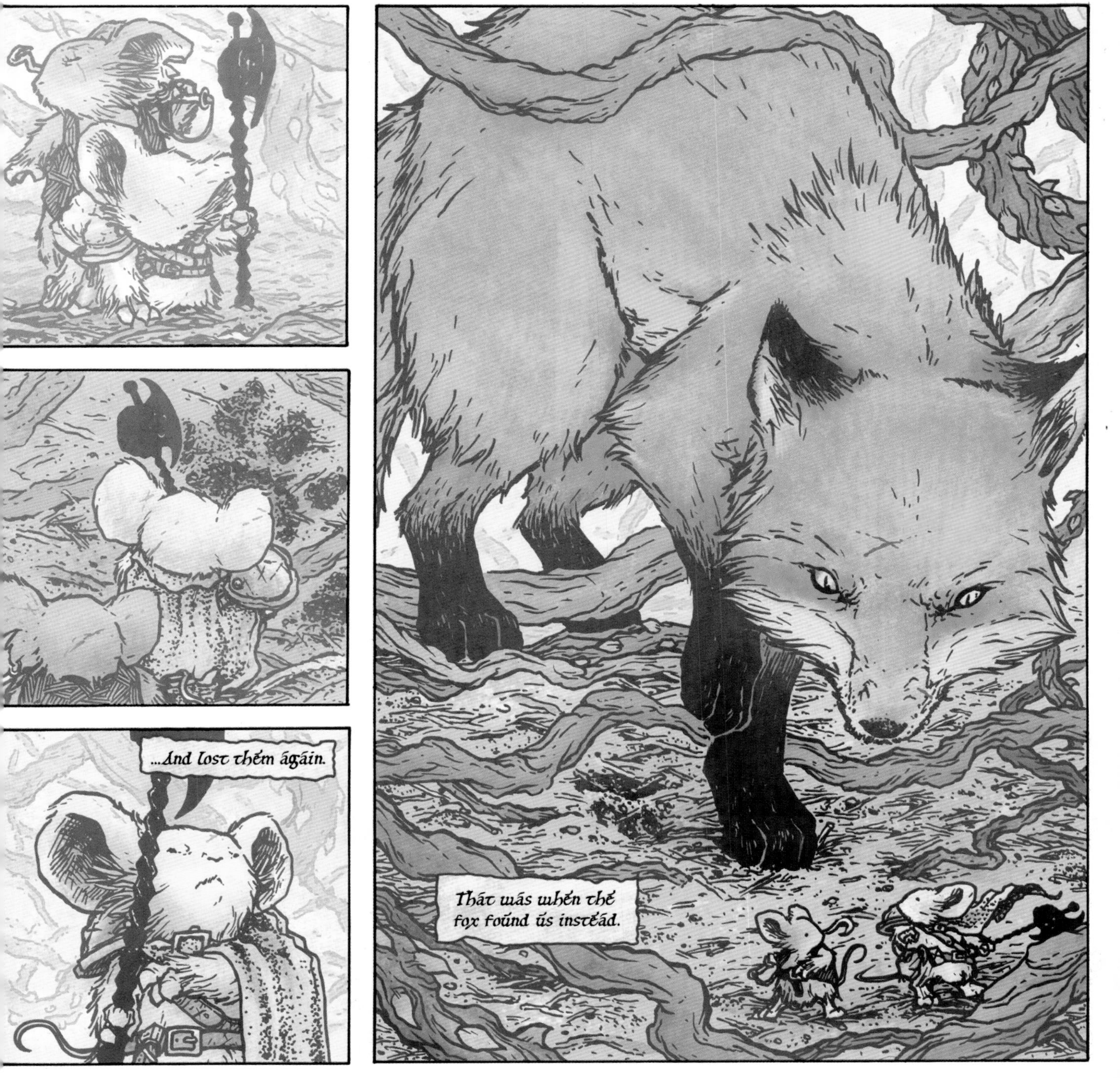
...And lost them again.
That was when the fox found us instead.

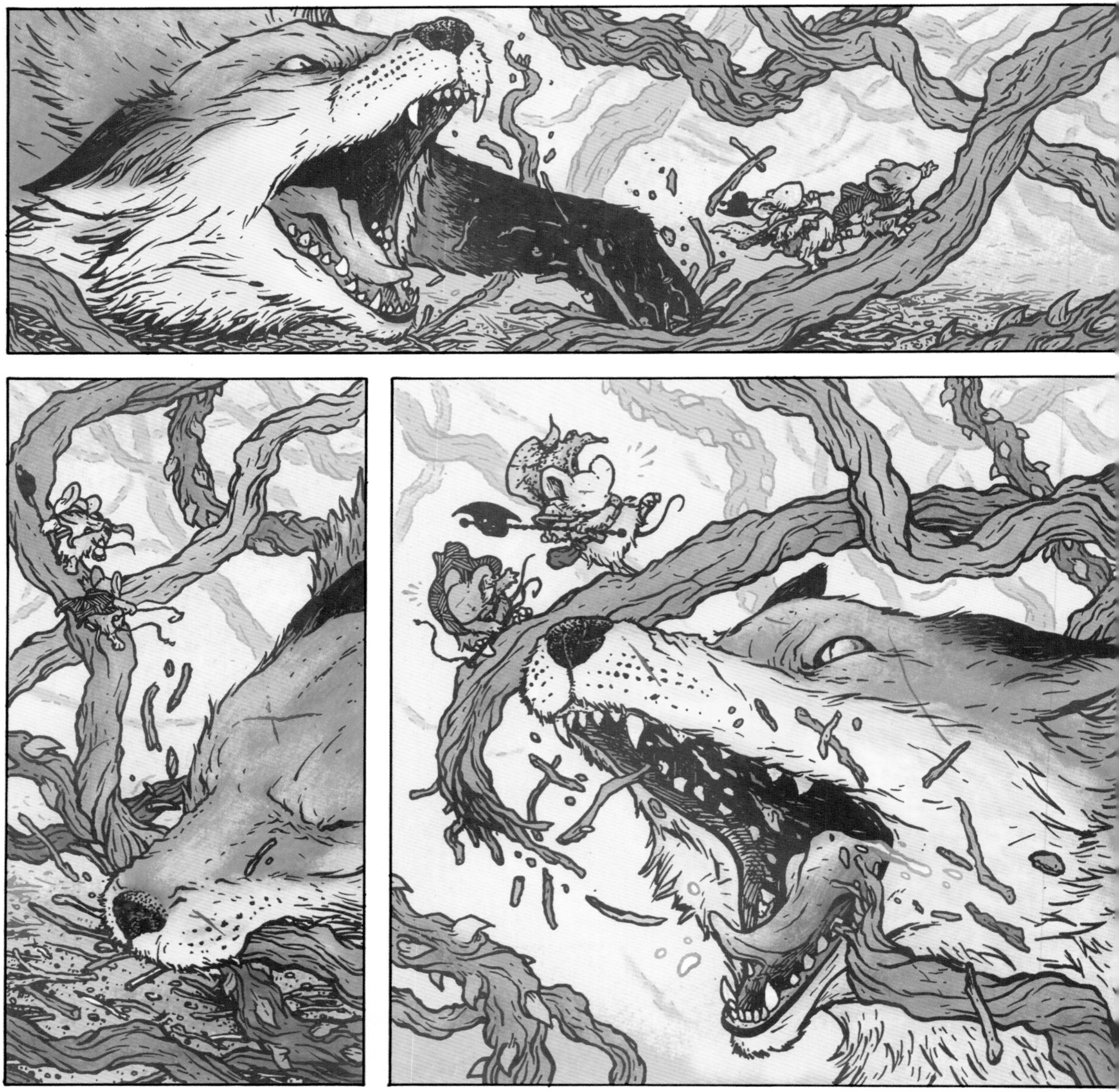

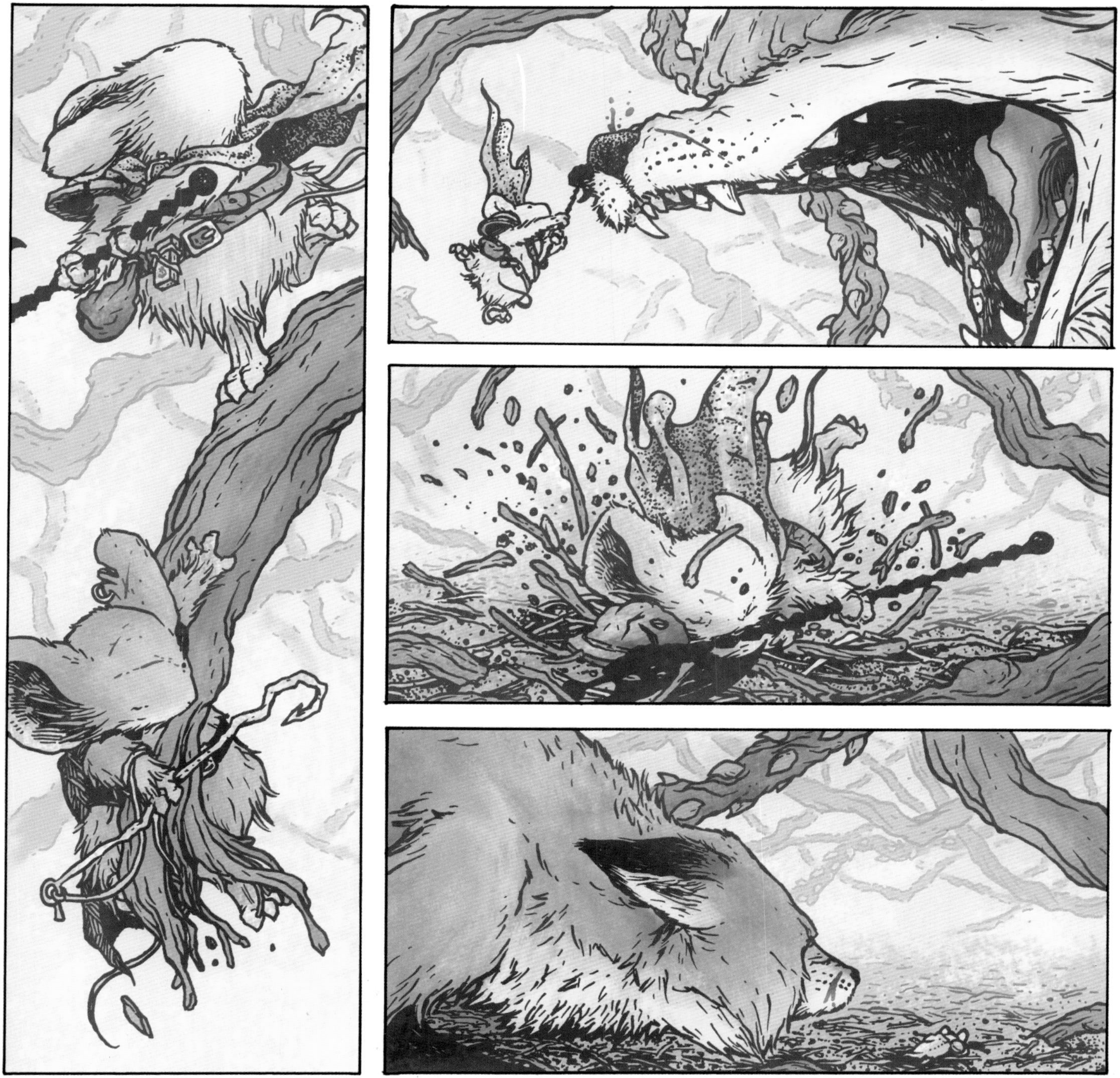

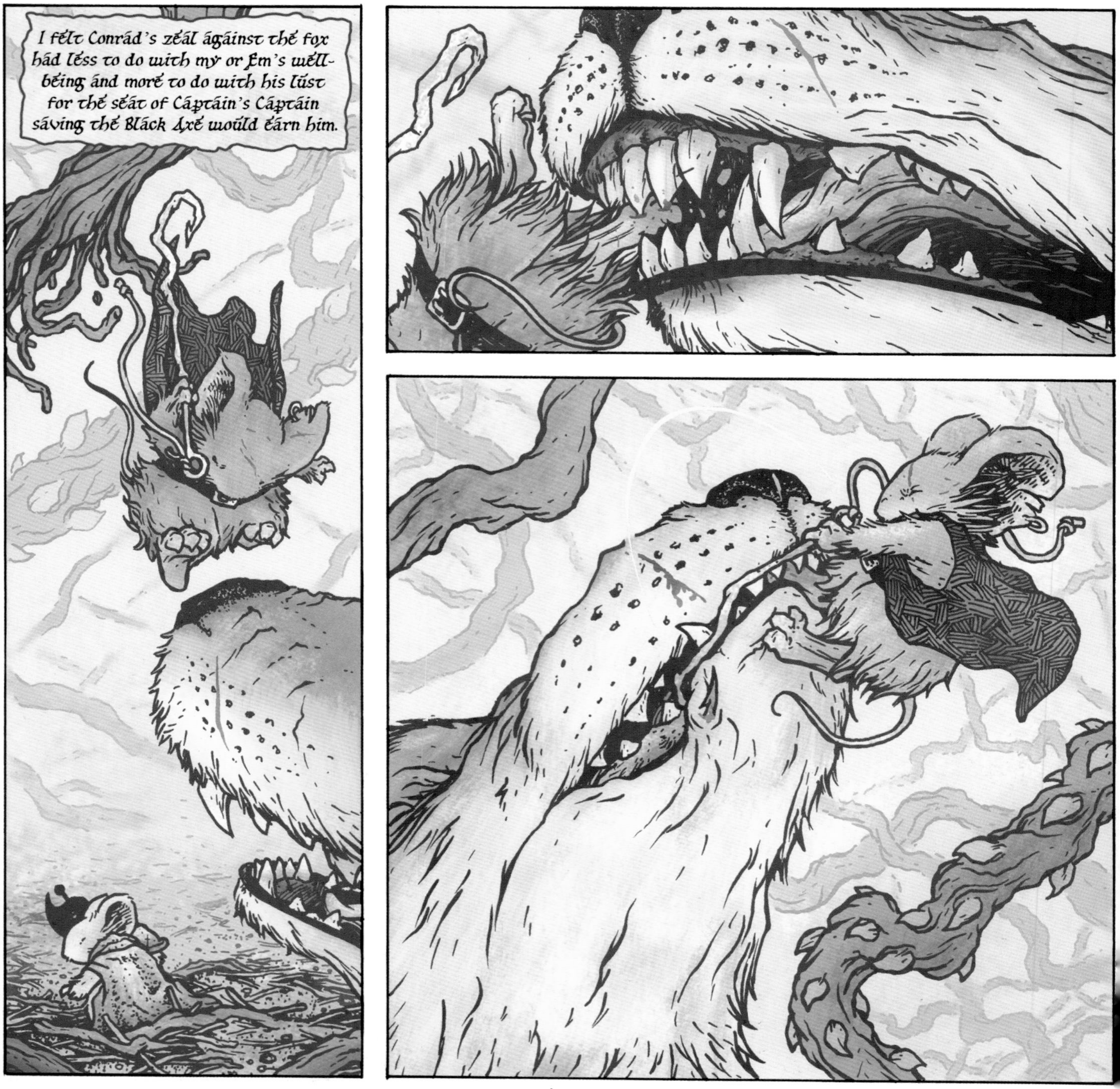
I felt Conrad's zeal against the fox had less to do with my or Em's well-being and more to do with his lust for the seat of Captain's Captain saving the Black Axe would earn him.

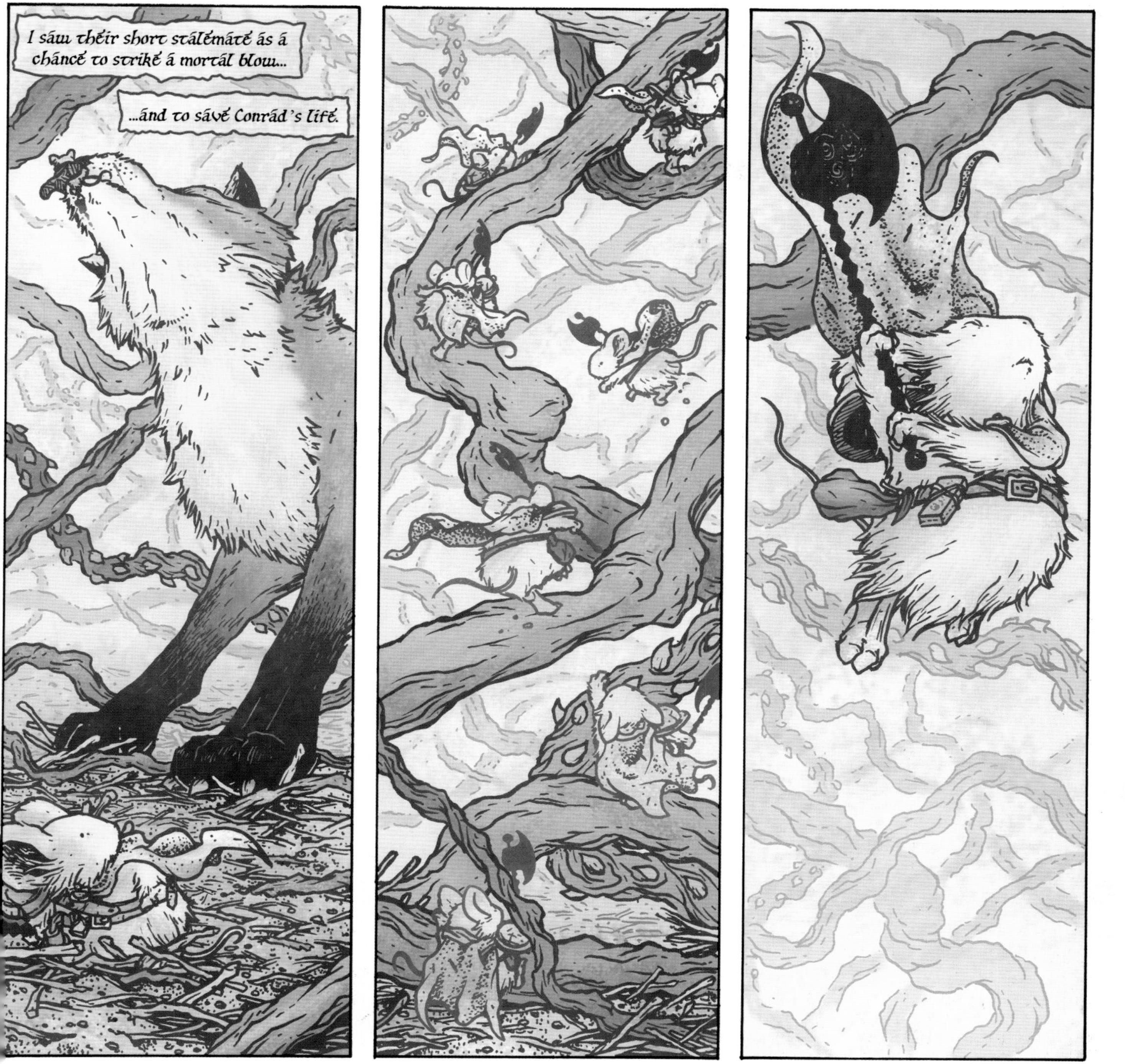

I saw their short stalemate as a chance to strike a mortal blow...
...and to save Conrad's life.

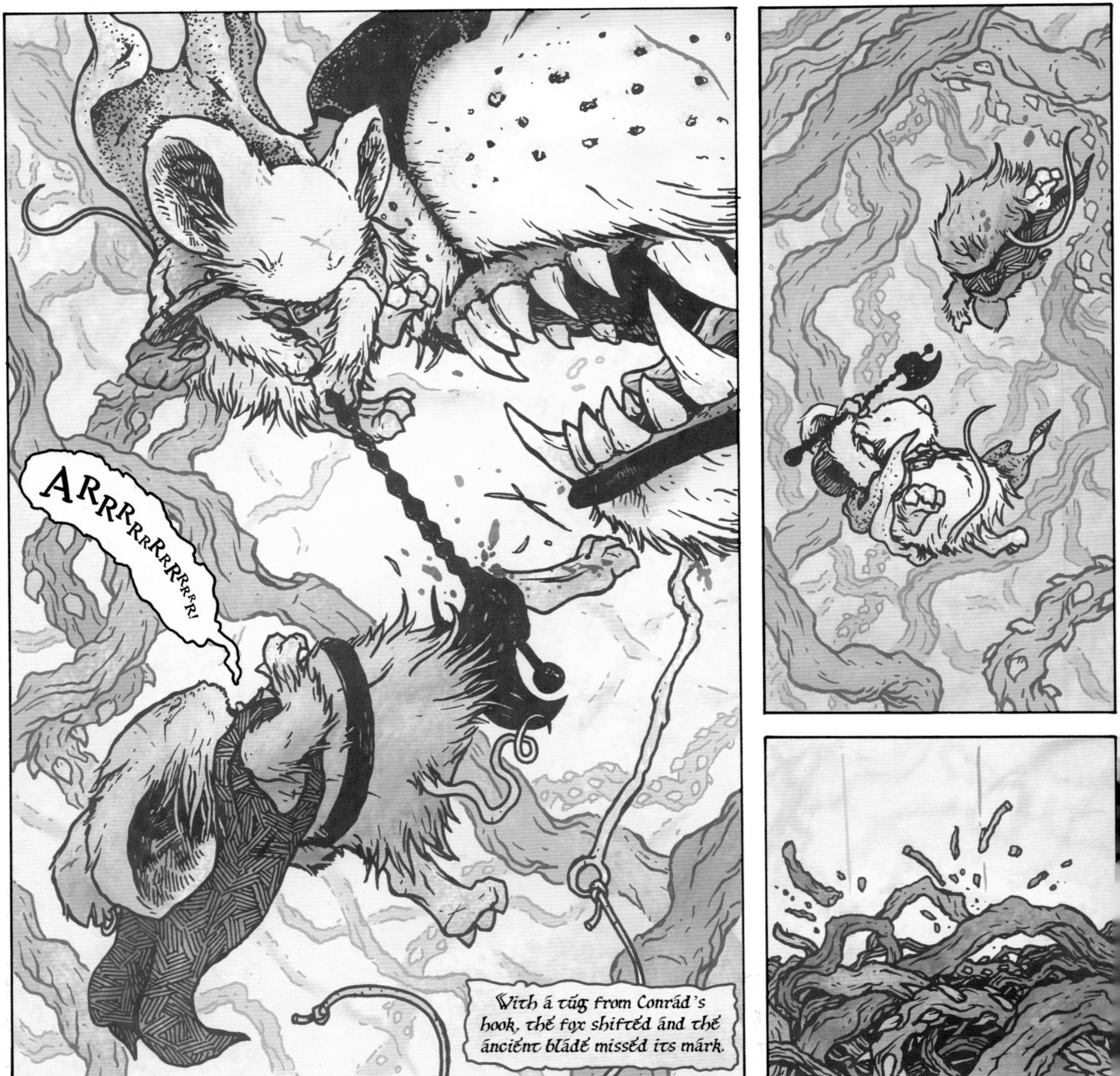

ARRRRRRRRRRRRR!
With a tug from Conrad's hook, the fox shifted and the ancient blade missed its mark.

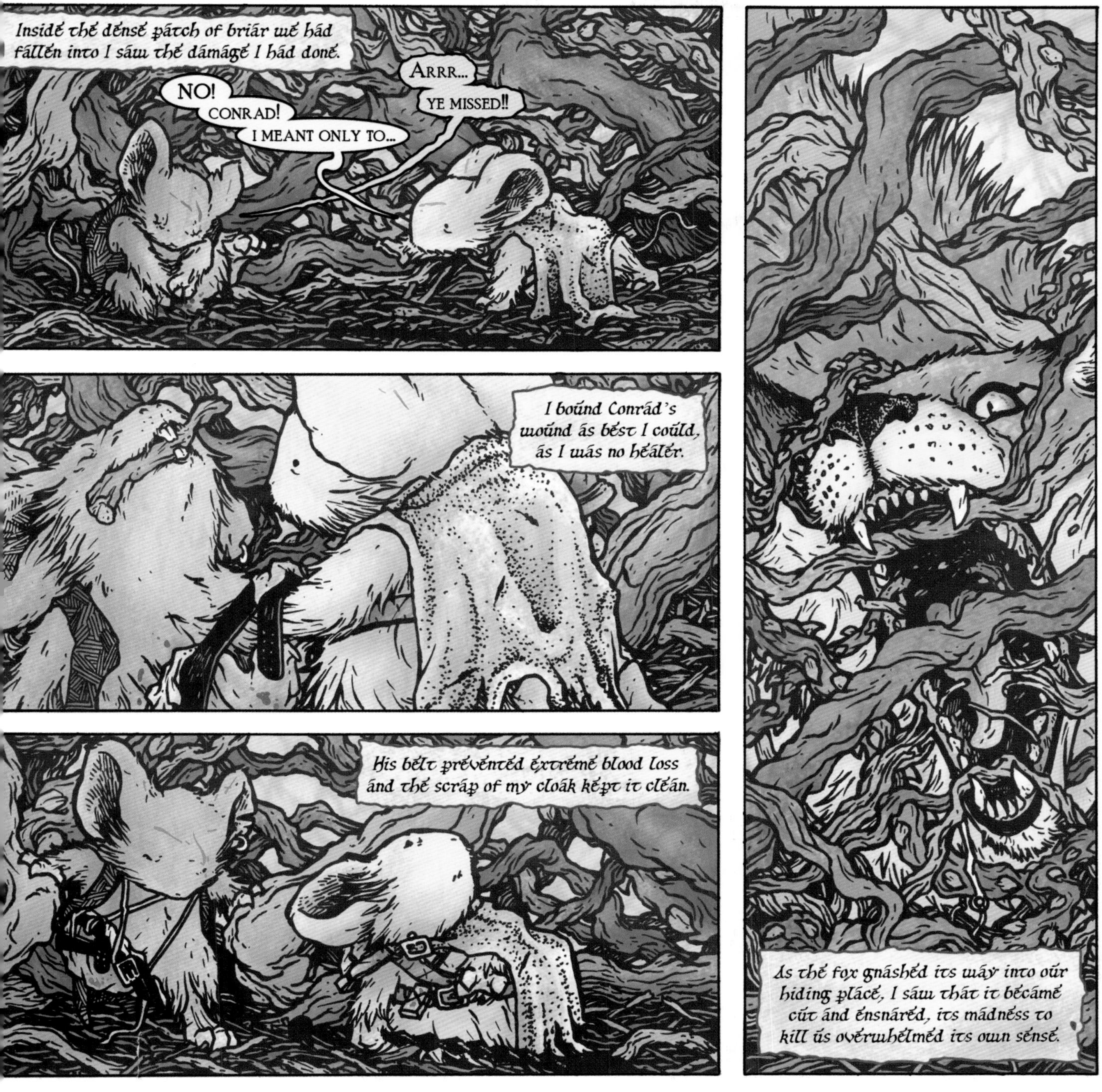

Inside the dense patch of briar we had fallen into I saw the damage I had done.
NO! CONRAD! I MEANT ONLY TO...
ARRR... YE MISSED!!
I bound Conrad's wound as best I could, as I was no healer.
His belt prevented extreme blood loss and the scrap of my cloak kept it clean.
As the fox gnashed its way into our hiding place, I saw that it became cut and ensnared, its madness to kill us overwhelmed its own sense.

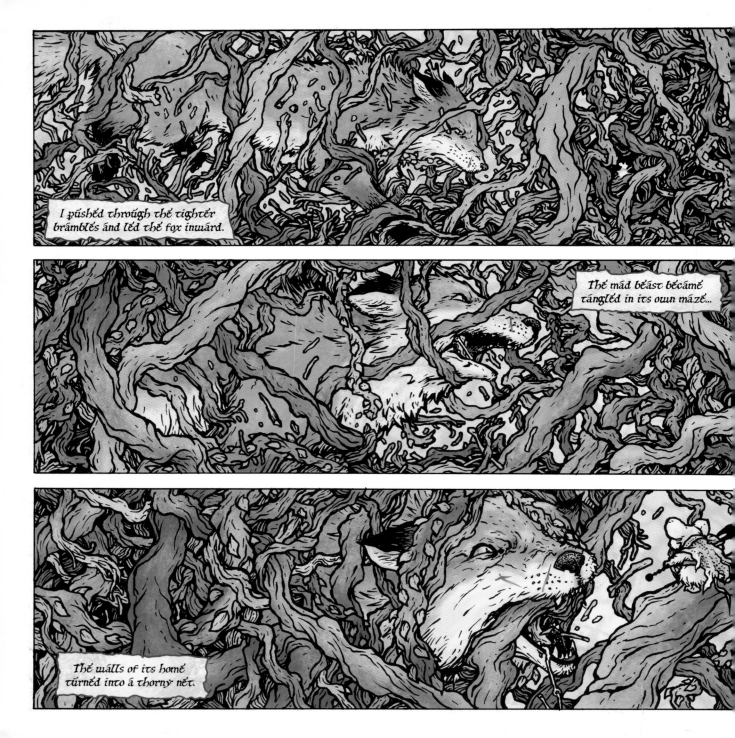

I pushed through the tighter brambles and led the fox inward.

The mad beast became tangled in its own maze...

The walls of its home turned into a thorny net.

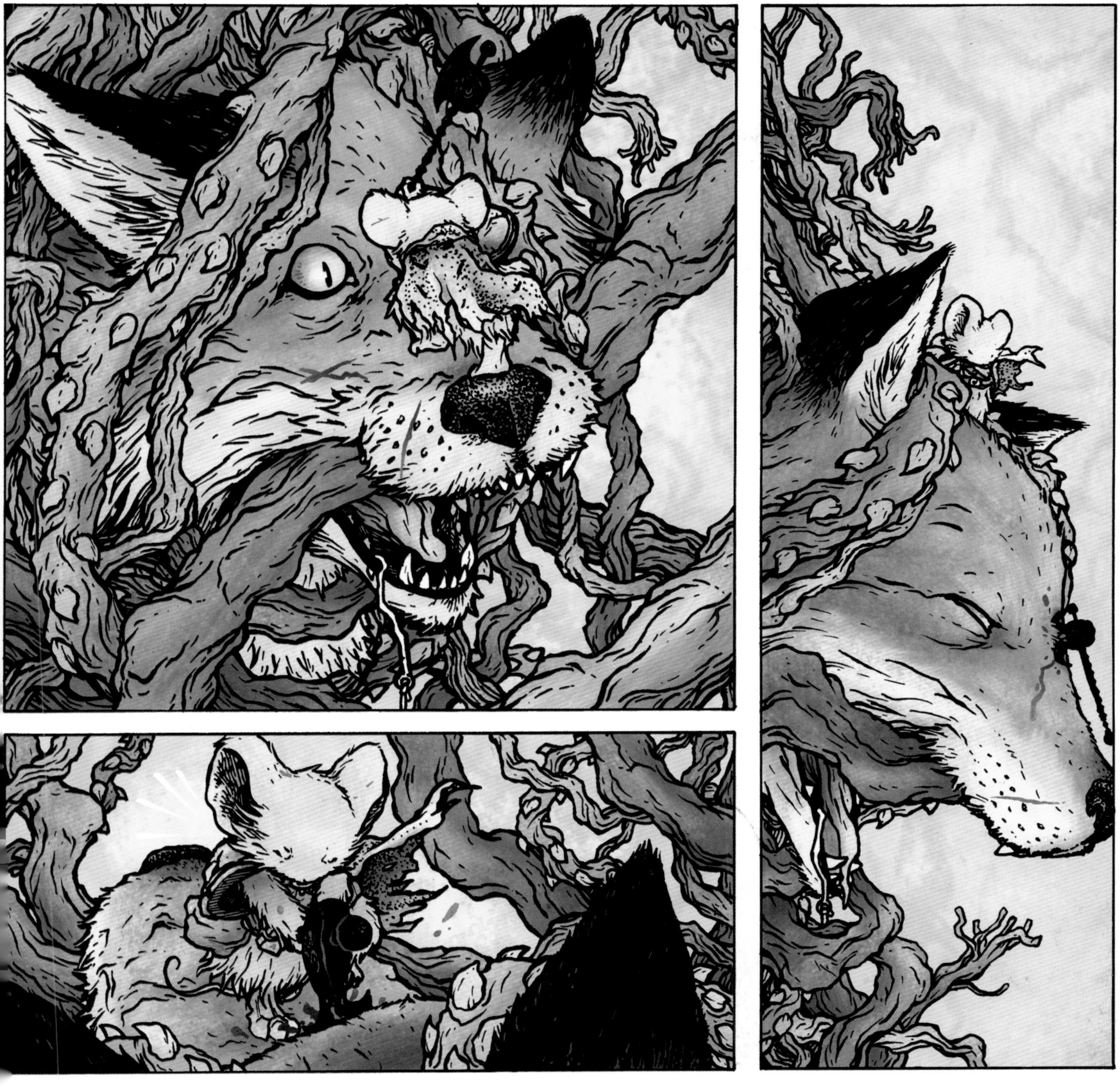

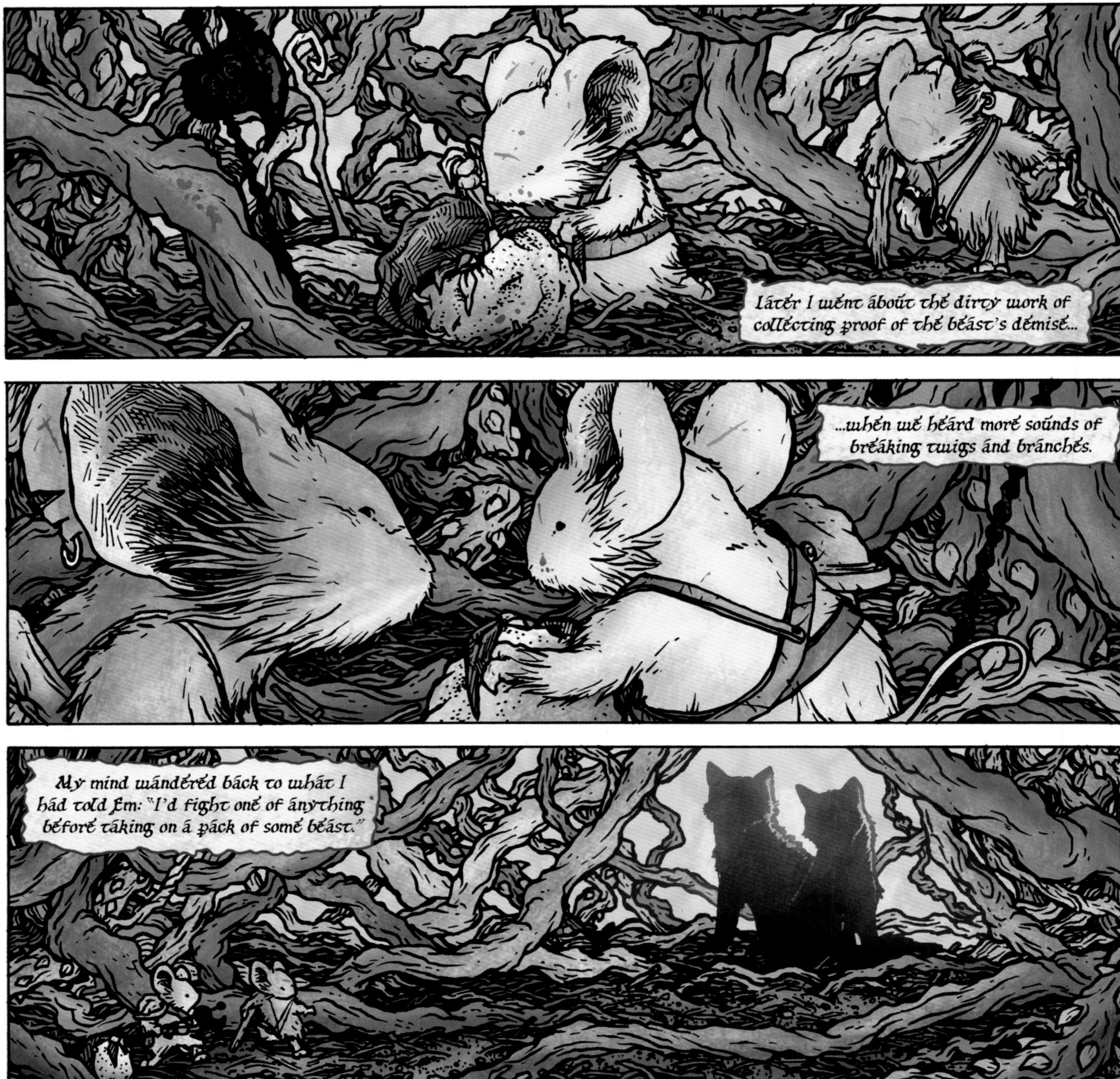
Later I went about the dirty work of collecting proof of the beast's demise...
...when we heard more sounds of breaking twigs and branches.
My mind wandered back to what I had told Em: "I'd fight one of anything before taking on a pack of some beast."

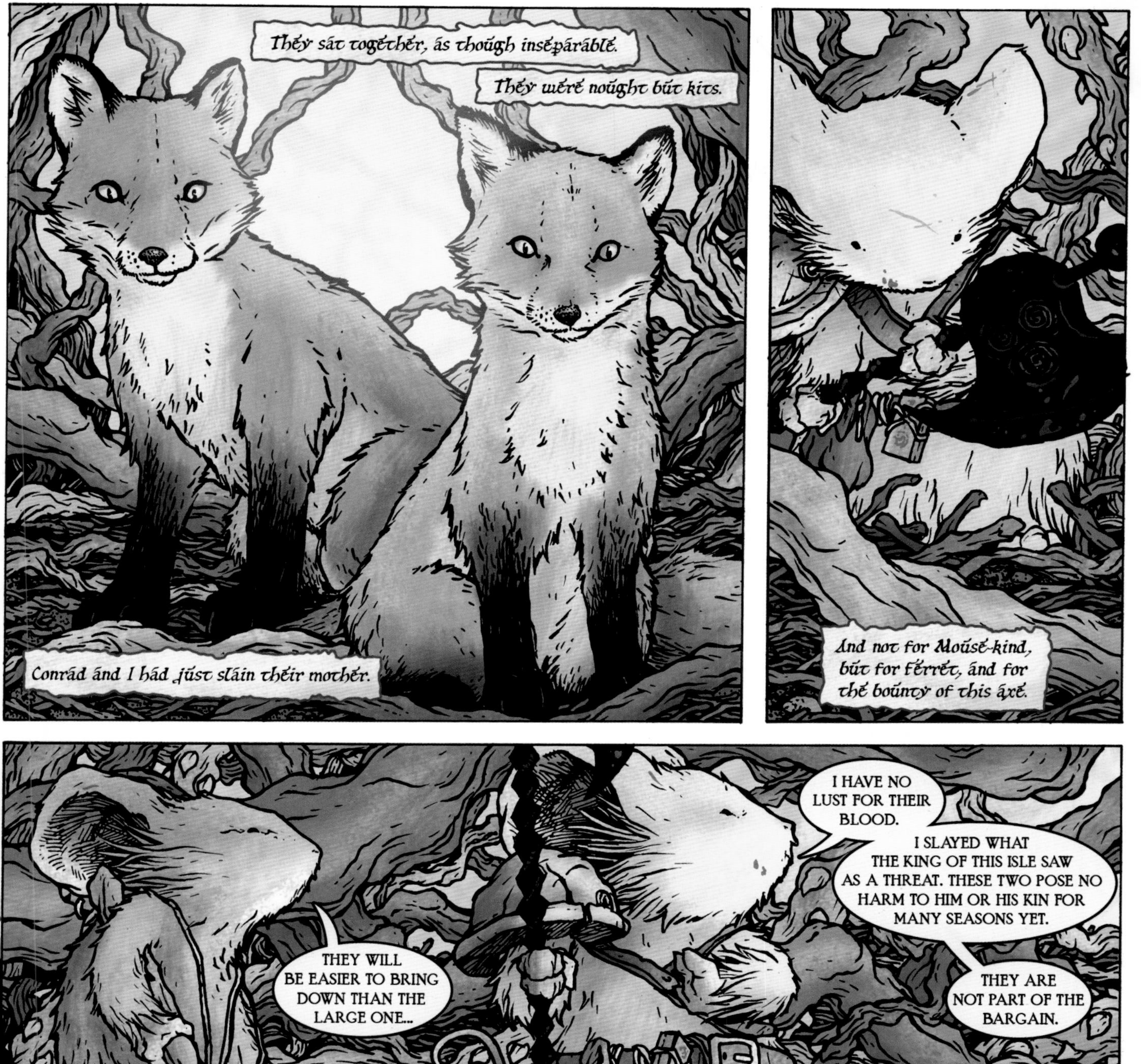

They sat together, as though inseparable.
They were nought but kits.
Conrad and I had just slain their mother.
And not for Mouse-kind, but for ferret, and for the bounty of this axe.
THEY WILL BE EASIER TO BRING DOWN THAN THE LARGE ONE...
I HAVE NO LUST FOR THEIR BLOOD.
I SLAYED WHAT THE KING OF THIS ISLE SAW AS A THREAT. THESE TWO POSE NO HARM TO HIM OR HIS KIN FOR MANY SEASONS YET.
THEY ARE NOT PART OF THE BARGAIN.

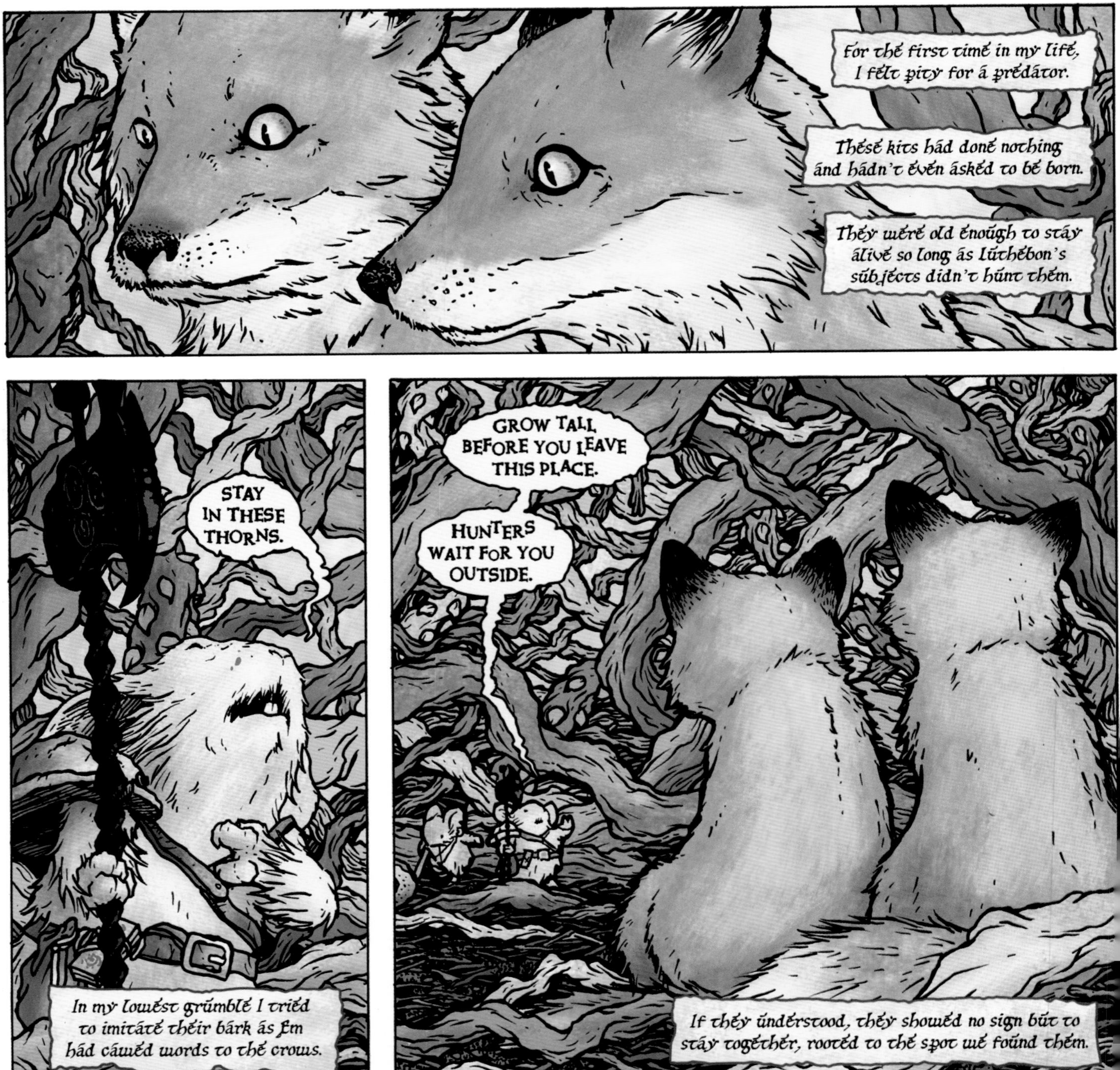

For the first time in my life, I felt pity for a predator.
These kits had done nothing and hadn't even asked to be born.
They were old enough to stay alive so long as Luthebon's subjects didn't hunt them.
STAY IN THESE THORNS.
In my lowest grumble I tried to imitate their bark as Em had cawed words to the crows.
GROW TALL BEFORE YOU LEAVE THIS PLACE.
HUNTERS WAIT FOR YOU OUTSIDE.
If they understood, they showed no sign but to stay together, rooted to the spot we found them.

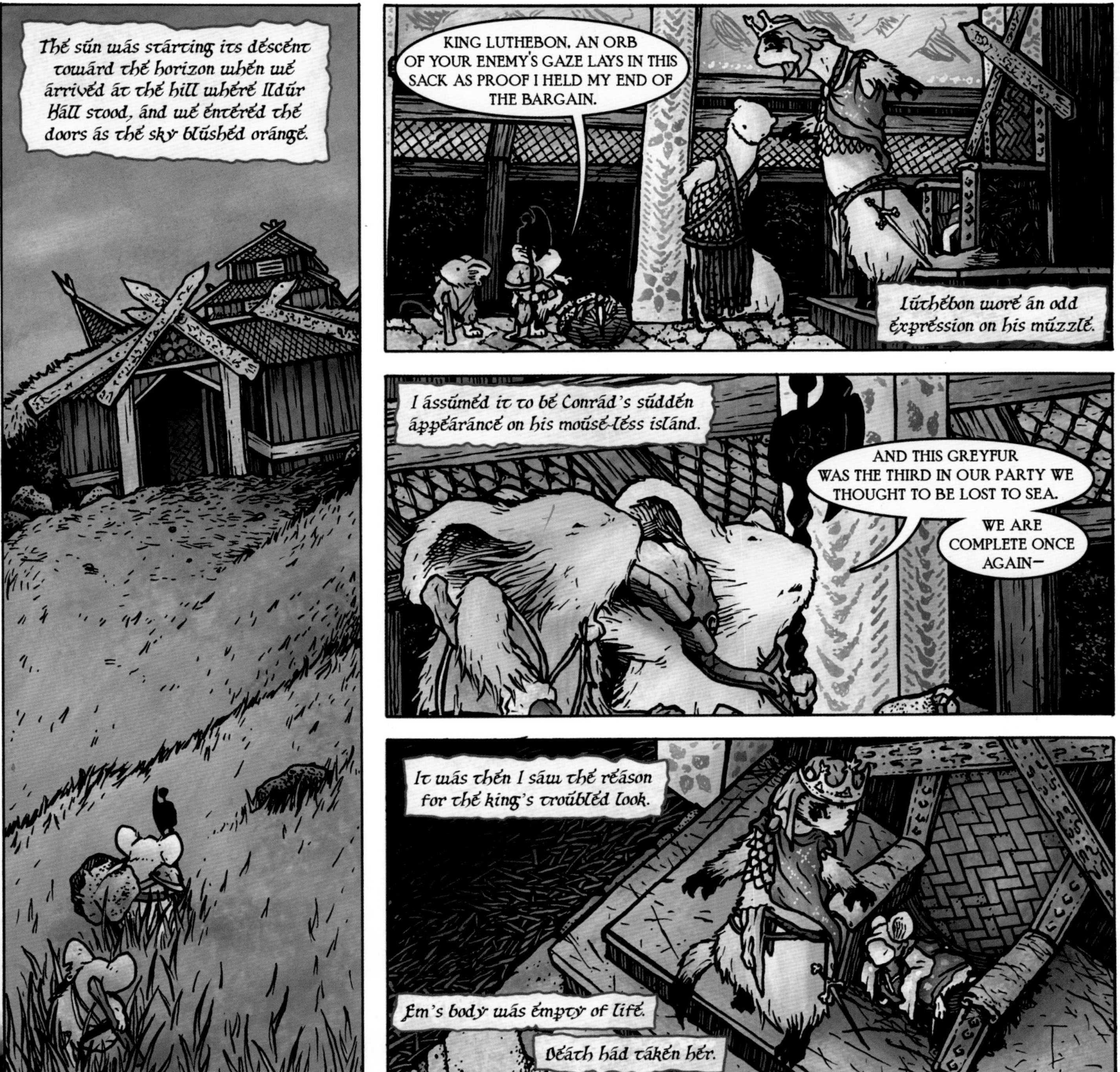
The sun was starting its descent toward the horizon when we arrived at the hill where Ildur Hall stood, and we entered the doors as the sky blushed orange.
KING LUTHEBON, AN ORB OF YOUR ENEMY'S GAZE LAYS IN THIS SACK AS PROOF I HELD MY END OF THE BARGAIN.
Luthebon wore an odd expression on his muzzle.
I assumed it to be Conrad's sudden appearance on his mouse-less island.
AND THIS GREYFUR WAS THE THIRD IN OUR PARTY WE THOUGHT TO BE LOST TO SEA.
WE ARE COMPLETE ONCE AGAIN–
It was then I saw the reason for the king's troubled look.
Em's body was empty of life.
Death had taken her.

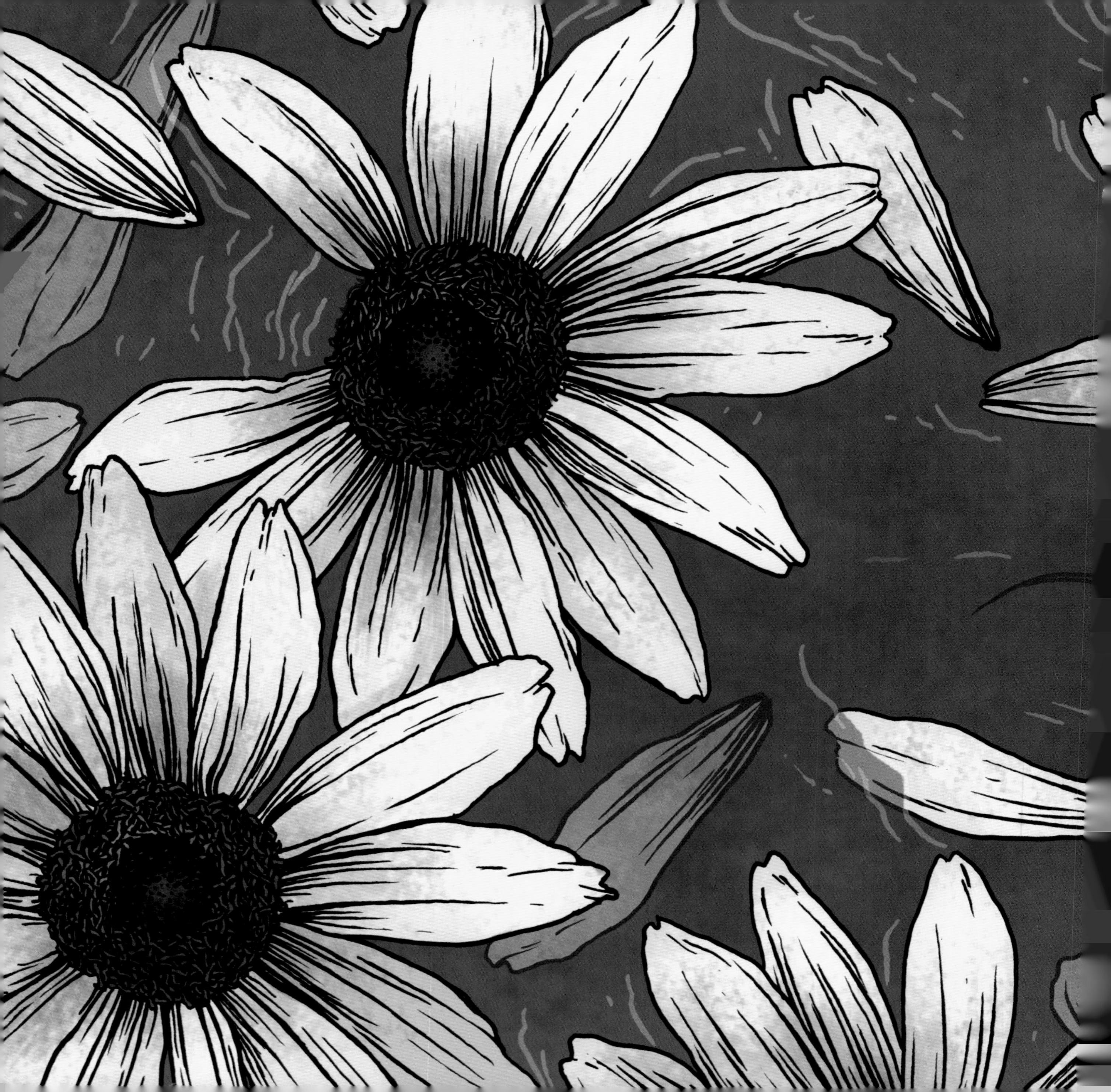

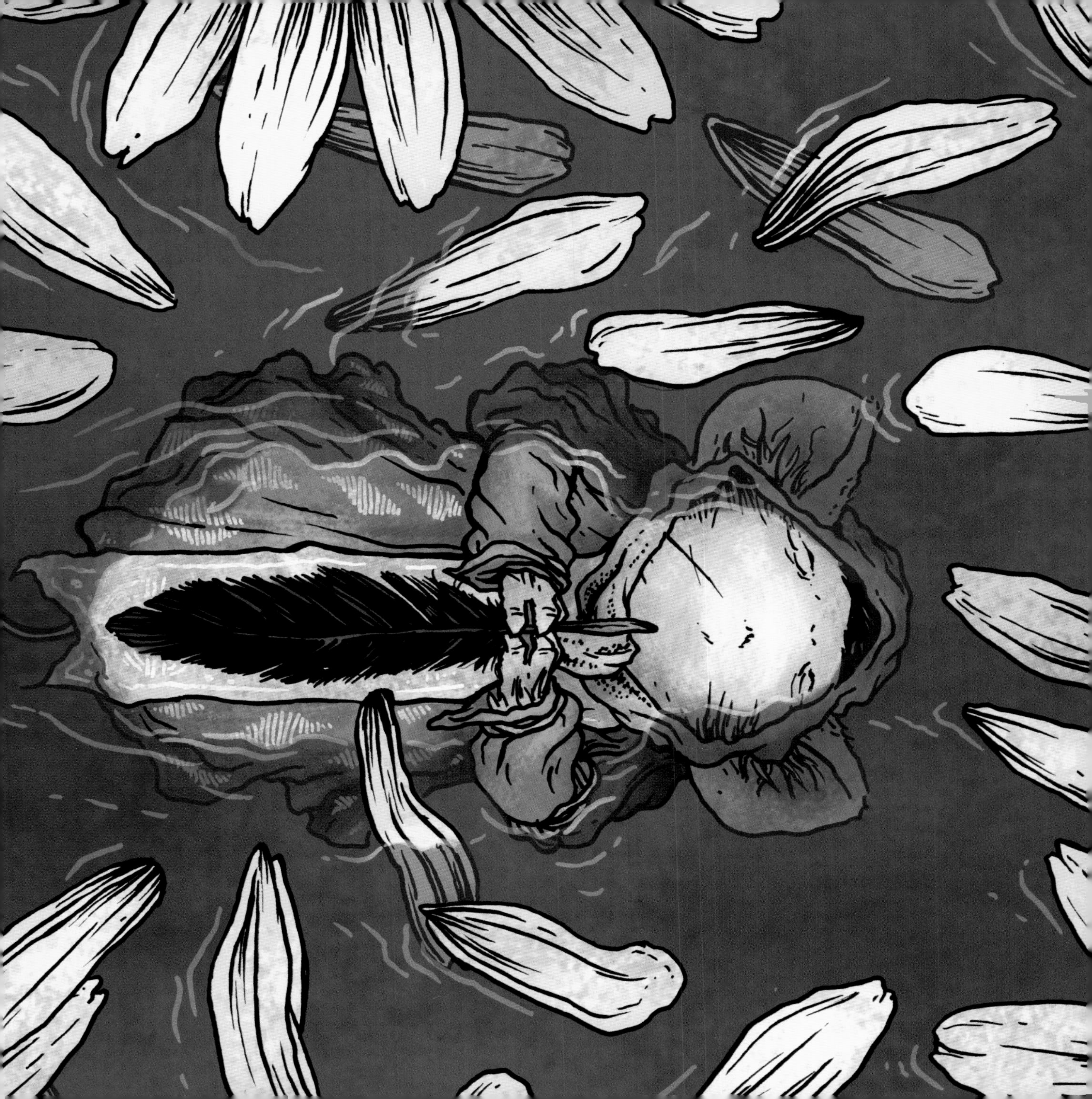

CHAPTER FIVE

After he had lost all loves, and seen the fruits of his work benefit all those around,

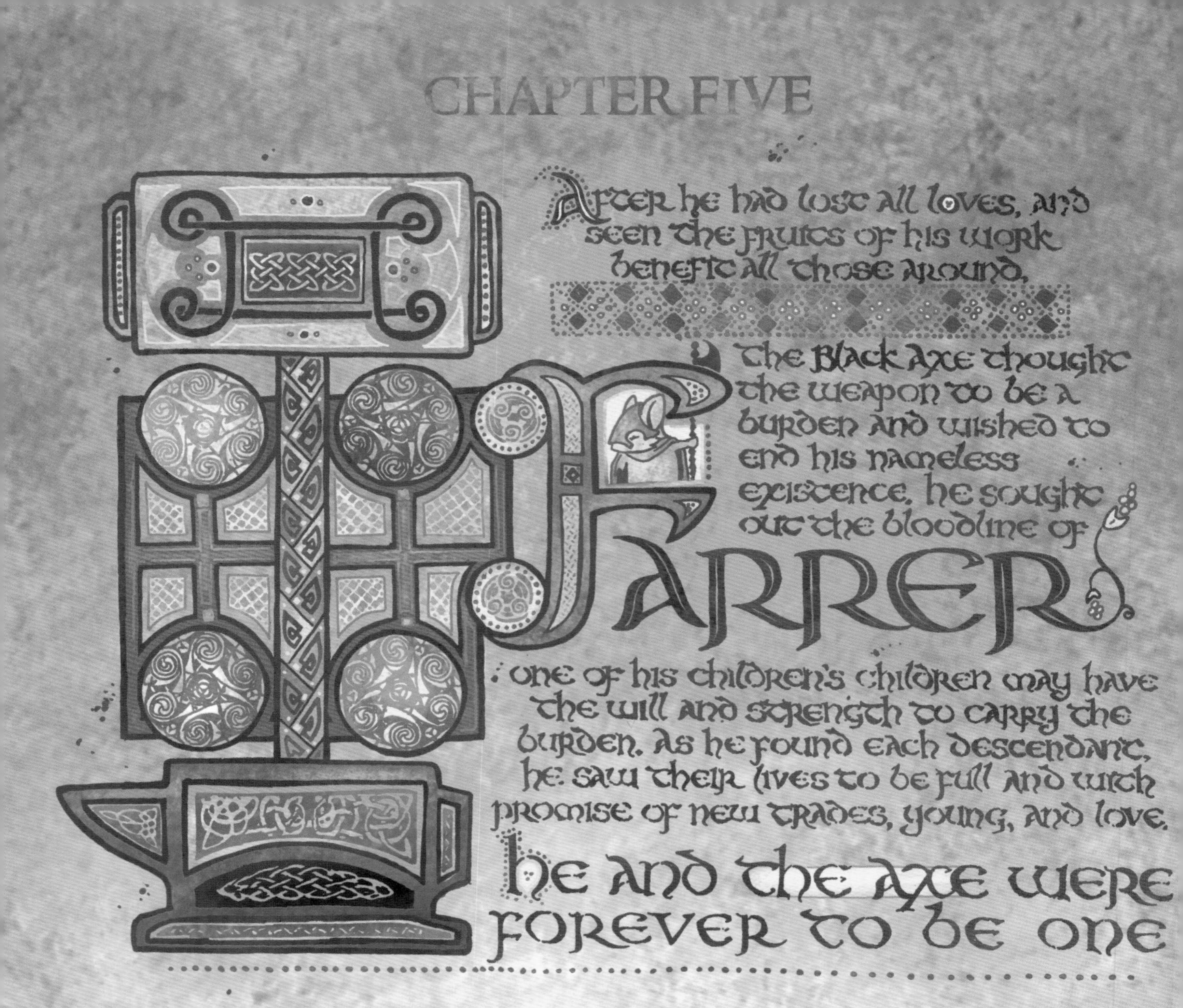

The Black Axe thought the weapon to be a burden and wished to end his nameless existence, he sought out the bloodline of

Farrer.

One of his children's children may have the will and strength to carry the burden. As he found each descendant, he saw their lives to be full and with promise of new trades, young, and love.

He and the axe were forever to be one

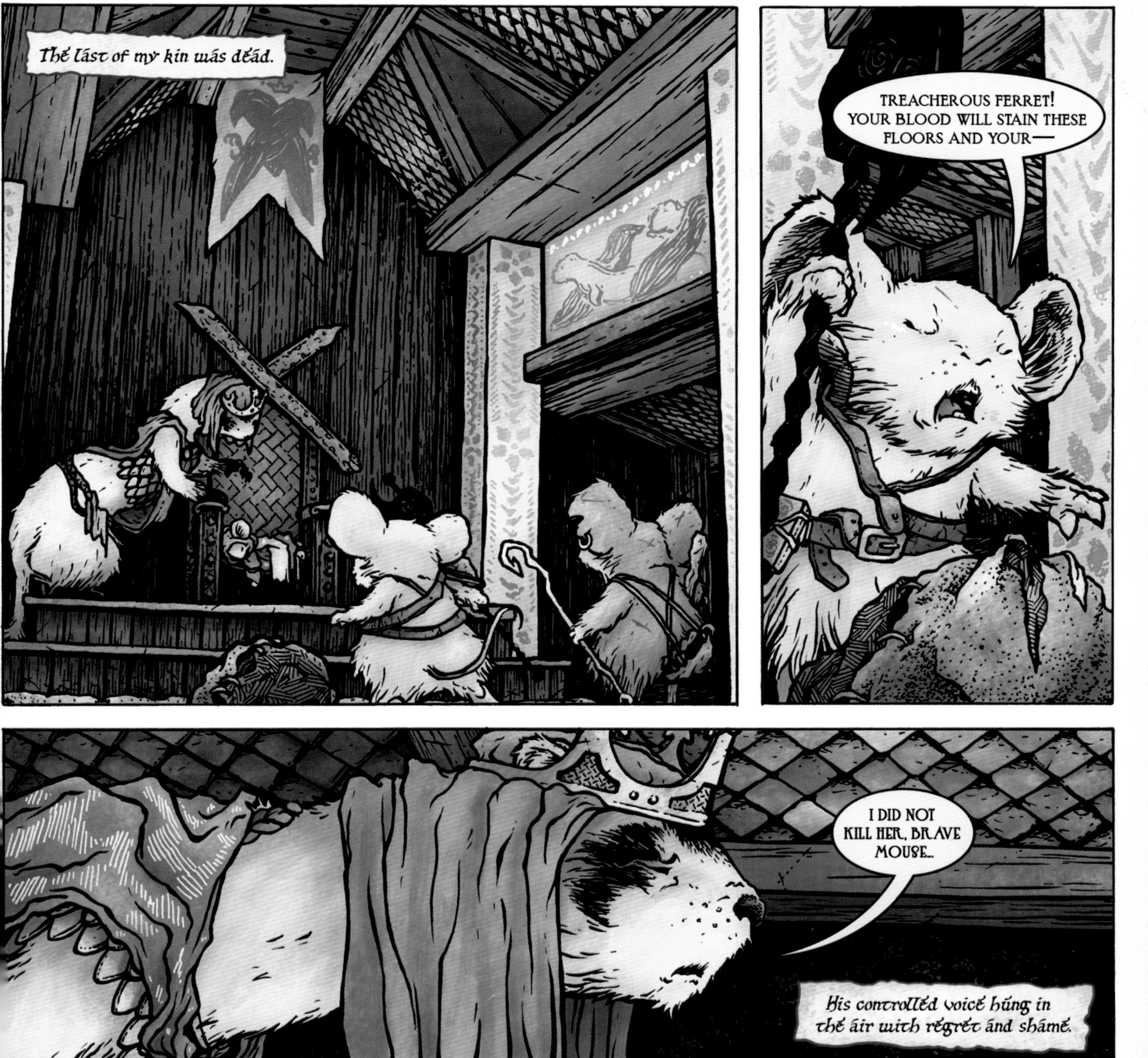

The last of my kin was dead.
TREACHEROUS FERRET! YOUR BLOOD WILL STAIN THESE FLOORS AND YOUR—
I DID NOT KILL HER, BRAVE MOUSE...
His controlled voice hung in the air with regret and shame.

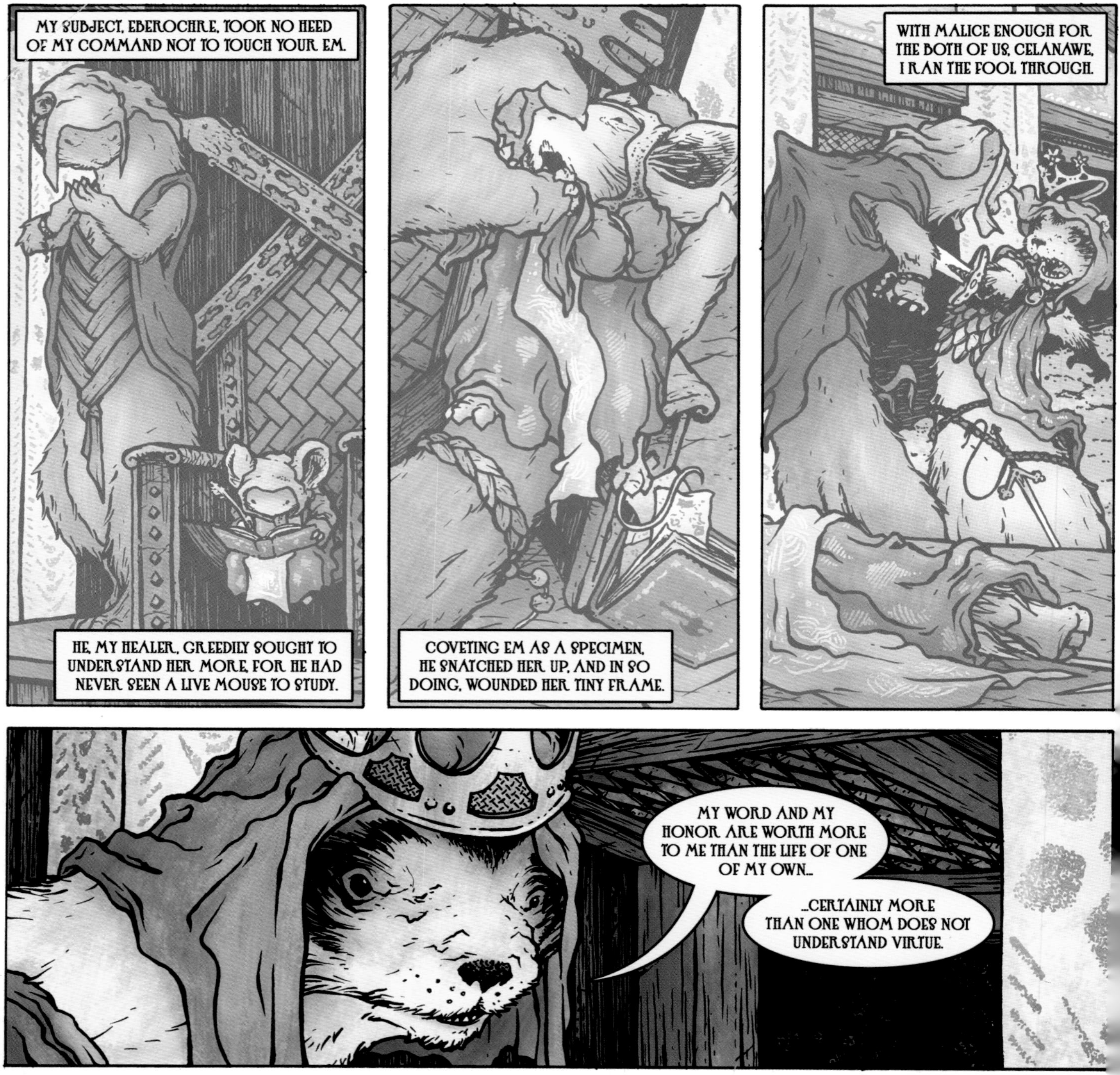
MY SUBJECT, EBEROCHRE, TOOK NO HEED OF MY COMMAND NOT TO TOUCH YOUR EM.
HE, MY HEALER, GREEDILY SOUGHT TO UNDERSTAND HER MORE, FOR HE HAD NEVER SEEN A LIVE MOUSE TO STUDY.
COVETING EM AS A SPECIMEN, HE SNATCHED HER UP, AND IN SO DOING, WOUNDED HER TINY FRAME.
WITH MALICE ENOUGH FOR THE BOTH OF US, CELANAWE, I RAN THE FOOL THROUGH.
MY WORD AND MY HONOR ARE WORTH MORE TO ME THAN THE LIFE OF ONE OF MY OWN...
...CERTAINLY MORE THAN ONE WHOM DOES NOT UNDERSTAND VIRTUE.

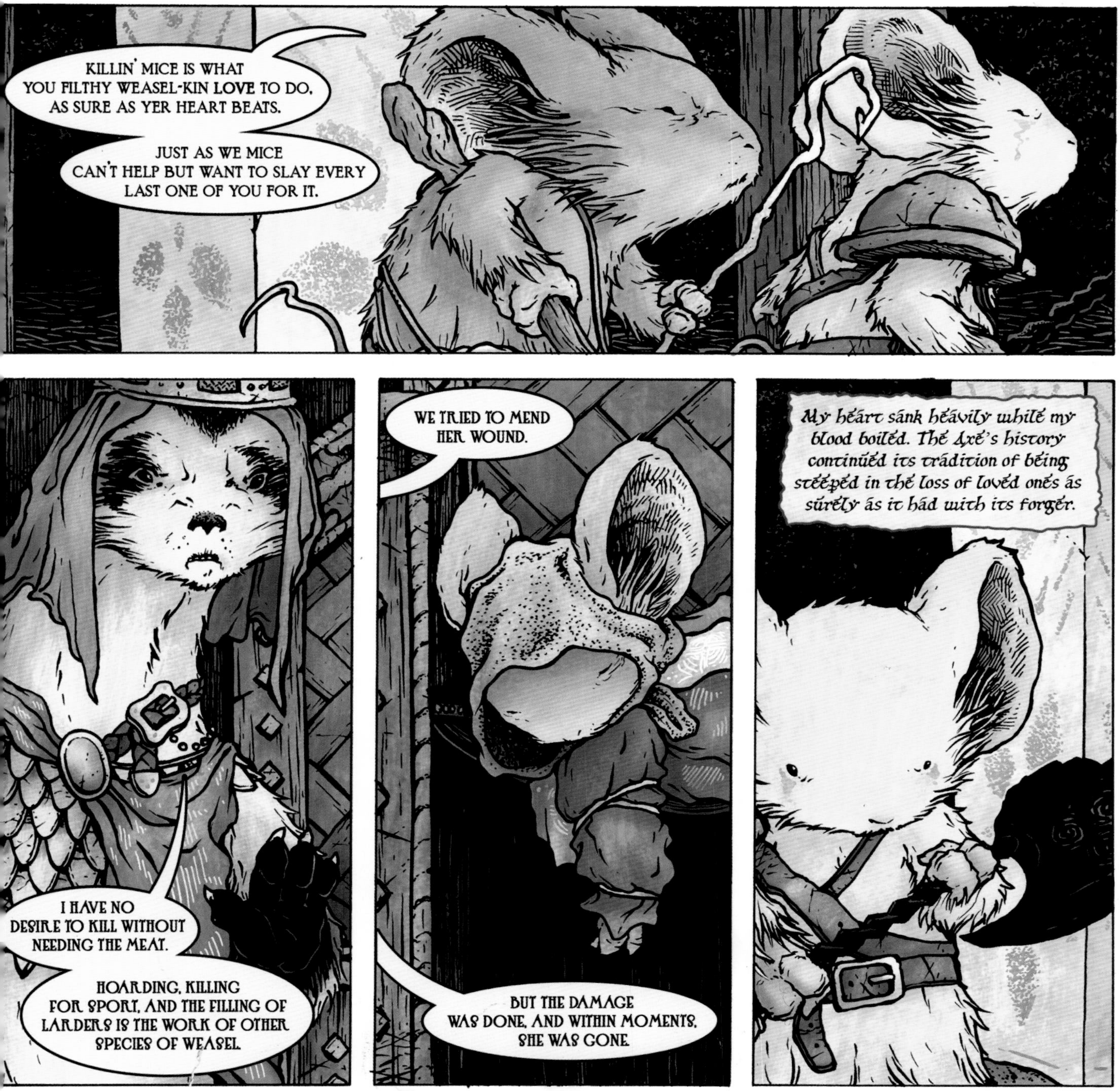
KILLIN' MICE IS WHAT YOU FILTHY WEASEL-KIN LOVE TO DO, AS SURE AS YER HEART BEATS.
JUST AS WE MICE CAN'T HELP BUT WANT TO SLAY EVERY LAST ONE OF YOU FOR IT.
I HAVE NO DESIRE TO KILL WITHOUT NEEDING THE MEAT.
HOARDING, KILLING FOR SPORT, AND THE FILLING OF LARDERS IS THE WORK OF OTHER SPECIES OF WEASEL.
WE TRIED TO MEND HER WOUND.
BUT THE DAMAGE WAS DONE, AND WITHIN MOMENTS, SHE WAS GONE.
My heart sank heavily while my blood boiled. The Axe's history continued its tradition of being steeped in the loss of loved ones as surely as it had with its forger.

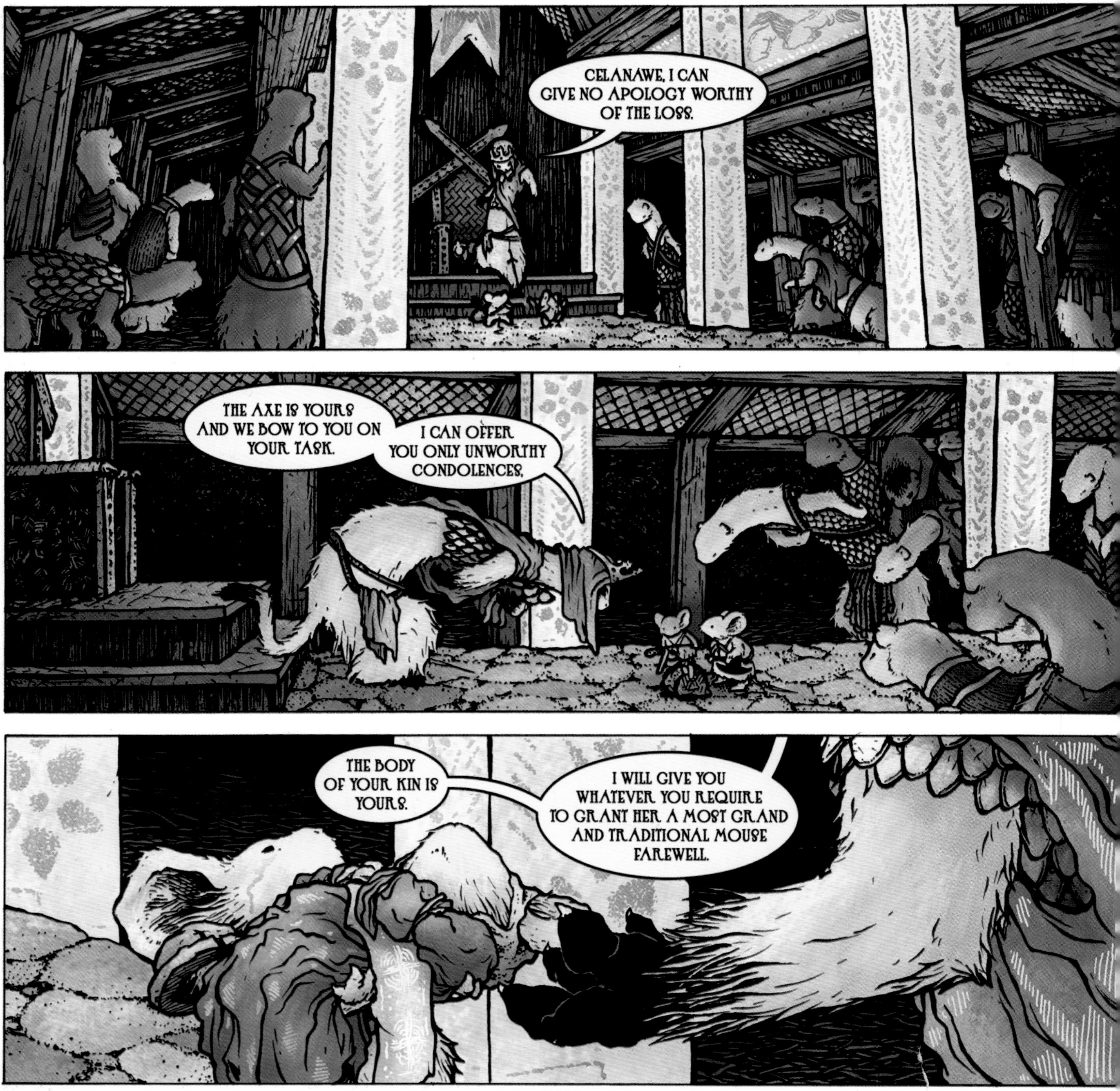
CELANAWE, I CAN GIVE NO APOLOGY WORTHY OF THE LOSS.
THE AXE IS YOURS AND WE BOW TO YOU ON YOUR TASK.
I CAN OFFER YOU ONLY UNWORTHY CONDOLENCES,
THE BODY OF YOUR KIN IS YOURS.
I WILL GIVE YOU WHATEVER YOU REQUIRE TO GRANT HER A MOST GRAND AND TRADITIONAL MOUSE FAREWELL.

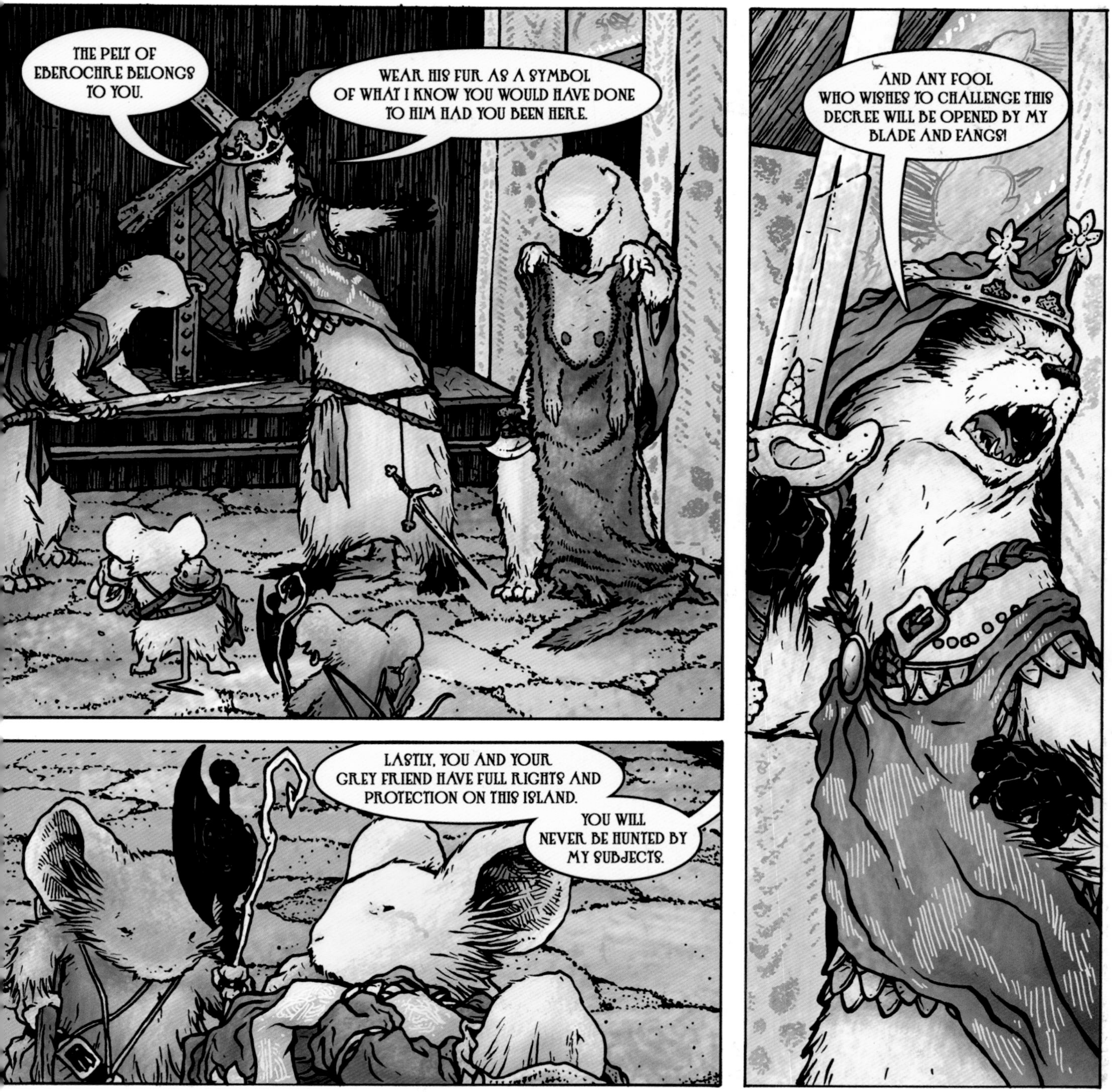
THE PELT OF EBEROCHRE BELONGS TO YOU.
WEAR HIS FUR AS A SYMBOL OF WHAT I KNOW YOU WOULD HAVE DONE TO HIM HAD YOU BEEN HERE.
LASTLY, YOU AND YOUR GREY FRIEND HAVE FULL RIGHTS AND PROTECTION ON THIS ISLAND.
YOU WILL NEVER BE HUNTED BY MY SUBJECTS.
AND ANY FOOL WHO WISHES TO CHALLENGE THIS DECREE WILL BE OPENED BY MY BLADE AND FANGS!

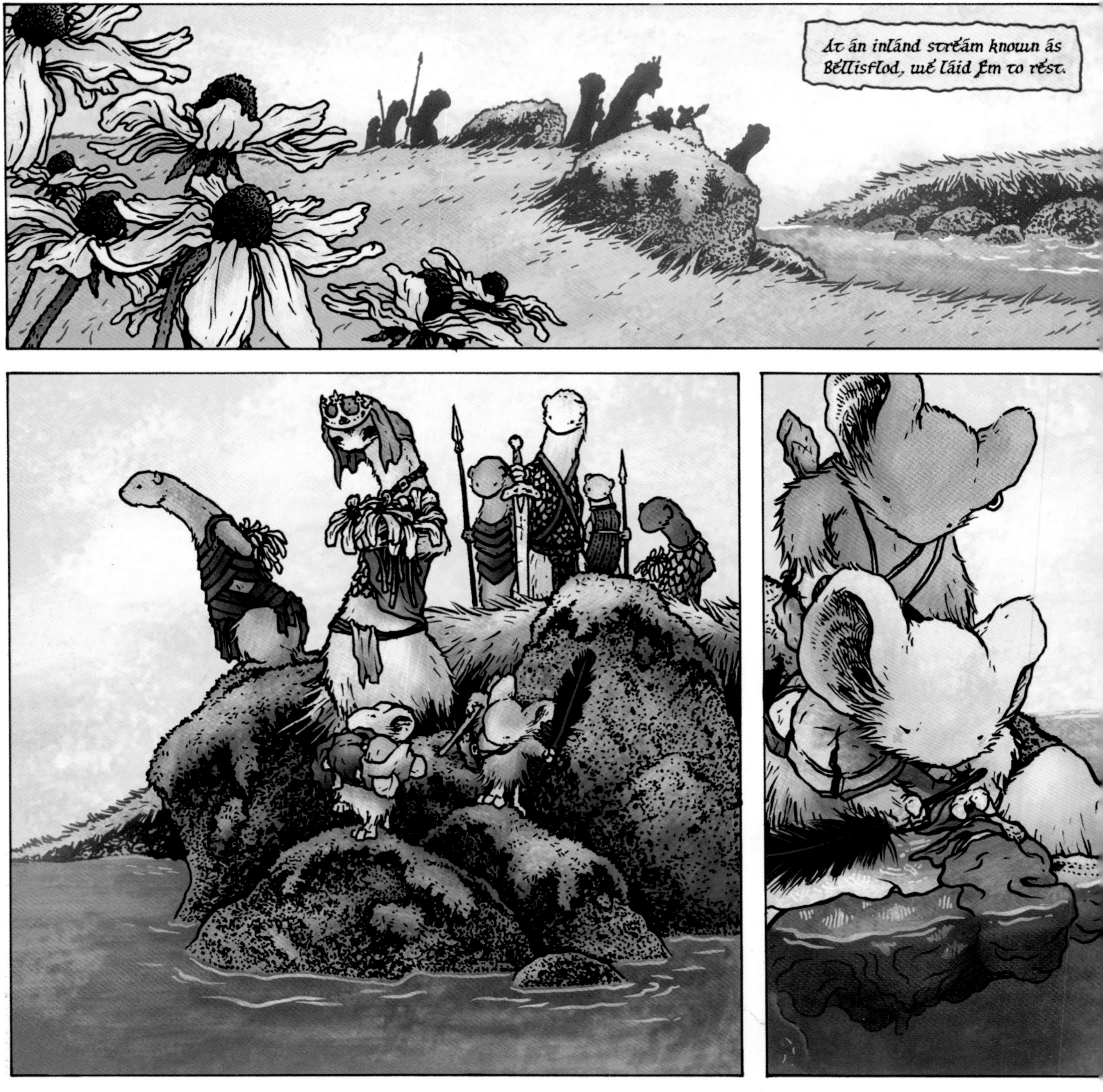
At an inland stream known as Bellisflod, we laid them to rest.

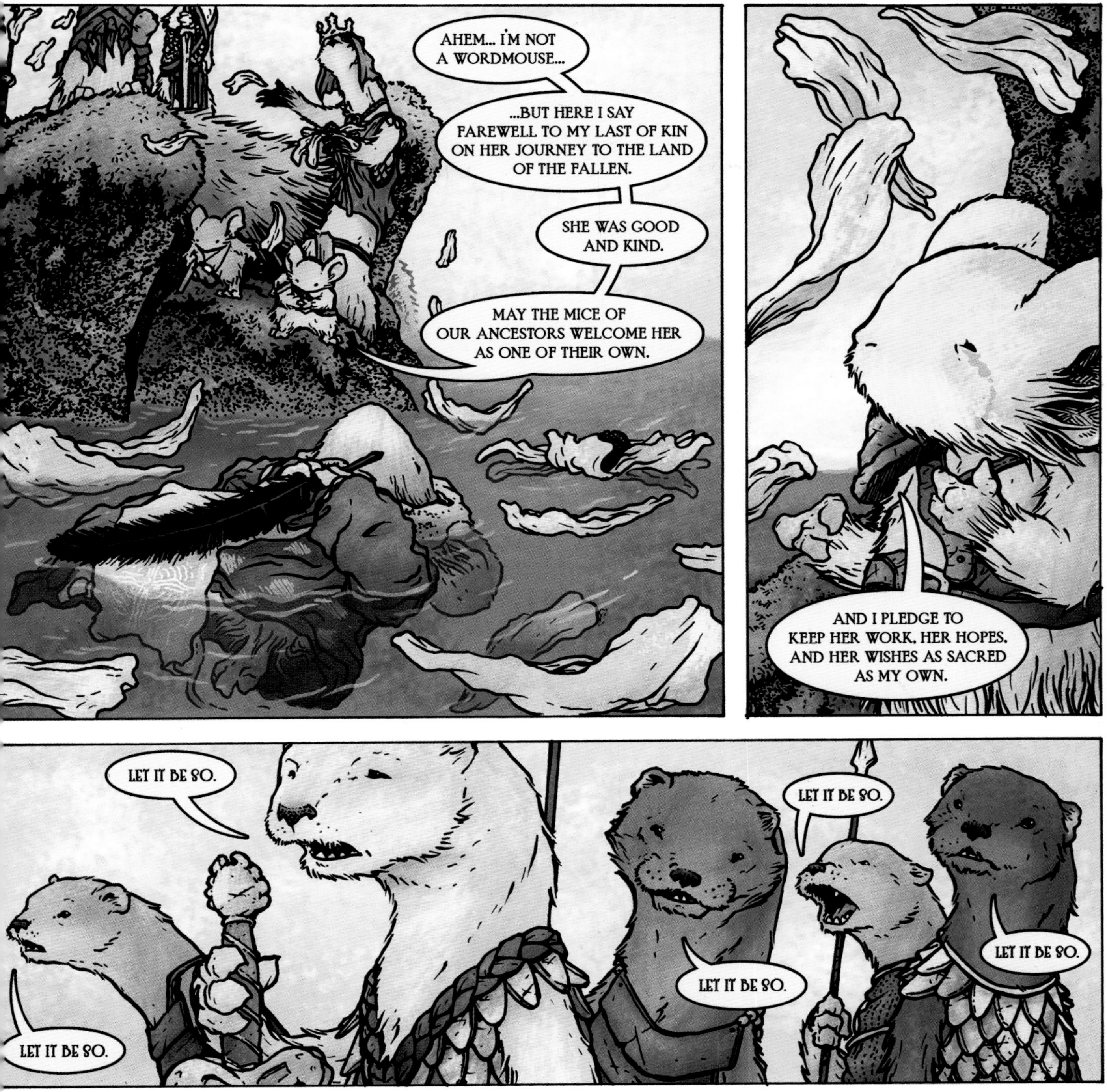
AHEM... I'M NOT A WORDMOUSE...
...BUT HERE I SAY FAREWELL TO MY LAST OF KIN ON HER JOURNEY TO THE LAND OF THE FALLEN.
SHE WAS GOOD AND KIND.
MAY THE MICE OF OUR ANCESTORS WELCOME HER AS ONE OF THEIR OWN.
AND I PLEDGE TO KEEP HER WORK, HER HOPES, AND HER WISHES AS SACRED AS MY OWN.
LET IT BE SO.
LET IT BE SO.
LET IT BE SO.
LET IT BE SO.
LET IT BE SO.

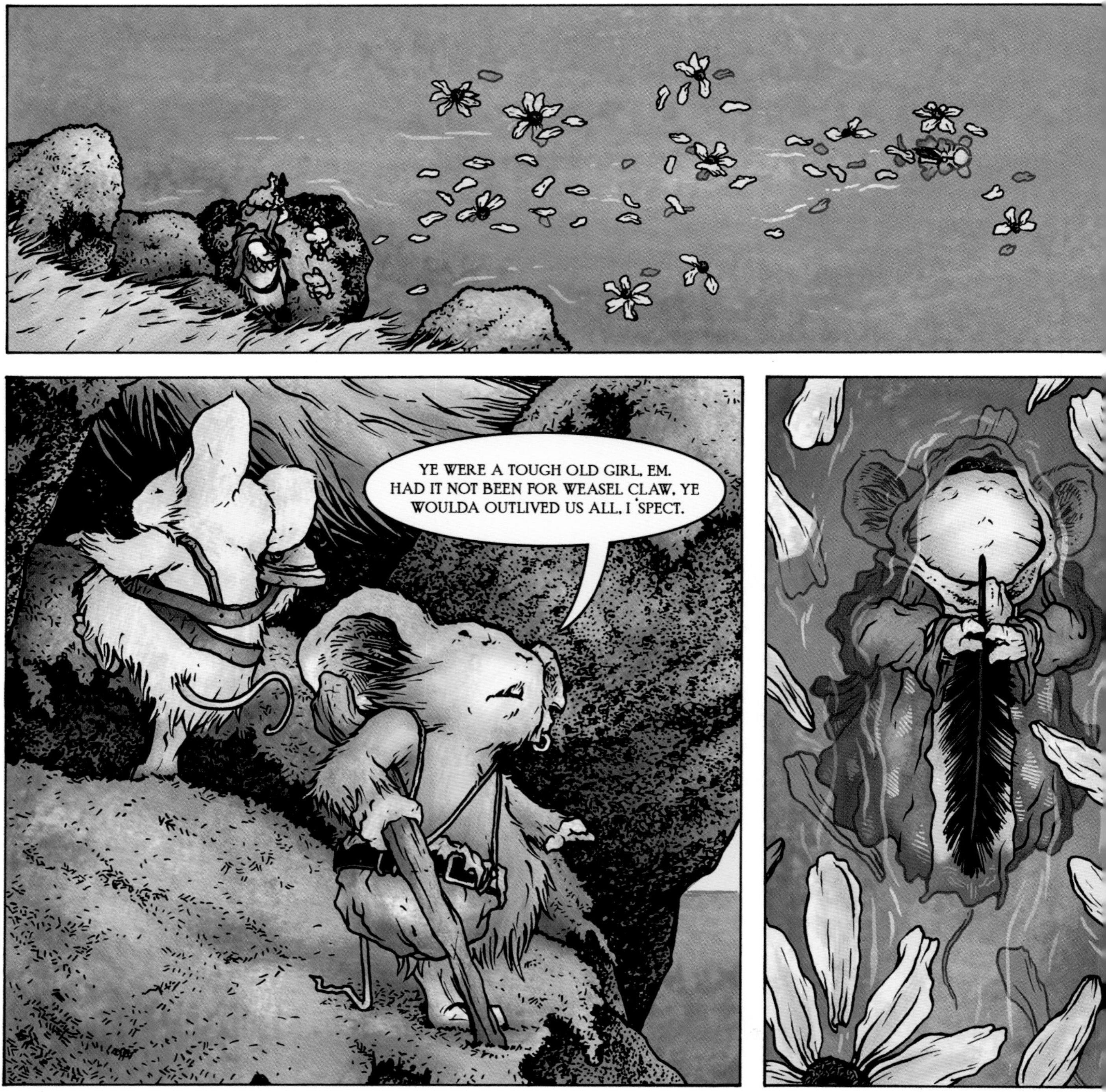
YE WERE A TOUGH OLD GIRL, EM. HAD IT NOT BEEN FOR WEASEL CLAW, YE WOULDA OUTLIVED US ALL, I 'SPECT.

Conrad and I kept clear of the ferrets in the following days.

I sat reading Em's journal on the Axe. I hoped its history, words, and pictures would give me an understanding of how recovering this ebony blade was worth the loss of her life.

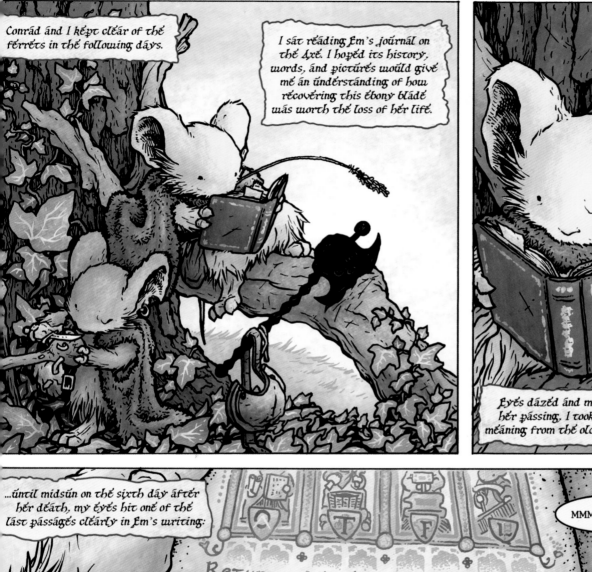

Eyes dazed and mind numb from her passing, I took in very little meaning from the old text and notes...

...until midsun on the sixth day after her death, my eyes hit one of the last passages clearly in Em's writing:

MMM... CONRAD....

RETURN WITH THE AXE TO SHORESTONE, SPEAK TO HAVEN GUILD, KEEPERS OF THE IDEALS OF LOCKE, OMARR, FARRER, AND THURSTON

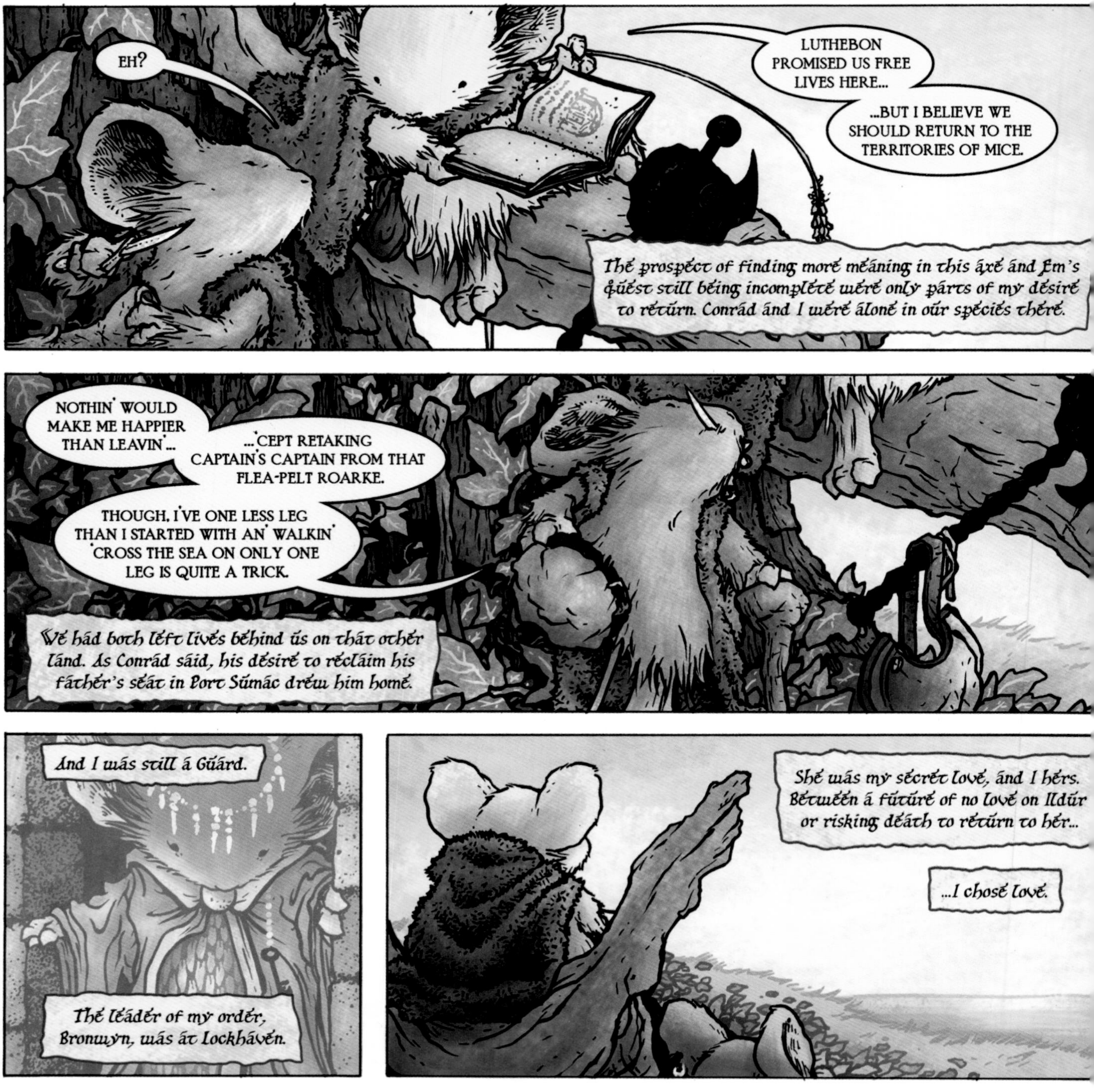
EH?
LUTHEBON PROMISED US FREE LIVES HERE...
...BUT I BELIEVE WE SHOULD RETURN TO THE TERRITORIES OF MICE.
The prospect of finding more meaning in this axe and Em's quest still being incomplete were only parts of my desire to return. Conrad and I were alone in our species there.
NOTHIN' WOULD MAKE ME HAPPIER THAN LEAVIN'...
...'CEPT RETAKING CAPTAIN'S CAPTAIN FROM THAT FLEA-PELT ROARKE.
THOUGH, I'VE ONE LESS LEG THAN I STARTED WITH AN' WALKIN' 'CROSS THE SEA ON ONLY ONE LEG IS QUITE A TRICK.
We had both left lives behind us on that other land. As Conrad said, his desire to reclaim his father's seat in Port Sumac drew him home.
And I was still a Guard.
The leader of my order, Bronwyn, was at Lockhaven.
She was my secret love, and I hers. Between a future of no love on Ildur or risking death to return to her...
...I chose love.

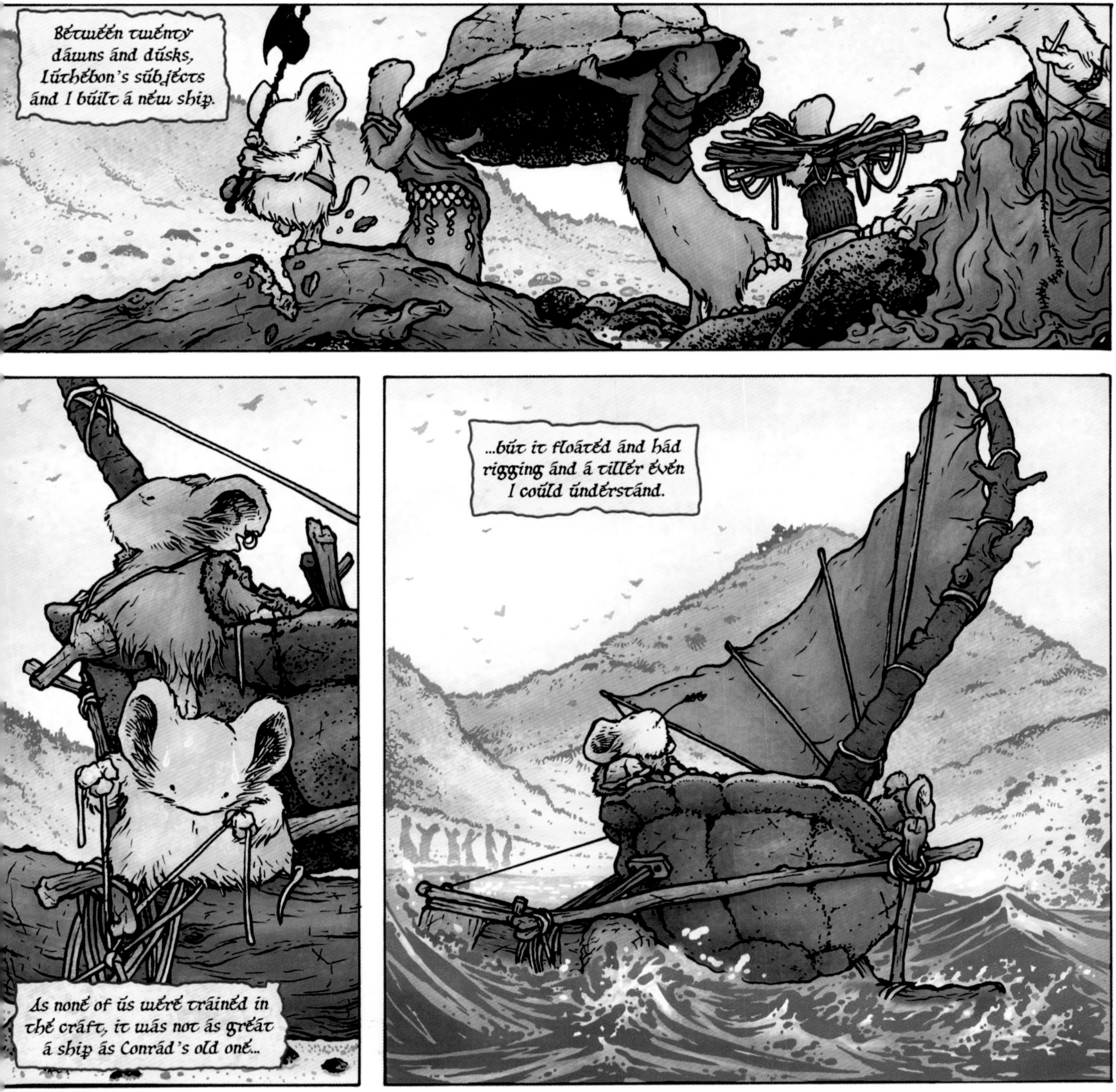
Between twenty dawns and dusks, Luthebon's subjects and I built a new ship.
As none of us were trained in the craft, it was not as great a ship as Conrad's old one...
...but it floated and had rigging and a tiller even I could understand.

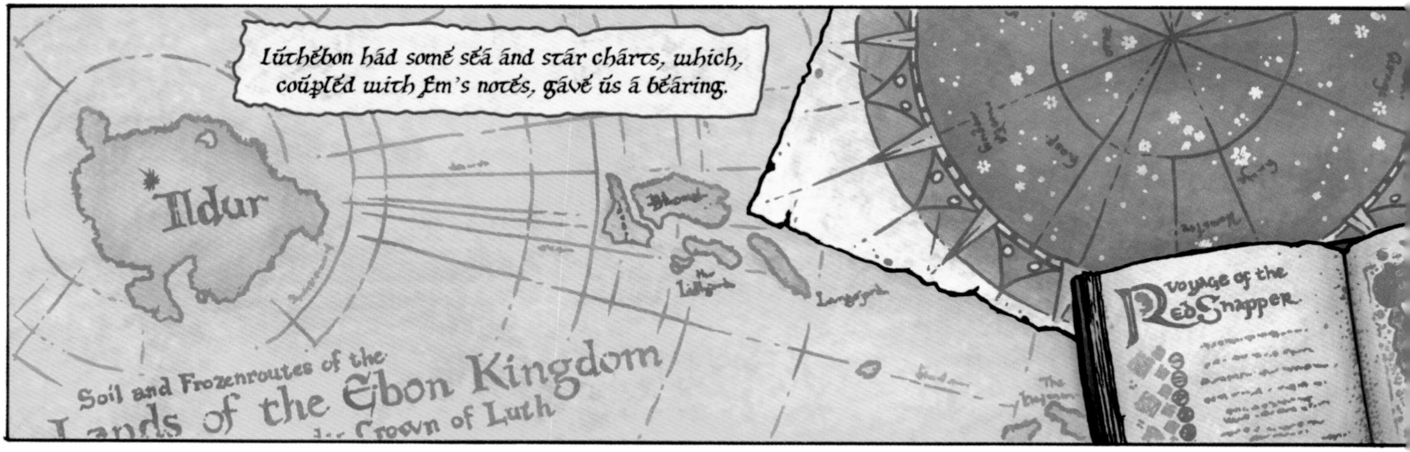
Luthebon had some sea and star charts, which, coupled with Em's notes, gave us a bearing.
Ildur
Soil and Frozenroutes of the
Lands of the Ebon Kingdom
Crown of Luth
Voyage of the RedSnapper

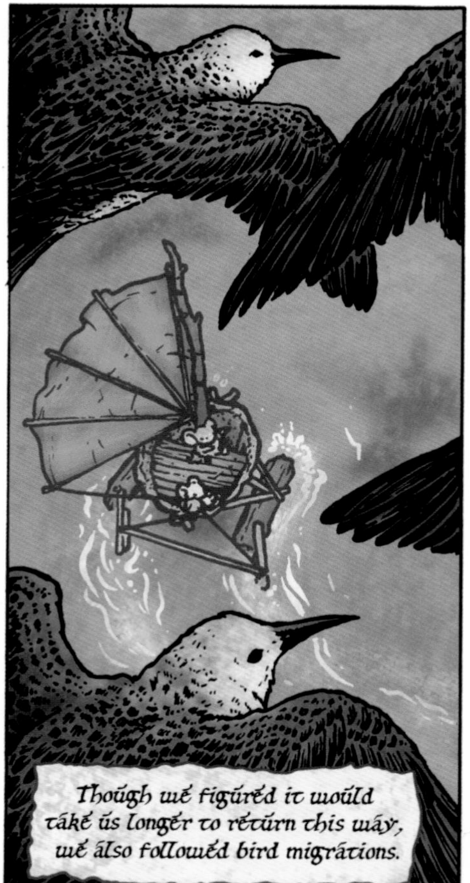
Though we figured it would take us longer to return this way, we also followed bird migrations.

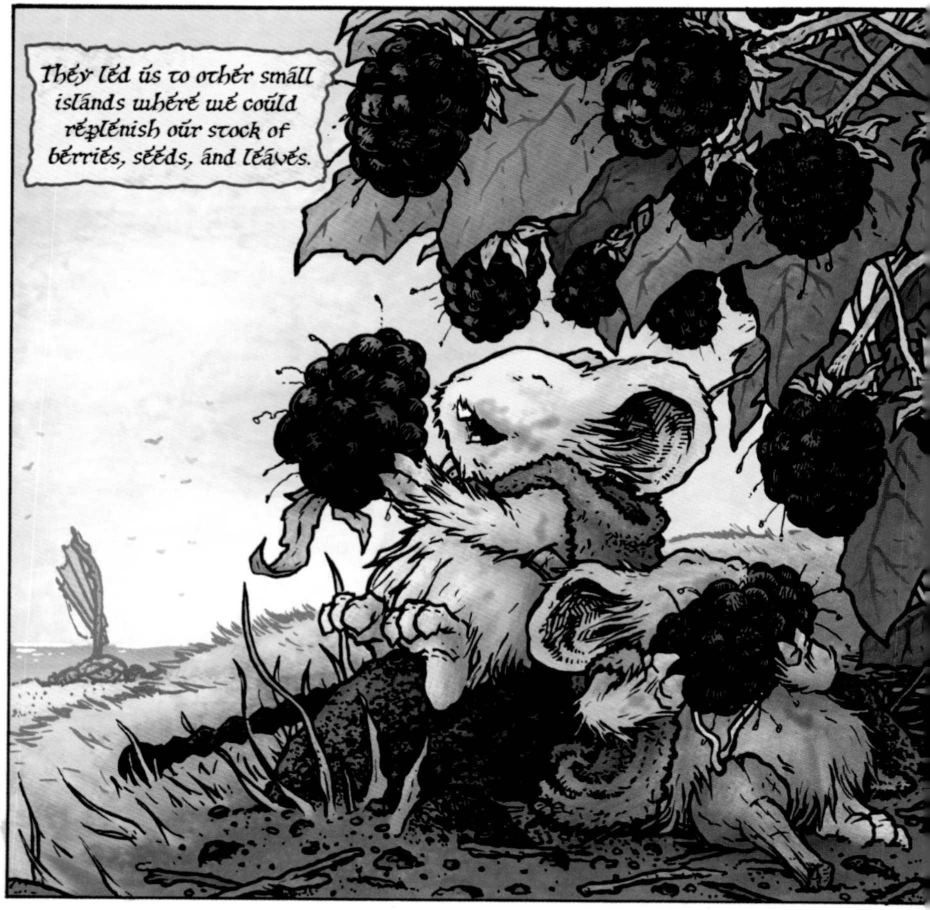
They led us to other small islands where we could replenish our stock of berries, seeds, and leaves.

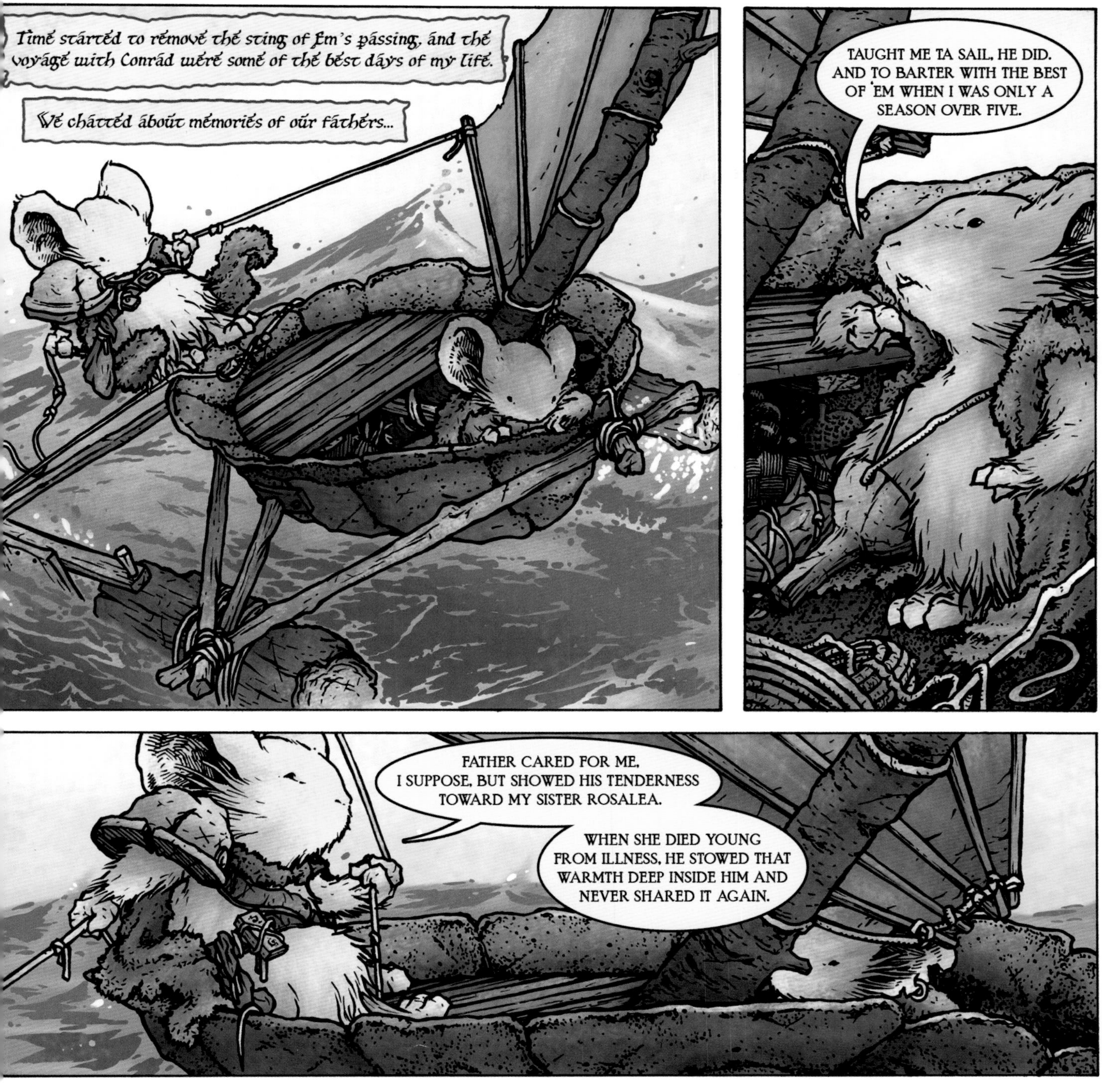
Time started to remove the sting of Em's passing, and the voyage with Conrad were some of the best days of my life.
We chatted about memories of our fathers...
TAUGHT ME TA SAIL, HE DID. AND TO BARTER WITH THE BEST OF 'EM WHEN I WAS ONLY A SEASON OVER FIVE.
FATHER CARED FOR ME, I SUPPOSE, BUT SHOWED HIS TENDERNESS TOWARD MY SISTER ROSALEA.
WHEN SHE DIED YOUNG FROM ILLNESS, HE STOWED THAT WARMTH DEEP INSIDE HIM AND NEVER SHARED IT AGAIN.

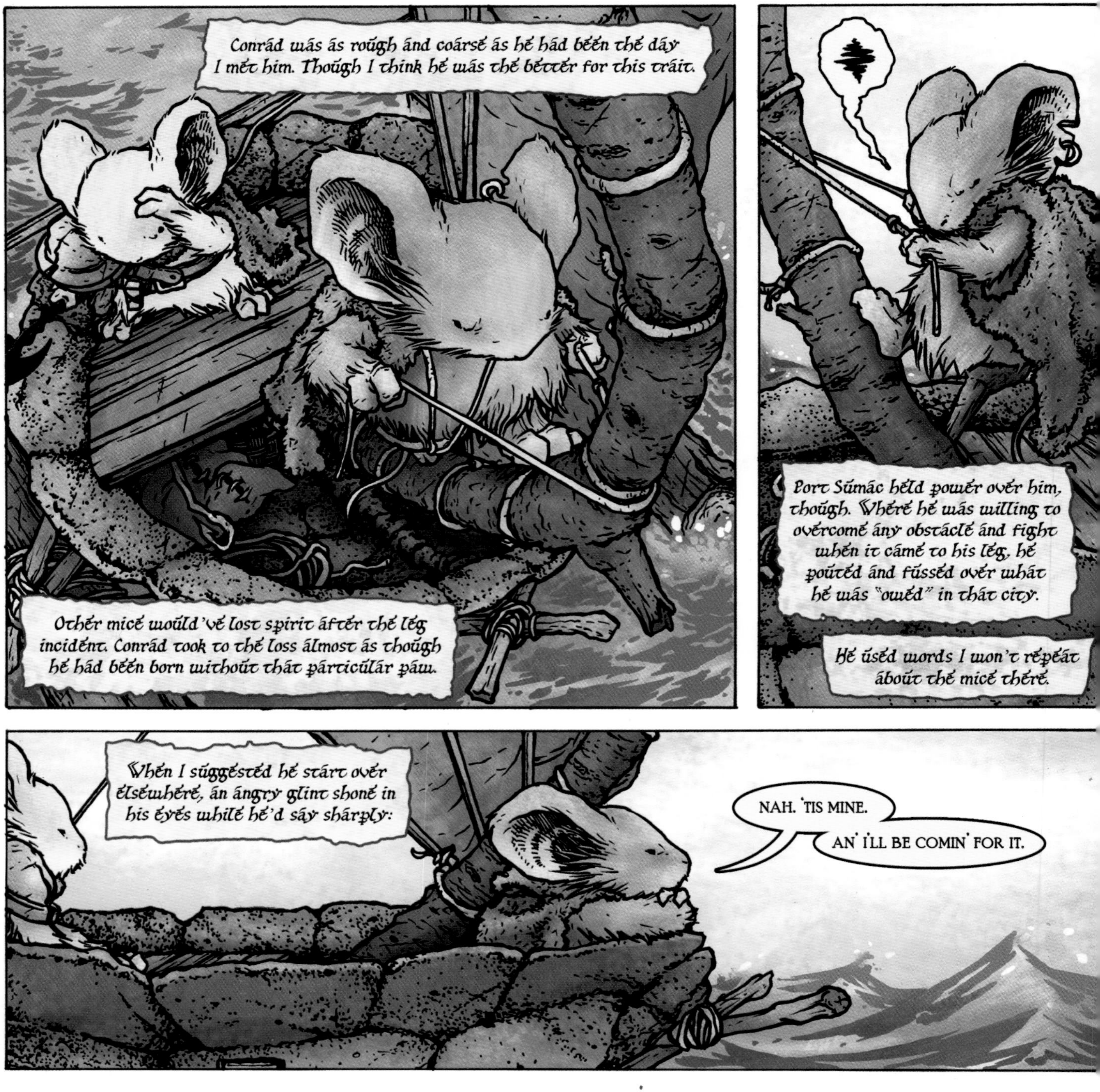
Conrad was as rough and coarse as he had been the day I met him. Though I think he was the better for this trait.
Other mice would've lost spirit after the leg incident. Conrad took to the loss almost as though he had been born without that particular paw.
Port Sumac held power over him, though. Where he was willing to overcome any obstacle and fight when it came to his leg, he pouted and fussed over what he was "owed" in that city.
He used words I won't repeat about the mice there.
When I suggested he start over elsewhere, an angry glint shone in his eyes while he'd say sharply:
NAH. 'TIS MINE.
AN' I'LL BE COMIN' FOR IT.

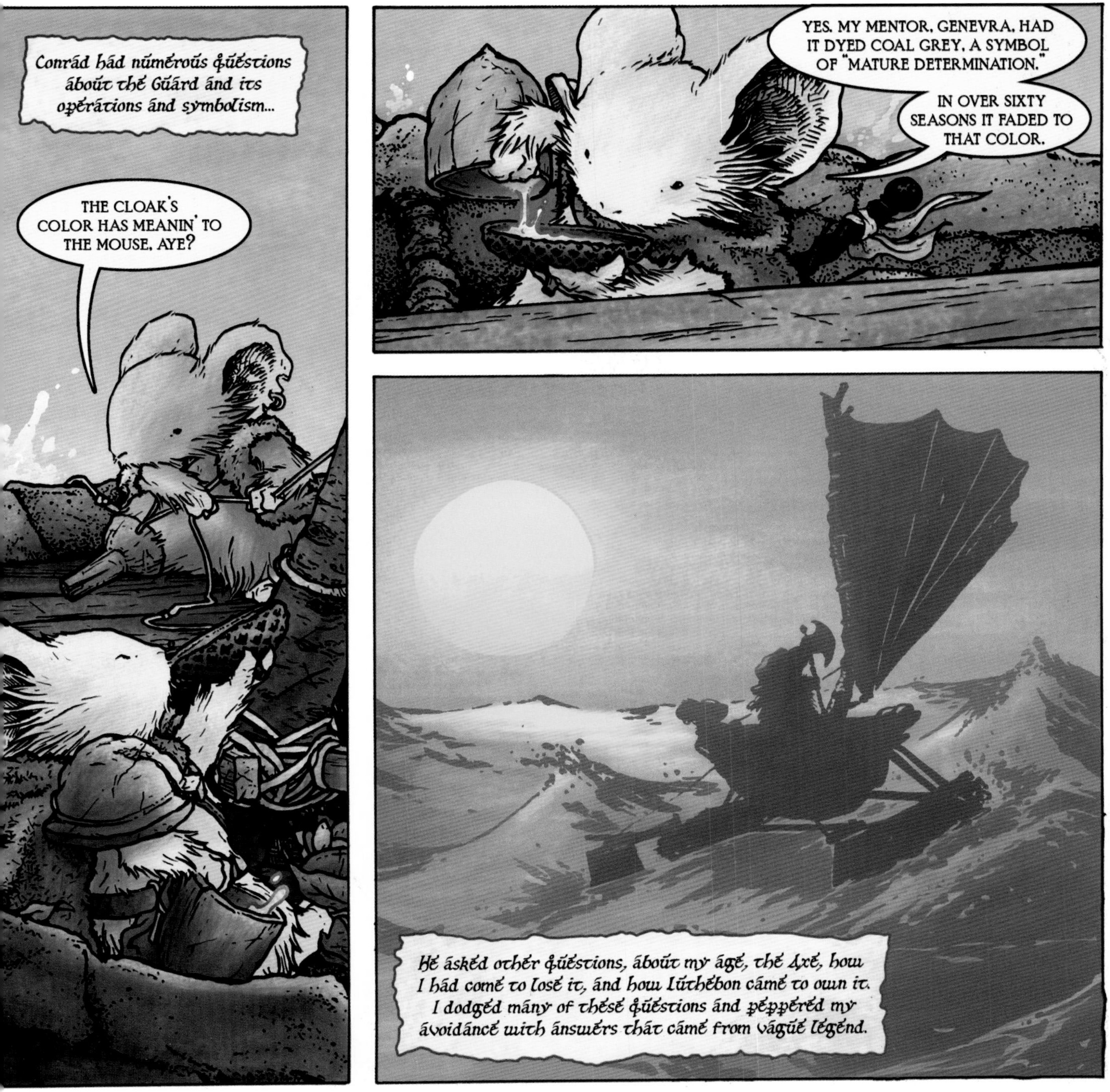
Conrad had numerous questions about the Guard and its operations and symbolism...
THE CLOAK'S COLOR HAS MEANIN' TO THE MOUSE, AYE?
YES. MY MENTOR, GENEVRA, HAD IT DYED COAL GREY, A SYMBOL OF "MATURE DETERMINATION."
IN OVER SIXTY SEASONS IT FADED TO THAT COLOR.
He asked other questions, about my age, the Axe, how I had come to lose it, and how Luthebon came to own it. I dodged many of these questions and peppered my avoidance with answers that came from vague legend.

We took better care to map our way...

...found small unplotted islands...

...camped two moon phases in the snow and ice...

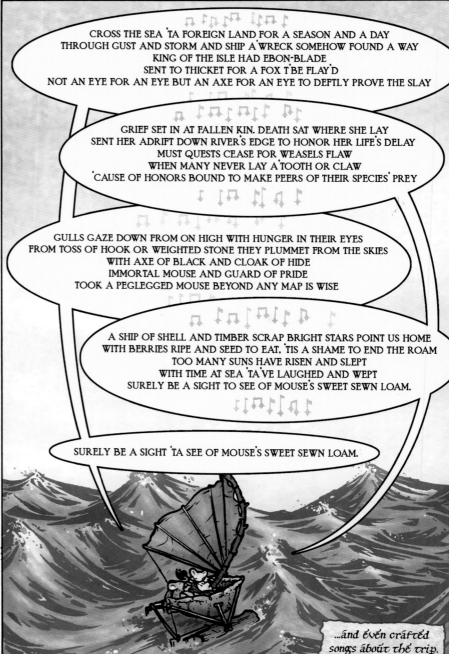

CROSS THE SEA 'TA FOREIGN LAND FOR A SEASON AND A DAY
THROUGH GUST AND STORM AND SHIP A'WRECK SOMEHOW FOUND A WAY
KING OF THE ISLE HAD EBON-BLADE
SENT TO THICKET FOR A FOX T'BE FLAY'D
NOT AN EYE FOR AN EYE BUT AN AXE FOR AN EYE TO DEFTLY PROVE THE SLAY

GRIEF SET IN AT FALLEN KIN. DEATH SAT WHERE SHE LAY
SENT HER ADRIFT DOWN RIVER'S EDGE TO HONOR HER LIFE'S DELAY
MUST QUESTS CEASE FOR WEASELS FLAW
WHEN MANY NEVER LAY A'TOOTH OR CLAW
'CAUSE OF HONORS BOUND TO MAKE PEERS OF THEIR SPECIES' PREY

GULLS GAZE DOWN FROM ON HIGH WITH HUNGER IN THEIR EYES
FROM TOSS OF HOOK OR WEIGHTED STONE THEY PLUMMET FROM THE SKIES
WITH AXE OF BLACK AND CLOAK OF HIDE
IMMORTAL MOUSE AND GUARD OF PRIDE
TOOK A PEGLEGGED MOUSE BEYOND ANY MAP IS WISE

A SHIP OF SHELL AND TIMBER SCRAP BRIGHT STARS POINT US HOME
WITH BERRIES RIPE AND SEED TO EAT. 'TIS A SHAME TO END THE ROAM
TOO MANY SUNS HAVE RISEN AND SLEPT
WITH TIME AT SEA 'TA'VE LAUGHED AND WEPT
SURELY BE A SIGHT TO SEE OF MOUSE'S SWEET SEWN LOAM.

SURELY BE A SIGHT 'TA SEE OF MOUSE'S SWEET SEWN LOAM.

...and even crafted songs about the trip.

Away for slightly more than four full seasons, our eyes caught sight of the northern coast of our homeland.

I departed from our sea-home just east of Dawnrock.

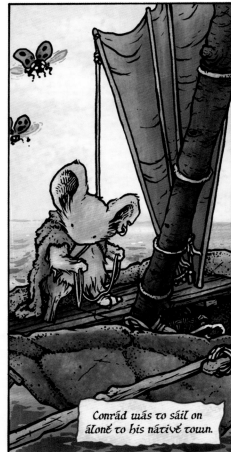

Conrad was to sail on alone to his native town.

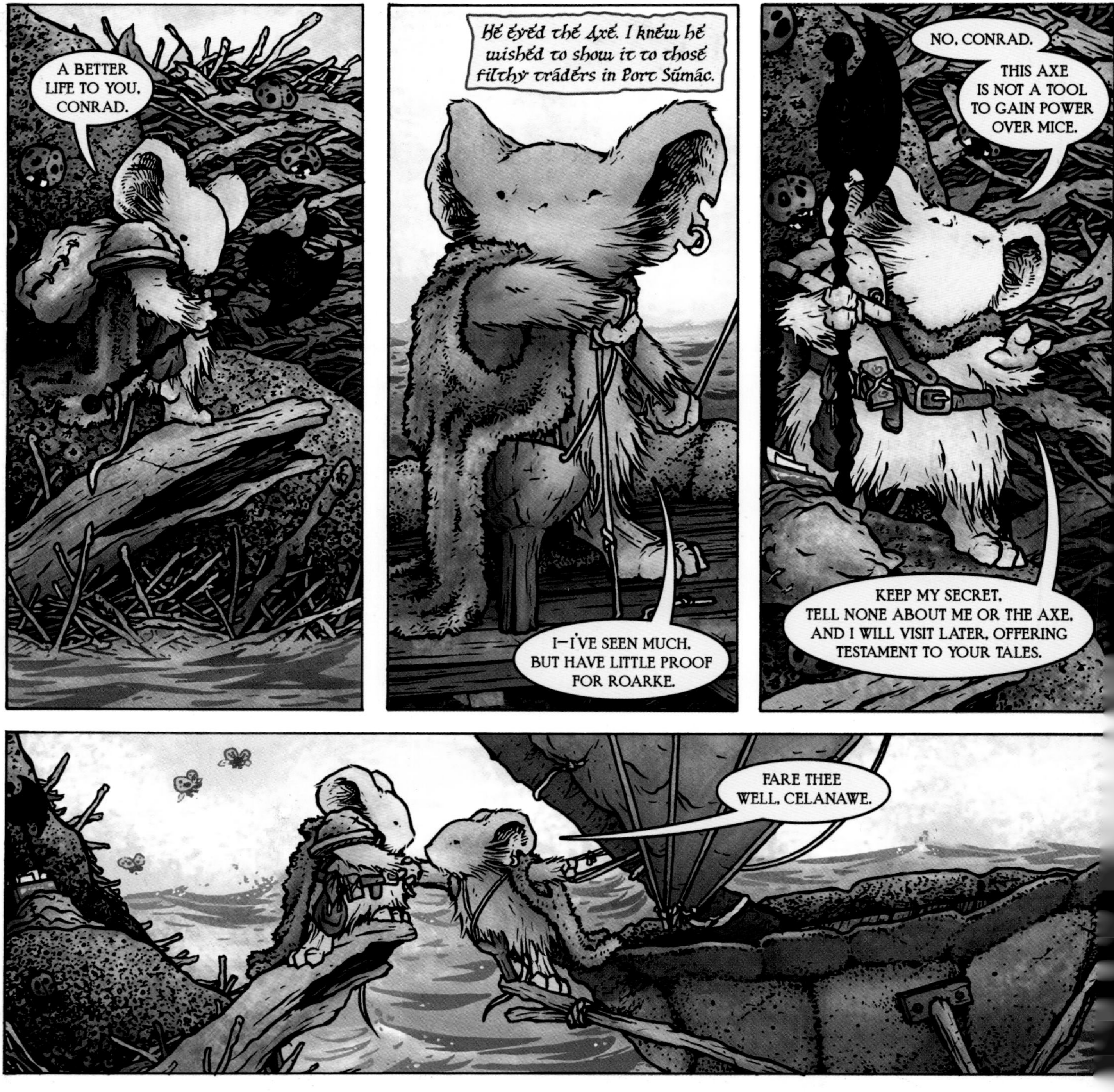
A BETTER LIFE TO YOU, CONRAD.
He eyed the Axe. I knew he wished to show it to those filthy traders in Port Sumac.
I—I'VE SEEN MUCH, BUT HAVE LITTLE PROOF FOR ROARKE.
NO, CONRAD.
THIS AXE IS NOT A TOOL TO GAIN POWER OVER MICE.
KEEP MY SECRET, TELL NONE ABOUT ME OR THE AXE, AND I WILL VISIT LATER, OFFERING TESTAMENT TO YOUR TALES.
FARE THEE WELL, CELANAWE.

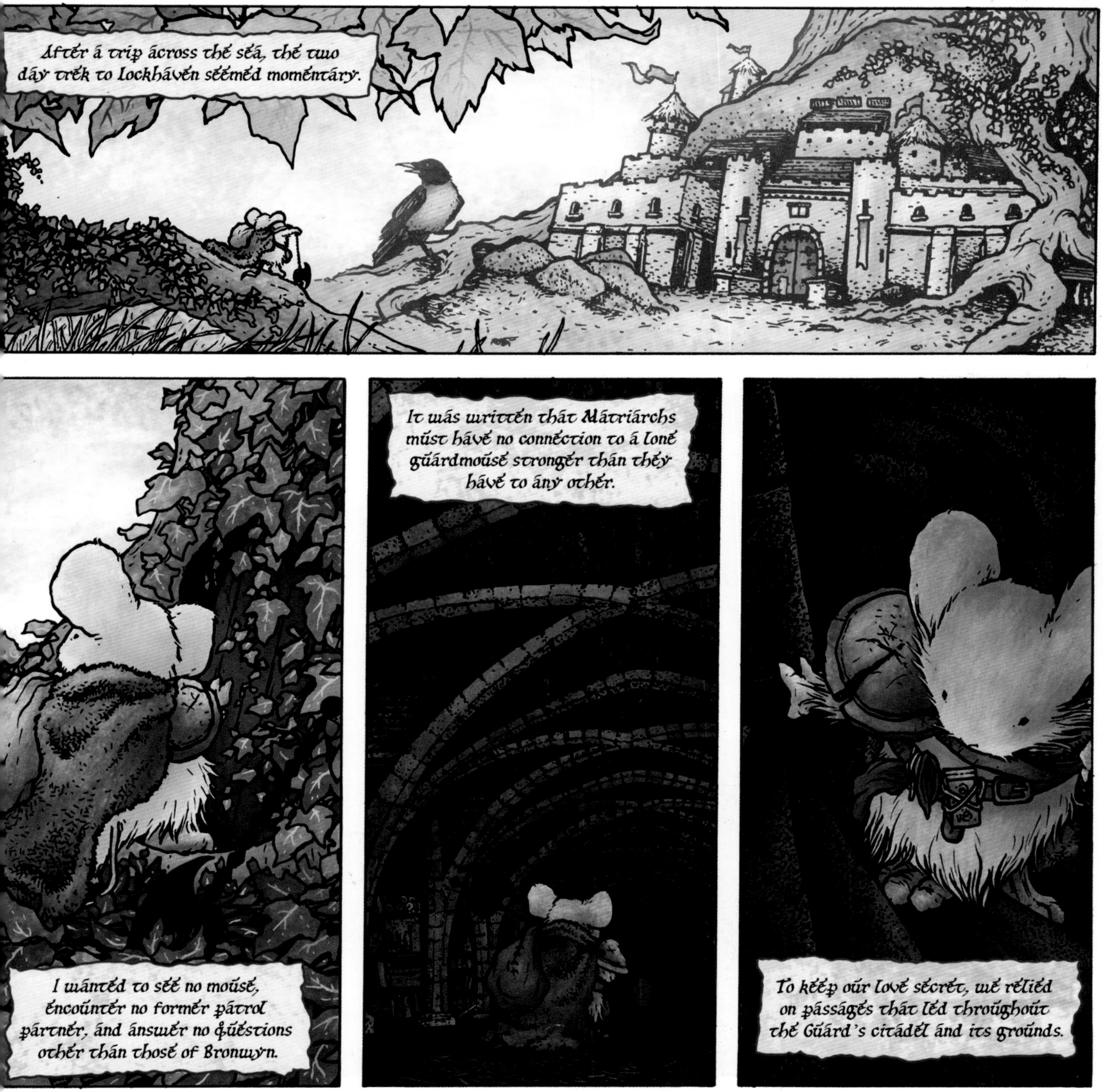
After a trip across the sea, the two day trek to Lockhaven seemed momentary.
I wanted to see no mouse, encounter no former patrol partner, and answer no questions other than those of Bronwyn.
It was written that Matriarchs must have no connection to a lone guardmouse stronger than they have to any other.
To keep our love secret, we relied on passages that led throughout the Guard's citadel and its grounds.

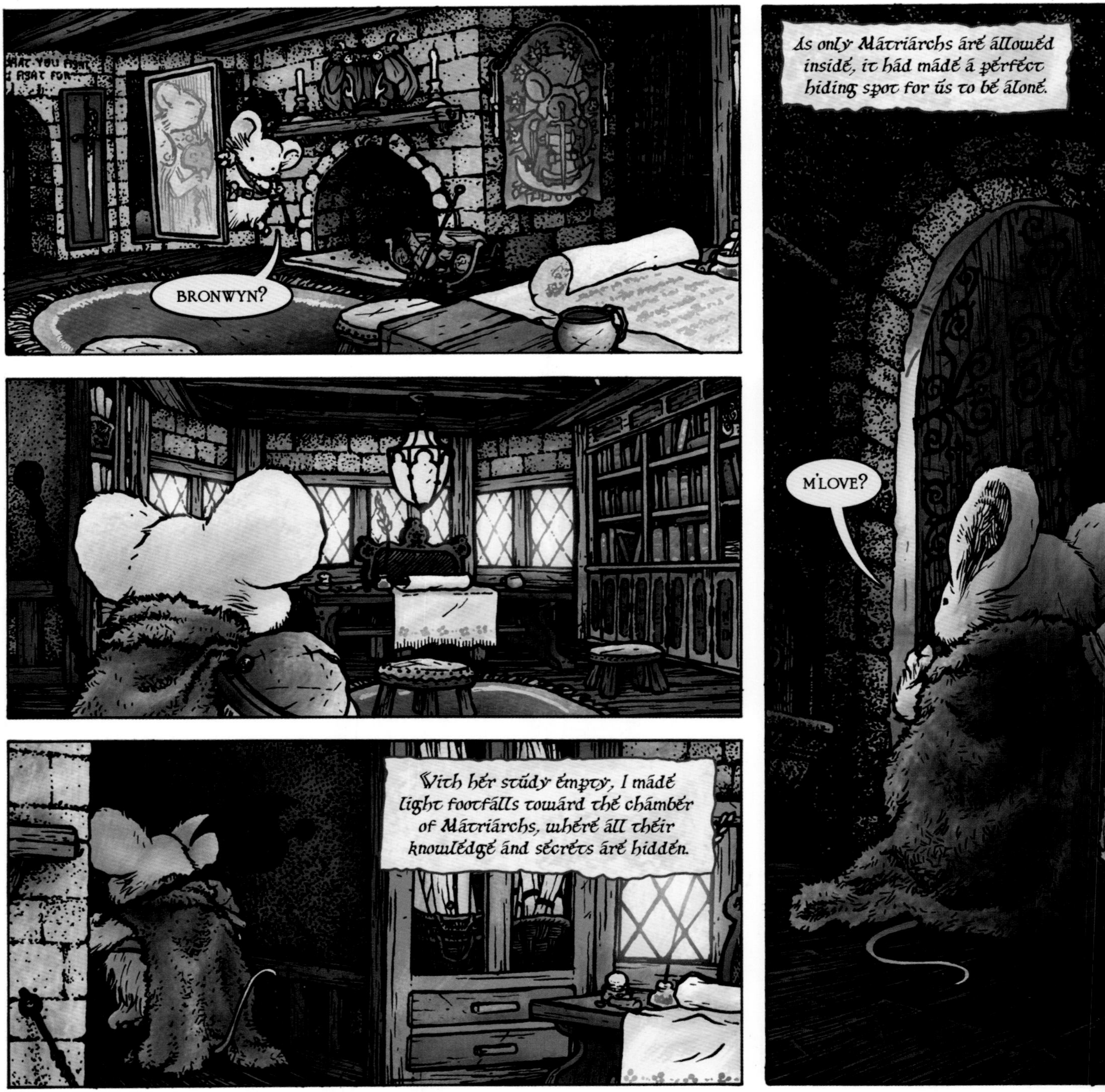
BRONWYN?
With her study empty, I made light footfalls toward the chamber of Matriarchs, where all their knowledge and secrets are hidden.
As only Matriarchs are allowed inside, it had made a perfect hiding spot for us to be alone.
M'LOVE?

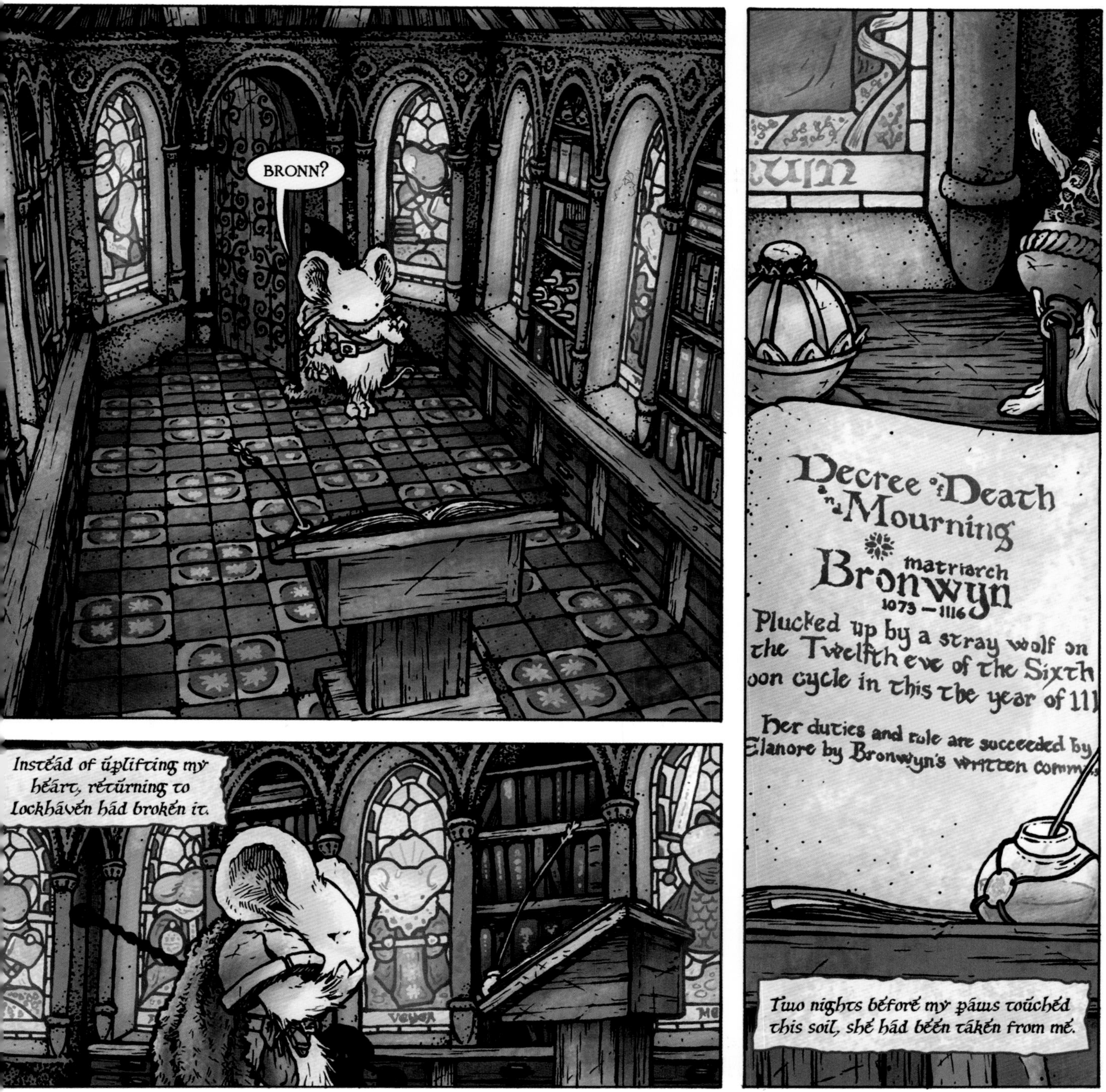
BRONN?
Instead of uplifting my heart, returning to Lockhaven had broken it.
Decree of Death and Mourning
matriarch Bronwyn
1073 — 1116
Plucked up by a stray wolf on the Twelfth eve of the Sixth
oon cycle in this the year of 111
Her duties and rule are succeeded by
Elanore by Bronwyn's written comm
Two nights before my paws touched this soil, she had been taken from me.

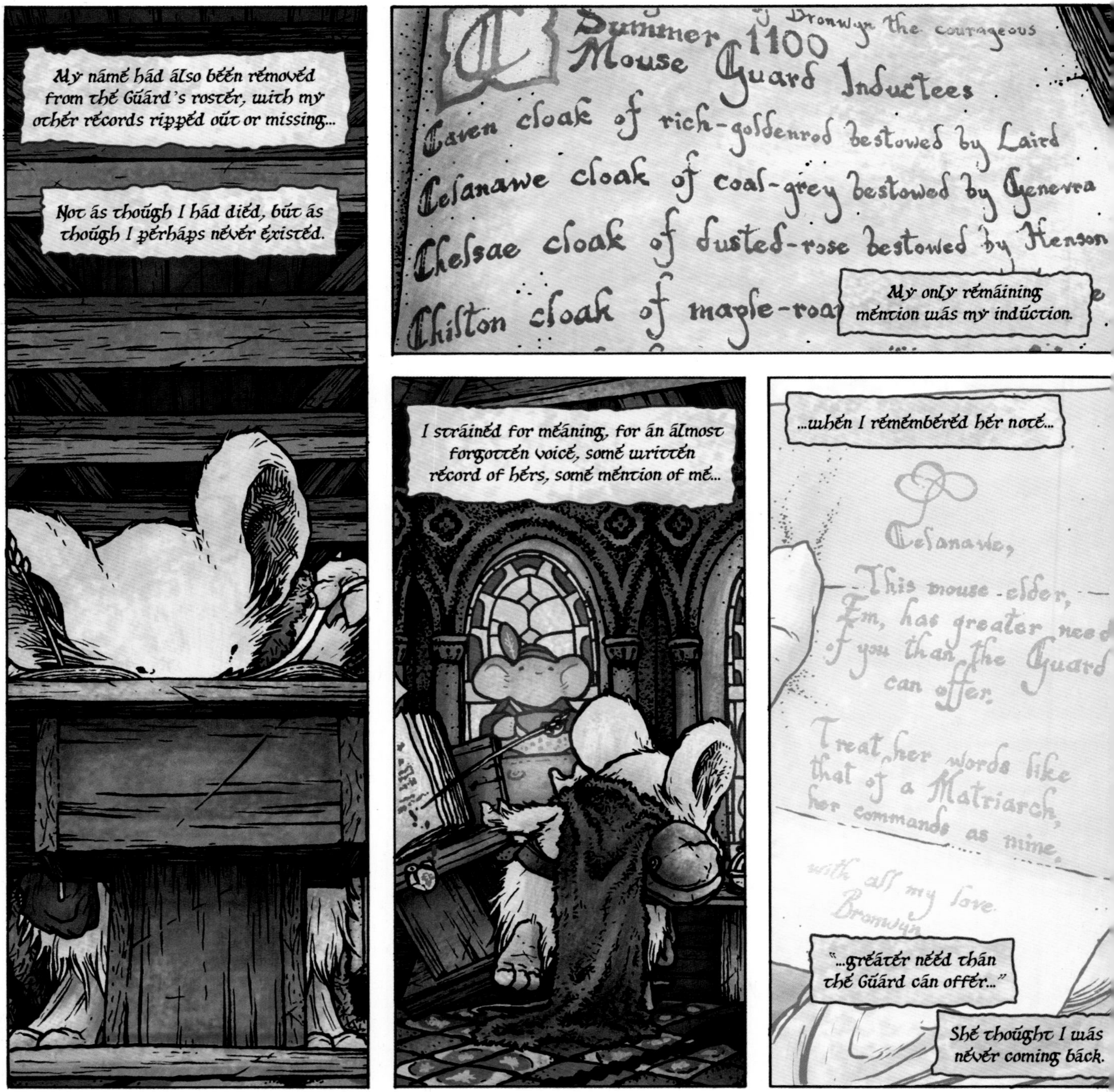

My náme hád álso béen rémoved from thé Gúard's róstér, with my óthér récords rípped óut or míssing...

Not ás thoúgh I hád died, bút ás thoúgh I pérháps névér éxísted.

by Bronwyn the courageous

Summer 1100
Mouse Guard Inductees

Caven cloak of rich-goldenrod bestowed by Laird

Celanawe cloak of coal-grey bestowed by Genevra

Chelsae cloak of dusted-rose bestowed by Henson

Chilton cloak of maple-roa...

My only rémáining méntion wás my indúction.

I stráined for méaning, for án álmost forgotten voice, some written récord of hérs, some méntion of mé...

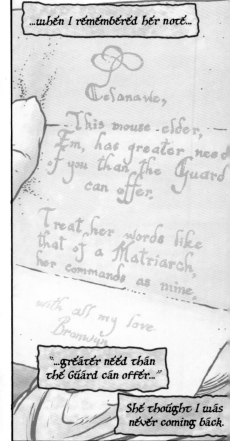

...whén I rémémbéred hér note...

Celanawe,

This mouse-elder, Em, has greater need of you than the Guard can offer.

Treat her words like that of a Matriarch, her commands as mine...

with all my love,
Bronwyn

"...gréatér néed thán thé Gúard cán offér..."

She thoúght I wás névér coming báck.

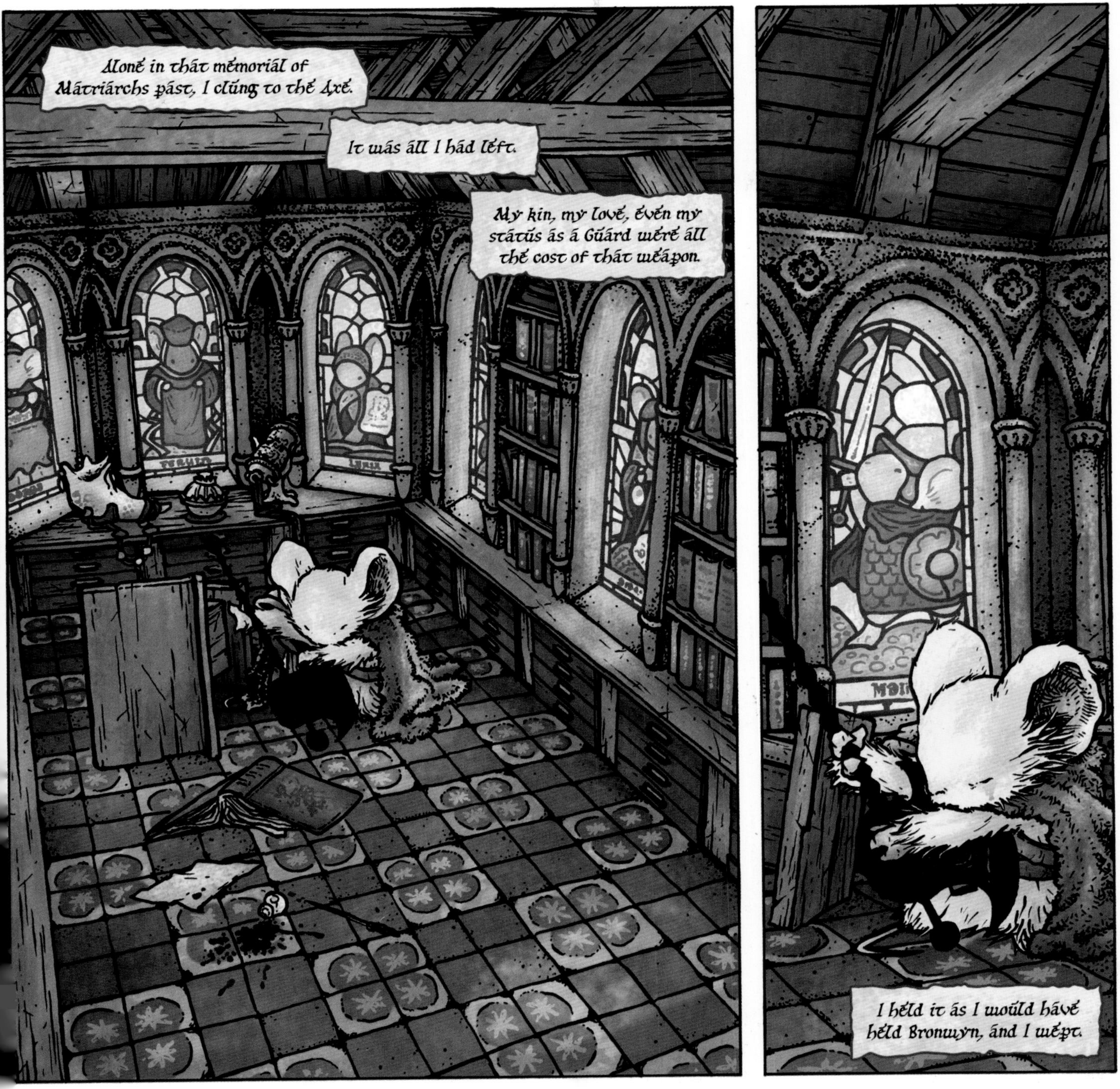
Alone in that memorial of Matriarchs past, I clung to the Axe.
It was all I had left.
My kin, my love, even my status as a Guard were all the cost of that weapon.
I held it as I would have held Bronwyn, and I wept.

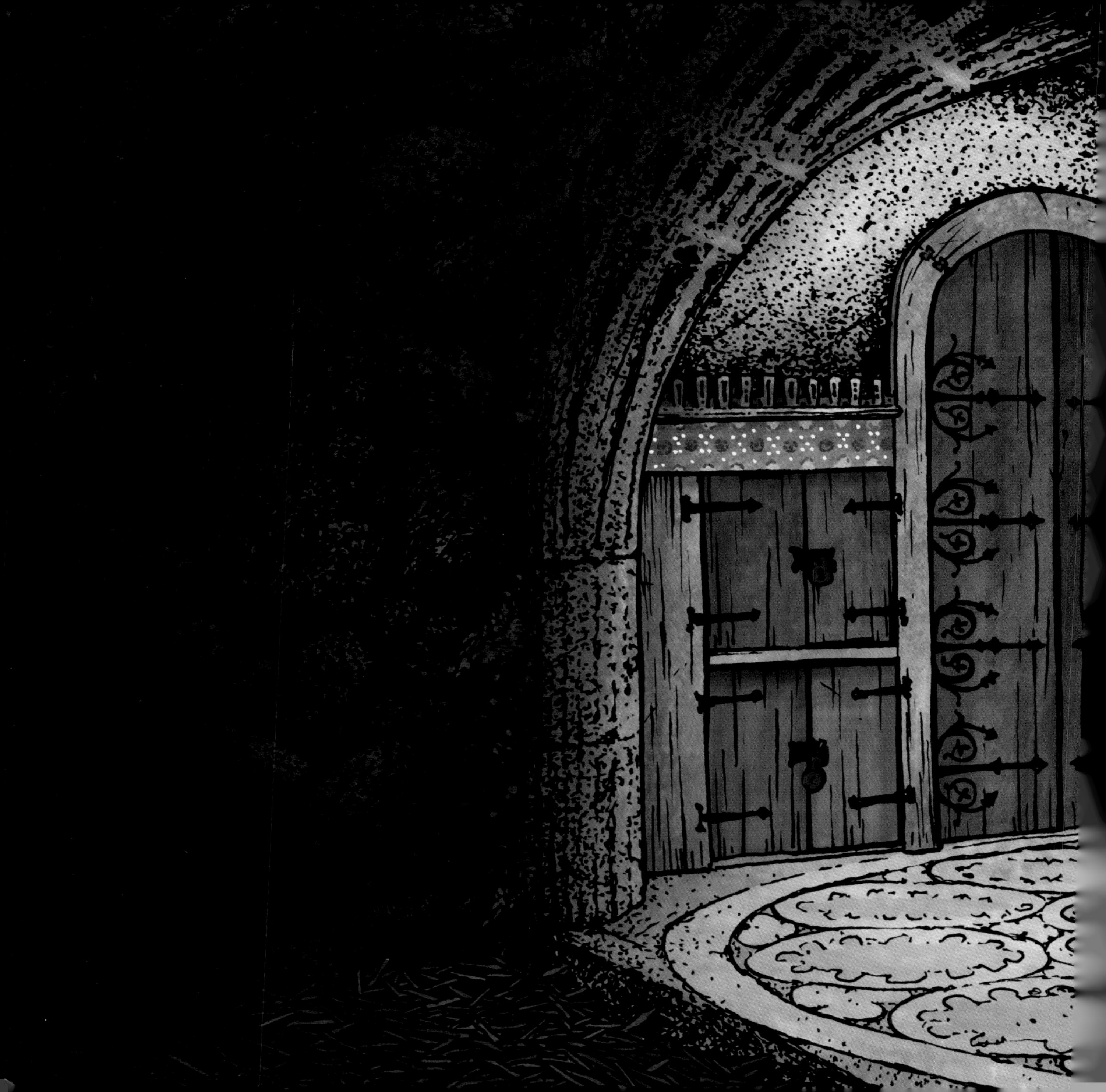

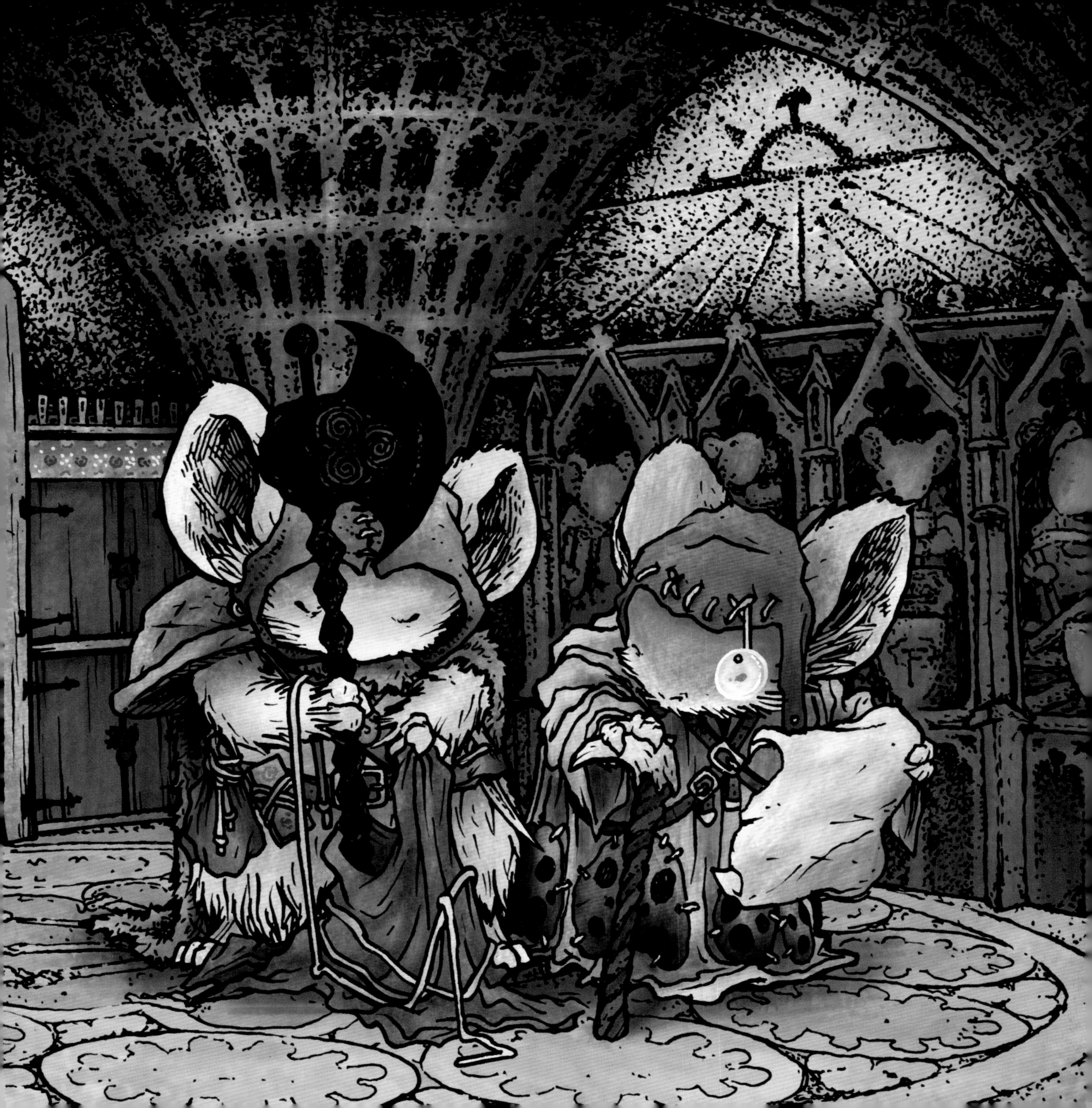

CHAPTER SIX

Even death could not stop the wielder of that axe.

The flora of the earth becomes

reborn after the ice and cold

pass from our land, so too does

the black axe. No grave will

ever mark his bed, for he shall

never rest, his work is unending

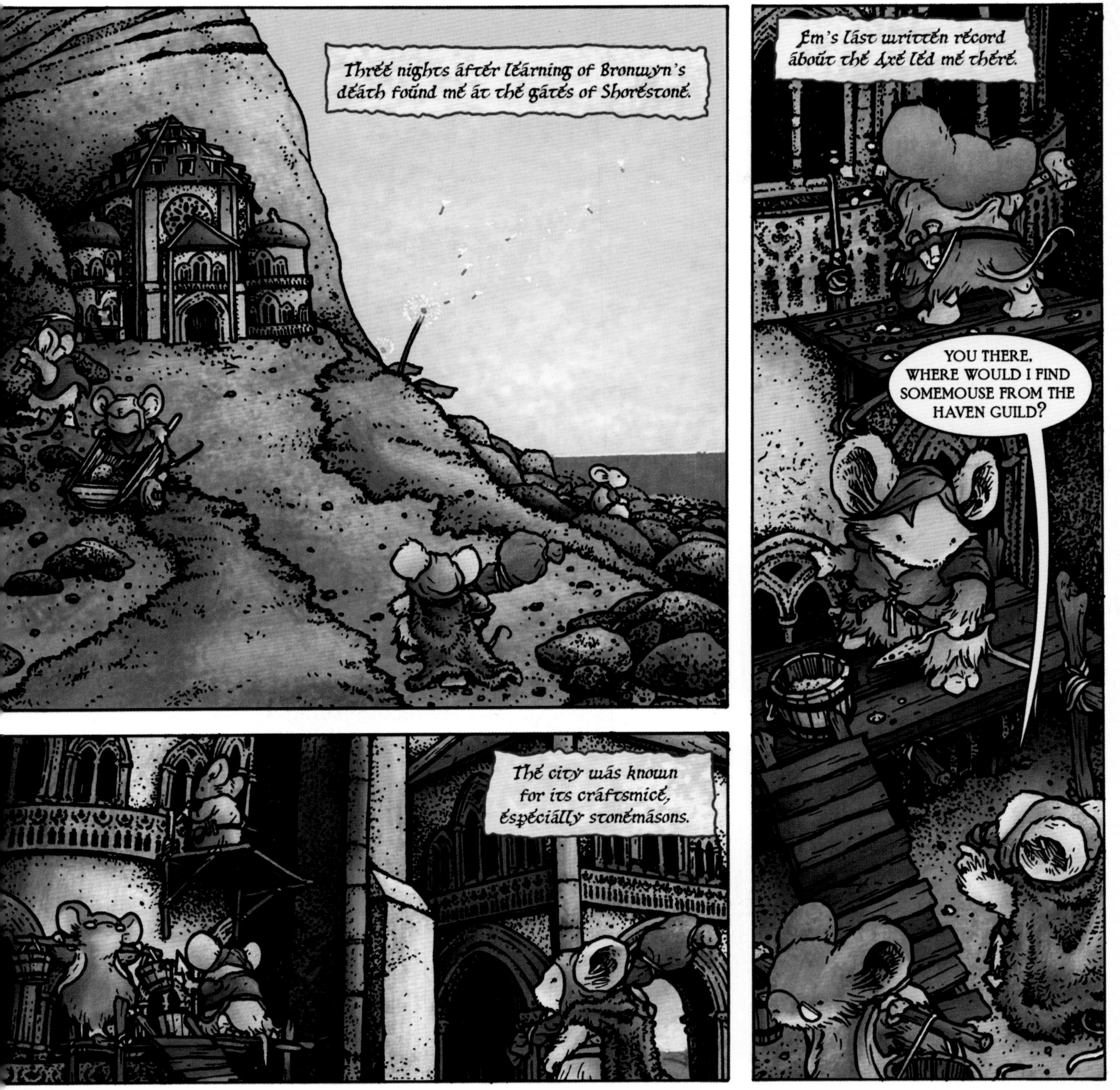

Three nights after learning of Bronwyn's death found me at the gates of Shorestone.
The city was known for its craftsmice, especially stonemasons.
Em's last written record about the Axe led me there.
YOU THERE. WHERE WOULD I FIND SOMEMOUSE FROM THE HAVEN GUILD?

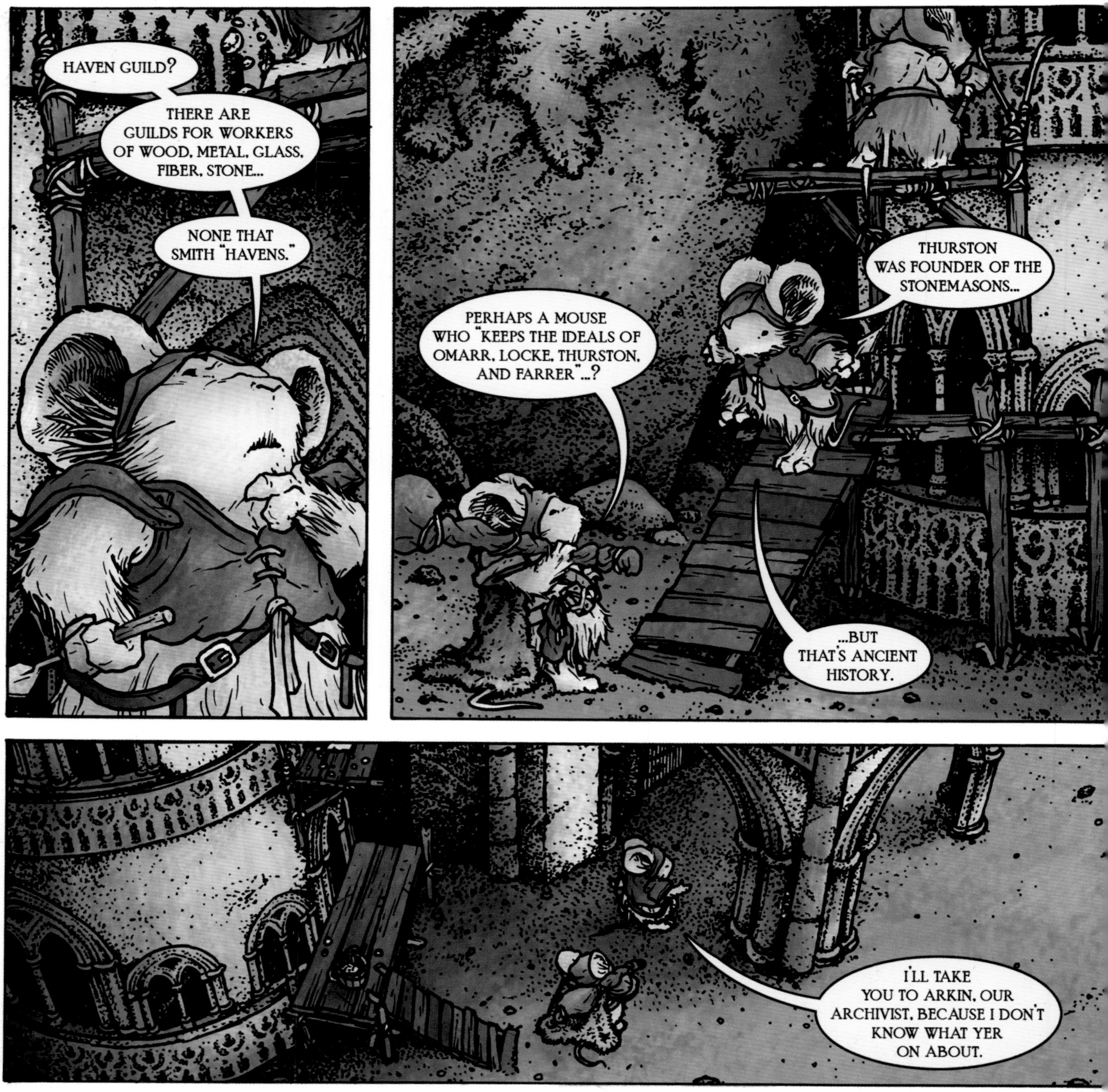
HAVEN GUILD?
THERE ARE GUILDS FOR WORKERS OF WOOD, METAL, GLASS, FIBER, STONE...
NONE THAT SMITH "HAVENS."
PERHAPS A MOUSE WHO "KEEPS THE IDEALS OF OMARR, LOCKE, THURSTON, AND FARRER"...?
THURSTON WAS FOUNDER OF THE STONEMASONS...
...BUT THAT'S ANCIENT HISTORY.
I'LL TAKE YOU TO ARKIN, OUR ARCHIVIST, BECAUSE I DON'T KNOW WHAT YER ON ABOUT.

Past its echoing entry...

...the mason led me through the huge stone city...

HAROLD'S KILN POTTERY

INKS & STAINS

THE HABERDASK PEDDLER

BOOKS

BRAIDS & ROPES

DWORK

...down into the skilled labor district...

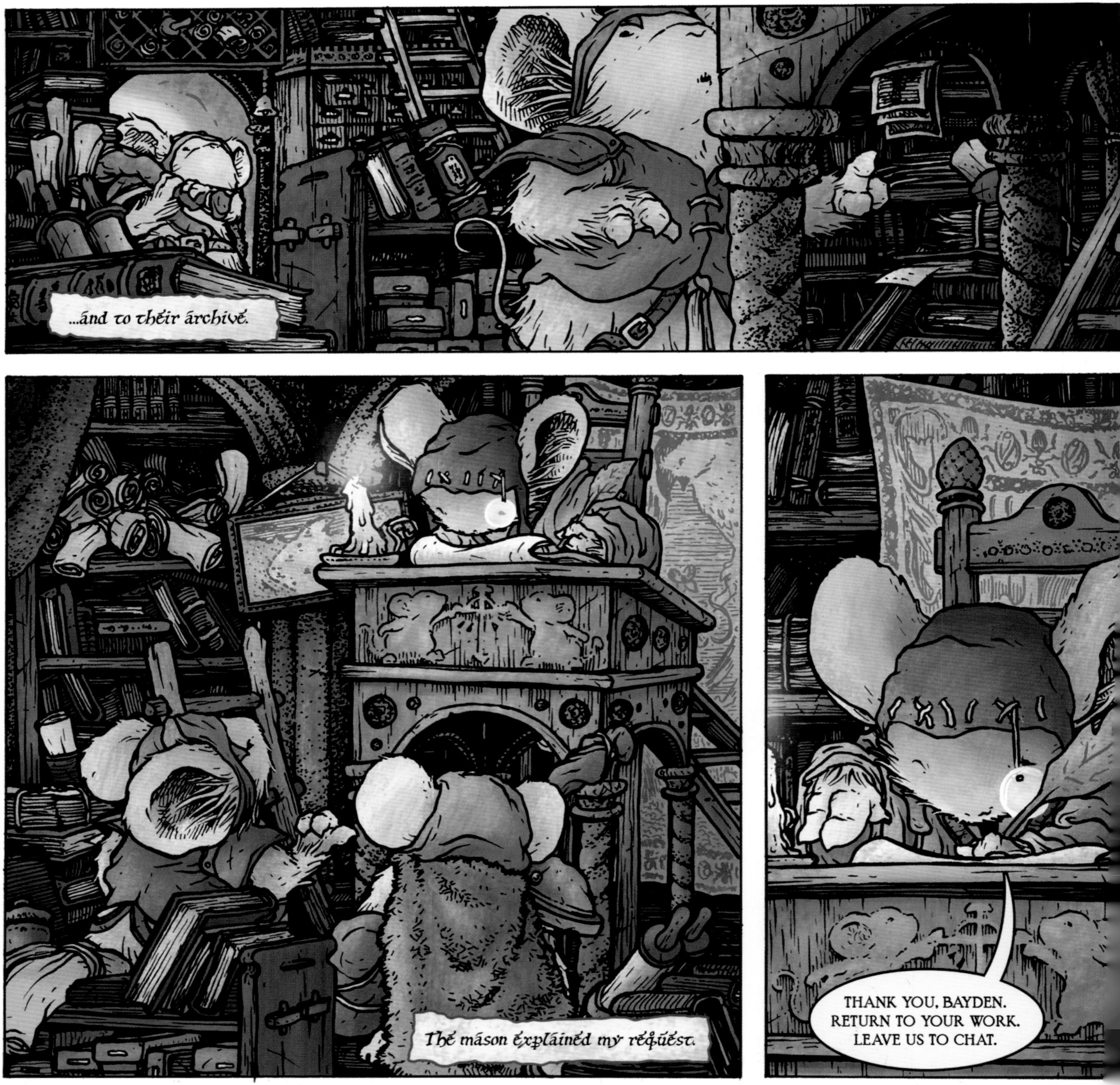
...and to their archive.
The mason explained my request.
THANK YOU, BAYDEN. RETURN TO YOUR WORK. LEAVE US TO CHAT.

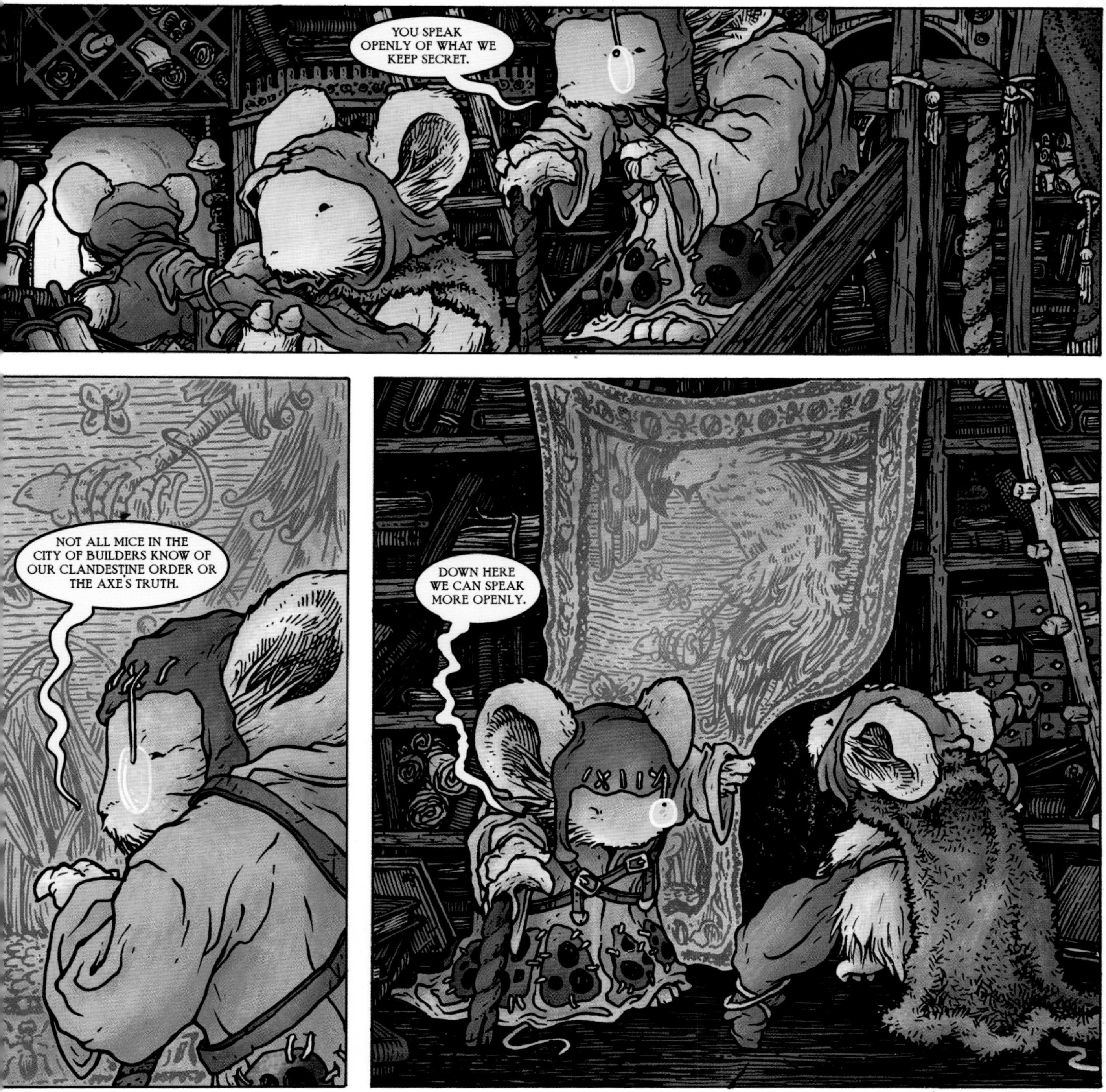
YOU SPEAK OPENLY OF WHAT WE KEEP SECRET.
NOT ALL MICE IN THE CITY OF BUILDERS KNOW OF OUR CLANDESTINE ORDER OR THE AXE'S TRUTH.
DOWN HERE WE CAN SPEAK MORE OPENLY.

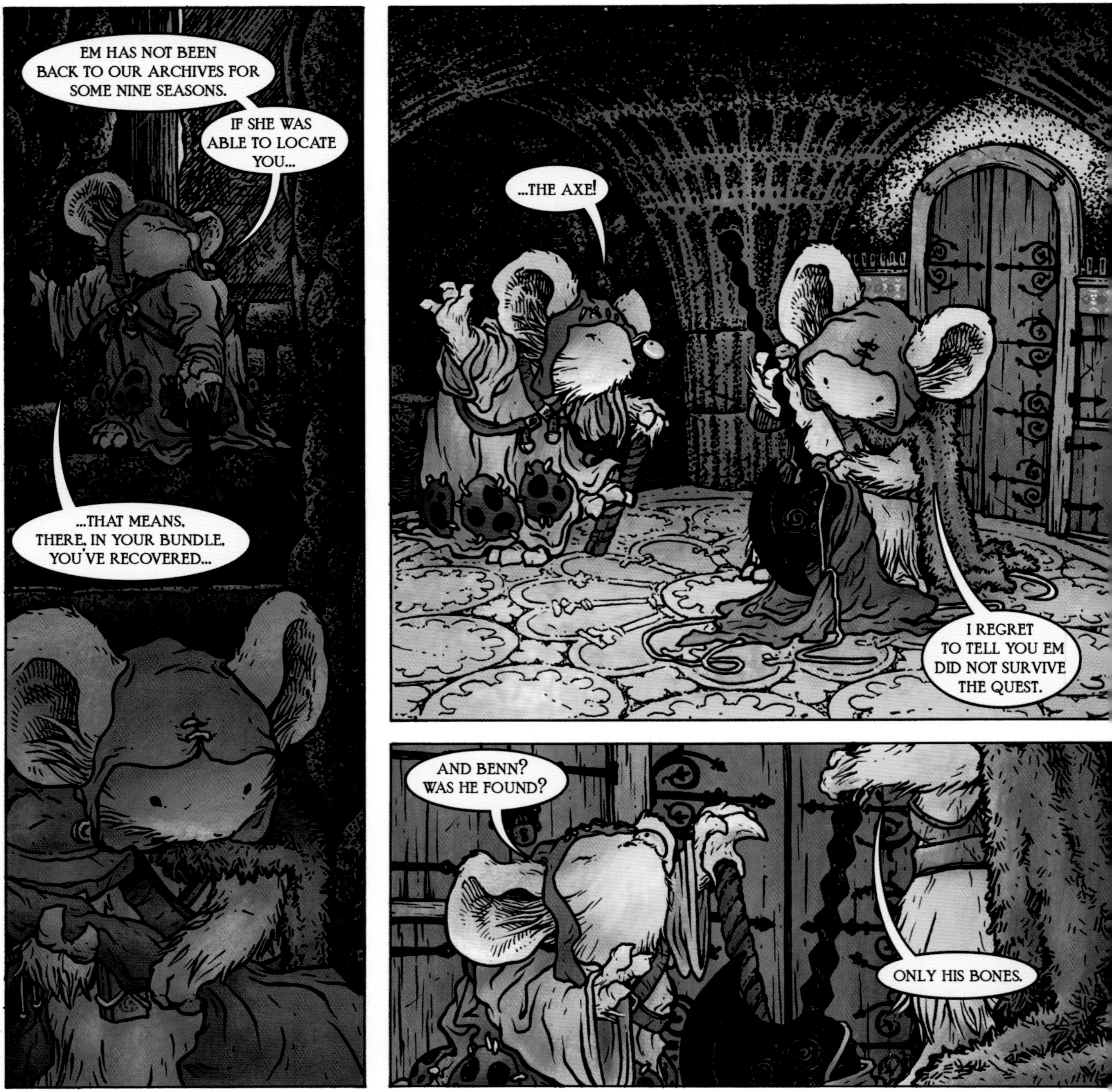
EM HAS NOT BEEN BACK TO OUR ARCHIVES FOR SOME NINE SEASONS.
IF SHE WAS ABLE TO LOCATE YOU...
...THAT MEANS, THERE, IN YOUR BUNDLE, YOU'VE RECOVERED...
...THE AXE!
I REGRET TO TELL YOU EM DID NOT SURVIVE THE QUEST.
AND BENN? WAS HE FOUND?
ONLY HIS BONES.

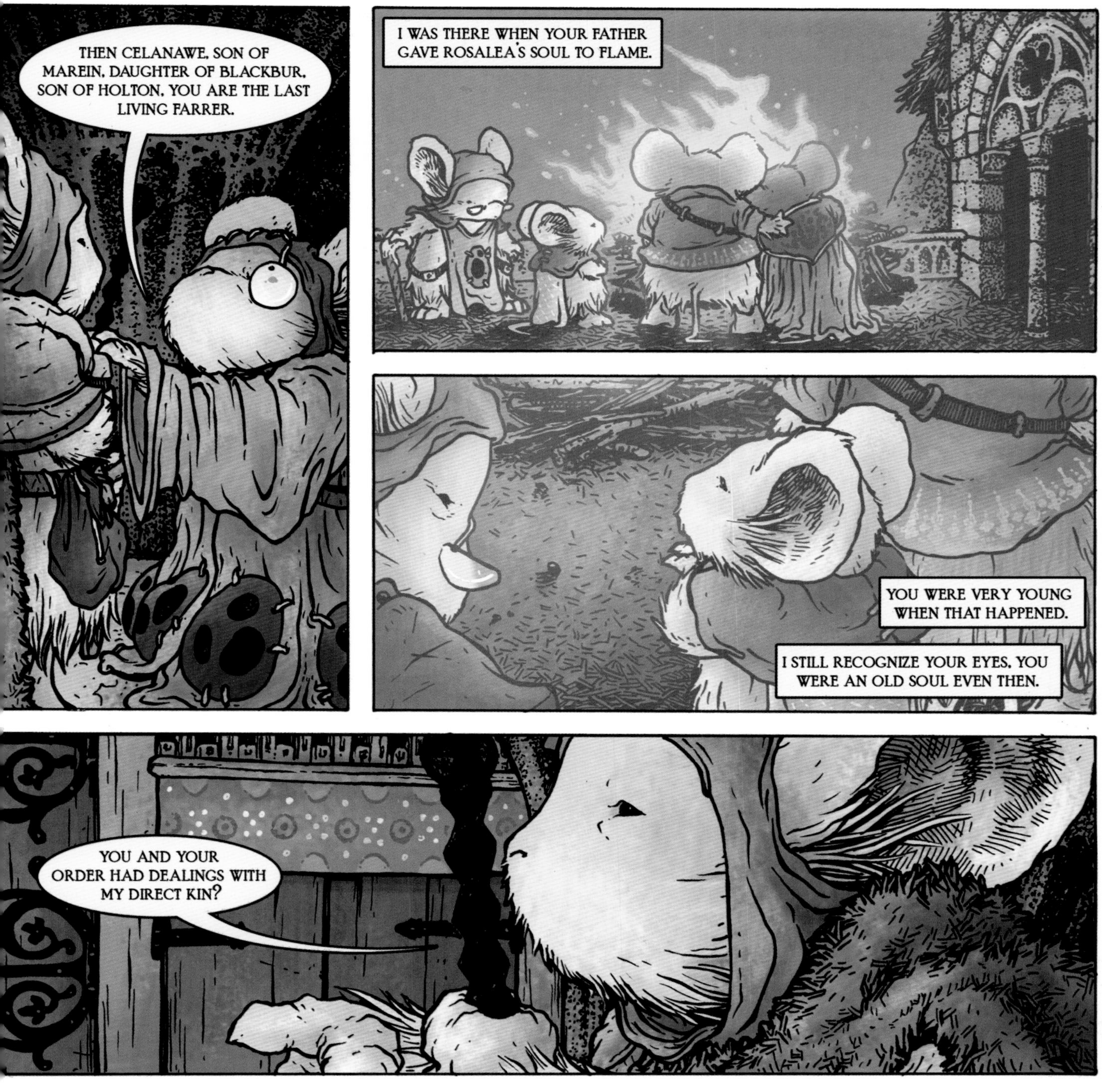

THEN CELANAWE, SON OF MAREIN, DAUGHTER OF BLACKBUR, SON OF HOLTON, YOU ARE THE LAST LIVING FARRER.
I WAS THERE WHEN YOUR FATHER GAVE ROSALEA'S SOUL TO FLAME.
YOU WERE VERY YOUNG WHEN THAT HAPPENED.
I STILL RECOGNIZE YOUR EYES. YOU WERE AN OLD SOUL EVEN THEN.
YOU AND YOUR ORDER HAD DEALINGS WITH MY DIRECT KIN?

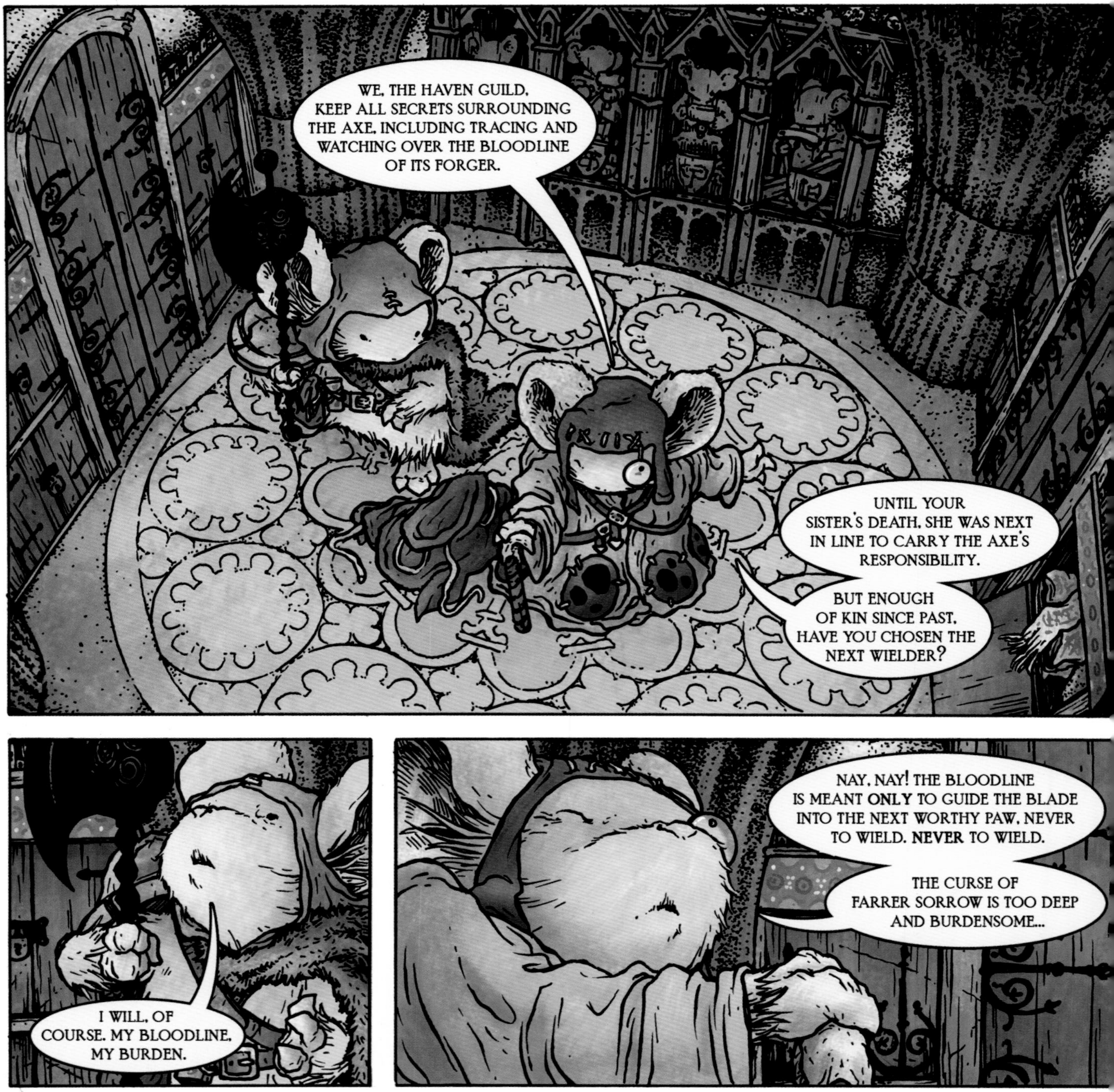
WE, THE HAVEN GUILD, KEEP ALL SECRETS SURROUNDING THE AXE, INCLUDING TRACING AND WATCHING OVER THE BLOODLINE OF ITS FORGER.
UNTIL YOUR SISTER'S DEATH, SHE WAS NEXT IN LINE TO CARRY THE AXE'S RESPONSIBILITY.
BUT ENOUGH OF KIN SINCE PAST, HAVE YOU CHOSEN THE NEXT WIELDER?
I WILL, OF COURSE. MY BLOODLINE, MY BURDEN.
NAY, NAY! THE BLOODLINE IS MEANT **ONLY** TO GUIDE THE BLADE INTO THE NEXT WORTHY PAW, NEVER TO WIELD. **NEVER** TO WIELD.
THE CURSE OF FARRER SORROW IS TOO DEEP AND BURDENSOME...

AS A WEAPON OF DEATH, THE AXE MUST ONLY BE CONTROLLED BY A MOUSE FULLY CAPABLE TO DELIVER DEATH AND FALL TO IT THEMSELVES.

FARRER	915	DARDRICK
LYTHER	935	ANKUR
CEARA	965	SOREN
BRYNNE	995	URKEN
DALEON	1011	ERROLL
ARDYN	1023	RUDYARD
THERA	1038	ZYNAN
BLACKBUR	1051	IVONNE
BENN	1085	MEREK

BENN GUIDED THE AXE INTO THE PAWS OF MEREK AND WATCHED OVER IT. JUST AS EIGHT MICE BEFORE HIM HAVE BEEN GRANTED USE OF THE AXE BY YOUR BLOODLINE.

FARRER STARTED THE TRADITION IN 915 BY TAKING THE AXE TO LOCKHAVEN FOR THAT FIRST WORTHY MOUSE.

IT WAS ONLY IN 1071 WHEN THE PROTOCOL OF A FARRER WEARING SMITH'S GLOVES TO TOUCH THE AXE BETWEEN WIELDERS WAS LIFTED.

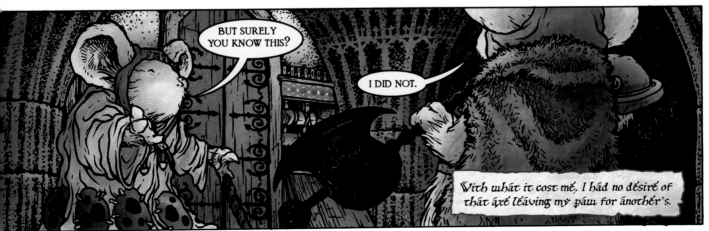

BUT SURELY YOU KNOW THIS?

I DID NOT.

With what it cost me, I had no desire of that axe leaving my paw for another's.

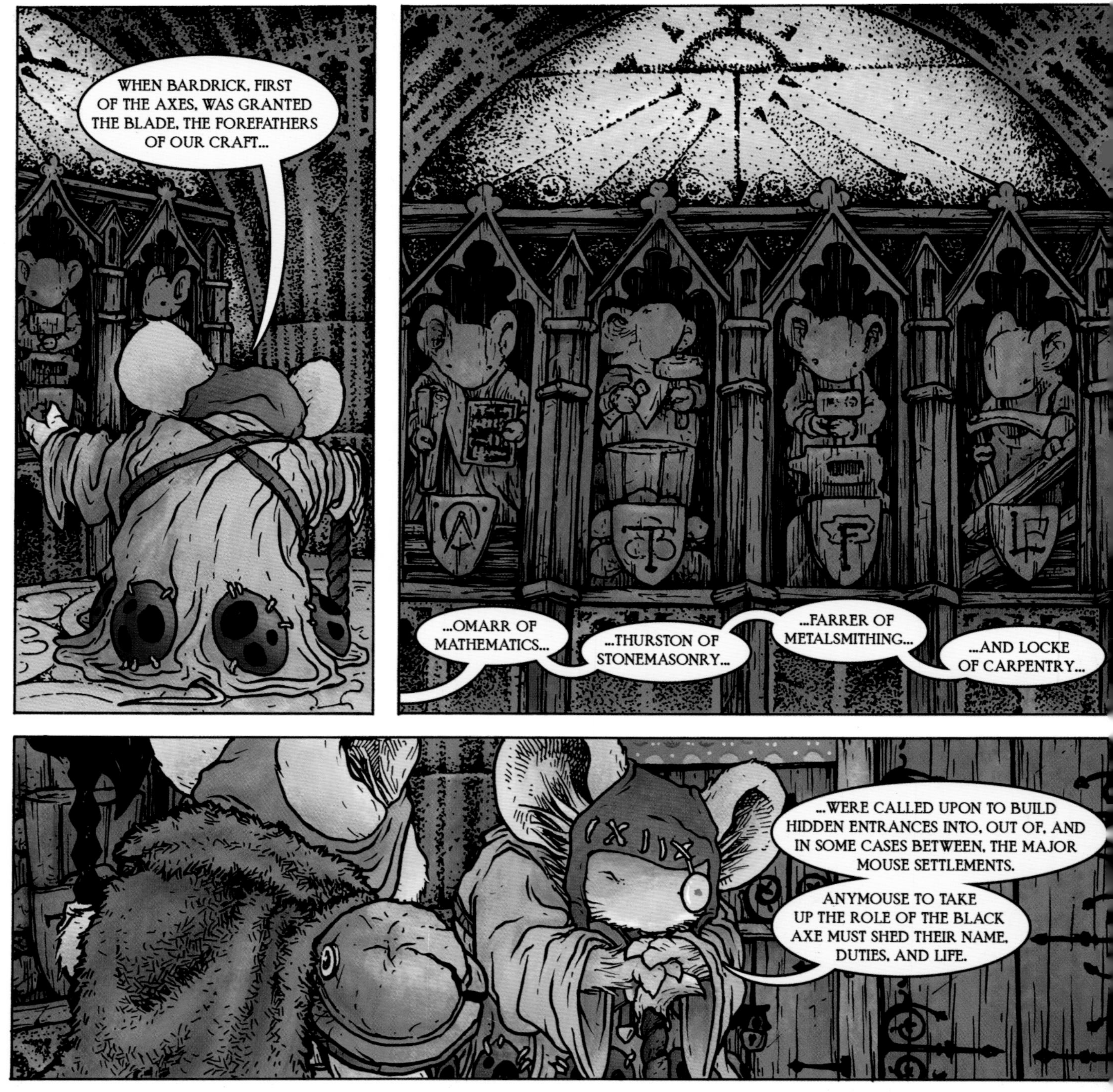
WHEN BARDRICK, FIRST OF THE AXES, WAS GRANTED THE BLADE, THE FOREFATHERS OF OUR CRAFT...
...OMARR OF MATHEMATICS...
...THURSTON OF STONEMASONRY...
...FARRER OF METALSMITHING...
...AND LOCKE OF CARPENTRY...
...WERE CALLED UPON TO BUILD HIDDEN ENTRANCES INTO, OUT OF, AND IN SOME CASES BETWEEN, THE MAJOR MOUSE SETTLEMENTS.
ANYMOUSE TO TAKE UP THE ROLE OF THE BLACK AXE MUST SHED THEIR NAME, DUTIES, AND LIFE.

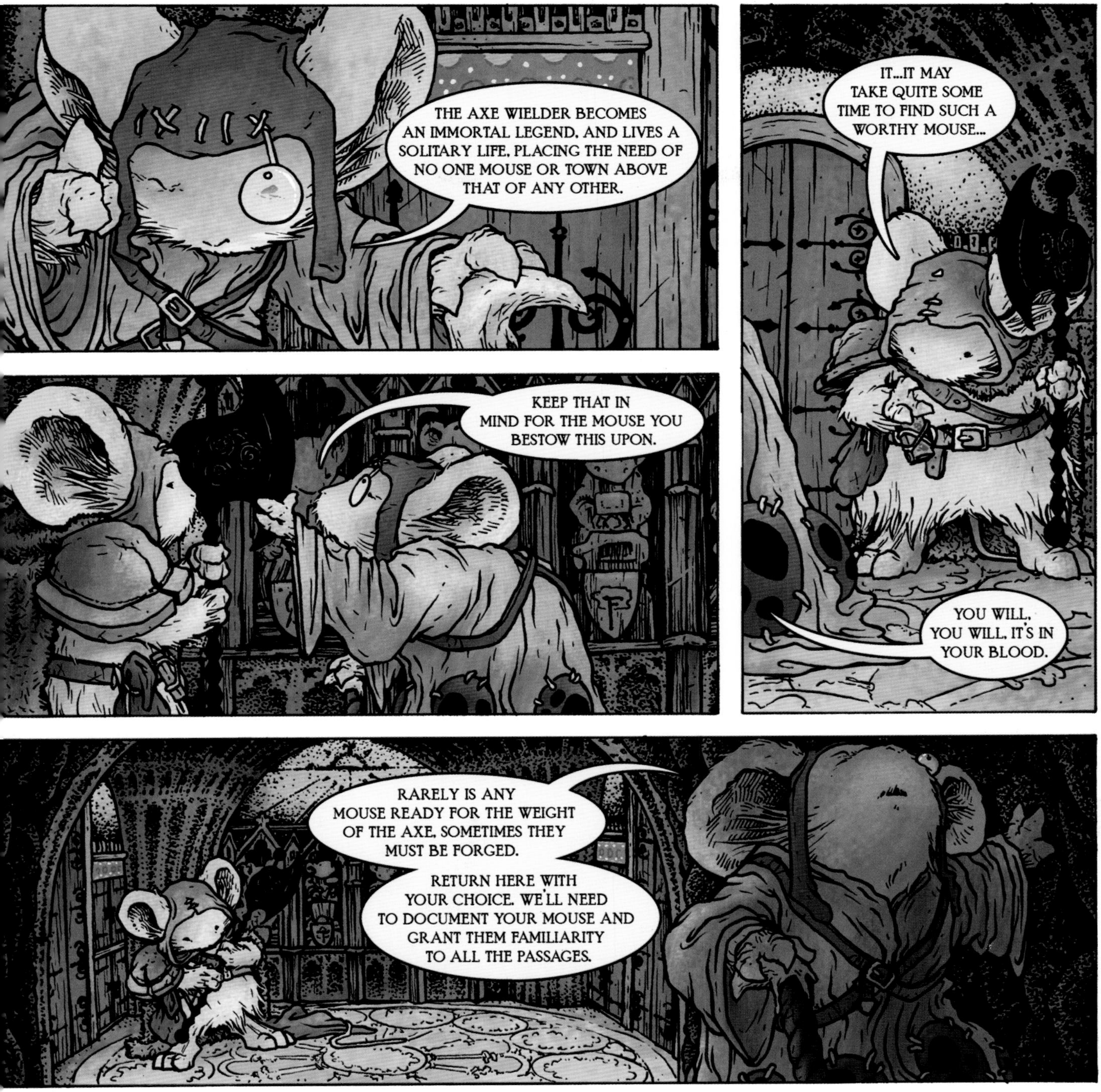

THE AXE WIELDER BECOMES AN IMMORTAL LEGEND, AND LIVES A SOLITARY LIFE, PLACING THE NEED OF NO ONE MOUSE OR TOWN ABOVE THAT OF ANY OTHER.
IT...IT MAY TAKE QUITE SOME TIME TO FIND SUCH A WORTHY MOUSE...
KEEP THAT IN MIND FOR THE MOUSE YOU BESTOW THIS UPON.
YOU WILL, YOU WILL, IT'S IN YOUR BLOOD.
RARELY IS ANY MOUSE READY FOR THE WEIGHT OF THE AXE, SOMETIMES THEY MUST BE FORGED.
RETURN HERE WITH YOUR CHOICE. WE'LL NEED TO DOCUMENT YOUR MOUSE AND GRANT THEM FAMILIARITY TO ALL THE PASSAGES.

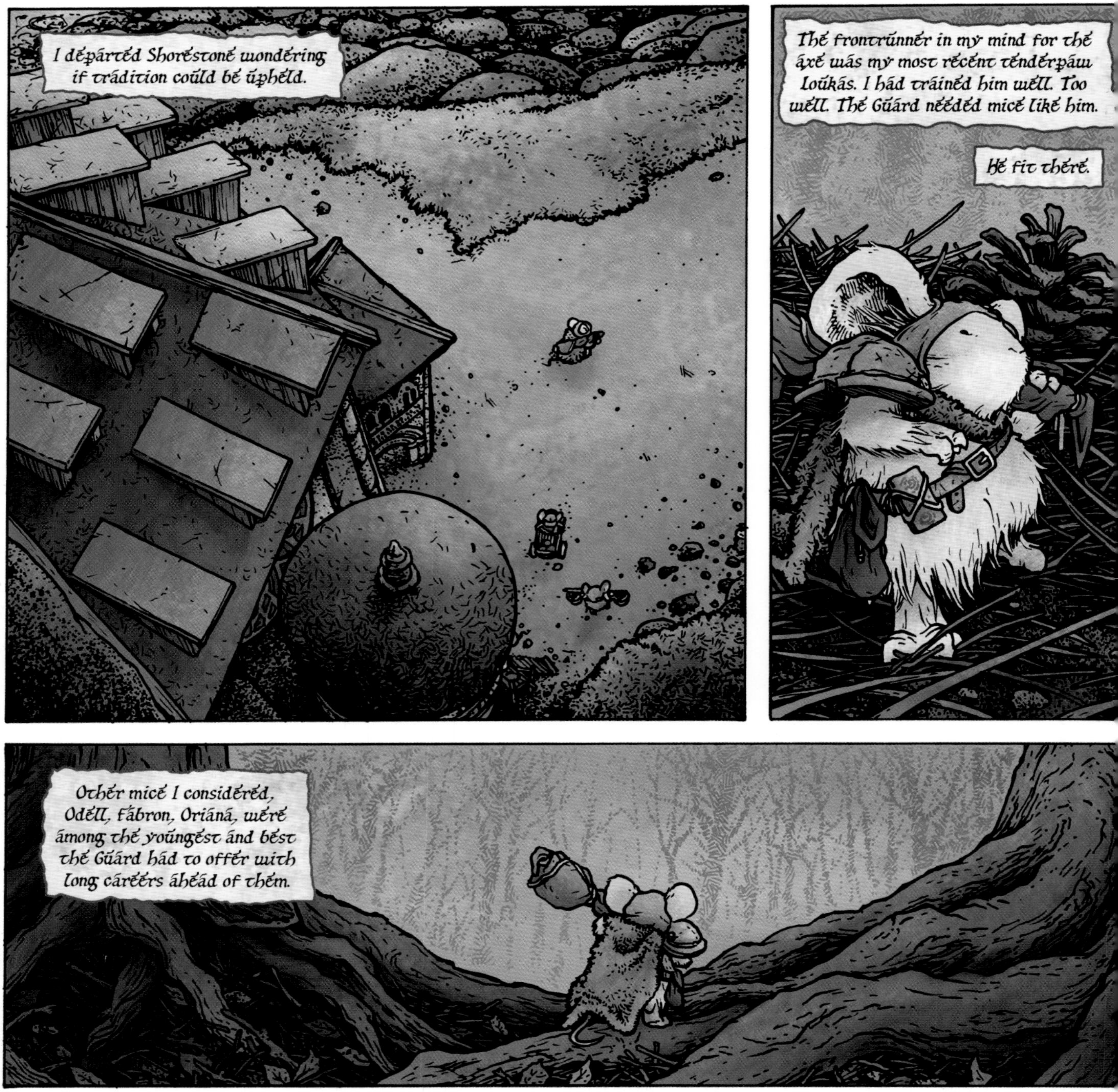
I departed Shorestone wondering if tradition could be upheld.
The frontrunner in my mind for the axe was my most recent tenderpaw Loukas. I had trained him well. Too well. The Guard needed mice like him.
He fit there.
Other mice I considered, Odell, Fabron, Oriana, were among the youngest and best the Guard had to offer with long careers ahead of them.

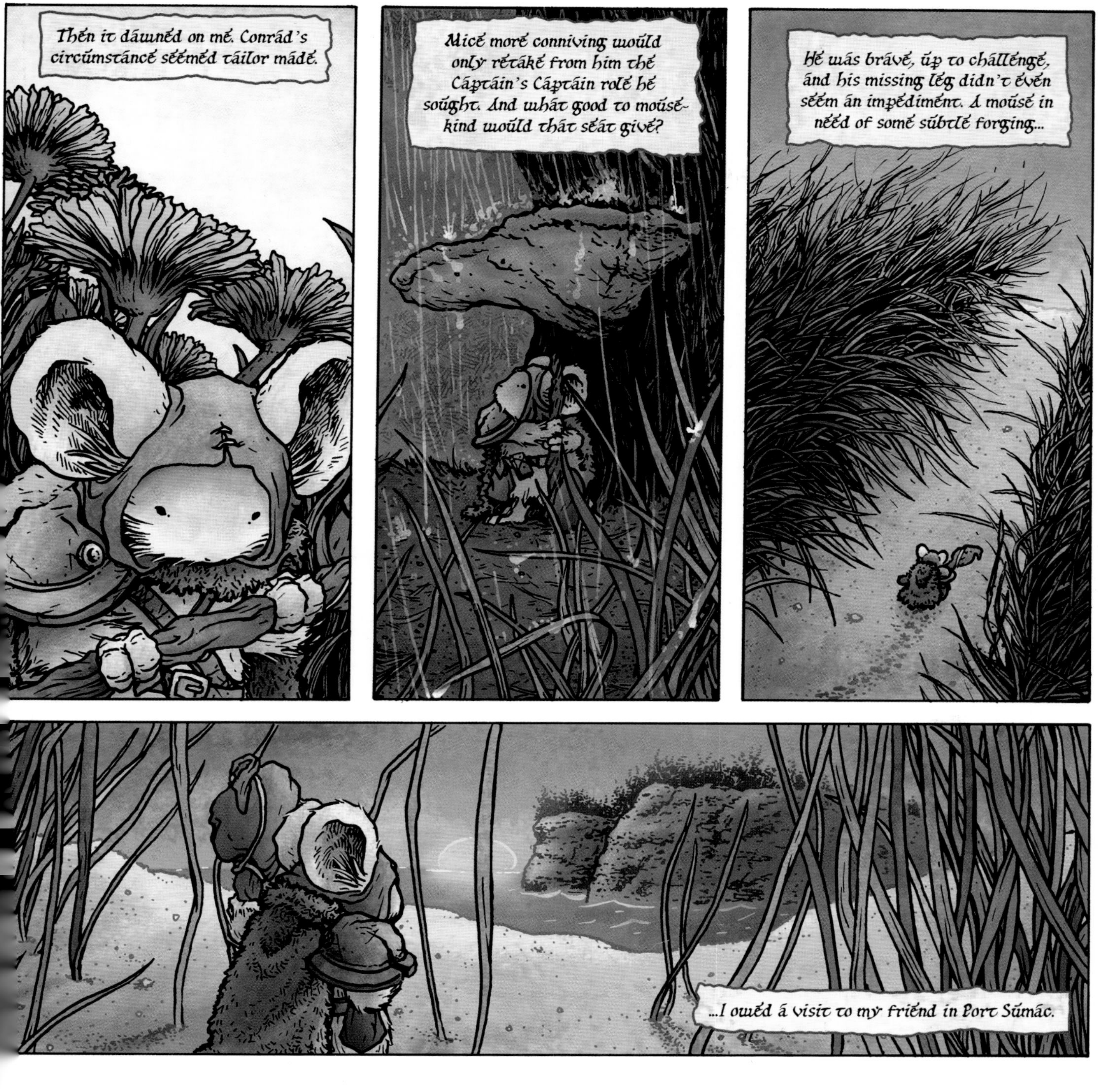

Then it dawned on me. Conrad's circumstance seemed tailor made.
Mice more conniving would only retake from him the Captain's Captain role he sought. And what good to mouse-kind would that seat give?
He was brave, up to challenge, and his missing leg didn't even seem an impediment. A mouse in need of some subtle forging...
...I owed a visit to my friend in Port Sumac.

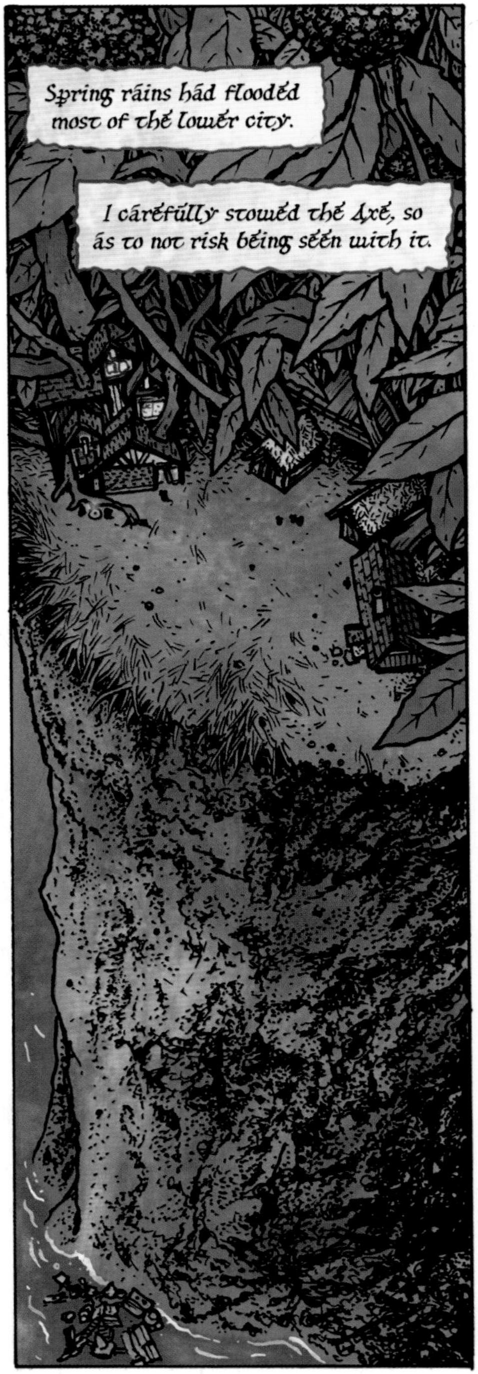
Spring rains had flooded most of the lower city.
I carefully stowed the Axe, so as to not risk being seen with it.

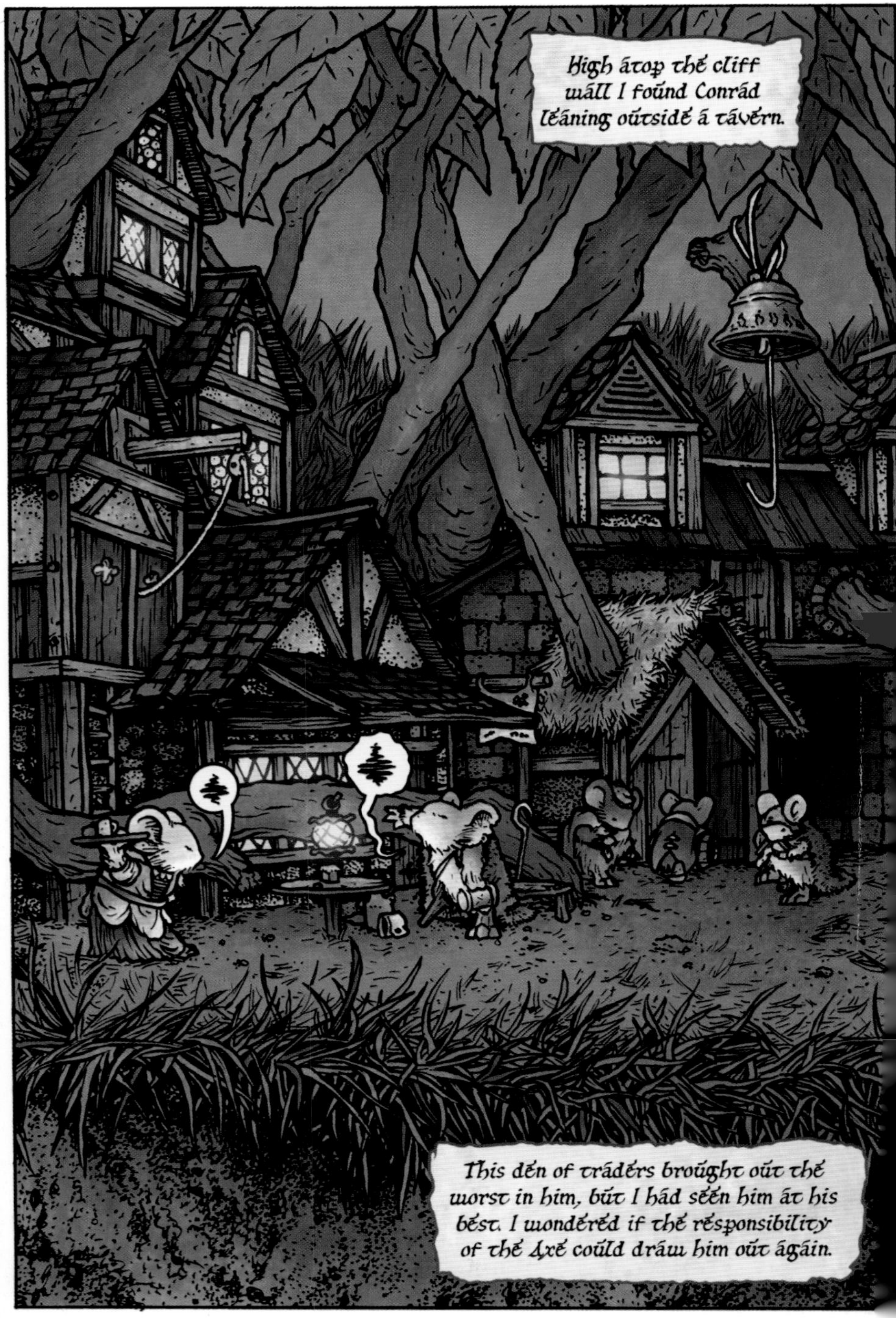
High atop the cliff wall I found Conrad leaning outside a tavern.
This den of traders brought out the worst in him, but I had seen him at his best. I wondered if the responsibility of the Axe could draw him out again.

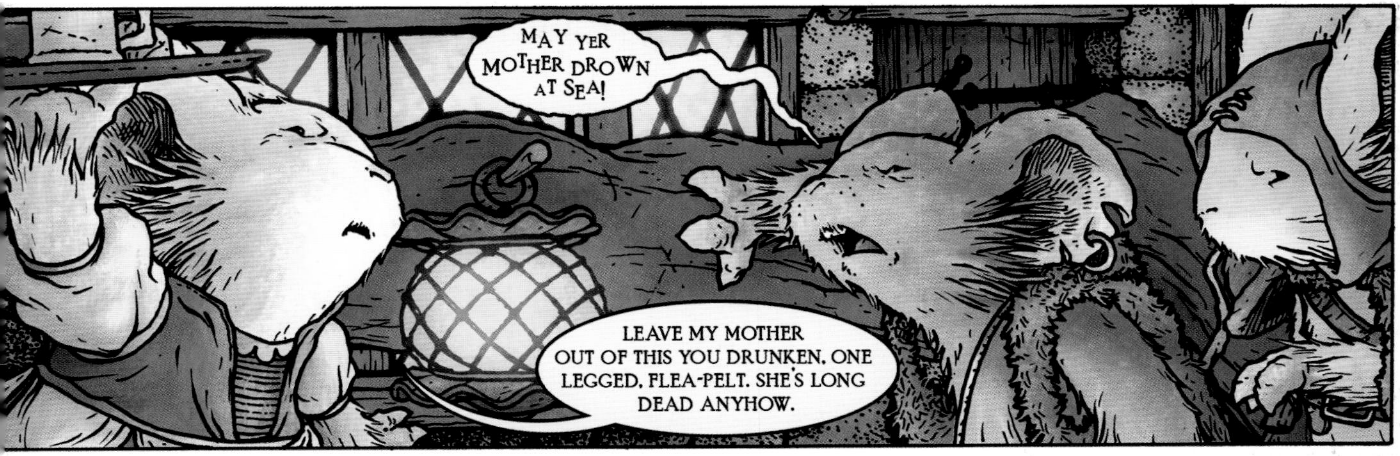

MAY YER MOTHER DROWN AT SEA!
LEAVE MY MOTHER OUT OF THIS YOU DRUNKEN, ONE LEGGED, FLEA-PELT. SHE'S LONG DEAD ANYHOW.

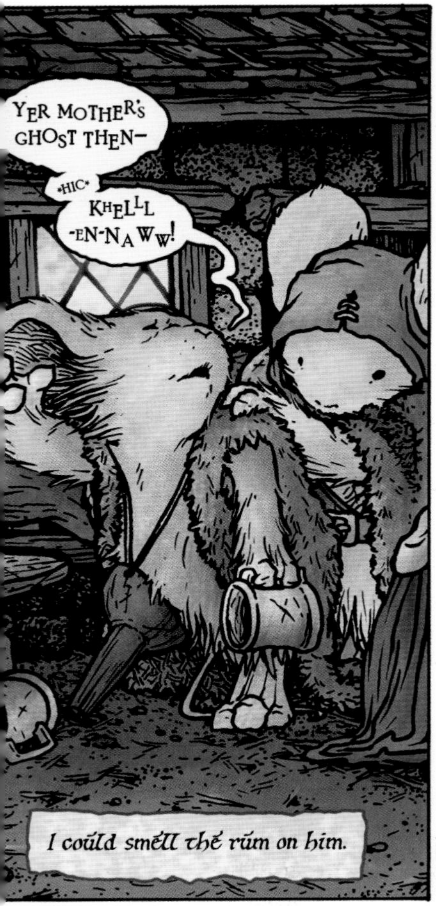

YER MOTHER'S GHOST THEN–
HIC
KHELLL -EN-NAWW!
I could smell the rum on him.

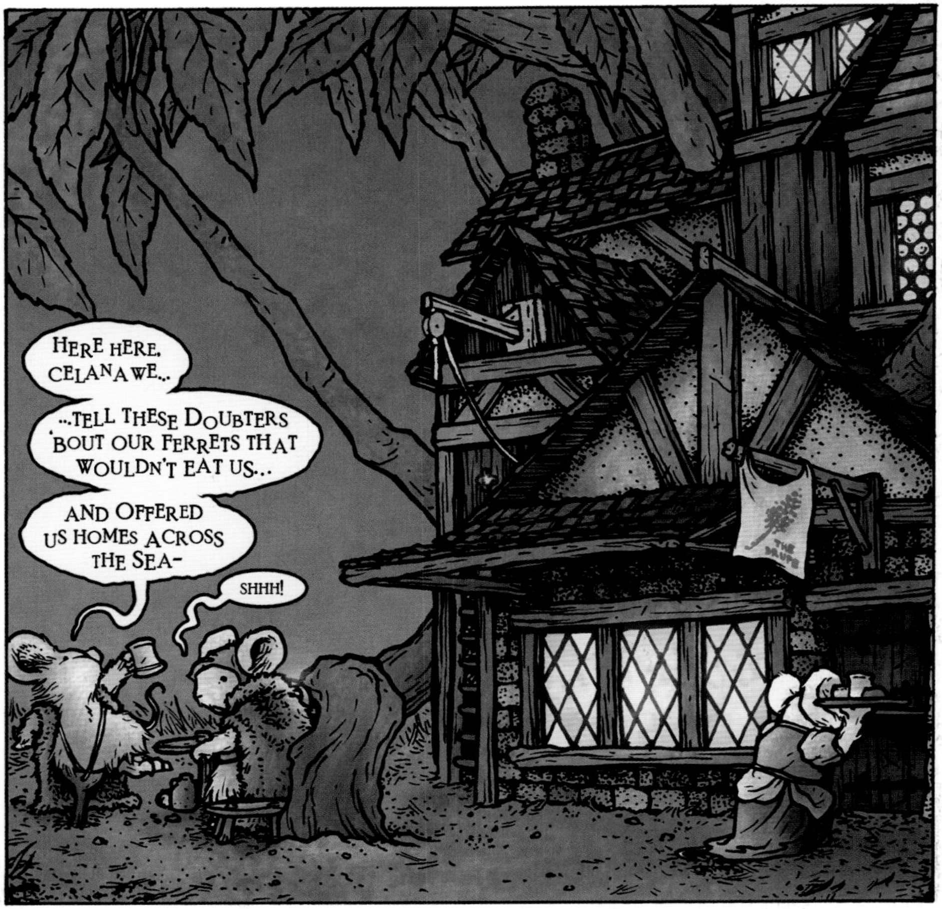

HERE HERE, CELANAWE...
...TELL THESE DOUBTERS 'BOUT OUR FERRETS THAT WOULDN'T EAT US...
AND OFFERED US HOMES ACROSS THE SEA-
SHHH!

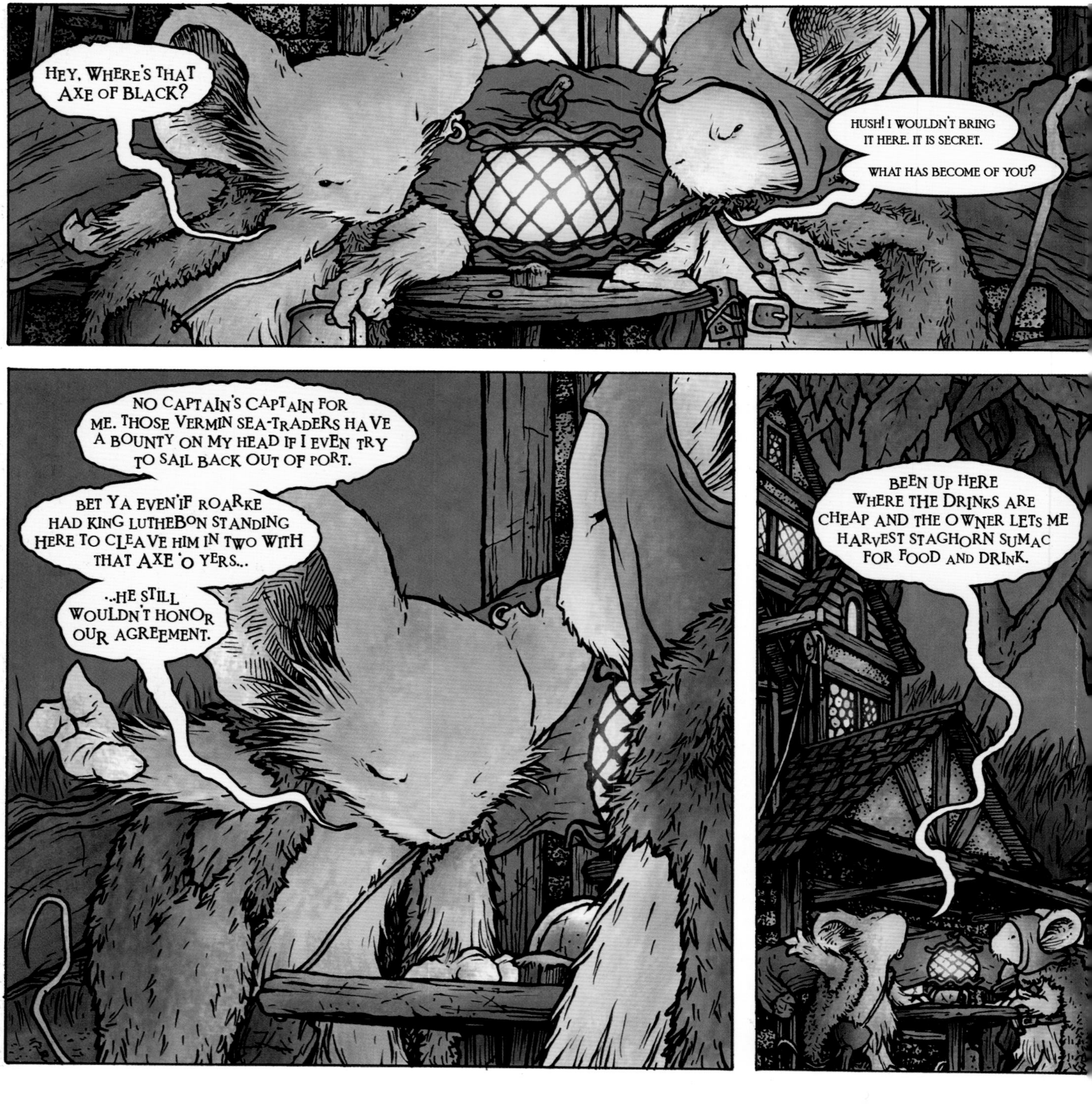
HEY, WHERE'S THAT AXE OF BLACK?
HUSH! I WOULDN'T BRING IT HERE. IT IS SECRET.
WHAT HAS BECOME OF YOU?
NO CAPTAIN'S CAPTAIN FOR ME. THOSE VERMIN SEA-TRADERS HAVE A BOUNTY ON MY HEAD IF I EVEN TRY TO SAIL BACK OUT OF PORT.
BET YA EVEN IF ROARKE HAD KING LUTHEBON STANDING HERE TO CLEAVE HIM IN TWO WITH THAT AXE 'O YERS...
...HE STILL WOULDN'T HONOR OUR AGREEMENT.
BEEN UP HERE WHERE THE DRINKS ARE CHEAP AND THE OWNER LETS ME HARVEST STAGHORN SUMAC FOR FOOD AND DRINK.

MOSTLY DRINK BY THE LOOK OF YOU, CONRAD. YOU ARE A BETTER MOUSE THAN THIS. SOBER UP AND MAKE SOMETHING OF YOUR LIFE.

LOT OF BABBLE FROM THE AXE WIELDER...

...YER THE MOUSE WHAT ROBBED ME OF MY LEG!

YE STOLE A YEAR OF ME LIFE, REDUCED M'FATHER'S SHIP TO SPLINTERS...

...MY LIFE IS WORSE FOR KNOWING YOU.

CONRAD...W—

AND EM'S LIFE IS GONE BECAUSE OF IT.

His eyes had flashed mean under that glaze of drink.

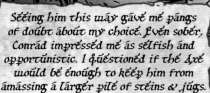

Seeing him this way gave me pangs of doubt about my choice. Even sober, Conrad impressed me as selfish and opportunistic. I questioned if the Axe would be enough to keep him from amassing a larger pile of steins & jugs.

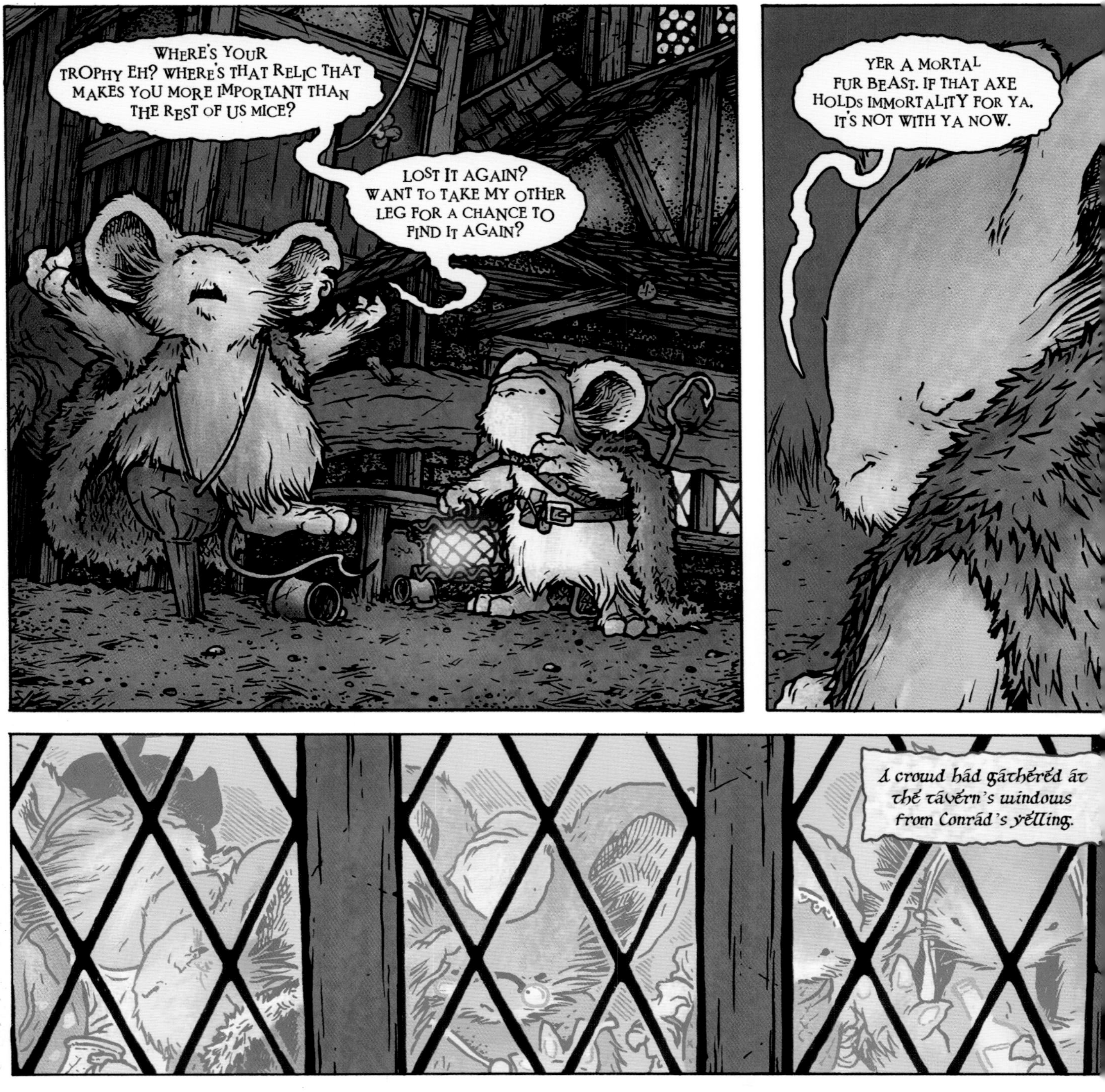
WHERE'S YOUR TROPHY EH? WHERE'S THAT RELIC THAT MAKES YOU MORE IMPORTANT THAN THE REST OF US MICE?
LOST IT AGAIN? WANT TO TAKE MY OTHER LEG FOR A CHANCE TO FIND IT AGAIN?
YER A MORTAL FUR BEAST. IF THAT AXE HOLDS IMMORTALITY FOR YA, IT'S NOT WITH YA NOW.
A crowd had gathered at the tavern's windows from Conrad's yelling.

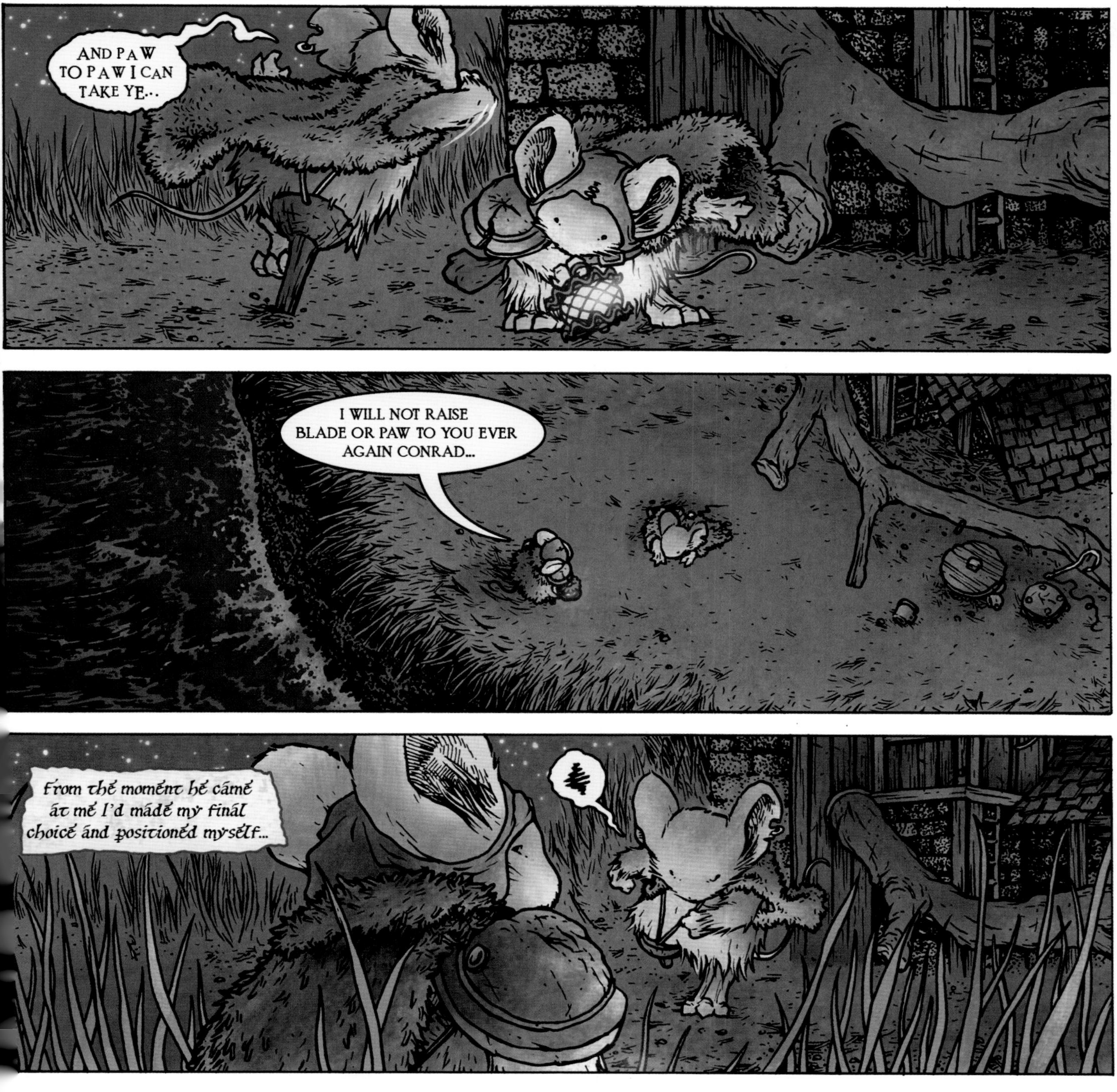
AND PAW TO PAW I CAN TAKE YE...
I WILL NOT RAISE BLADE OR PAW TO YOU EVER AGAIN CONRAD...
From the moment he came at me I'd made my final choice and positioned myself...

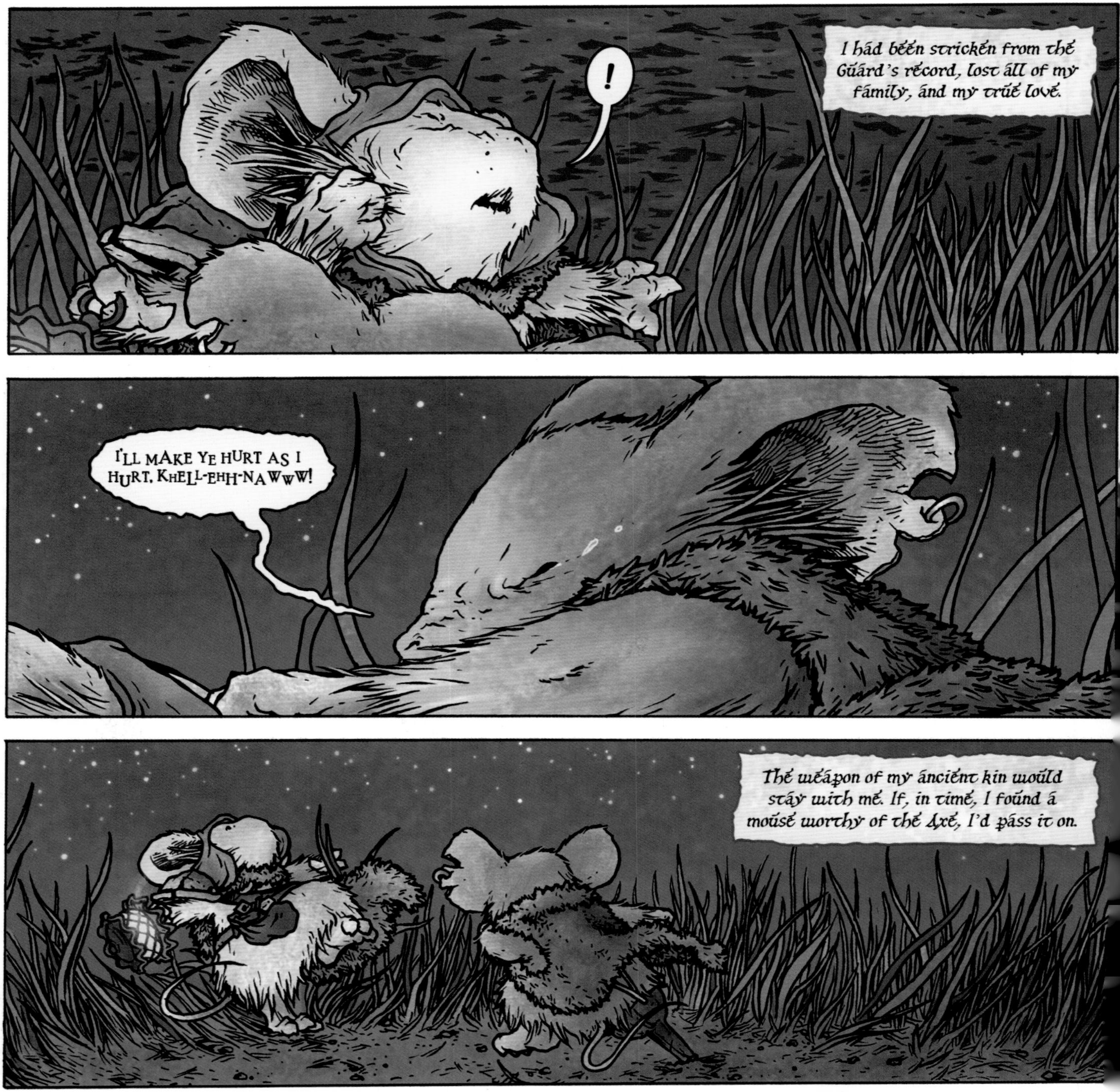
I had been stricken from the Guard's record, lost all of my family, and my true love.
!
I'LL MAKE YE HURT AS I HURT, KHELL-EHH-NAWWW!
The weapon of my ancient kin would stay with me. If, in time, I found a mouse worthy of the Axe, I'd pass it on.

Until then I would shed my name and become the mouse known as the Black Axe.

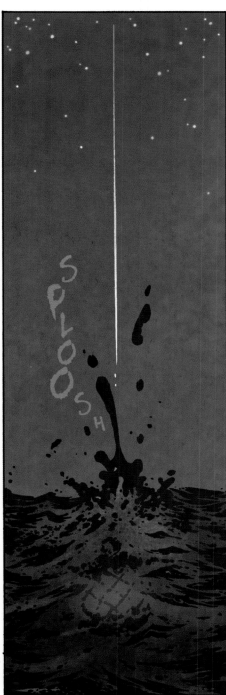

SPLOOSH

Hidden, I'd work outside the structures of guild, guard, or town government for the greater good of all mice.

guard, or town goverment. The greater good of all mice.

Conrad was the last living mouse outside of the haven guild that could connect me to the axe.

he needed to think the same...

"HE NEEDED TO THINK THE SAME AS EVERY OTHER MOUSE, THAT I WAS DEAD."

CELANAWE LEFT THE AXE TO ME.

SOUTH OF LOCKHAVEN
SUMMER 1153

KENZIE. SAXON. YOU ARE THE ONLY TWO MICE I TRUST MY SECRET TO.

I'VE BEEN OFF LIVING ALONE, DOING THE WORK THIS AXE WAS FORGED FOR...

...THE WORK CELANAWE ENTRUSTED ME TO DO.

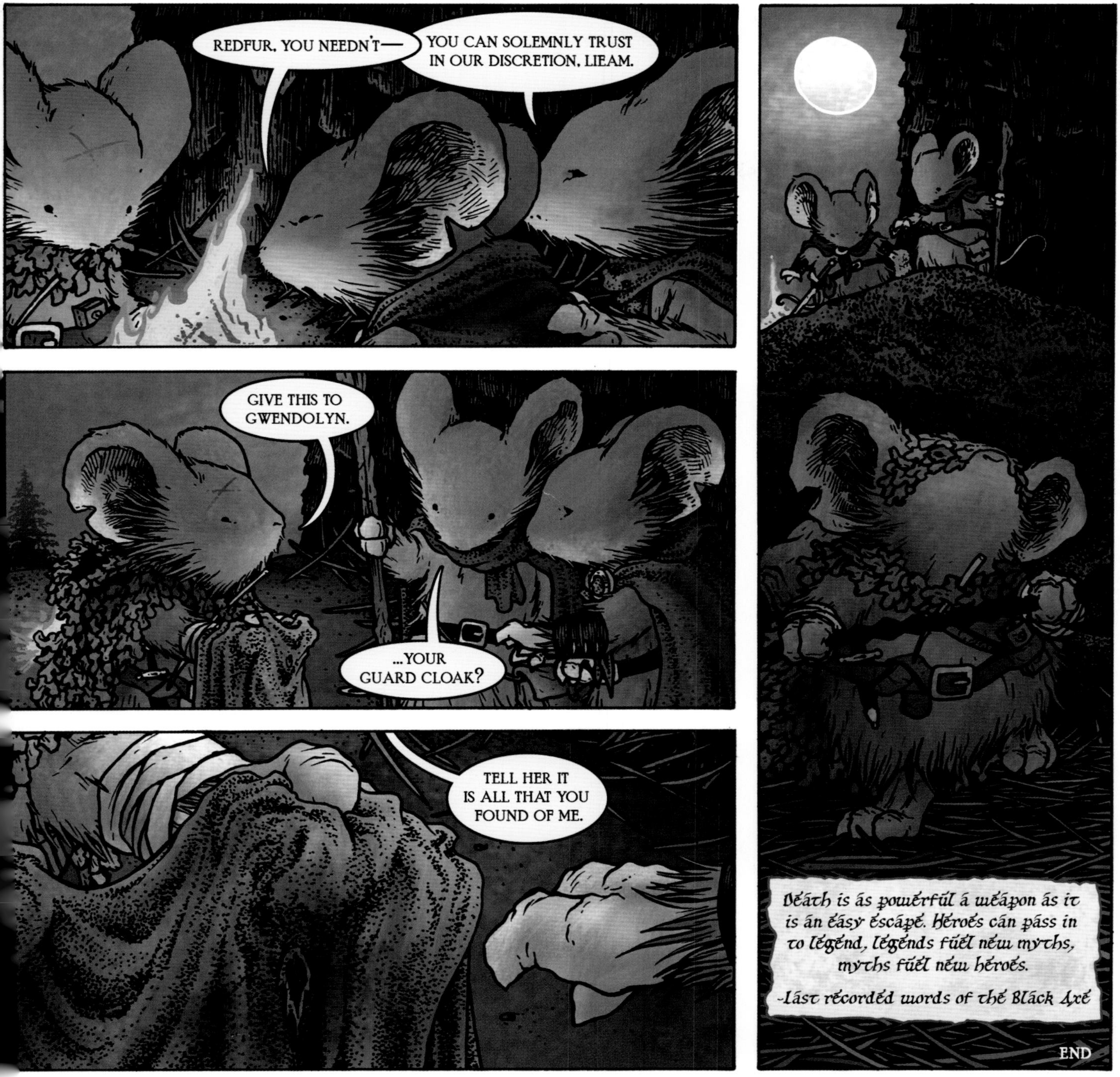
REDFUR, YOU NEEDN'T—
YOU CAN SOLEMNLY TRUST IN OUR DISCRETION, LIEAM.
GIVE THIS TO GWENDOLYN.
...YOUR GUARD CLOAK?
TELL HER IT IS ALL THAT YOU FOUND OF ME.
Death is as powerful a weapon as it is an easy escape. Heroes can pass in to legend, legends fuel new myths, myths fuel new heroes.
-last recorded words of the Black Axe
END

EPILOGUE

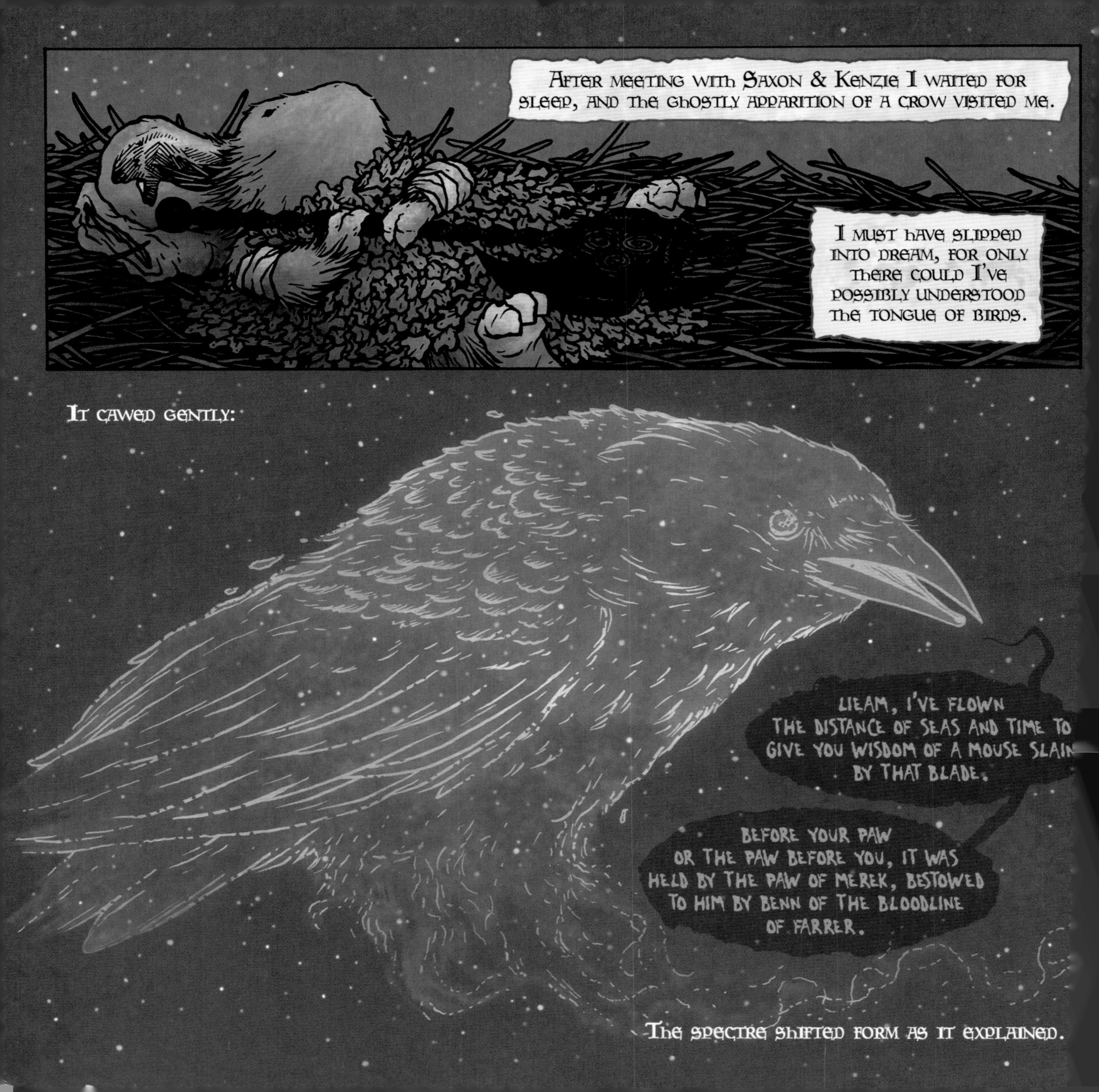
After meeting with Saxon & Kenzie I waited for sleep, and the ghostly apparition of a crow visited me.
I must have slipped into dream, for only there could I've possibly understood the tongue of birds.
It cawed gently:
LIEAM, I'VE FLOWN THE DISTANCE OF SEAS AND TIME TO GIVE YOU WISDOM OF A MOUSE SLAIN BY THAT BLADE.
BEFORE YOUR PAW OR THE PAW BEFORE YOU, IT WAS HELD BY THE PAW OF MEREK, BESTOWED TO HIM BY BENN OF THE BLOODLINE OF FARRER.
The spectre shifted form as it explained.

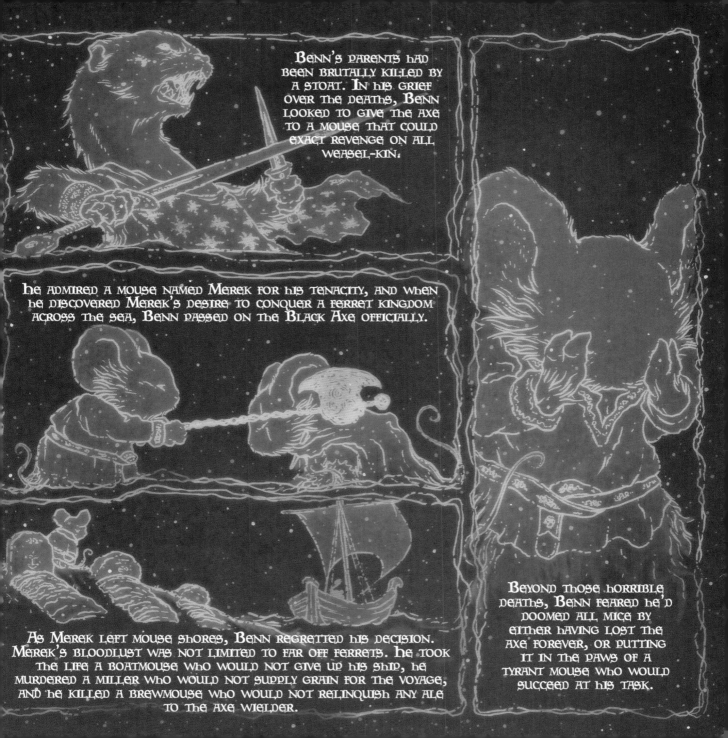

BENN'S PARENTS HAD BEEN BRUTALLY KILLED BY A STOAT. IN HIS GRIEF OVER THE DEATHS, BENN LOOKED TO GIVE THE AXE TO A MOUSE THAT COULD EXACT REVENGE ON ALL WEASEL-KIN.

HE ADMIRED A MOUSE NAMED MEREK FOR HIS TENACITY, AND WHEN HE DISCOVERED MEREK'S DESIRE TO CONQUER A FERRET KINGDOM ACROSS THE SEA, BENN PASSED ON THE BLACK AXE OFFICIALLY.

AS MEREK LEFT MOUSE SHORES, BENN REGRETTED HIS DECISION. MEREK'S BLOODLUST WAS NOT LIMITED TO FAR OFF FERRETS. HE TOOK THE LIFE A BOATMOUSE WHO WOULD NOT GIVE UP HIS SHIP, HE MURDERED A MILLER WHO WOULD NOT SUPPLY GRAIN FOR THE VOYAGE, AND HE KILLED A BREWMOUSE WHO WOULD NOT RELINQUISH ANY ALE TO THE AXE WIELDER.

BEYOND THOSE HORRIBLE DEATHS, BENN FEARED HE'D DOOMED ALL MICE BY EITHER HAVING LOST THE AXE FOREVER, OR PUTTING IT IN THE PAWS OF A TYRANT MOUSE WHO WOULD SUCCEED AT HIS TASK.

FEELING A BLOOD TIE TO GUIDE THE AXE, BENN ARRANGED BIRD TRANSPORT ACROSS THE STORVAND SEA WHERE HE MET MEREK ON THE SHORES OF THE DISTANT LAND.

OOHG HROOO ÆHR.

KROU GRAAHHGH HAR

ARHH KWOUUGH URK

MEREK HAD BEEN SPEAKING IN THE TONGUE OF BEASTS BUILDING UP THE INHABITANTS' FEAR ABOUT HIS PLANNED SLAUGHTER OF THE FERRET KING AND ALL HIS SUBJECTS.

WITH TEARS IN HIS EYES BENN PLEADED WITH MEREK TO CEASE. HE SPOKE WITH COMPASSION AND ELOQUENCE ABOUT THE COST OF MOUSE LIFE AND THE SENSELESSNESS OF MEREK'S PLAN.

BUT MEREK WAS UNYIELDING AND SAW BENN AS ONLY ONE MORE BARRIER TO A GLORIOUS KINGDOM OF MOUSE PROSPERITY HE AND THE AXE COULD CARVE. SCOLDING BENN FOR PREVENTING THE DEATHS OF THE KIN OF HIS PARENT'S MURDERERS, MEREK MURDERED BENN RIGHT THERE ON THAT DISTANT ROCKY WATER'S EDGE.

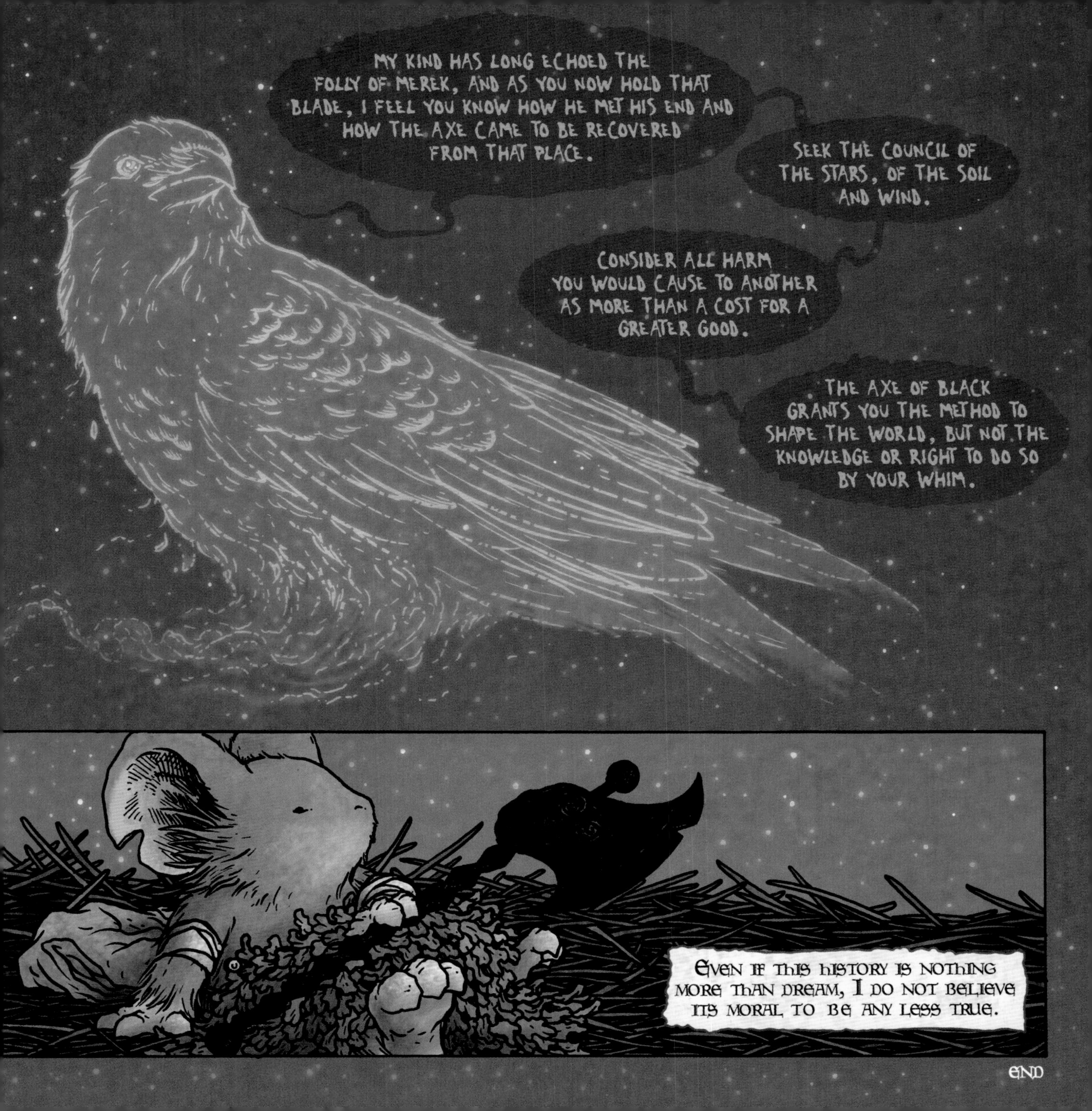
MY KIND HAS LONG ECHOED THE FOLLY OF MEREK, AND AS YOU NOW HOLD THAT BLADE, I FEEL YOU KNOW HOW HE MET HIS END AND HOW THE AXE CAME TO BE RECOVERED FROM THAT PLACE.
SEEK THE COUNCIL OF THE STARS, OF THE SOIL AND WIND.
CONSIDER ALL HARM YOU WOULD CAUSE TO ANOTHER AS MORE THAN A COST FOR A GREATER GOOD.
THE AXE OF BLACK GRANTS YOU THE METHOD TO SHAPE THE WORLD, BUT NOT THE KNOWLEDGE OR RIGHT TO DO SO BY YOUR WHIM.
EVEN IF THIS HISTORY IS NOTHING MORE THAN DREAM, I DO NOT BELIEVE ITS MORAL TO BE ANY LESS TRUE.
END

MAPS,
GUIDES, AND
ASSORTED
EXTRAS

the **North Sea**

Dawnrock

Whitepine

Thistledown

Wildseed

Elmwood

Shaleburgh

Lockhaven

Ironwood

Barkstone

Ivydale

Blackrock

Woodruff's Grove

Elmmoss

Ferndale

Copperwood

Rooty

Sprucetuck

Shore

Darkheather

Walnutpeck

Dorigift

Applelofte

Gilpledge

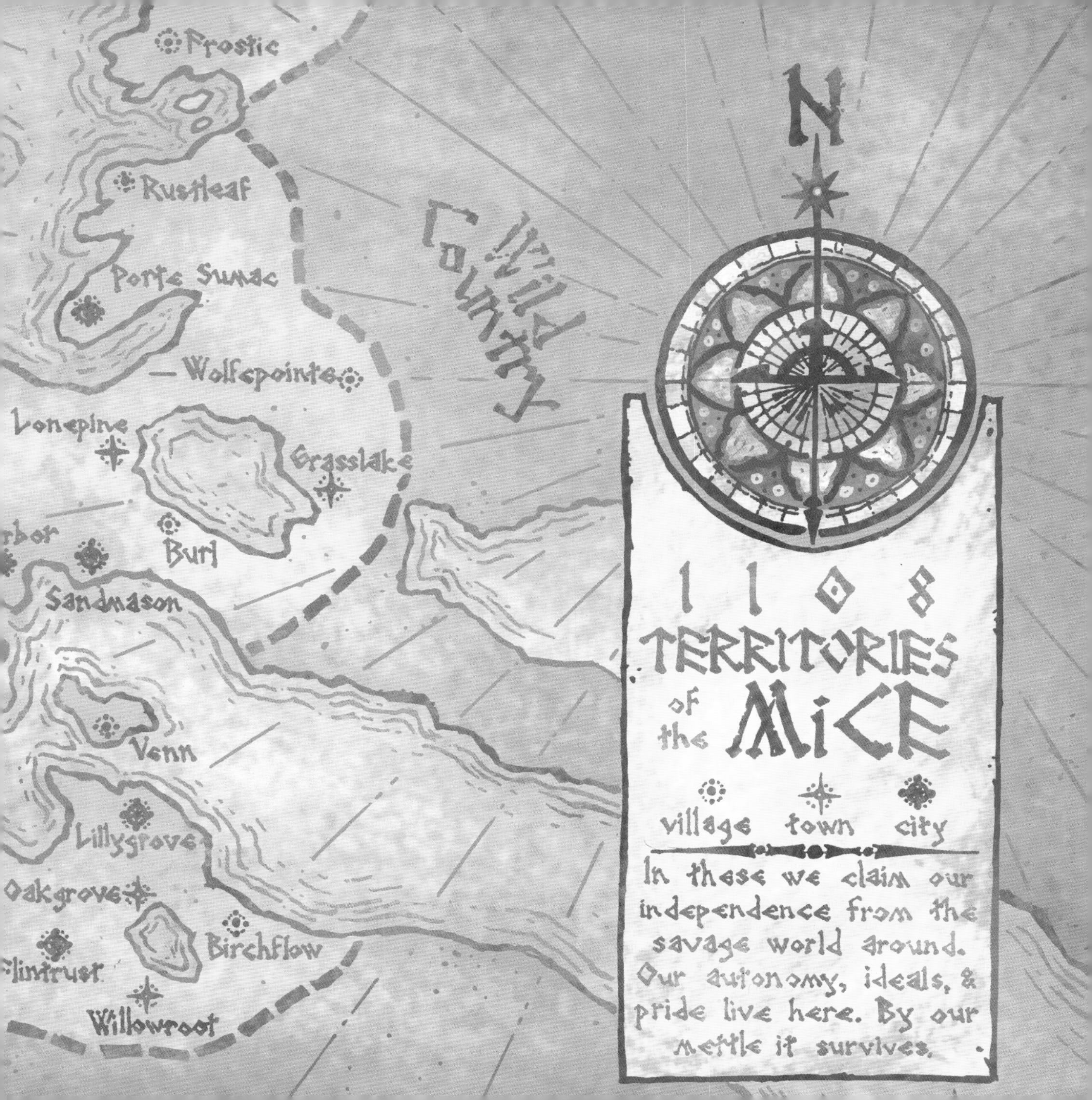
Frostic
Rustleaf
Porte Sumac
Wolfepointe
Wild Country
N
Lonepine
Grasslake
rbor
Burl
Sandmason
Venn
Lillygrove
Oakgrove
Birchflow
Flintrust
Willowroot
1 1 0 8
TERRITORIES of the MICE
village town city
In these we claim our independence from the savage world around. Our autonomy, ideals, & pride live here. By our mettle it survives.

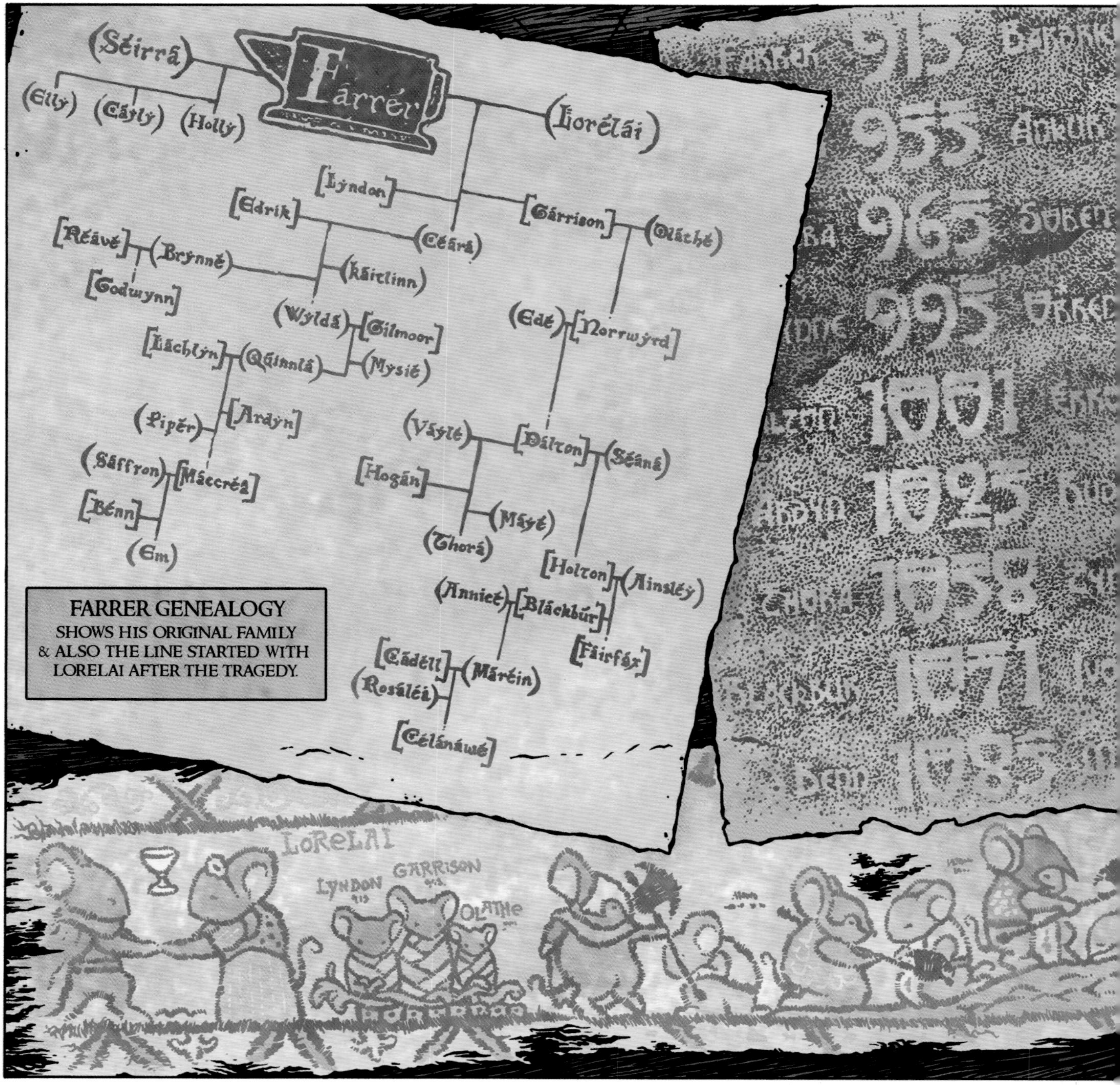
Seirra
Elly
Catly
Holly
Farrer
Lorelai
Lyndon
Edrik
Garrison
Ceara
Olathe
Reave
Brynne
Kaitlinn
Godwynn
Wylda
Gilmoor
Ede
Norrwyrd
Lachlyn
Quinnla
Mysie
Piper
Ardyn
Vayle
Dalton
Seana
Saffron
Maccrea
Hogan
Benn
Maye
Em
Thora
Holton
Ainsley
Anniet
Blackbur
Fairfax
Cadell
Marcin
Rosalea
Celanawe
955
965
1001
1025
LORELAI
LYNDON
GARRISON
OLATHE

FARRER GENEALOGY
SHOWS HIS ORIGINAL FAMILY
& ALSO THE LINE STARTED WITH
LORELAI AFTER THE TRAGEDY.

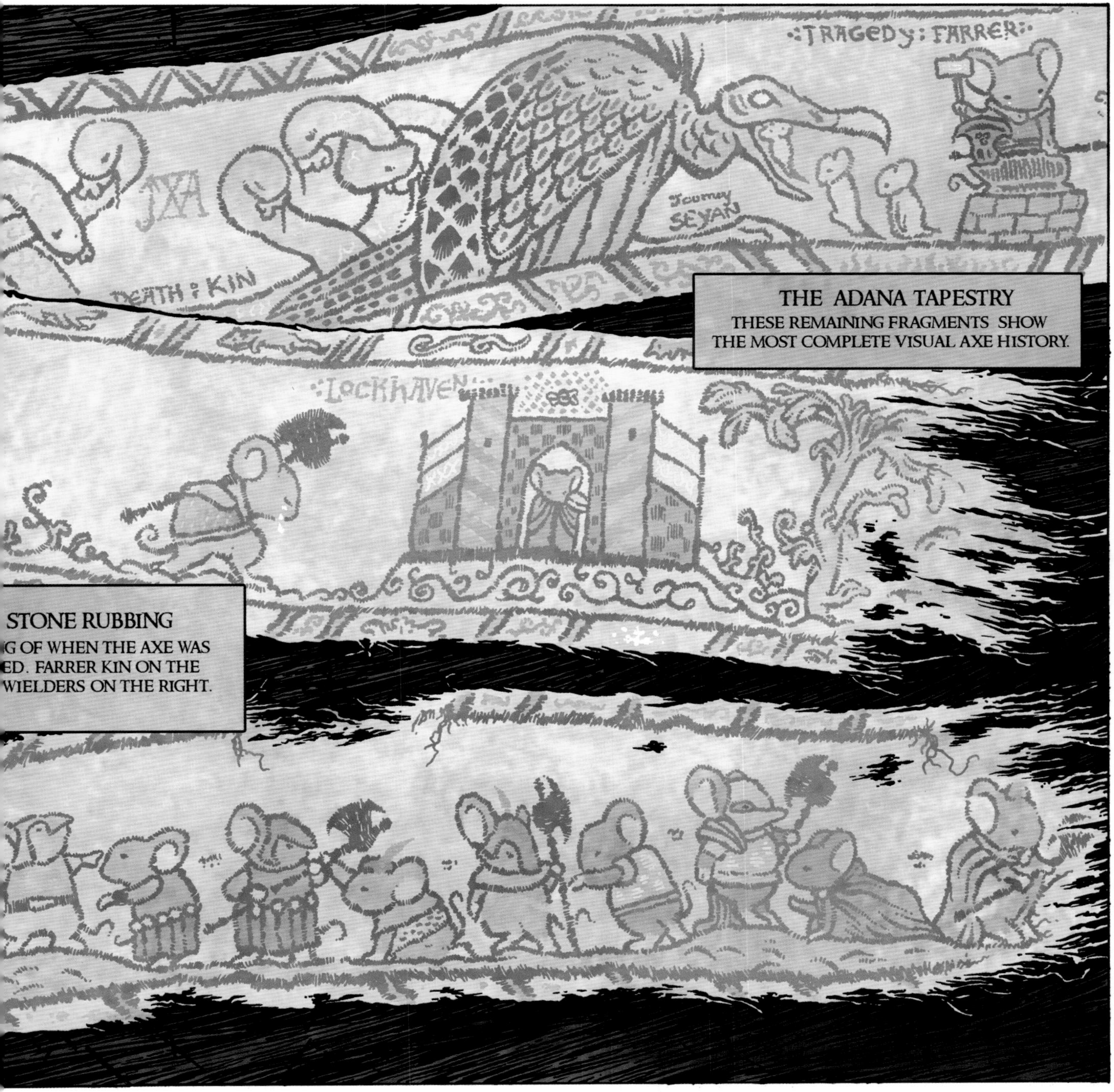

:TRAGEDY: FARRER:
DEATH : KIN
SEYAN
THE ADANA TAPESTRY
THESE REMAINING FRAGMENTS SHOW THE MOST COMPLETE VISUAL AXE HISTORY.
:LOCKHAVEN:
STONE RUBBING
G OF WHEN THE AXE WAS
ED. FARRER KIN ON THE
WIELDERS ON THE RIGHT.

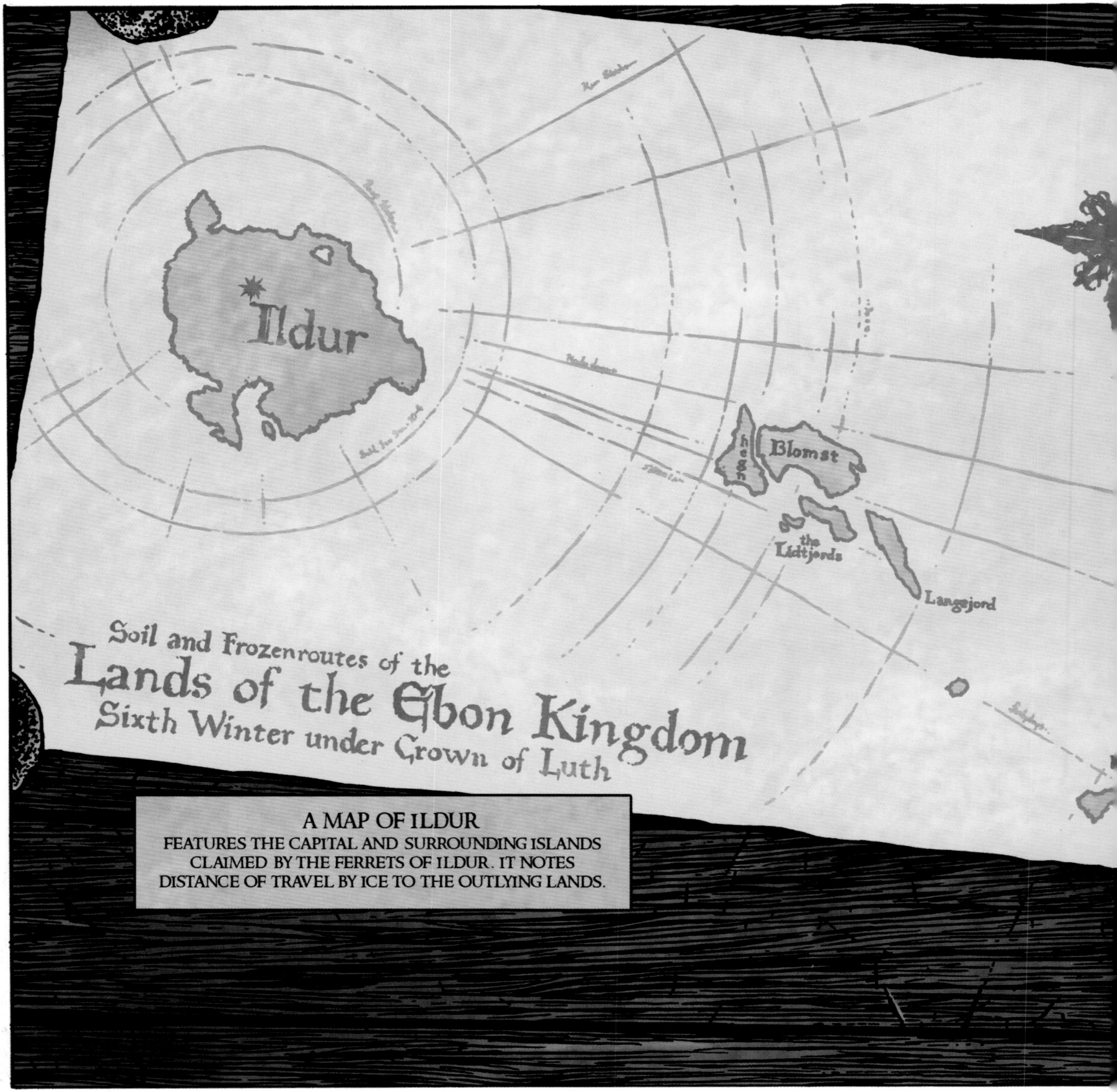
Ildur
hegn
Blomst
the Lidtjords
Langejord
Soil and Frozenroutes of the
Lands of the Ebon Kingdom
Sixth Winter under Crown of Luth

A MAP OF ILDUR
FEATURES THE CAPITAL AND SURROUNDING ISLANDS CLAIMED BY THE FERRETS OF ILDUR. IT NOTES DISTANCE OF TRAVEL BY ICE TO THE OUTLYING LANDS.

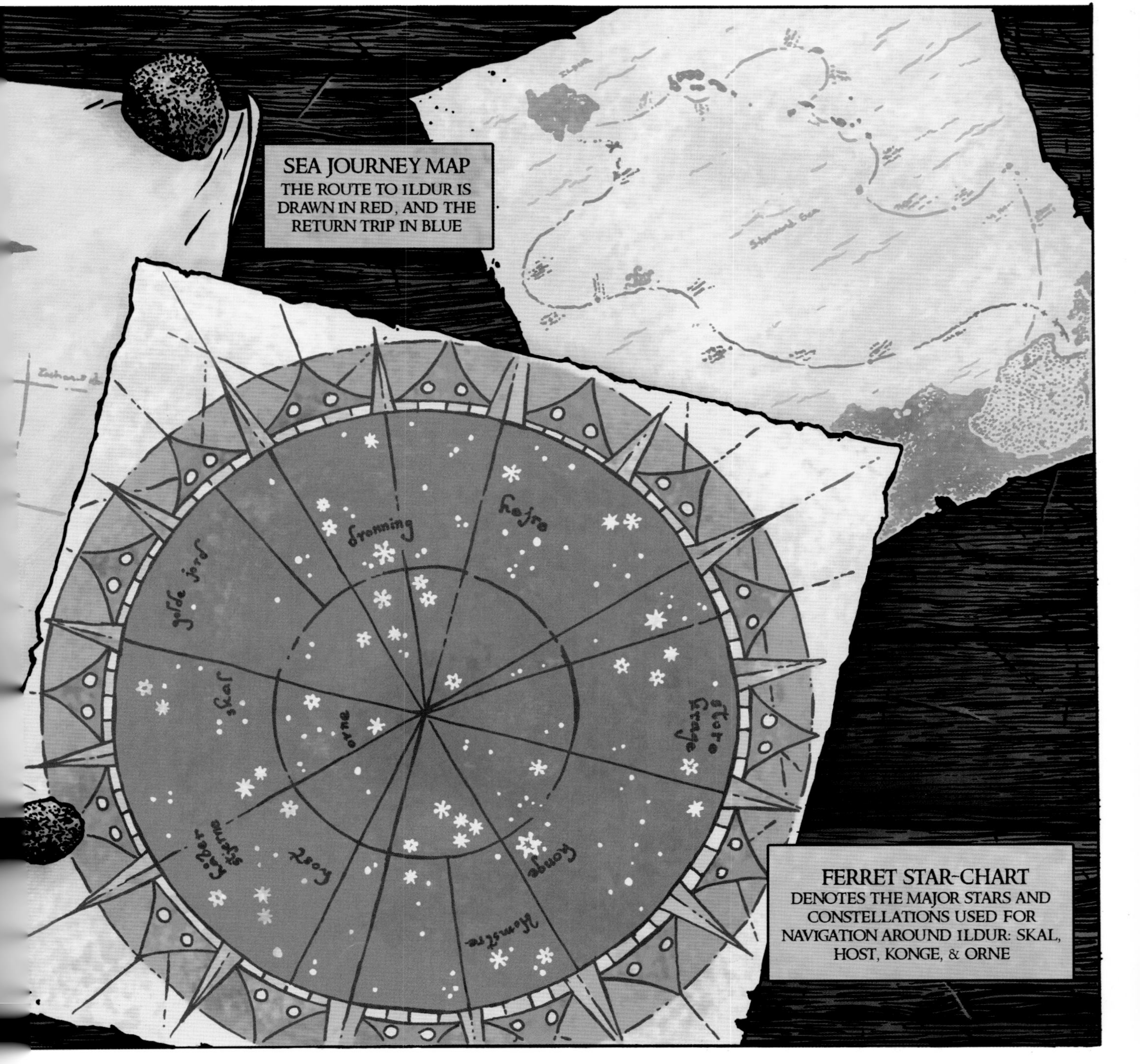
SEA JOURNEY MAP
THE ROUTE TO ILDUR IS DRAWN IN RED, AND THE RETURN TRIP IN BLUE
dronning
hejre
gylde jord
skal
orne
store grage
host
konge
FERRET STAR-CHART
DENOTES THE MAJOR STARS AND CONSTELLATIONS USED FOR NAVIGATION AROUND ILDUR: SKAL, HOST, KONGE, & ORNE

THE RED SNAPPER

Was originally built in 1101 for Conrad's father Strom by the Darkwater boat builders Kelton & Son. The ship has a large storage hold under the main deck. The sheet ropes, used to contol the tautness of the sail, as well as the tiller ropes are all tied down and accessible by a single mouse under the aft deck. Strom sailed the Snapper from Port Sumac to the waterfront towns of the Territories transporting cloth, ale, and pottery.

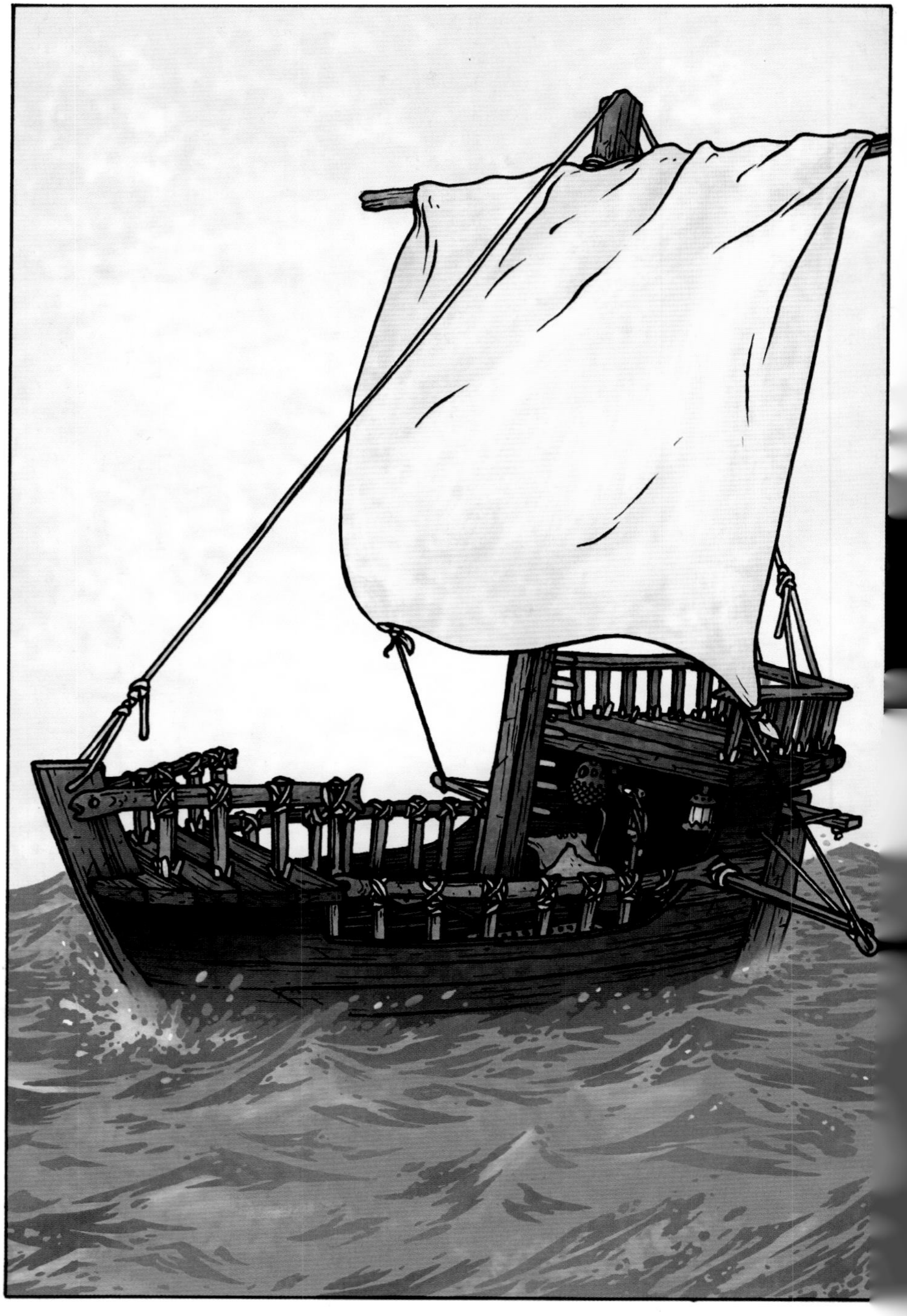

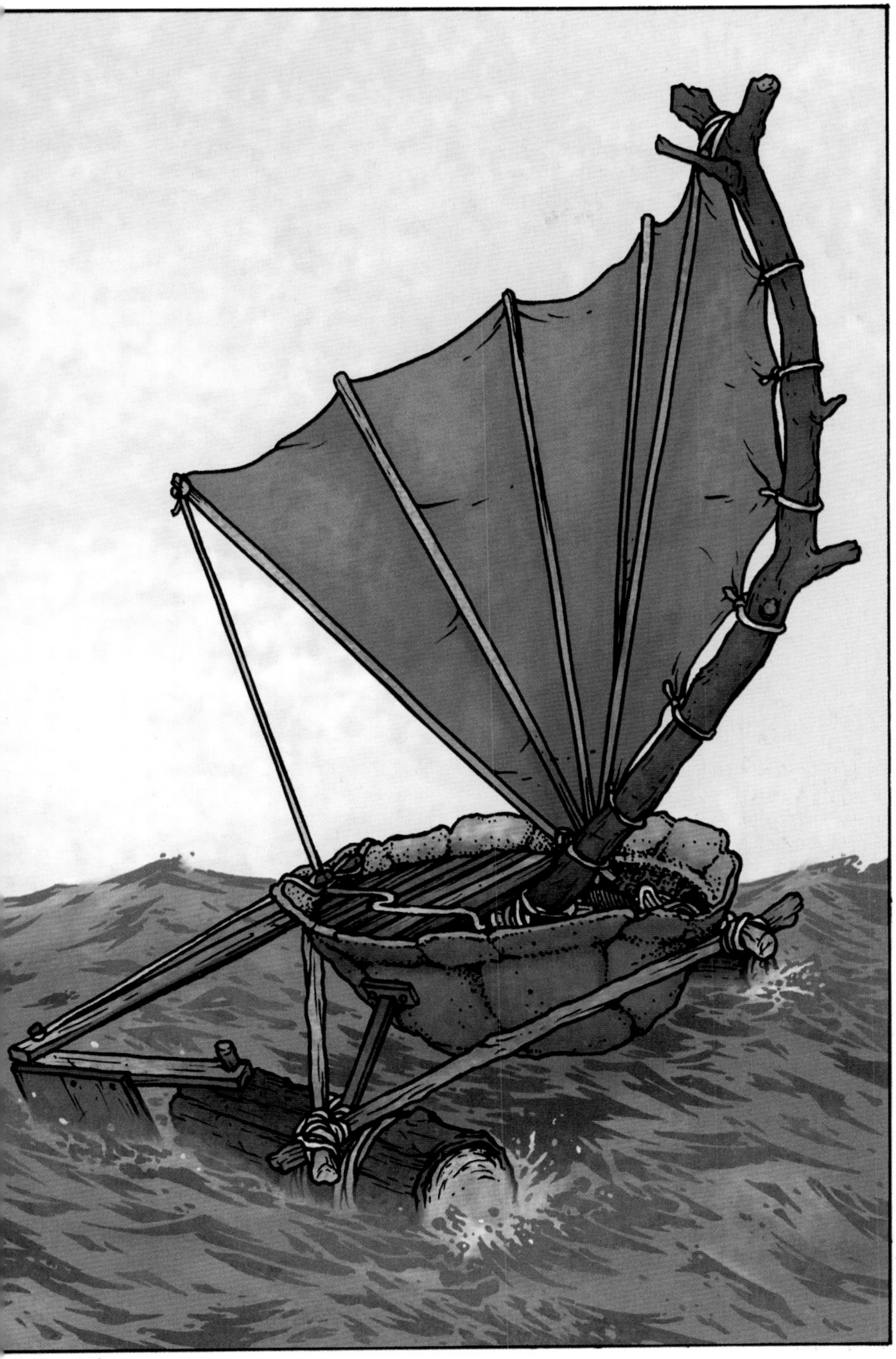

A Ship of Shell & Timber Scrap

Built in twenty days from scavenged materials, this ship was crafted by the ferrets of Ildur after the Red Snapper was destroyed. Outrigged timbers provide bouyancy for the turtle shell hull. Fewer provisions could be stored here than on their previous vessel, but the route Conrad & Celanawe, returned home by offered more stops to hunt for provisions.

ILDUR HALL

Atop the highest hill on the Isle of Ildur stands the entrance to Ildur Hall, the chief dwelling of ferret kingdom there. The main hall sits just below the grass, but buried below the hall is a network of tunnels & chambers used by the ferrets for storage, metal-smithing, and private residence. A central firepit in the hall provides warmth & a cookery for the celebratory feasts the ferrets prepare after any successful hunt.

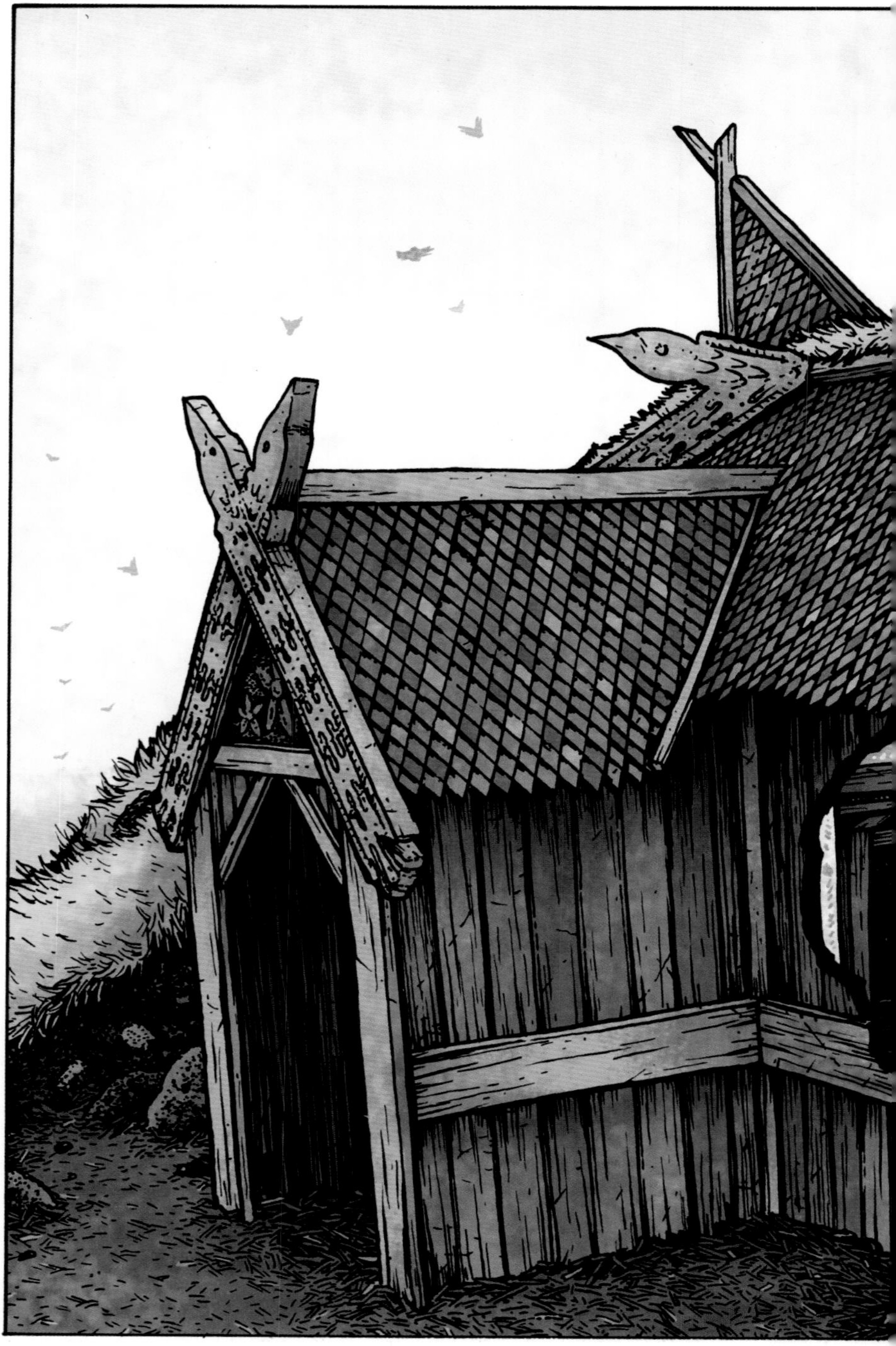

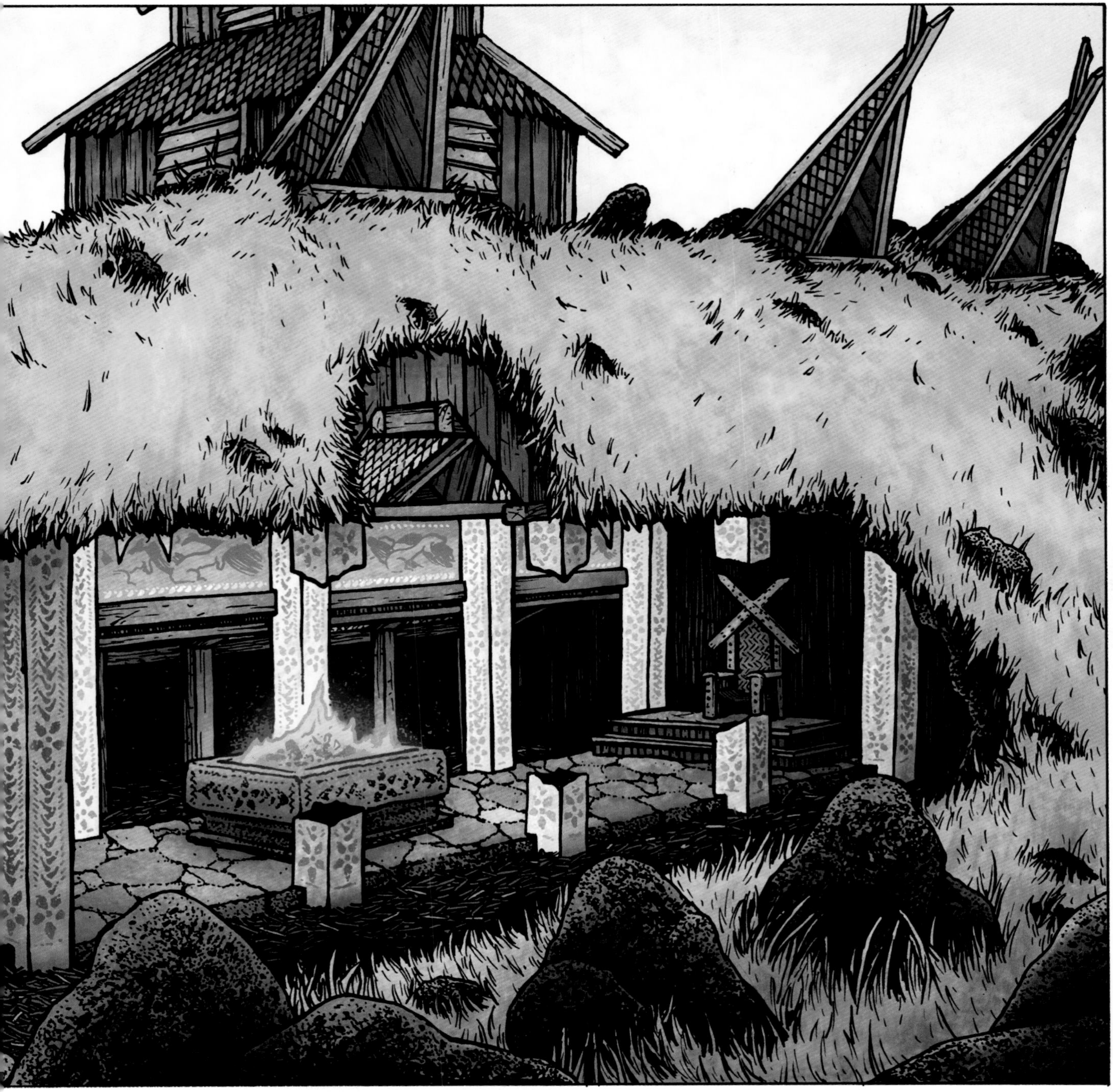

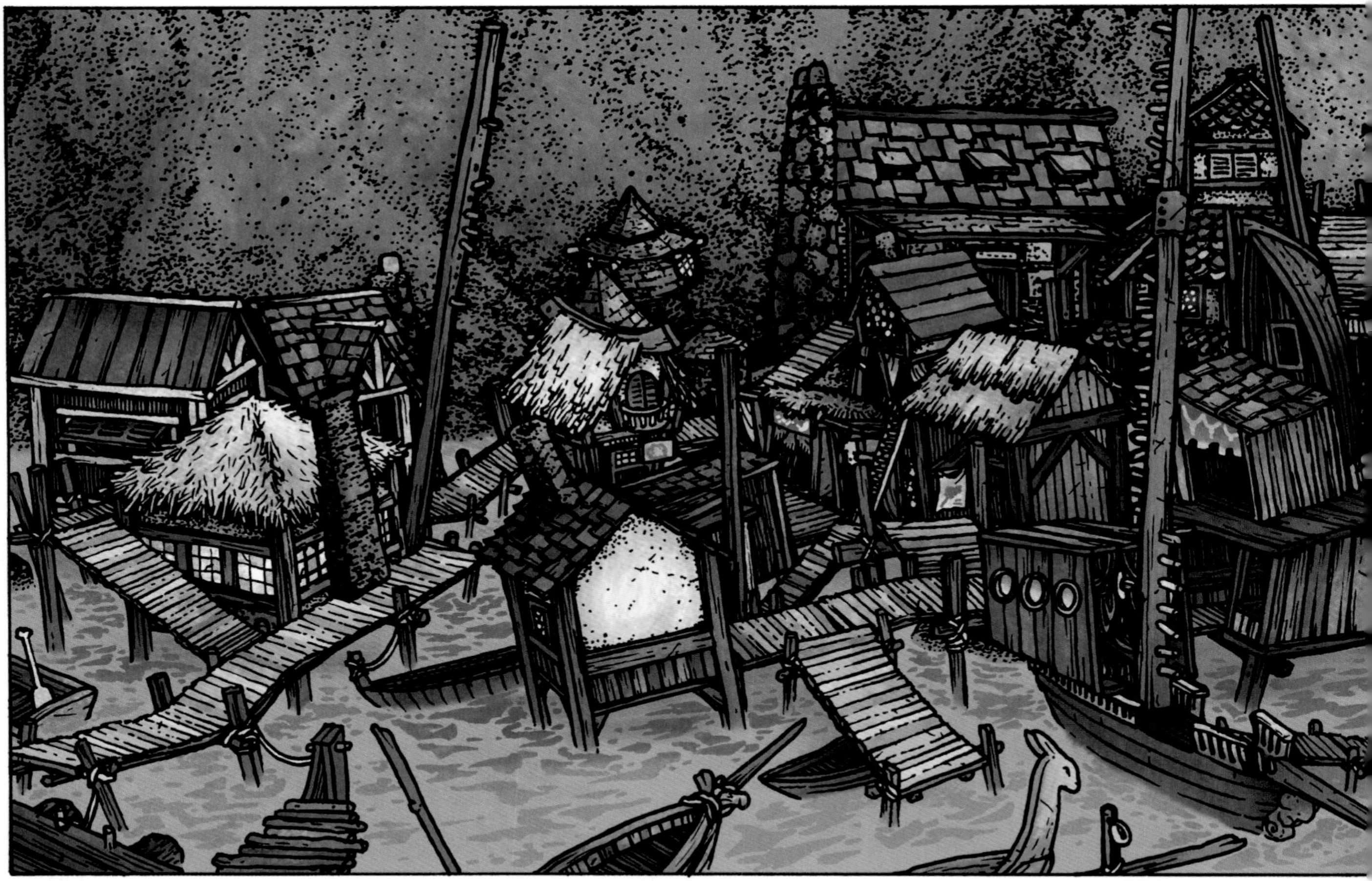

LOWER PORT SUMAC:

This shipping and trading town is lashed together out of wrecked and moored ships, stilted dwellings made of scrap, and docks linking them all together. It is governed by a council of ship captains, the most profitable of the previous season holds the chair of "Captain's Captain." Boatcraft is a profitable trade in the port, as is dealing in cloth, ale, dyes, rope, or grain.

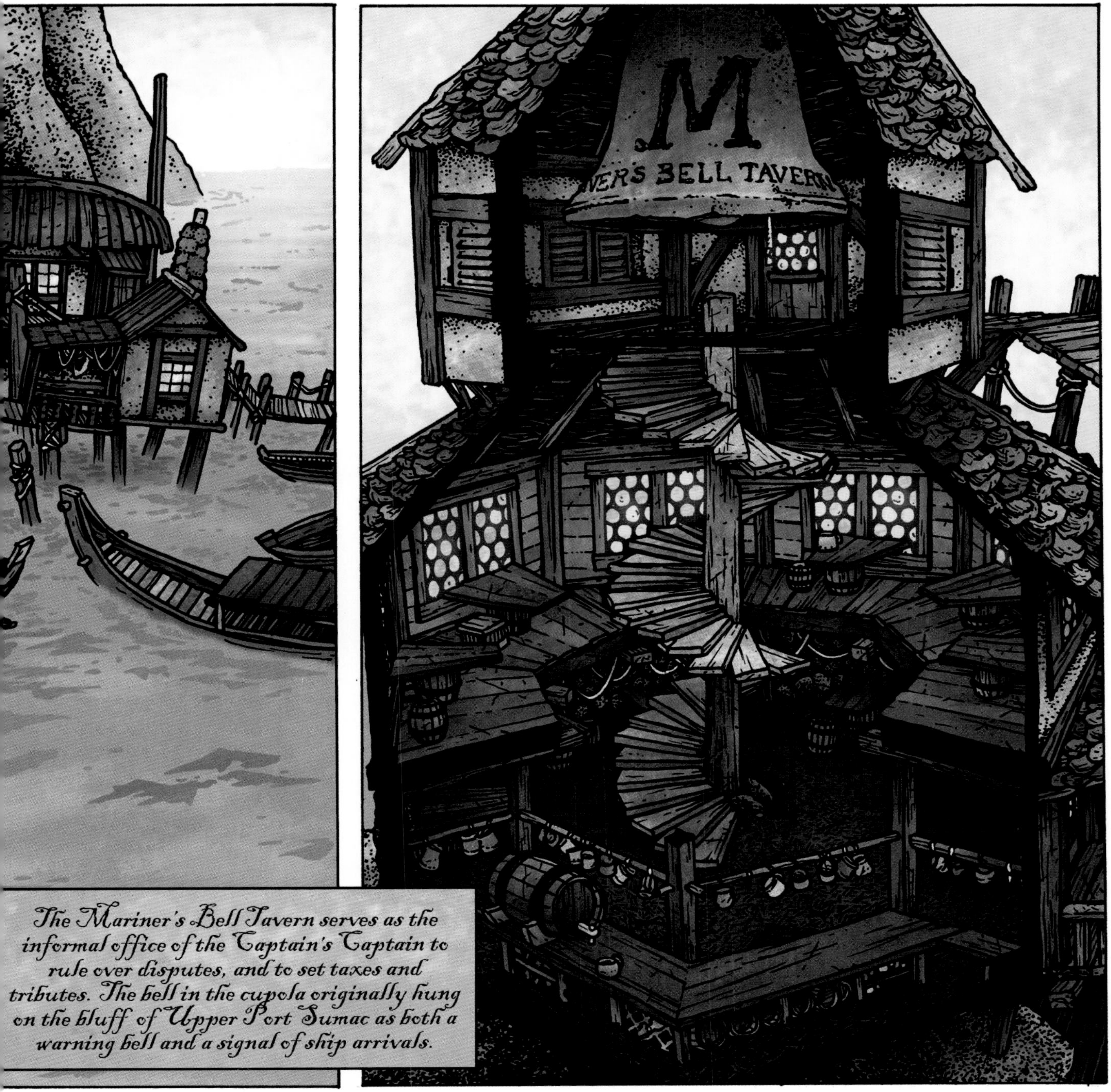
The Mariner's Bell Tavern serves as the informal office of the Captain's Captain to rule over disputes, and to set taxes and tributes. The bell in the cupola originally hung on the bluff of Upper Port Sumac as both a warning bell and a signal of ship arrivals.

UPPER PORT SUMAC:

On the cliff overlooking Lower Port Sumac only three of the upper city's buildings are visible. Most of the residents live beyond the main gates in underground homes. The canopy of Staghorn Sumac provides shelter and the source of the key ingredient in their prized Rhus Ale. Harvesters scale the branches while listening for the city's bell warning of predators.

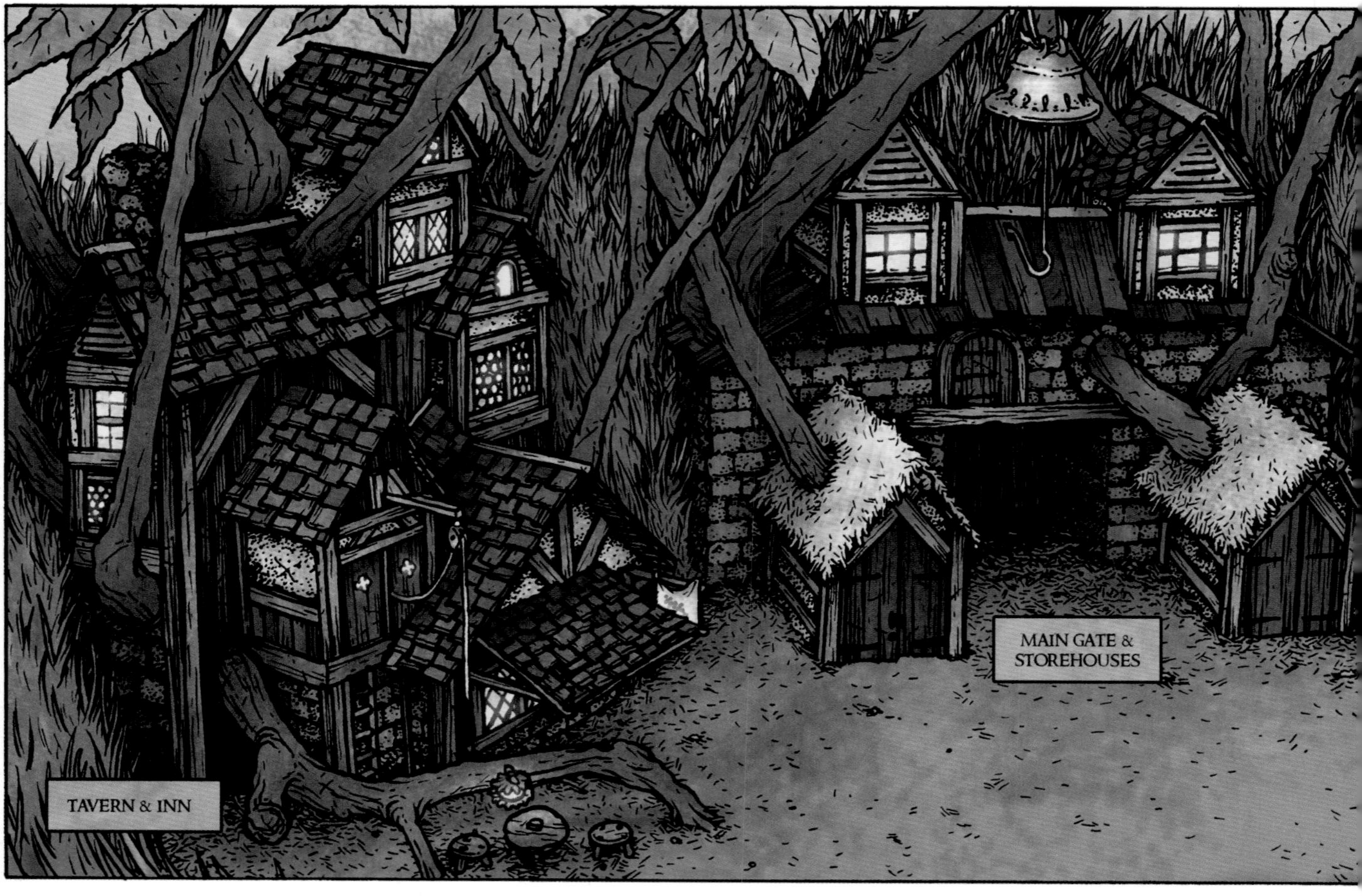

MAIN GATE &
STOREHOUSES
TAVERN & INN

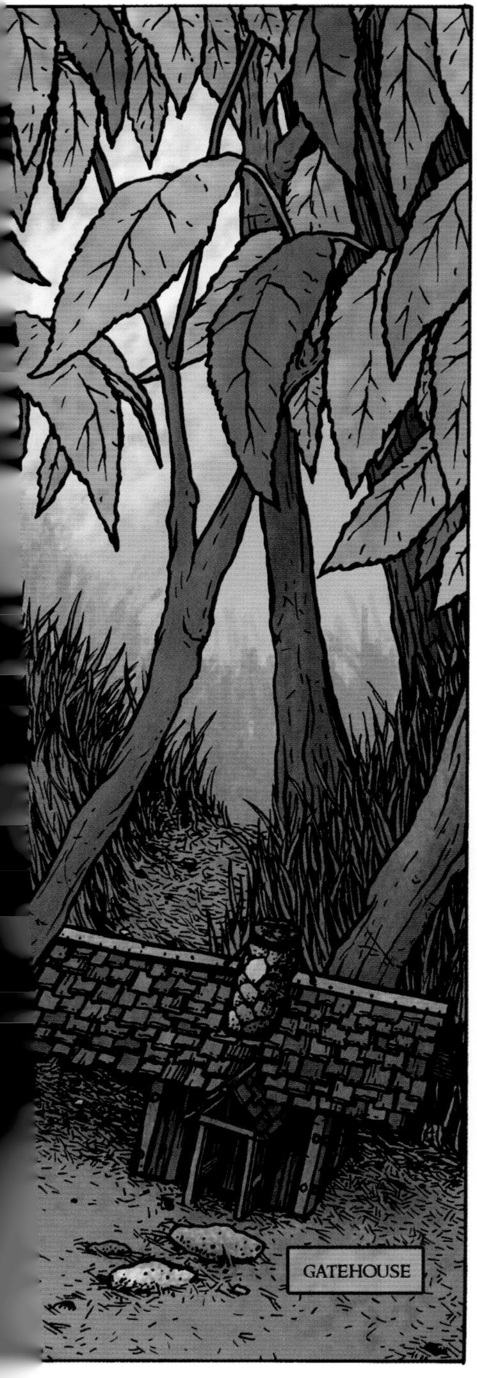
GATEHOUSE

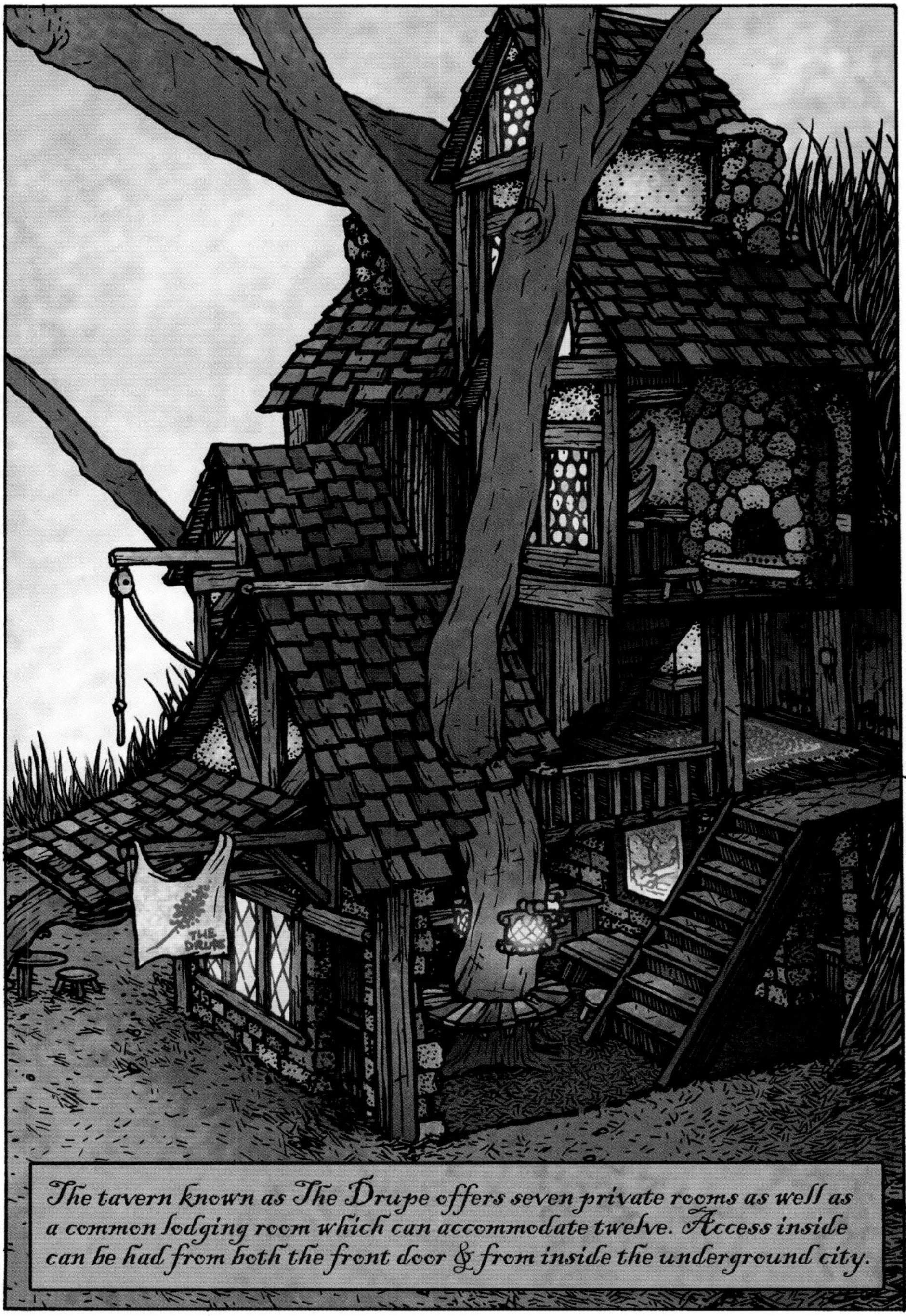
THE DRUPE
The tavern known as The Drupe offers seven private rooms as well as a common lodging room which can accommodate twelve. Access inside can be had from both the front door & from inside the underground city.

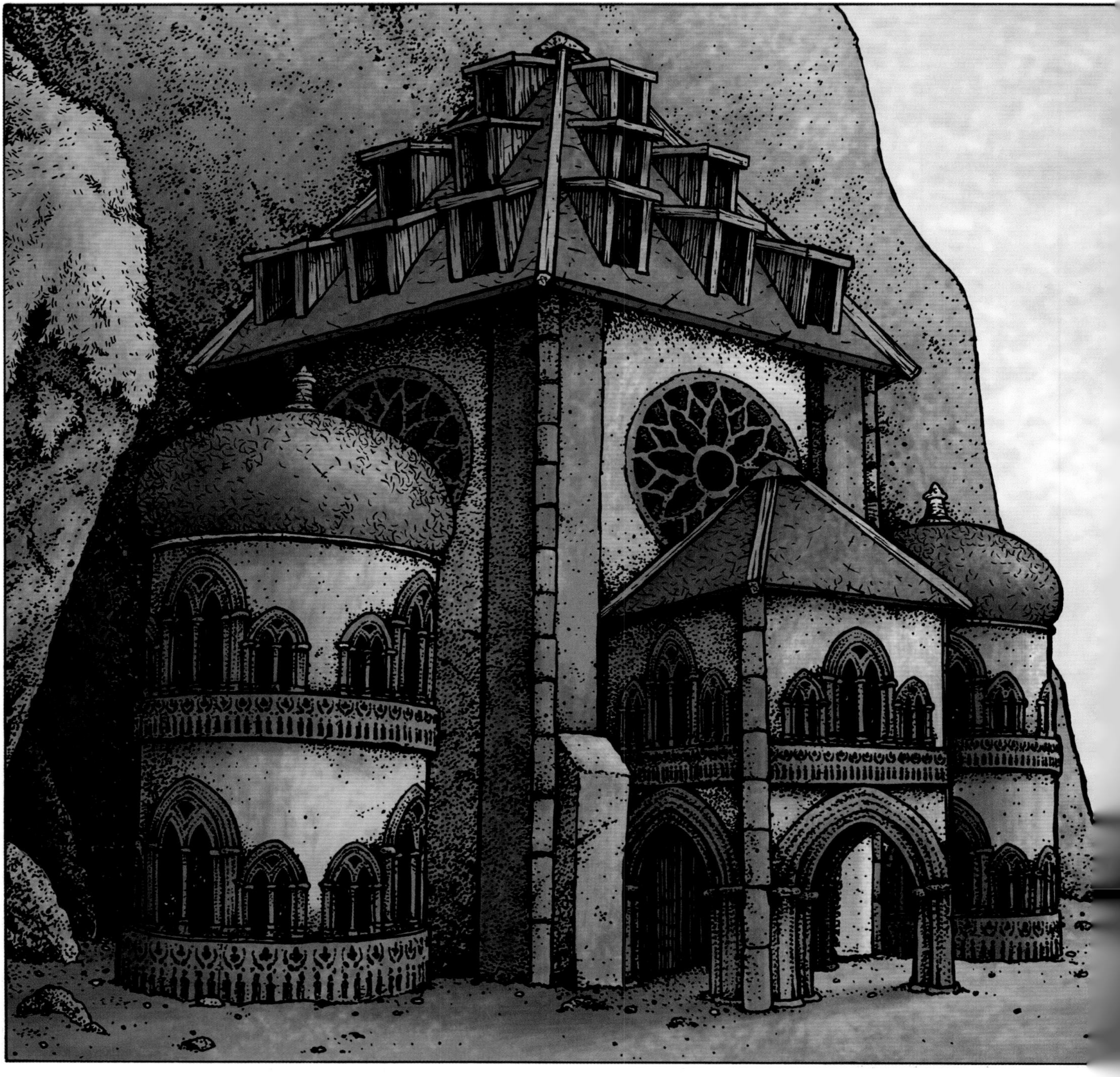

SHORESTONE:

A city on the eastern shore of the mouse territories known for highly skilled craftsmice. The front facade is a grand display of masonry, metalwork, carpentry, & design, but is only a small glimpse of the sprawling city & its beauty. While other crafts are taught & practiced here, these four are the cornerstones:

STONE MASONRY

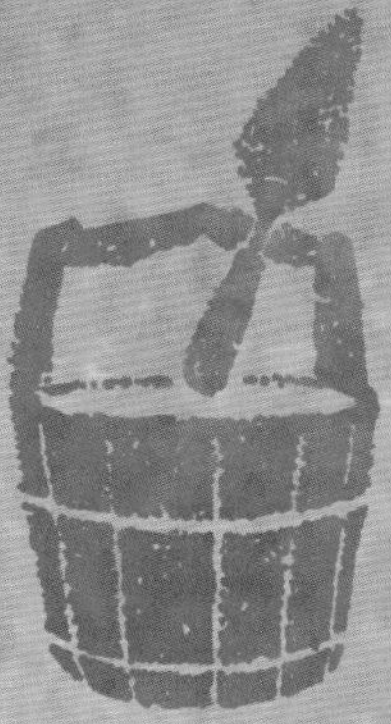

Mice who quarry, shape, pile, & mortar stone do back breaking work. It requires the right blend of physical strength, skilled paws, and a clever mind to form stone into stable, steadfast structures

METAL SMITHING

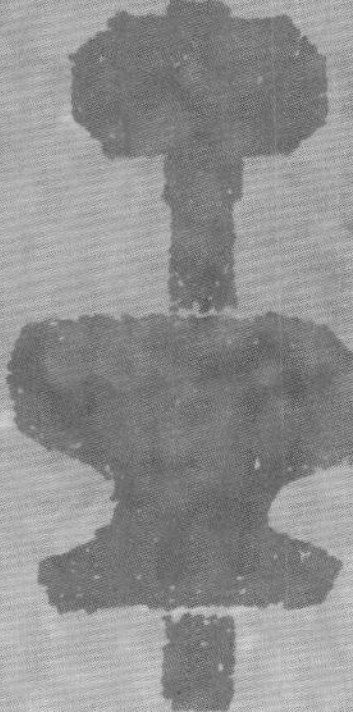

The guild of metalsmiths are more than just hammerers of iron. They are metallurgists who know how to select the right ore, smelt it in the correct heat, form it into shape, and temper it to last.

MATHEMATICS

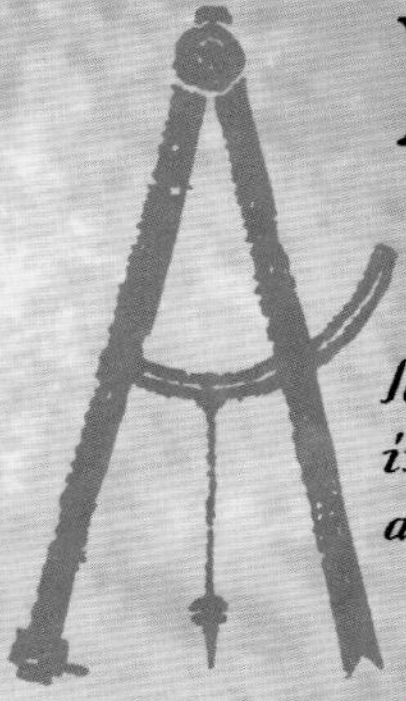

Planning is needed throughout an architectural build. Guild members are learned mice good with numbers in theory and in practice. They are also expected to become seasoned draftsmice who put their ideas to parchment.

CARPENTRY

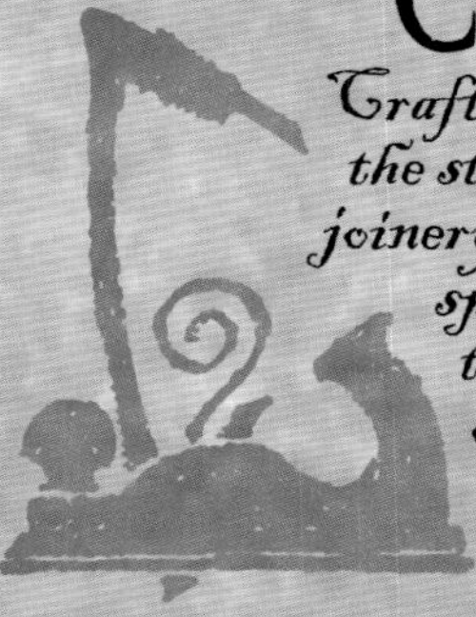

Crafting wood into items is only the start of this trade. Skills in joinery, selecting appropriate species of material, and treating it to stand the test of time are all important on items as small as a bowl and as large as a home.

INSIDE SHORE-STONE

Beyond the rocky facade, the city opens into an echoing arched gallery of skilled labor guilds and trades. The various guilds have been commissioned for their beautiful work by so many of the settlements in the Territories, they fly the banners of cities current and long since past as a testament to their own craft. While the front of the city is all commerce, a residential area lies further in.

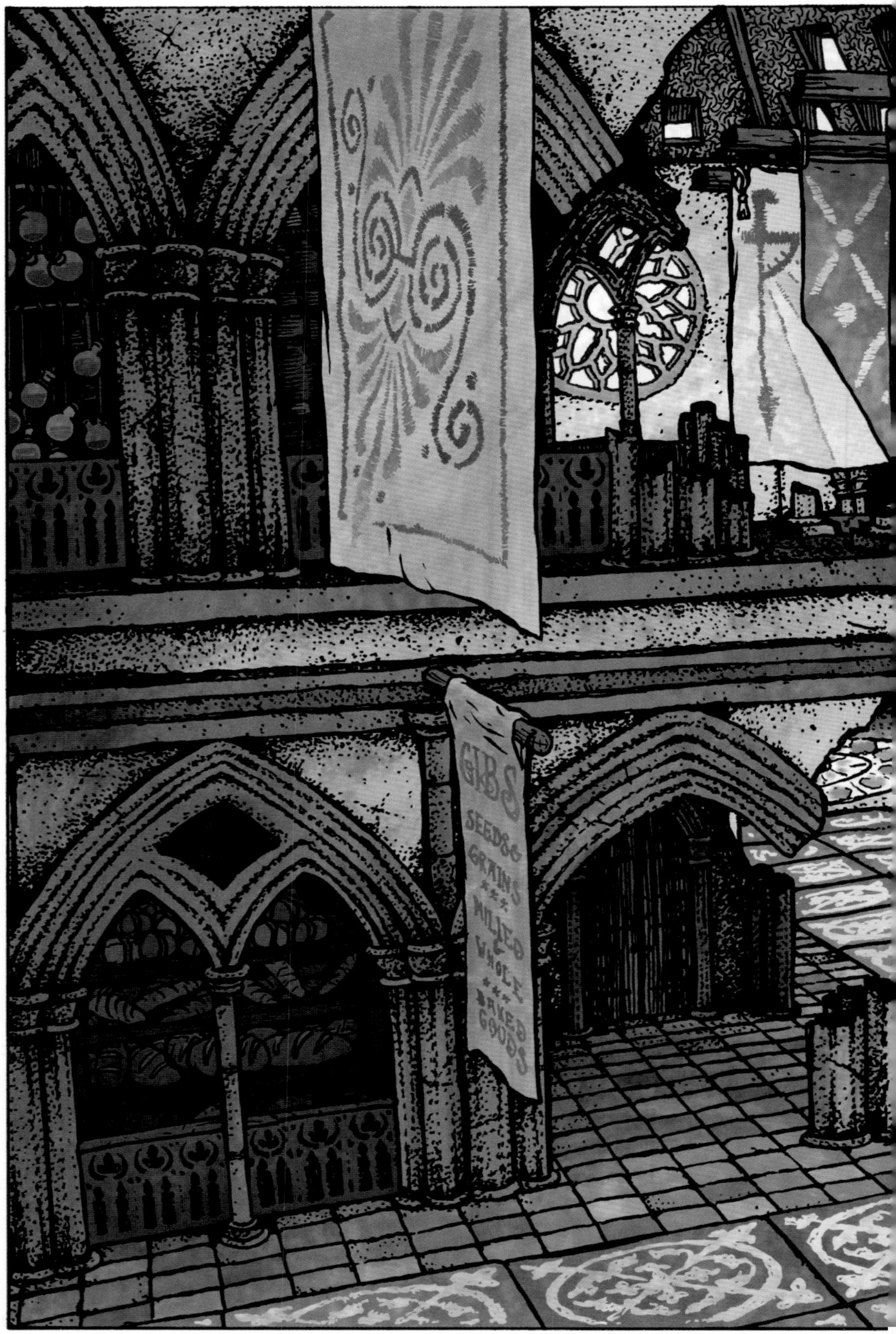
GIBBS
SEEDS &
GRAINS
MILLED
&
WHOLE
BAKED
GOODS

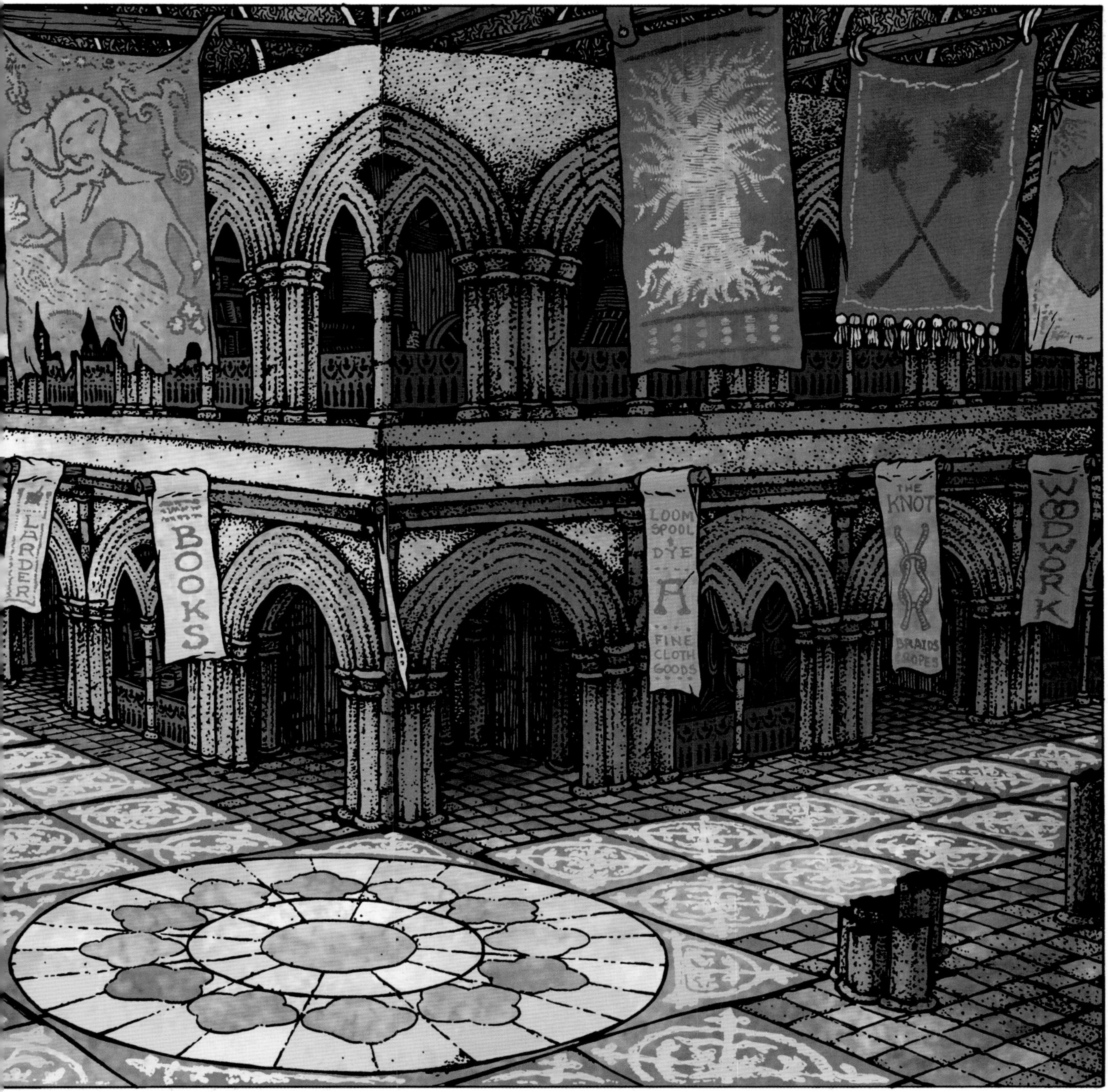
LARDER
BOOKS
LOOM SPOOL & DYE
FINE CLOTH GOODS
THE KNOT
BRAIDS & ROPES
WOODWORK

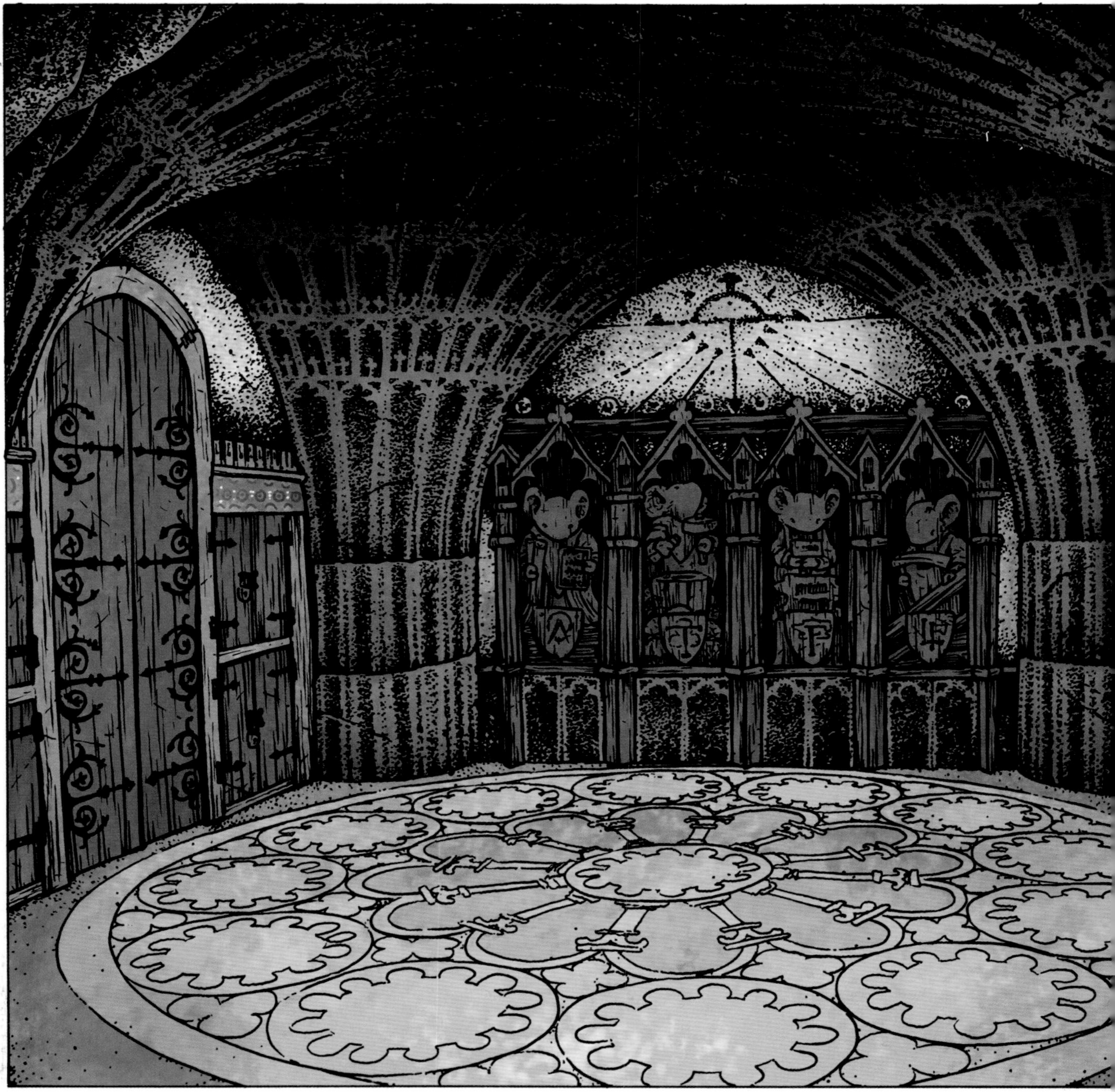

OMARR

Integrated the use of mathematics in building design and architecture more than any other mouse before him. Omarr wrote three volumes on geometry both in theory and in practice. He also made common the idea of accurate scale plans and the archiving of them.

FARRER

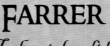

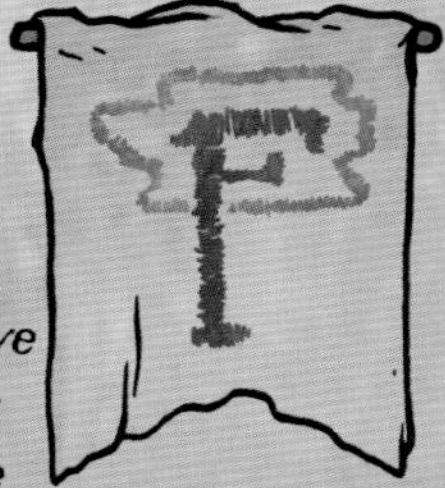

Took metal craft beyond its use for utility objects like brackets and nails to decorative art and design. While mostly now known as the forger of the mythic Black Axe, he studied the science of metals and developed techniques for smelting, tempering, and smithing known only to him.

THURSTON

Crafted stone to reach higher and stay more stable than his mason predecessors. Working with such heavy materials, he was a model of efficiency. He preferred to move stone as little as possible and only by exerting the least energy. Masons since swear by his recipe for mortar as "unimprovable."

LOCKE

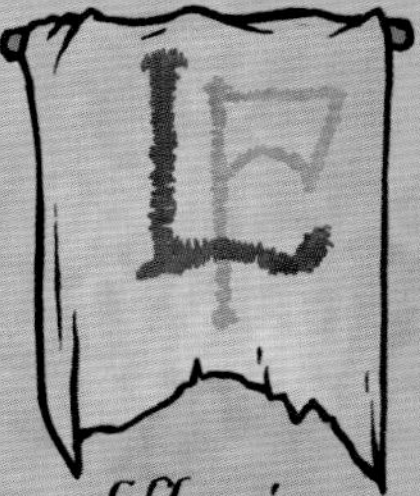

Often overlooked as a cabinet maker, Locke perfected wood joinery that allowed timber structures to be more than surface detail, but as the bones and flooring of many a mouse city. In his younger days he worked closely with an elderly Thurston to rig scaffolding, levers, and braces for stonework.

THE HAVEN GUILD ROOM

Hidden beneath the Shorestone Archive is a room in tribute to the four most celebrated craftsmice of history. The secretive Haven Guild passes down their most advanced and cherished techniques and, not just in the case of Farrer, also protect their artifacts.

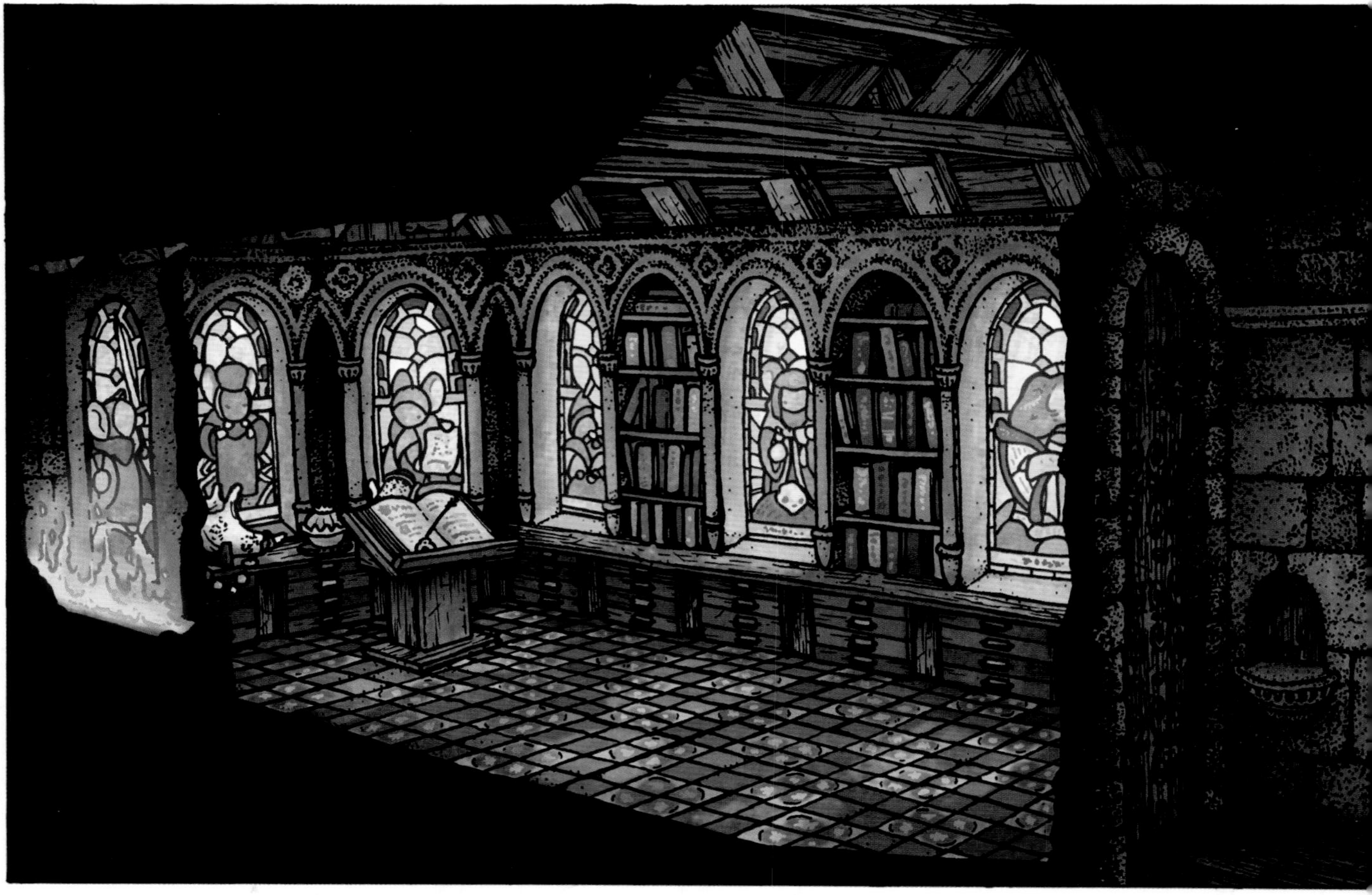

THE MATRIARCH'S PRIVATE CHAMBER

Located just off of her office in Lockhaven, this private chamber, only accessible by the Matriarch, is a room for the Guard's history. Her logs join the records of all past Matriarchs as well as many sacred artifacts from past Guardmice. The eleven stained glass windows, which depict eleven exemplary Matriarchs of long ago, are illuminated by a trough of lit oil that runs inside the walls of the room

FERUIN — **DAYANA** — **LARIA** — **SIOBHAN** — **ALLYSON**

A weaver who started the tradition of cloaked Guardmice	Her botanical studies were the most complete in Guard history	Expanded Lockhaven three separate occasions in her time	Healer who took on any and all ill. "To mend is our duty"	A learned writer, thinker, and poet. Her words adorn the office wall.

MOIRA — **ADELLE** — **RAINA** — **CAYLYN** — **DORYS** — **VEYGA**

Slayed a tyrant king over the murder of her beloved	Tamed the first bees brought into the Lockhaven apiary	Set her logs of the Guard to the melody of her harp	Commissioned the first accurate mapping of the Territories	Fed the masses & was more often in the kitchen than in her office	Pushed for the development of star navigation & mapping

A GALLERY OF PINUPS

BY ESTEEMED AUTHORS & FRIENDS

AS PRESENTED IN THE
ORIGINAL MOUSE GUARD SERIES

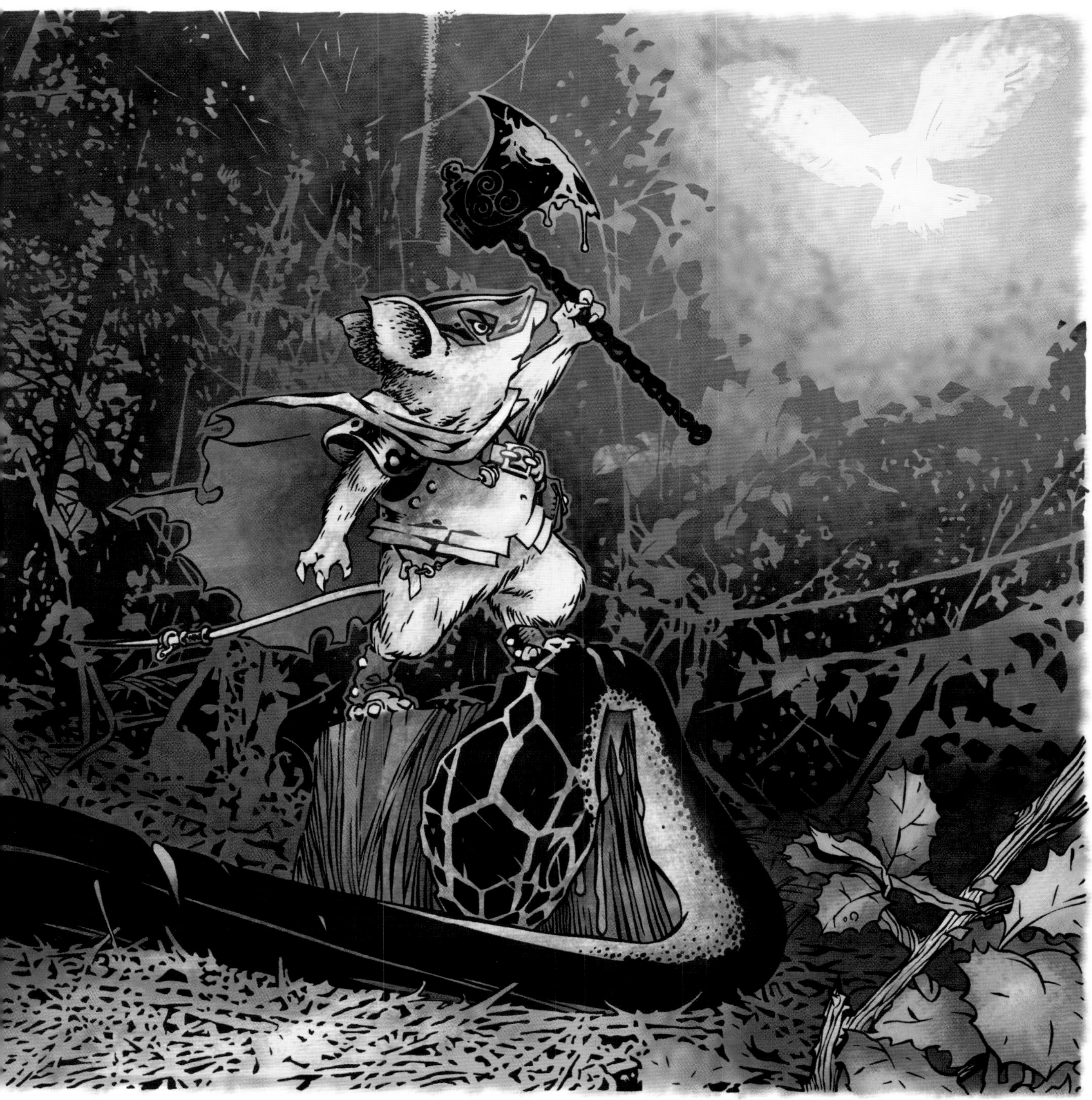

PINUP BY ALEX SHEIKMAN

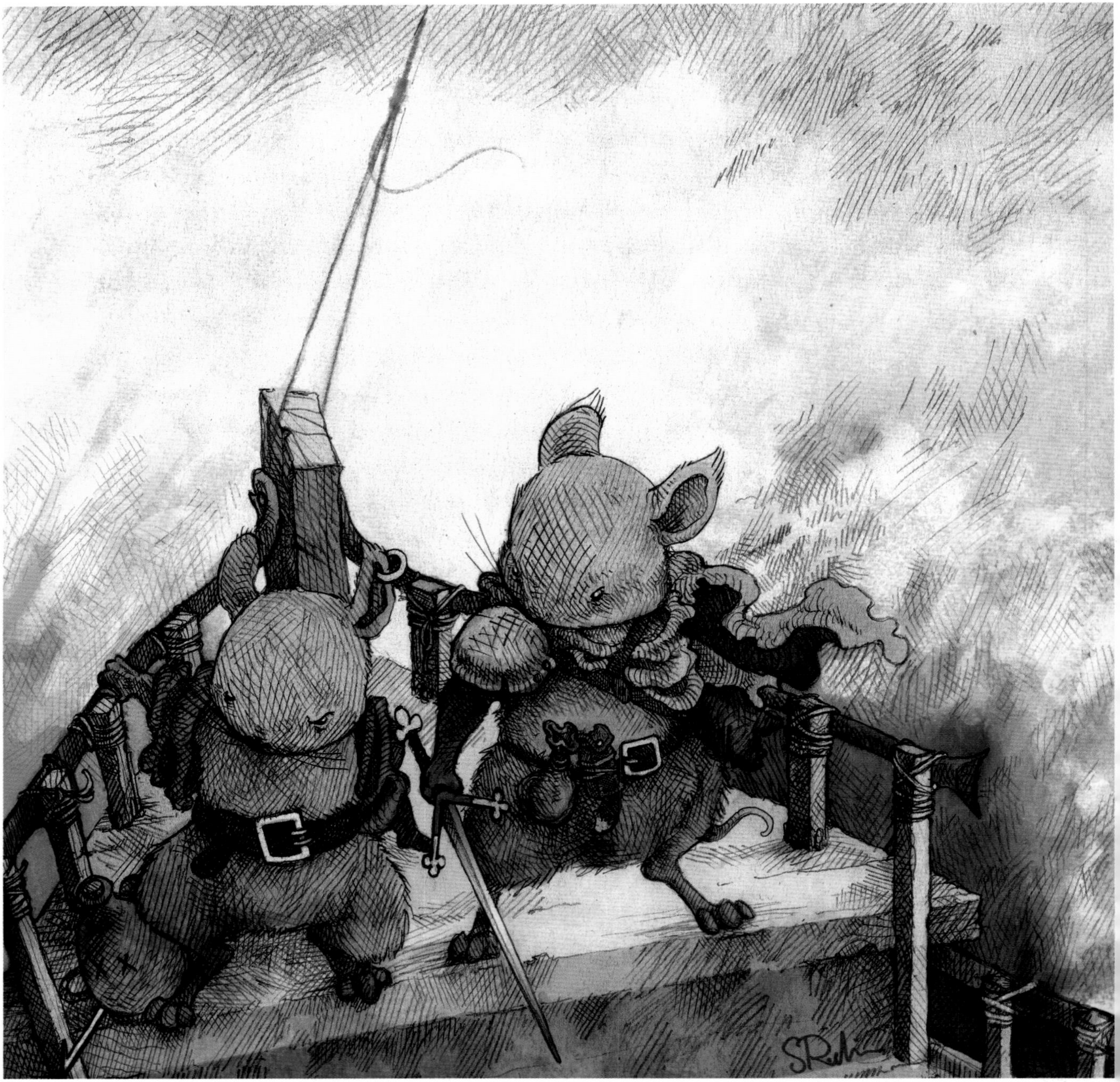

PINUP BY SEAN RU

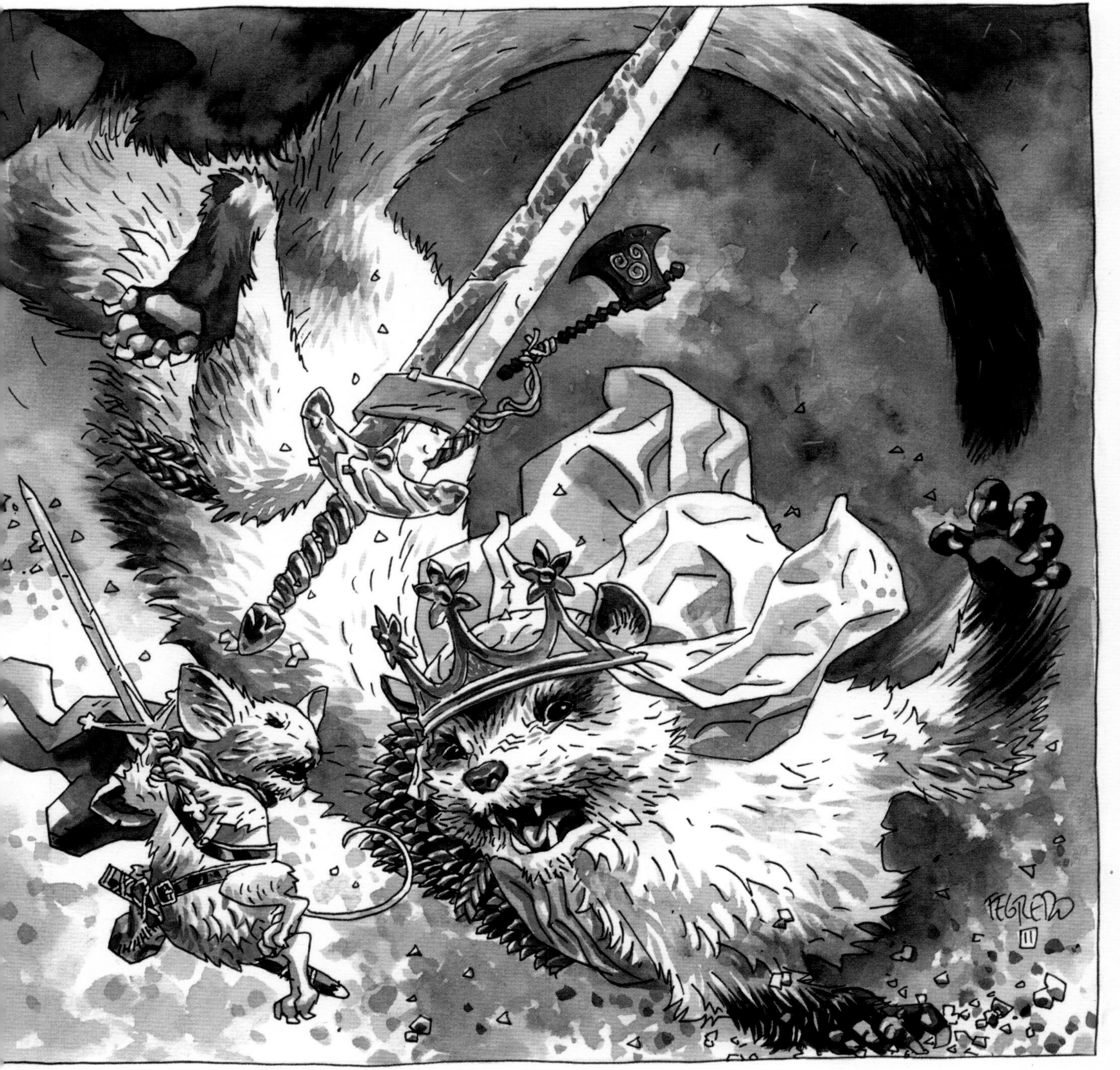
FEGREDO
11

PINUP BY DUNCAN FEGREDO

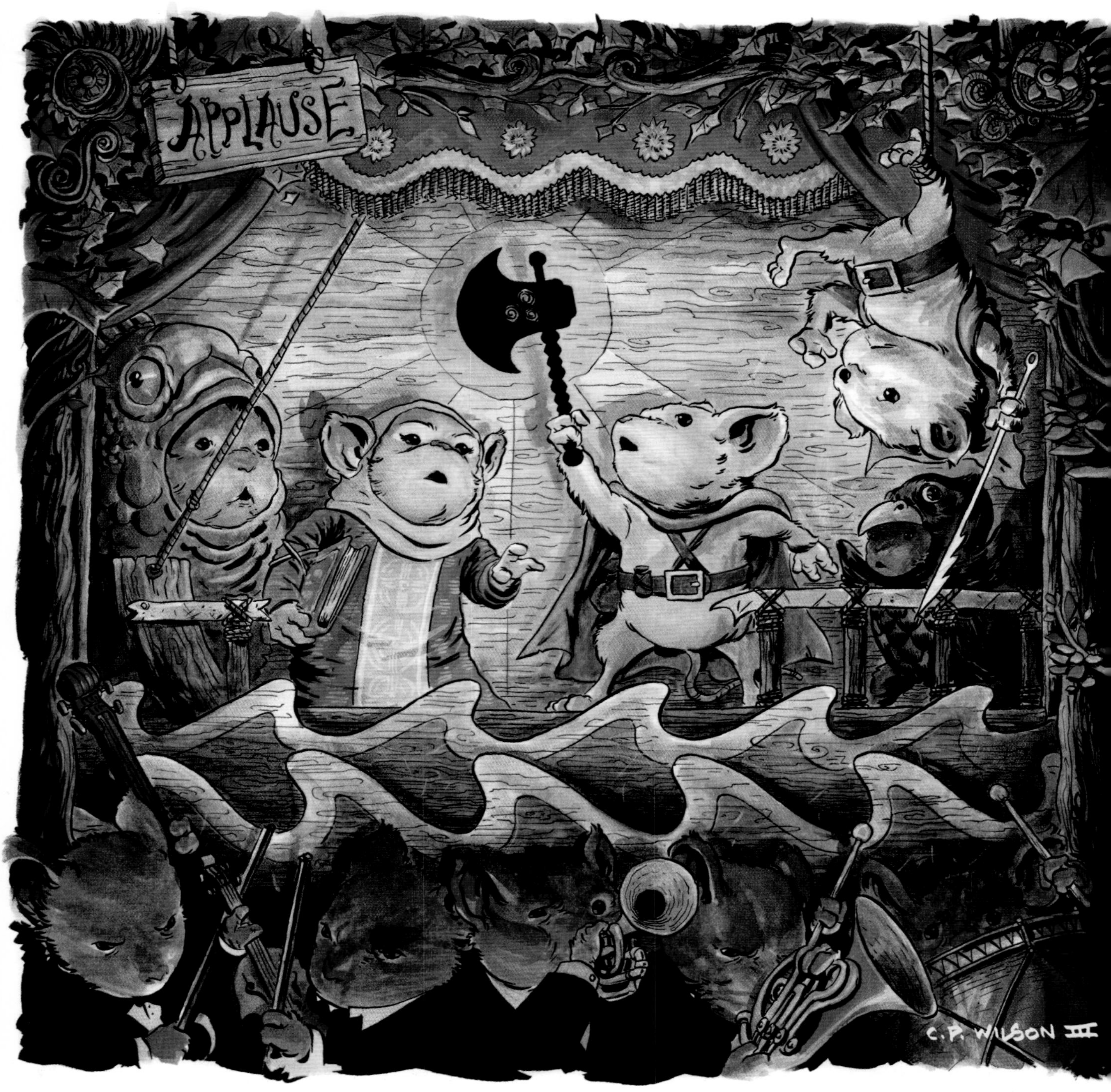
APPLAUSE
C.P. WILSON III

PINUP BY CHARLES PAUL WILSON

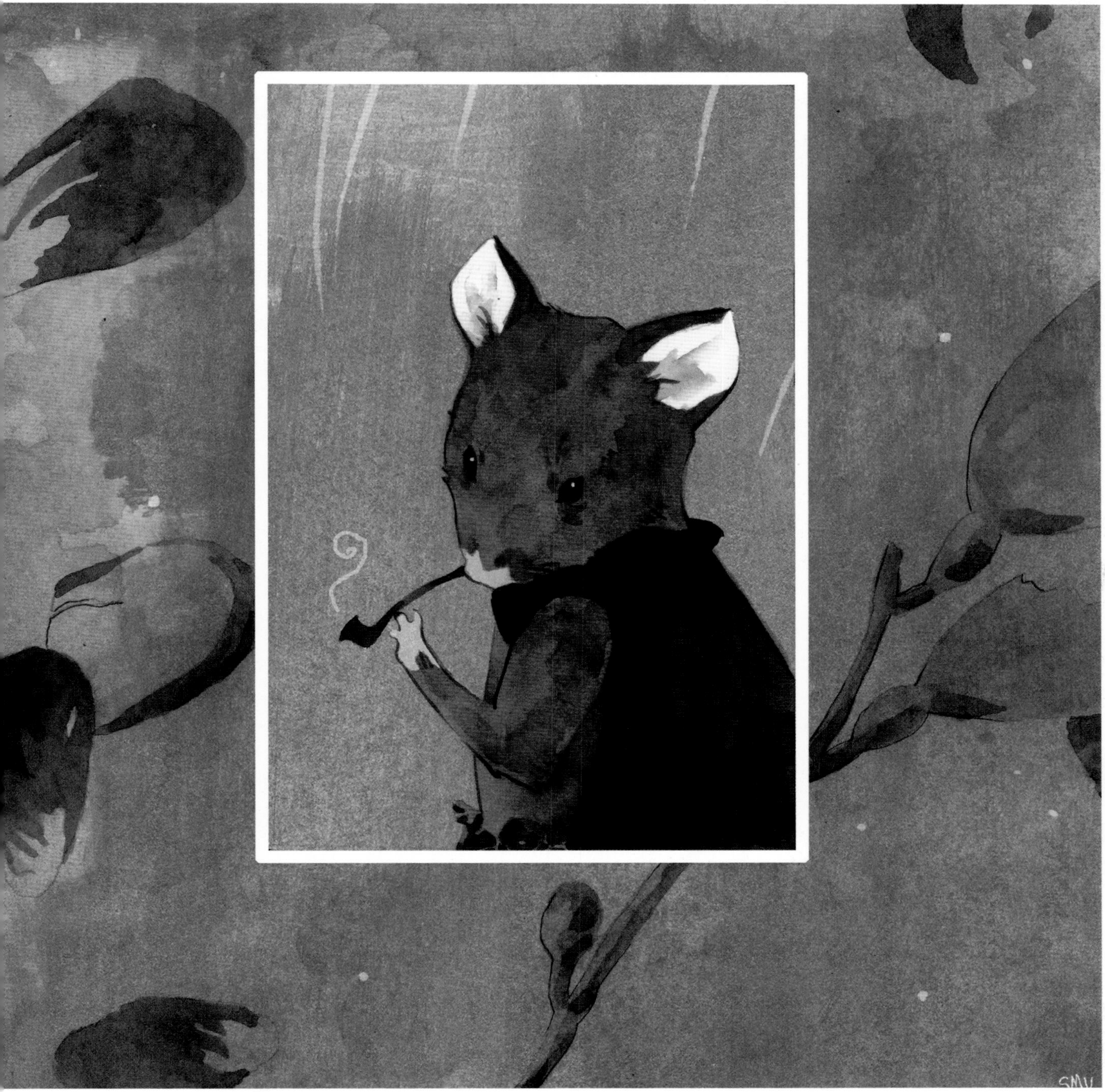
SMV

PINUP BY SHANE-MICHAEL VIDAURRI

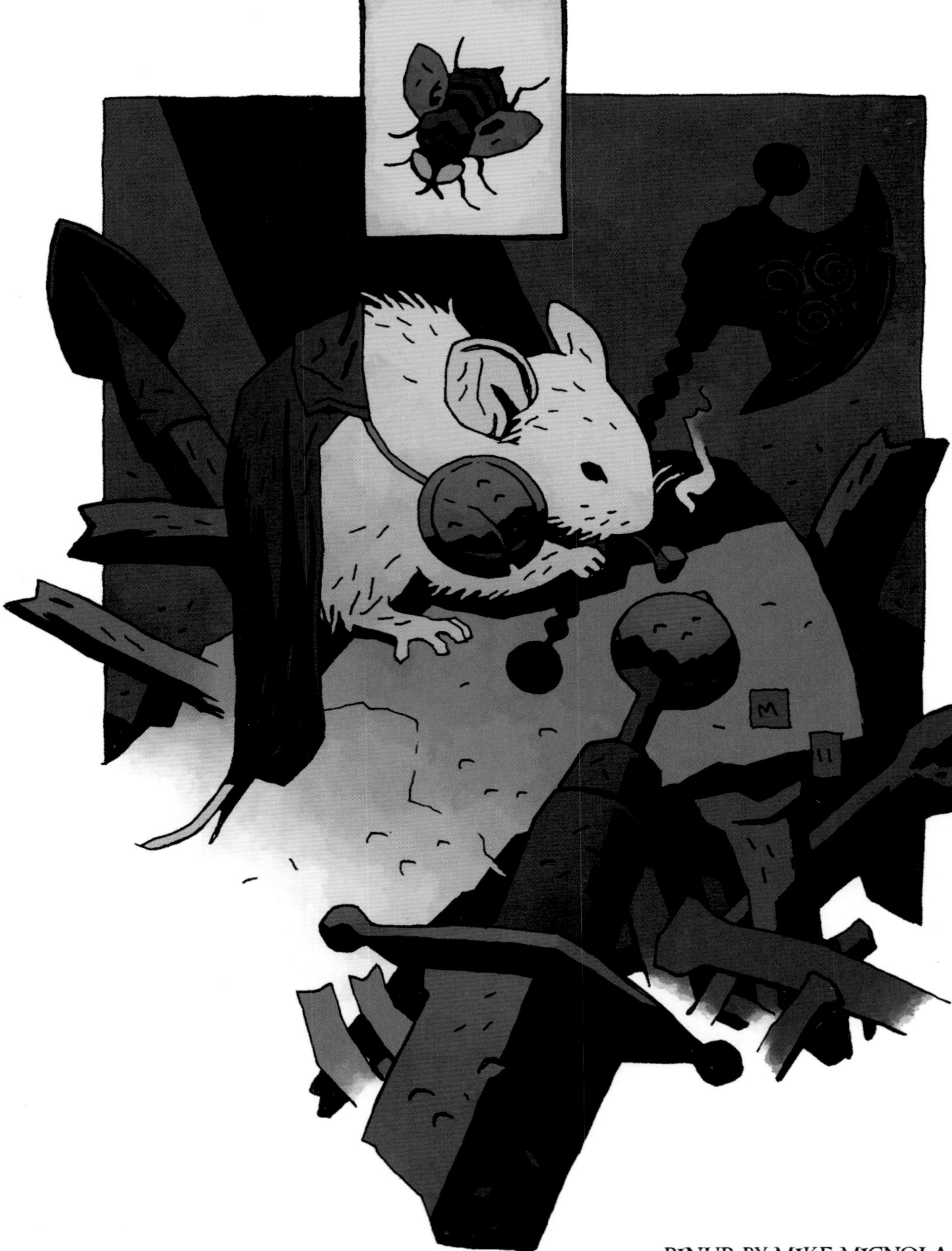

PINUP BY MIKE MIGNOLA & DAVE STEWA

ABOUT THE AUTHOR

David Petersen was born in 1977. His artistic career soon followed. A steady diet of cartoons, comics and tree climbing fed his imagination and is what still inspires his work today. David was the 2007 Russ Manning Award recipient for Most Promising Newcomer, and in 2008 won Eisner Awards for Best Publication for Kids *(Mouse Guard Fall 1152 & Winter 1152)* and Best Graphic Album – Reprint *(Mouse Guard Fall 1152 Hardcover)*. He received his BFA in Printmaking from Eastern Michigan University where he met his wife Julia. They continue to reside in Michigan with their dog Autumn.

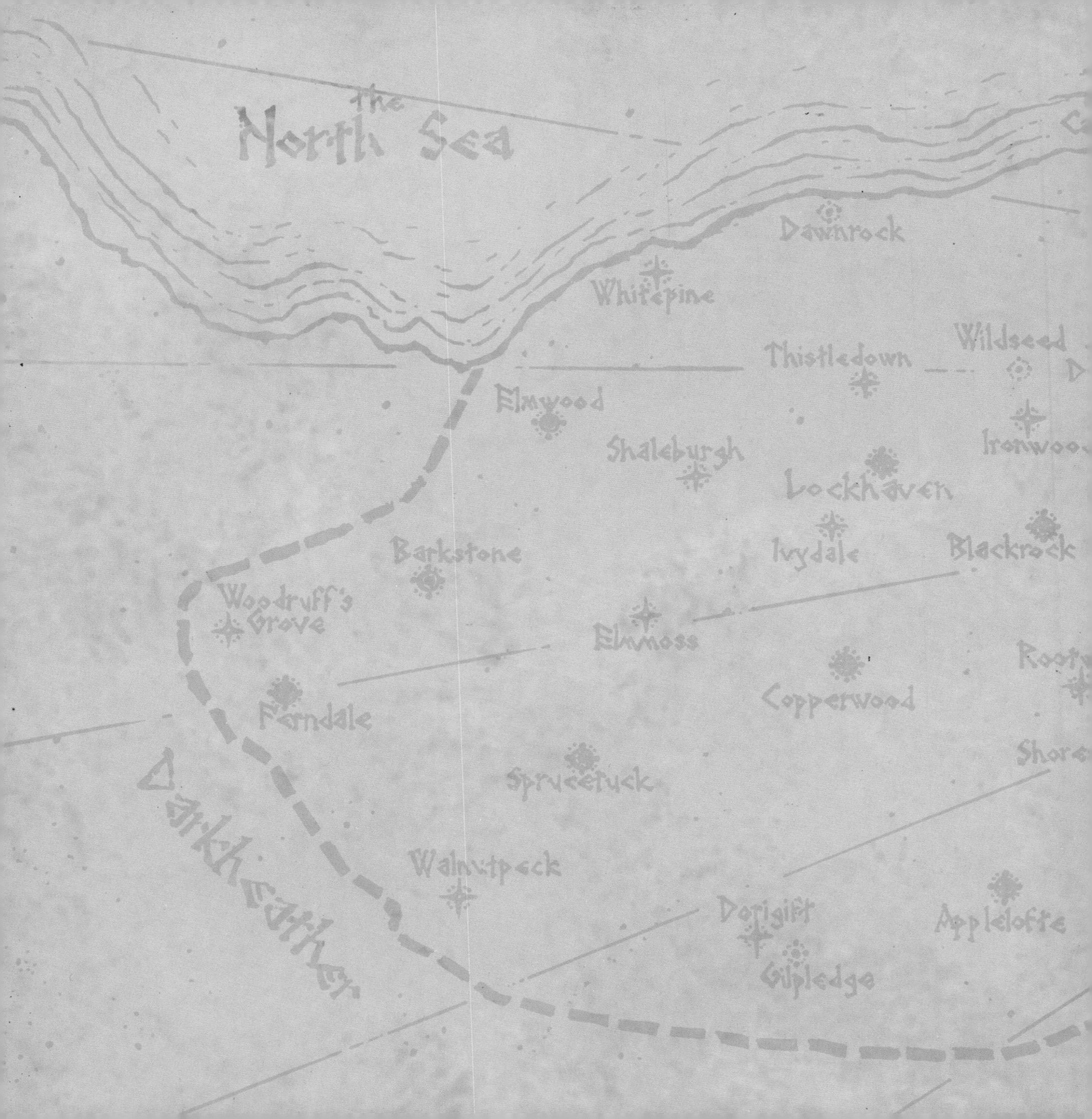
the North Sea
Dawnrock
Whitepine
Thistledown
Wildseed
Elmwood
Shaleburgh
Lockhaven
Barkstone
Ivydale
Blackrock
Woodruff's Grove
Elmmoss
Copperwood
Ferndale
Sprucetuck
Darkheather
Walnutpeck
Dorigift
Gilpledge
Applelofte